Readers of Mazo de la Roche's celebrated Jalna saga will enjoy this new collection. Included are a novelette and nine stories of love, devotion, sacrifice, humor — the entire range of human emotions — told simply and movingly against a variety of colorful settings here and abroad.

The title story is a full-length novelette which describes the hysterical world of two aging spinsters who live in an isolated country hamlet, behind a façade of charm and gentility. Into this world comes Eddy, a lame thirteen-year-old Cockney boy reclaimed from a home for delinquent children. And in Eddy two lives find their violent climax.

In "Auntimay," after a life of continual sacrifice for parents and family, May Baxter is abandoned by all and left to her own devices. But while modeling in a fashionable tearoom she sees a distinguished gentleman, and from the moment their glances cross, her future is inextricably bound to his.

"Twa Kings" is the story of little Geordie MacQueen, who shared the birthdate of the King, and whose whole life was changed by a tremendous Jubilee medal from London.

But Mazo de la Roche needs no introduction. Since 1927, when *Jalna* first appeared, her heart-warming novels have won for her the admiration and devotion of readers all over the world. And A BOY IN THE HOUSE is just as rewarding as Miss de la Roche's previous work.

A BOY IN THE HOUSE

AND OTHER STORIES

A Boy in the House

AND OTHER STORIES

by
MAZO DE LA ROCHE

An Atlantic Monthly Press Book
Little, Brown and Company · Boston

The author wishes to thank the editors of *Harper's Bazaar* (London) and *Good Housekeeping* (London) for permission to reprint stories which first appeared in their magazines; also the editors of the *Canadian Home Journal* for permission to reprint "Twa Kings."

ATLANTIC–LITTLE, BROWN BOOKS
ARE PUBLISHED BY
LITTLE, BROWN AND COMPANY
IN ASSOCIATION WITH
THE ATLANTIC MONTHLY PRESS

To
Norah
with love

Contents

A BOY IN THE HOUSE
AND OTHER STORIES

Auntimay

M AY BAXTER had been invaluable to her family. Not one of
them knew what they would have done without her. She was not
one of those unmarried women who pour out their love and their
strength for their families without getting gratitude for it. Neither
was she the sort who, under the pretext of self-sacrifice, domi-
nates the lives of those nearest and dearest to her. What she had
done she had wanted to do. She often told herself this. There
had been no sacrifice about it. She had devoted herself heart and
soul to her family and they had loved her and been grateful to
the point of making her exclaim, "Now, now, I don't want to be
thanked! I like doing it!"

Few women who have the spirit of devotion in them have had a
wider field for its expression than May Baxter. There were seven
in the family besides herself, and every single one of them needed
her. First there were the parents. She could not remember the
time when her mother had not been an invalid. The first needle-
work she had done, as a little girl, was the embroidering of a
tray cloth for her mother's birthday. When she should have been
playing with other children she had sat by her mother's bedside
stroking the weary forehead, reading aloud in her low, sweet
voice. Her mother could not bear anyone else to read aloud to
her. All other voices irritated her. Her mother could not bear to
send her daughter away to school. So the loved child was edu-

cated by a governess who came in for a few hours daily. They lived in a nice dim old house in one of the small streets near Buckingham Palace.

They had always lived there and almost the first thing May could remember was being taken by her nurse to see the changing of the Guard. How her little heart had quickened when she heard the strains of the military band, saw the marching of soldiers in the Palace Yard! Best of all were the mounted Guards, with their gleaming black Arab horses, their silver breastplates and drooping white plumes. She had stared up wondering into the faces of the scarlet-coated sentries. Now, perhaps, in these days, she saw the grandsons of the sentries she had admired in childhood, for she was fifty.

She had read several introspective articles about the feelings of people when they had reached the age of fifty, some of them quite courageous and wise, all more or less depressing. Curiously, she herself did not feel at all different from the days of her youth. She woke each morning with the same feeling of expectancy towards what the day might bring her. And, year after year, the days mounting, mounting into decades, brought her practically the same thing. Only more of it.

While she was still a girl her father, after a too violent participation in politics, had a stroke of paralysis and never walked again. Neither was his mind very clear. But it was clear enough for him to enjoy *The Times* and the *Spectator,* and the reading of these to him was added to May's other duties.

She went from one parent's room to the other like a ray of sunshine, as they often remarked. The comparison was all the more apt because of her extreme fairness. She was very tall, very slender and very straight, in spite of the long hours she passed bent over newspapers or books or the writing of long letters to her mother's many old friends.

Her brother Frederick married and brought home his wife.

Her name was Viola and she was the daughter of a solicitor. She lost no time in having three children, who all adored their aunt. They were always calling her: "Auntimay! Auntimay!" And the grown-up members of the family began also to call her by that name.

What a joy it was to escape — no, escape was not the right word, for it made her seem to have been unhappy — to emerge, then, from the pensive air of the invalids' rooms into the gaiety and clamor of the nurseries! The children clung to her more and more. Her sister-in-law clung to her too, for one needed support in the business of bearing three babies, overseeing their upbringing and going into society. Viola liked going into society, but she did it from a sense of duty also, for Frederick, like his father, had political ambitions.

May was proud of her brother and did everything in her power to help him. She studied the political situation earnestly, and Frederick would have been loath to acknowledge how much she really helped him with his speeches. Not that he was not grateful. He thought her the best sister a man ever had. They were a united family.

Of the three children May could not possibly have told you which was her favorite. Daphne, the eldest, was very like herself, and grew even more so as she developed into girlhood. But there was one big difference. Daphne didn't care for sickrooms or domesticity. She was all for expressing herself in the pleasures of life.

Ralph, the second, was a studious boy who showed a talent for architecture before he had outgrown his building bricks. It was Auntimay who went with him from church to church in his first excursions for the study of ecclesiastical buildings, but, when he was old enough to go abroad, it was his mother who accompanied him.

Possibly it was Willy, the youngest, who was really May's

favorite. He was delicate and was taught at home. He was not only an imaginative child, but he seemed to have drawn to himself the best physical points from both sides of the family. He fascinated May. She dreamed of a wonderful but vague future for him in which he would, at the height of great achievement, declare that he owed it all to her understanding and devotion.

One thing she could not imagine was any great change in her own life. When her parents died she would still have her brother and sister-in-law. When they died she would still have the children. So secure did she feel that she never thought of the possibility of dying herself. She thought of herself as the perennial strength and guiding hand of a clinging family.

But everything did change for her and with a startling swiftness. When she was fifty her parents died within a few weeks of each other. They were past eighty and the end came gently to both. The two rooms between which she had spent the greater part of her life were suddenly vacant.

Within a few months of this bereavement her brother had a decisive political defeat in a by-election on which he had built his hopes. He threw up all his political ambitions and retired into a rather petulant private life. He had spent a great deal of money and also he had lost a considerable part of his income, which had been invested in South American stocks. He found himself at fifty-four facing a distinct need for retrenchment.

He had no further need of May. Neither had his wife. She was going less into society and her children were almost grown up. Daphne was studying dramatic art. Ralph was absorbed by modern architecture. Even Willy became suddenly independent of May. His health improved and he was eager for the experience of school. When his trunk was carried out to the taxi May could not help crying. It annoyed Willy's mother to see her, for she was sensibly glad to feel that her boy was now strong enough to do as other boys.

"Really," she said to Frederick, "it's rather stupid the way May goes on about Willy leaving. One would think he was her son instead of mine."

"She always has been more maternal than you," said Frederick with the slight vindictiveness that was the result of his short political career.

May tried almost desperately to find something to occupy her. The silence in the house oppressed her. The length of the days almost frightened her. She simply could not settle down to do next to nothing, like Frederick and Viola. There was no outlet for her vitality such as the three young ones had. Instinctively, in her mind, she classed herself with them. She was young. She wanted to do things.

She had always loved the theater and she now began to wonder if it were too late for her to go into the profession of acting. She had a lovely figure. She knew that. And she had a lovely speaking voice. She had a wonderful memory.

She broached the subject to Daphne. The young girl could scarcely restrain her astonishment.

"Why, Auntimay —" there were not words to convey her sense of May's unfitness. But her expression was enough.

May felt some chagrin.

"Of course, dear, I mean in a part suitable to my age."

"But — Auntimay, the theater is *overflowing* with actresses of *experience* who are simply *panting* for jobs!"

"Don't you think I should stand a chance?"

"Not a *shadow* of one!"

May did not believe her. She experienced a slight feeling of resentment towards Daphne. A faint suspicion crossed her mind. Was Daphne trying to keep her down?

But she refused to be kept down. She had heard through

Daphne of a play about to go into rehearsal in which there was one attractive small part for a middle-aged woman. The play was a revival. She had seen it and well remembered the part of Mrs. Ashley. "I should make a perfect Mrs. Ashley," she thought.

In the morning she went to the theater where the play was to be put on and inquired at the box office for the producer. She was asked if she had an appointment with him. She was so disarming and confidential in her admission that she had only her extreme desire to see him that the man in the box office showed her into a little room where two middle-aged actresses and one very young one were also waiting.

"I suppose you're after the part of Mrs. Ashley," said one of the older women, looking her over.

"Yes," May admitted. "I suppose you are too."

The actress nodded. Then she said, "I shall not have a chance against you. You absolutely *are* Mrs. Ashley!"

The other woman said, "I don't seem to remember you. Yet I thought I knew everyone on the London stage."

"I have been off it for some years," answered May.

The young girl broke in. "Oh, I must have the part of Phyllis! I know I can make a marvelous success of it. If only Mr. Birks will hear me read some of the lines, he'll be sure to take me on! But I've been here eleven times and he's never seen me yet."

A mop-headed girl looked in at the door.

"Miss Foster, please," she said, in a voice of supreme indifference.

One of the older actresses went out with an anxious air.

"I'm as nervous as a cat," said the other, when the door had closed. "I never get used to these interviews. Have a cigarette?"

"Thank you. I don't smoke," answered May.

She saw the young girl's eyes fixed eagerly on the cigarettes and wished that one had been offered to her, but the woman snapped the case shut with an abstracted air.

They waited, almost in silence, for a space. Then Miss Foster returned, with an air of disappointment.

"Well, I'm out of it," she said briefly. "There's nothing to do now but try for another job."

The mop-headed girl again looked in at the door.

"Miss Baxter," she said, even more indifferently than before.

May followed her through a swing door as in a dream. They went up steps, through a passage lighted by a single unshaded light, into a tangle of ropes, canvas and carpenters' tools. From there, half dazed, May was led onto the stage. The girl handed her a few pages of typescript and vanished. Before her May could see the twilit theater, the seats swathed in buff linen. Two figures sat in one of the front rows. One of them spoke.

"Please read Mrs. Ashley's lines."

May could scarcely see the typescript, her hand had begun to shake so. At last she made out that there was a conversation between Mrs. Ashley and someone named George.

"Shall I read George's lines, too?" she asked, in a husky voice, quite unlike her own.

"Oh, just make sounds for them."

May gathered all her strength and steadied the paper. She made a few sounds for George.

Distinctly she heard one of the two figures say, "Who the deuce is she? I don't know her."

"Neither do I," came the answer. "But she's exactly what we want — if she can act."

May was thrilled, for she knew she could act. She put all the feeling of which she was capable into Mrs. Ashley's lines, her voice ringing out loud and strong. She raised one hand to emphasize the words. Her eyes, now more used to the dim light, saw two faces round-eyed with astonishment.

When she had finished, one of the men said, with a crack in his voice:

"Please do it again."

He asked in just the way the children used to beg her to repeat something that had charmed them.

She did it again.

This time a strange gasping sound came from the man who had asked her to repeat the reading. The other said, very politely, "Thank you. If we decide to take you on, we'll write. Please leave your address."

She was in the street again. Her spirits were raised by this contact with the theatrical world. She wondered, too, if she were doing right in competing with these women who so obviously needed the engagement.

But she need not have feared superseding them, for no word came from the theater. When, a month later, the play was produced and May sat on the first night in one of the front rows, an actress she had not seen before took the part of Mrs. Ashley.

During that month she became more and more restive in the narrow scope of her life, more determined to find some outlet. She answered all sorts of advertisements without success. She had no money to put into chicken farming or boarding kennels for dogs. She had not the necessary qualifications for a secretary, though she had often been told by her mother's friends what an ideal one she would make. By humiliating degrees she found out that, for all her efficient activities in her own home, there seemed nothing for her to do in the outside world.

And she wanted to do something so badly. The glimpses she had had of a life so different from her own had exhilarated her into an almost fierce determination to escape from her past.

It was impossible for her to conceal all her efforts from her family. Envelopes bearing the names of various agencies came addressed to her. She had obscure telephone calls. At last she confessed that she was trying to get a position. She actually said "job," glorying in the rough worldliness of the word.

She was hurt by the way the news was received. Frederick and Viola showed complete skepticism as to her ability to do anything but be a companion to some old lady or invalid. At this suggestion May felt, for the first time in her life, anger deep and resentful.

"I've had enough of that sort of life, thank you!" she exclaimed hotly.

Frederick and Viola were nothing less than shocked.

Daphne and Ralph were just as unsympathetic. Daphne smiled, tolerantly amused, then began to talk about her own affairs and the stupid injustice of awarding a prize medal to another girl, over her head. Ralph scarcely troubled to listen to her. He had discovered that he had made a mistake in his choice of a career. He now wanted to throw up architecture and go into flying. He begged Auntimay to use her influence with his father.

"I have no influence with your father," answered Auntimay tartly.

She wrote, pouring out her heart, to her beloved Willy. He answered from school, without any reference to her hopes and schemes. He was full of a cricket match in which he was to play.

May felt herself suddenly as nothing in the house where she had so long been in hourly demand. Nobody needed her. Nobody wanted her. One day she overheard Viola and Daphne discussing her, laughing at her schemes. A few days later Frederick and she had words and he remarked that, as he had always given her a home, he was prepared to go on doing so to the end. The idea of being considered an object of charity by her family made May's brain reel. She who had been their staff and their prop! She felt so desperate that she determined to take a long walk and not come back to tea.

As she was walking along the Mall she saw a car approaching from the direction of St. James's Palace. She saw the policeman on duty salute. A man walking swiftly, stopped and took off his hat. Then she saw the Prince of Wales sitting alone in the car, bareheaded and smoking a short pipe. His boyish face was brown. He had a look of resolve, of calm pleasure in his pipe and the fresh sunny day.

For a moment May felt a deep envy of him. Everybody wanted him. No one wanted her. Then she remembered that he too had his problems, that probably he too had known ingratitude and disillusion.

Ingratitude! It was the first time she had let that hateful word enter her mind. She put it resolutely from her, straightened her back and looked up at the glistening gulls that swooped above St. James's Park.

She had tea in the restaurant of one of the largest shops. It was a delicious tea of toasted scones and little walnut cakes. The handsome restaurant was full of people. Two beautiful models in evening gowns were gliding among the tables. They were charmingly conscious of how well the expensive dresses suited them.

May heard a woman at the next table remark: "Curves are coming in. Neither of those girls is quite so thin as was fashionable a while ago."

"Yes," her companion agreed. "But why do they never show the fashions on middle-aged women? They'd make many a good sale, if only they would."

After tea May inquired the way to the business office of the gowns department and offered herself as a model.

It happened that that very week an expensive evening dress had been made for a wealthy customer who had refused to take it when finished, because of some fancied fault in the fitting. It seemed that the dress was to be on their hands, a loss. Someone suggested that this unusual applicant should be allowed to show the dress in the restaurant. It was too matronly for any of the other models.

And May had such a graceful carriage! When, the next day, she stepped out of the dressing room, the gold tissue of the lovely gown flowing about her, she felt dazed for a moment, but she knew she was looking well, she knew she had a walk that would admirably set off this particular gown. She moved forward, graceful as a swan, among the tables of tea drinkers.

Heads turned to look at her. She had not walked the length of the restaurant when every eye was on her. There was something about her, so gracious, so simple, so pleasant in her curves, so unstudied. And the gown! Before the tea hour was over it was sold, and May was engaged to display more dresses.

The fear of being laughed at kept her from telling of her success. She was silent and preoccupied in the house, like a young girl in love. At night she lay awake, picturing, over and over again, her elegant progress among the tables.

Frequenters of the restaurant began to look for the new model. They began to talk about her to their friends. Middle-aged and elderly ladies began to crowd the tables, with visions of what they themselves might look if only they were properly clothed.

Then some old friends of the family (May never had had time to make friends of her own) discovered her, scarcely believing their eyes. Now she knew that Frederick and Viola must hear of what, to them, would seem the silly escapade of a woman old enough to know better.

But the family discovered her in quite an unexpected way. She met Daphne face to face in the restaurant, not as a patron but as another mannequin, wearing a cruising suit of red and white.

Aunt and niece started back, staring at each other, forgetting their studied pose of obliviousness to their surroundings. Daphne's jaw dropped. May was the first to recover. With a little smile at Daphne she sailed on, the flowing sleeves of her dove-gray tea gown seeming to bear her gently onward, like wings.

"I've never heard of anything so ridiculous in my life!" exclaimed Frederick that evening, his little grizzly mustache bristling with anger.

"Why is it ridiculous for me and not for Daphne?" asked May serenely, though her heart beat hurriedly.

"Good heavens, woman, compare your ages!"

"I compare our selling ability. There are hundreds of girls who can show off cruising suits, but I am almost unique in my line."

May did not say this in a conceited way, but merely as stating a fact. Yet the remark was the opening to a quite disagreeable scene. Viola reached the point of intimating that May was taking the bread out of Daphne's mouth, and Frederick openly said that she was leading a double life and that he was ashamed to face his friends.

The Baxters had always been such an agreeable family that they did not know how to make up a quarrel. They felt deeply ashamed, yet rigid. They could not make advances towards reconciliation.

"If May is going to make herself a figure of fun at Mills and Shermans," said Frederick to Daphne, "I cannot have you parading about at the same time. You'll have to give it up. I never did like it."

"Lots of girls do it," Daphne complained bitterly. "And how else can I make some money?"

"A fat lot of good your dramatic work is doing you!" said Ralph.

"How can I help it if others get in ahead of me! And did you stick at your architecture?"

"If only you had kept out of politics," moaned Viola to Frederick, "all this would never have happened!"

Auntimay, who had been the moral prop of the family, had sown these seeds of its disintegration.

Within three months Daphne married a young actor who only now and again had engagements. Ralph had joined a flier who traveled about taking country folk for short flights at agricultural fairs, and Willy had written home to say that he wanted to be a puppet showman.

One day, at the lunch hour, May was gliding through the restaurant in an oyster-colored satin evening gown, looking the picture of Edwardian graciousness. She carried with her the very breath of those spacious days. In one hand she held an ostrich-feather fan. People forgot to eat their Japanese fruit salad or poached egg on spinach and stared. The young girls in beach costumes might well have been on some distant beach, for all the notice that was taken of them.

At a table in a corner, eating the most substantial lunch the menu provided, sat the handsomest elderly gentleman May had ever seen. His head was really magnificent, with its waves of silvery hair and its noble, almost unlined, forehead. His features were regular, but at the same time expressive, and his blue eyes held a look of both benevolence and amusement. He watched May's progress along the narrow aisle between the crowded tables with grave attention, his eyes traveling slowly from the silken folds of her dress to her perfectly arranged hair. Their eyes met and they exchanged a look, calmly admiring on his part, suddenly rather shy on hers. She wondered what such a man was doing there, in that throng of chattering, gobbling women. She felt suddenly embarrassed.

She went the length of the first restaurant and moved slowly through the second, stopping now and again when ladies questioned her as to the price of the gown or fingered its texture. She thought, looking down into their upturned faces, how unattractive most of them were, how badly they would have shown off the gown she was wearing. But there they were, securely seated at table, choosing what they fancied from the menu, while she paraded up and down, up and down, with the one object — of interesting them in what she wore!

No, that was not quite true. There was now another object in her progression. She wanted to pass by the handsome elderly man again and find out if she had been mistaken in thinking that he was at a table alone. It was quite probable that he was accompanied by some dowdy female who would be completely overshadowed by him. As May threaded her way among the tables she went straight in his direction, ignoring the other side of the room.

Since she had passed that way the empty table next him had been taken by four stout women, so that he looked more than ever surrounded by their sex, but, at his own small table, he was alone. A glass of sherry had just been set down by his hand.

This time May approached him from behind. First she saw his broad shoulders and well-shaped head, then his hand, white and strong, on which he wore a heavy seal ring. She gave a swift look down over his face as she passed, but he did not see her and she returned to the dressing room with a feeling of disappointment.

She was to change from the gown she had worn into a black velvet dinner dress with a full skirt. The fullness of the skirt showed to advantage her long, slender waist and her carriage, which was authentically Victorian and not produced by exigent muscular effort. She moved more quickly than usual, afraid that he might already have finished his lunch and gone.

But he had not finished. He was looking somewhat critically at the underripe pear on his plate when she approached. He raised his eyes to hers and made a little arresting gesture with his hand.

"What a charming gown," he said.

May stopped and the heads of the women at the surrounding tables turned.

"Yes, isn't it?" she answered. Her voice, even in that confusion, conveyed an atmosphere of gentleness and repose. She wondered if she should speak of the gown and its style to one who so obviously could not wear it or whether she should sail on leaving him to the further investigation of his pear. But her legs refused to move. She simply stood there smiling down at him, enjoying the looks of him, thinking how different he was from her brother Frederick or any other of the few men she knew.

He said, "I am looking for just such a dress for my wife."

"Your wife!" She should not have said that! She followed it immediately with, "Yes, I am sure she would like it. It is one of our latest models and so comfortable, and — " she spoke rather gaspingly.

"She is just your height," he said, "and your coloring. Can you tell me how much the dress is?"

"Only twenty guineas. Perhaps I could arrange a fitting for her."

"I am afraid she cannot come to be fitted. She is an invalid. She is up and about, you understand, but she cannot leave the house. Might I see the back of the dress?"

May turned round slowly in front of him, showing off both the gown and herself. The consumption of food in the restaurant entirely ceased while all eyes were fixed on May and the handsome elderly gentleman.

She was embarrassed and yet rather pleased with herself, even haughty, as she continued her progress among the tables. She saw him pay his bill, saw him in conversation with the head waitress. Was he, possibly, asking to be directed to the reception rooms?

He was. May was recalled from her promenade and summoned to display the dress before him and the head of the gowns' department in the seclusion of a private room. He sat on a green velvet settee, watching her judicially as she paraded up and down the room. He liked the dress, he said. He liked it very much, but he was not at all sure that it would be the thing for his wife. They lived so quietly. Could he be shown something more in the nature of a teagown?

A charming tea gown in a combination of mauve and pink was selected, and May had never appeared to more advantage than in it. Mr. Wycherley, for he had given his name, was impressed by the tea gown. It seemed that he could never have too much of looking at it. The manageress became a trifle restive and asked him if he would like to see some other model.

Regretfully Mr. Wycherley parted from the tea gown. It was beautiful, he said, but his wife disliked mauve. Could he see a gown in a brighter color? He could and did. May was quite tired by the time she had shown off more tea gowns, more dinner dresses and a negligee. Mr. Wycherley liked them all, but he could decide on nothing till he had talked with his wife. He would come back the next day.

May could not get the thought of him out of her head or the remembrance of his admiring gaze, which she was quite sure had not been only for the clothes she wore. She lay in bed thinking of him and his invalid wife. "If only I had had the time," she thought, "the freedom, he is the very sort of man I should have liked to marry! Distinguished, tranquil, gentle and yet commanding. Oh, how I wish that wife of his would die! Then — somehow or other — I would get him for myself! Nothing should stop me!"

She had said the words out loud and she was shocked to hear them. Why, she was little better than a murderess! Wishing a poor, innocent sick woman in her grave!

But though she stifled the words, the wish remained. The first thought that came into her head the next morning was, "Oh, I hope I shall see Mr. Wycherley today! Perhaps . . . perhaps . . . Mrs. Wycherley died last night!"

But he was not in the restaurant, which seemed unusually noisy and crowded that day. She paraded through one room after another in one gown after another. She completely forgot to stop and smile when her gown was admired. She just swept up and down the narrow aisles between the tables searching for Mr. Wycherley. The only face she knew was that of her sister-in-law, who was lunching with an old school friend and who radiated disapproval from behind her vitamin salad. May kept away from that corner. She hated to think of the remarks Viola would make that night. A stormy revolt against her home life and its restrictions suddenly rose in her, sharpened by the conviction that she would never see Mr. Wycherley again.

But she did see him. He was standing, with a very subdued air, near the door by which she passed from the restaurant. He stepped forward, then hesitated. She started backward, then hesitated. They stared at each other, mutually embarrassed. Then she gathered her forces and asked, in a pleasant voice:

"Is your wife interested in any of the gowns I showed you?"

His answer came so low that she had to strain her ears to catch it. "I am afraid not. You see — she died last night."

May felt that she was about to fall in a faint. But she had been so well trained through long years of thinking of everyone but herself that she kept her nerves under control. She put her hand on a table where a display of artificial flowers was arranged and steadied herself. She fixed her mind on the dead Mrs. Wycherley and thrust away from it the thought that that death might have been forwarded by her wish. She said:

"Oh, I am so sorry! I am so very sorry! Surely it is very sudden."

"Very sudden," he answered gravely.

"I hope she did not suffer much," said May.

"She did not suffer at all. She was glad to go."

Glad to go! And yet she had not suffered! Then why was she glad to go? Was it possible that she was glad to leave Mr. Wycherley? Looking into his kindly handsome face May could not believe that. She repeated:

"I am so very sorry, but still — if she was glad to go — I suppose one should not wish her back."

"No, no," he answered, "I could not wish her back. It is better so."

"It is a good thing," said May, who was practical as well as sentimental, "that you did not buy any of the dresses."

"I suppose it is," he agreed.

There seemed nothing more to say. Then the beautifully arranged flowers on the table suggested something to May. Could she send flowers to the dead Mrs. Wycherley whom she had never known? Still, her husband seemed almost a friend. Surely she could! She touched a spray of white lilac. Its dry unresponsiveness reminded her that the flowers were artificial. She asked almost timidly:

"Would you be willing — I should like very much to send some flowers if . . ."

Mr. Wycherley's eyes also rested on the flowers on the table. "Not these," he said. "She liked real ones."

"Oh, naturally!" cried May. "I never thought of anything but real ones." She looked about her bewildered. Did they keep real flowers in the store? She thought not. She could not remember.

He came to her help. "It is very kind of you. There is a small shop near by where we could get them. I could meet you outside when you are free. It is so very kind of you to think of it."

He was waiting for her in the lobby of the store. They looked a distinguished pair as they passed into the street. He guided her carefully through the crowd, but it was some time before he could find the florist's shop.

"What flowers were her favorites?" she asked.

"Violets," he answered, "just a little bunch of violets."

The violets were in sixpenny buttonhole bouquets. May bought eight of these. The assistant took off the wires and made them into one bunch. Mr. Wycherley took it gratefully from May's hand.

"I am going to be very lonely," he said.

She could only whisper, "I am so sorry."

They looked at each other across the bunch of violets. He said, with a slight tremor in his voice, "I wonder if I shall ever see you again."

"I shall still be in the restaurant."

"Perhaps I shall see you there."

They bowed and parted. A fortnight passed. Then one morning, before the rush hour, he appeared at the same table, a substantial lunch and a glass of sherry before him. May's heart gave a leap, for he had scarcely been out of her mind in the past weeks. Again she was struck by his good looks, his open, frank expression.

"Such a man," she thought, "could never deceive a woman. His lips simply could not utter a falsehood."

Yet on that very day she discovered that he had lied to her.

Gladly she had accepted his invitation to take tea with him at Richmond that afternoon. The weather was lovely. Mr. Wycherley had a smart car driven by an admirable chauffeur. As they sat at a small table, within sight of the river, in air scented by white lilacs, he confessed to her that he had lied about his wife. He had never had a wife. He had invented her on the spur of the moment in order to see more of May. He had killed her off as he had invented her when her existence became embarrassing.

May broke into sudden hysterical laughter. "Thank Heaven!" she exclaimed. "You have taken a weight off my mind. I wished the poor woman was dead and I was horrified when you told me — " Then May colored deeply and stared in speechless confusion at Mr. Wycherley.

"You wished her dead!" he cried. "You wished her dead! You really meant that — in all that her death would signify?"

May's head drooped. The color flooded her face, for she still blushed as she had at twenty.

Frederick and Viola appeared to take her engagement to Mr. Wycherley as a personal affront. The fact that Mr. Wycherley was a wealthy bachelor who had spent his life in the collecting of rare stamps moved Frederick to indignation. If he had had the authority to forbid the marriage he would have done so. As it was, May and Mr. Wycherley slipped quietly into a registry office one morning and came out man and wife.

Now May began to do all the things she had never before had time to do. She went to concerts, the theater and art exhibitions. She traveled, and that with a companion alive and interested in everything he saw. Mr. Wycherley was as delighted by May's companionship as she was by his. He realized that he had wasted a great part of his life in seclusion and the collecting of stamps. Now he wanted to make up for it. Like a newly discovered and exceedingly rare stamp, May's image was imprinted on his life. In truth, he was perfectly happy.

But May was not perfectly happy. One thing was lacking to her. That was the dependence her family had always placed on her. She was strong, she was resilient, she was made to support others, and Mr. Wycherley scarcely leaned on her at all. They were equal. Sometimes she would wander about the handsome house where she was now mistress, a nagging little yearning at her heart. She remembered how she had always been solving the children's problems for them, always helping them with this and that, with never time to think of herself.

One day, more than a year after her marriage, she was driving along Park Lane in her car when she saw a beautiful young girl rather shabbily dressed waiting for a bus. She saw that it was Daphne — and that she was carrying a baby. And she had never been told that Daphne had a baby!

Frantically she signaled the chauffeur to stop. She let down the window and waved her hand to Daphne. She called her by name and the young girl darted from the curb, almost dropping the baby, and was helped into the car by the chauffeur.

"Daphne, is it yours?" cried May.

"Oh, Auntimay, it is! George and I are separated! We were just too incompatible and he earned simply nothing! And I just can't live at home with Mother and Dad! They make such a fuss when Baby cries! Dad has given me a tiny allowance — a mere pittance — and I'm trying to get in the movies. Oh, how lovely you look! And how wonderful your furs are! I should have hunted you up long ago, only Mummy and Dad told me you had married a horrid old stamp collector and I pictured you living in poverty almost as great as my own and I thought I'd better keep away!"

"My poor darling! Let me see the baby! Is it a boy or girl?"

"A girl."

May took the tiny thing in her arms. It snuggled against the the warmth of the furs. May's blood seemed to turn to some mild fluid, sweet and exhilarating. Oh, surely her husband would not deny her this! Surely when he saw Daphne and her baby he would take them in!

"What is her name?" she asked.

"She's never been called anything but Baby. But her name is to be May — after you! I do want it to be May — if you don't mind."

Mind! May was in seventh heaven! She felt the baby's body like a tiny tendril twining about her life. She felt Daphne's dependence on her stronger than ever.

"What is the baby's surname?"

"Baxter. I've discarded George's name. She is simply May Baxter."

Another little May Baxter! Auntimay hugged her close. Daphne poured out in staccato phrases all that had happened to her since they had last met.

One look at Daphne's anxious young face, her shabby clothes, her tiny child, and from there into his loved wife's pleading eyes, was enough for Mr. Wycherley. He himself felt no lack in his life, but, if May wanted this young niece and her infant in the house, and apparently she wanted them very much, he was willing that she should have them.

A charming bedroom was arranged for Daphne. A most modern nursery created for young May, who behaved from the first as though she were the heir apparent and center of the establishment. She soon had Mr. Wycherley just where she wanted him, and that was at her diminutive pink feet!

The Celebration

Oh, I can't believe it! I can't believe it!" Mrs. Evans almost screamed in her hilarity. "Oh, it seems too good to be true." And she sat down and burst into tears.

Her son Robert looked down at her with mingled sympathy and grudging. It was all very well for her to be excited but there was no need to go on like this. Jimmy had had a wonderful piece of luck. Robert only wished it might have been himself.

"Do you really think he'll get the money?" Mrs. Evans quavered, raising her streaming eyes to his.

"Sure. Those Irish Sweepstakes always pay up. They're O.K."

His mother reached out and took his hand. "I hope he'll do something nice for you, Bob," she said. "You've had an awful lot to contend with."

"I'm not counting on that," he returned gruffly. "You're the one he ought to do something for."

"No, no, I don't want anything out of it. I just want to see my children get on. Sakes alive, won't your father be surprised?"

"You bet. And the girls. It'll all come out in the evening papers. The reporters are up at Jim's place already. They'll be photographing him and Lyla."

His mother gasped. "Photographing them for the papers! Oh, my goodness! Won't Lyla be conceited?"

"It's a pity Lyla isn't prettier. Now, if it was *my* wife she'd be worth taking a picture of."

His mother gave an embarrassed laugh and he remembered the unwieldy bulk of Lizzie, who was soon to have a child, her fourth. He said, in a grumpy tone, "Anyhow, she has a pretty face."

Mrs. Evans agreed. "Yes, and she's not ten years older than her husband — the way Lyla is. When I think of that boy of eighteen marrying a woman of twenty-eight, it makes me mad."

"They've been married a year now and she's got him just where she wants him — her and her parents."

"Jimmy's a real affectionate boy," cried his mother. "My, I wish he'd come and see me. I want to give him a big hug."

The words were scarcely out of her mouth when Jimmy walked into the room. He was flushed and excited.

"Hello, Ma," he stammered, in a voice that cracked, the way it did when it was changing. "Say — w-what d'you think of the Irish Sweepstakes now? Th-thirty thousand bucks! How d'you like havin' a millionaire for a son?"

She took him in her arms and almost hurt him with the strength of her hug. He was a fragile little fellow. She looked at her two boys, Bob stocky and reliable, a family man at twenty-six, finding it hard to make ends meet, what with doctors' bills and the high cost of living, Jimmy, married far too young, to a woman far too old, and now the sudden possessor of such wealth as none of them had ever dreamed of. She thought of her two married daughters and their husbands, of her youngest girl who was only fifteen, and the baby of the family, a boy of nine. They all would be proud of Jimmy's good fortune. And their father — what would he say — he who felt himself so superior to his family?

"Say, Ma," said Jimmy. "I can't stay long. Lyla wants me to go out with her and buy some clothes."

"For you or her?"

"For both of us. Everybody will be looking at us."

"Oh, Jimmy, are you sure you'll get the money?"

"Course I shall. This thing's O.K. Look." He took the notification of his prize winning from his pocket and spread it before her.

"Get my glasses, dearie."

He brought them and she perused the document. Bob leaned over her, his blunt features rigid with envy.

"It's sure swell," he said. He rubbed his head against his mother's as though to remind her that he too was her son.

The little boy, Ronnie, came running in from school. He was told the news and stared at Jimmy, as though he were a marvel of perspicacity. Then he burst out — "Show us the money!"

"He left it at home — with Lyla," grinned Bob.

The telephone rang. Jimmy sprang to answer it. Bob exchanged a look with his mother. "I'll bet it's her," he said.

It was. "I'm to go right home," Jimmy got out breathlessly. "It's another reporter. Gosh, what a life!"

His mother caught him by the arm. "Listen, Jimmy. I'm going to have a celebration for you — and for Lyla, of course — tomorrow night. We'll have the whole family. Be here early for supper, will you? And Lyla's father and mother too, if they'd like to come."

"Lyla's ma don't go out at night and he won't go without her. But we'll come."

"Come early."

"Sure."

"Bring your appetites with you. I'll bake the things you like."

With difficulty he wrenched his mind from his own affairs. "Corn fritters, Ma?"

"All you can eat. And the lemon custard cake Lyla likes. Be sure and come early."

He promised, half dazed by excitement, kissed her, freed himself and left.

The Evanses lived in a flat above a small undertaking establishment. They acted as caretakers and, in return, had their quarters rent free. These rooms were the best they had ever lived in, fine hardwood floors, clean new decorating throughout, excellent plumbing. The undertaking business on the ground floor was Jewish and the funeral services held there were, at first, rather disturbing and strange to the Gentile family. Mr. Katz, the undertaker, was a kind man. He was interested in Henry Evans, whom he looked on as a man of superior intelligence and education. They had long talks together in the room where the coffins were stored. Henry Evans had a good deal of spare time.

Mrs. Evans had wanted to keep the great news till her husband returned from the printers, where he had a part-time job, so that she might have the thrill of telling it to him herself. But on the way home he bought a newspaper and the first thing his eye lighted on was the picture of his son Jimmy, taken with his wife and parents-in-law. He read the heading: NINETEEN-YEAR-OLD MILK-TRUCK DRIVER WINNER IN IRISH SWEEPSTAKES.

He did not know the man sitting next him but he showed him the picture, trying to keep the hand that held the paper steady. Soon all the other passengers were looking at the same picture in their own papers. "He's always been a good boy," declared the father proudly," except that he wouldn't go to college."

He felt that people looked at him with more respect after that. He almost believed that he could have afforded to send Jimmy to college. His step was light as he hurried along the street and turned in at the door above which hung the sign KATZ FUNERAL PARLORS. His wife met him at the top of the stairs. She saw at once that he had heard the news.

Her face fell. "Oh, Henry, who told you?" she cried. Then she saw the newspaper. "But you hardly ever buy one!"

The evening paper was delivered to them by their own son, Ronnie, as they were on his route.

"I guess some instinct told me to buy it." Evans spoke in rather precise accents. His education, his manner of speaking, set him apart from his family, made the humorous things he said seem more humorous, the sarcastic things more sarcastic. He was lightly built and carried himself very straight. Mrs. Evans was stocky and reliable. Bob took after her.

"Isn't it wonderful?" she quavered, her eyes full of happy tears. "Our Jimmy — thirty thousand dollars — just for the price of one ticket!"

"Have you seen him?"

"Yes. He was here and Bob too. Jimmy couldn't stay. I guess he hardly knows if he's standing on his head or his heels."

"We'll go to his place and see him after supper," said her husband. "I hope he'll do something nice for you out of the money."

The small boy put in, "Can I come too? Do you think he'll do something for me?"

"Certainly," answered his father. "He'll probably buy you a fine bicycle."

"Now don't go putting ideas in the child's head." But Mrs. Evans herself was quivering with ideas.

The fifteen-year-old daughter who was rather an objectionable teen-ager, came tearing in. She could not wait to be told details but flew to the telephone to spread the news among her friends. This prevented her two married sisters from getting on the line. After repeated attempts they gave up and, after eating a sketchy evening meal, hastened with their husbands to the flat.

Nothing could have pleased Mrs. Evans better. She wanted all her children about her in this hour of triumph. She looked on her two sons-in-law as her children also, for one of them was an orphan and the other came from the West and had no relations of his own in the city. She hugged all four and told them the amazing news over again, as if they did not already know it. She repeated it, right from the moment when Jimmy had told her he had bought a ticket for the Sweeptakes and she had said he was foolish to waste his money that way, to the coming of Bob with the announcement of the lucky draw.

"I guess Bob wishes it was him," said her son-in-law, Bill Clark, "with three kids and another on the way."

"There's nothing jealous about Bob," declared the mother. "He's just glad Jimmy's had such luck."

"That old wife of his will be more stuck-up than ever," put in the teen-ager.

The two elder sisters laughed, rather maliciously. The pretty one said, "You'll see Lyla with a fur coat and a diamond ring before long, mark my words."

The plain one added, "*And* a car. I bet they buy one inside of a week."

"I know of a good secondhand car for sale," said Bill Clark, "I can get a commission on it if I find a buyer. I'll phone Jim before someone else gets in ahead of me." He sprang to the telephone. There was silence in the room as the family, one and all, listened avidly to his end of the conversation. Jimmy and his wife, from being nobodies, had become of breath-taking importance.

"Hello," Bill was saying genially. "Is that Lyla? . . . Oh, hello, Lyla — congratulations. This sure is wonderful news. . . . Yeah, aren't you the lucky pair? And you certainly deserve it. . . . Yeah, everybody's saying how glad they are. . . . Huh-huh, we're all here. The whole damn family — wish you and Jim were here. . . . Say, could I speak to Jim? Got to congratulate him personally. . . . Oh — tired, is he? No wonder — all those newspaper guys . . . Sure . . . but I'll just keep him a minute. . . . Too tired to talk? Well, I'll be darned. What's he doing? . . . *Gone to bed?* For the love of Mike!

Well — I just wondered if he's thinking of buying a car. I know of a dandy secondhand one. . . . *What?* You've ordered a new one? *Already?* By golly, you haven't wasted much time. But I'm certainly glad. I just thought if you wanted a secondhand one — what make did you order? I'd just like to know so's I can tell the folks. . . . A new model Buick! Well — that sounds good. Everybody here'll be tickled when I tell them. . . . Sure, tickled pink. . . . Well, remember us poor relations to Jim. Be seeing you tomorrow night. Bye-bye, Lyla." He hung up the receiver.

A volley of questions met him when he rejoined the circle. Though they had heard every word he said and guessed pretty accurately what Lyla had said, they wanted it repeated. Bill, who was quite a mimic, imitated Lyla's drawling, nasal tones.

"They're not wasting any time spending the money," said Henry Evans. "Believe me, they'll run through it in no time."

"But a new *Buick,*" cried his pretty daughter, pink with envy. "They must be crazy."

"I thought Lyla'd have more sense," the plain one added, "seeing that she's nine years older than Jimmy."

"She's a stuck-up old thing," declared the teen-ager.

"Why did Jimmy go to bed?"

"I guess the poor lad's tired out," said the mother.

Bill Clark gave a hoot. "I wish I was that kind of tired," he said.

The pretty sister gave herself a searching glance in the looking glass above the sideboard.

"It must be awful," she said, "to have photographers pushing right into your apartment to take your picture."

Everyone stared at her, thinking how she would have loved it.

"You'd certainly take a prettier picture than Lyla," said her father. He gave her an appreciative look, noting her resemblance to himself. He was, in fact, pleased with all his family at this moment. He looked forward to tomorrow morning at the printing office, when he would speak with nonchalance of his son's "bit of luck."

The quiet son-in-law, who had acquired a reputation for wisdom by almost never speaking, now opened his lips.

"I'm kind of thirsty," he said.

Mrs. Evans sprang up. "I'll make coffee for everybody."

"No, no, Mother." Bill Clark laid a restraining hand on her arm. "The kid can go to the corner and get some ginger ale." He drew silver from his pocket and gave it to Ronnie.

"I'd sooner have a coke," said the teen-ager.

"You'll drink what the rest do," said her father. In these days he disapproved of this girl. He disliked the way she dressed, the way she talked, the way she looked — almost ready to burst with health. Now she threw herself back in her chair, stretched out her legs, in their turned-up slacks and crumpled white socks, and sulked.

Her mother gave her a propitiatory look. "There's a coke in the icebox, Joanne."

The girl ignored this, for she wanted to continue with her sulking. The little boy had already run off.

"I wish Bob and Lizzie were here," remarked the plain sister. "I'd like to know what Bob thinks about it all."

"You'll see them tomorrow night," Mrs. Evans said happily. "I'm having a celebration. You've all got to be here early. There'll be lots to eat."

"And drink too," added Evans.

There was so much to say, so many speculations about Jimmy's future, that it was midnight before the married couples left, but as neither pair had any children, they had no need for anxiety on that score.

It was a restless night that Henry Evans and his wife spent. As they lay side by side in the dark, one of them would no sooner begin to get drowsy than the other would renew the talk about Jimmy and the prize money. By three o'clock they still hadn't closed their eyes. Jimmy's new situation in life was considered from every angle. They planned exactly what they themselves would have done had such a fortune come their way. Henry felt that his son should be equipped for such a responsibility and he told his wife how he was going to take the boy in hand, right from tomorrow, and guide him in the way of prudent investment and careful living. He enumerated the points in which he would give Jimmy counsel. It was then that Mrs. Evans grew sleepy. Soon he was left awake in the dark alone.

He scarcely realized that he had slept when the alarm went off at six-thirty. Yet when he set out for the printers he was brisker than usual. He bought a morning paper and, chuckling in a half-apologetic way, pointed out the picture of Jimmy and Lyla to the other passengers in the streetcar. There was an article in which Lyla was described as a slim blonde.

Mrs. Evans had a morning paper too and when she read that laughed out loud. "Slim blonde," she exclaimed. "She's no more a slim blonde than I am." She pictured Bill Clark greeting Lyla tonight with "Hello, slim blonde!" And she wondered how Lyla would take it. She hoped there'd be no unpleasantness.

It was hard to get on with her housework this morning, for her friends and relations kept ringing her up. Some dropped in to congratulate her. Added to this, her excitement made her less efficient. She kept letting things slip out of her hands. She broke her best cake plate. Ronnie developed a cold in the head and the teen-ager disappeared with her friends and did nothing to help. The lemon custard for the cake was inclined to run. At the fruit store she went quite wildly extravagant and bought four boxes of expensive strawberries. She bought ham and pressed veal and salad stuff. Everyone in the shop knew about Jimmy.

All day long she kept expecting Lyla or Jimmy to ring her up. She knew how busy they were, yet she still kept expecting it.

Every time the telephone rang she was sure it was one of them on the line. She kept counting the hours till six o'clock. That was the time she had set for the celebration. Half an hour before that time she was dressed in her best and the teen-ager had, under pressure, consented to set the table. Everything looked inviting, Henry Evans thought when he came into the room. He gave an admiring glance at his wife, at her flushed cheeks and bright eyes. He himself wore his Sunday suit and the tie she had given him on his birthday. He looked spruce and dignified. He said, "I've been thinking we ought to have some flowers for Lyla. It'd show her we know how to do things in good style."

"A corsage, you mean," put in the teen-ager.

He stared at her. "*I* call it a bunch of flowers."

"Corsage," she repeated.

"Flowers cost a lot," said his wife. "I've spent enough on this supper as it is. Anyhow Lyla didn't do anything. It was Jimmy bought the ticket."

"This is no time for economy," laughed Henry.

He hurried out, down the stairs, through the undertakers and into the street which seemed to wear an air of gaiety that evening. He bought three orchids, tied with a bow of chiffon, at the florists. He bought something else too — when his wife saw it, she cried, "You shouldn't have brought that stuff home. I've got plenty of ginger ale and Bill's sent a case of beer."

"This is just for us old folks," he grinned.

"I won't touch it. You know that."

"I mean Lyla and me."

She had to laugh but she was annoyed at him, both because of the expense and because of her fear that he might take too much of the stuff. He was not a man who could carry liquor well.

He took the quart bottle of whiskey into the kitchen and uncorked it. The small boy knelt on a chair beside the table watching with interest.

"May I taste, Dad?" he asked.

"Sure."

Ronnie picked up the cork and gingerly licked it. He made a face. "I don't like it."

"Stay that way," advised his father.

"Do you like it?"

"Once in a while when I want to celebrate."

"Like tonight?"

"Yes, like tonight."

"Dad, now Jimmy's rich do you s'pose he'll help you and Mamma?"

"I hope so."

"If I was rich, I would."

"I'll bet you would."

The first to arrive were Bob and his wife. Lizzie looked tired but her pretty face was lighted by an excited smile. She was a favorite with her parents-in-law and was kissed by each of them in turn.

"I thought you'd have brought the kiddies," said Mrs. Evans. "I've set places for them at the table."

"Goodness' sakes," Lizzie gave a big sigh, "I get enough of their noise. We left them at my mother's."

She looked admiringly at the table, carefully set out with good things to eat and, laid by Lyla's plate, the three orchids. She picked them up and examined them.

"What do you think of that?" asked her mother-in-law.

"Well, I've certainly never had an orchid."

Evans spoke from the doorway. "I'll buy you one when your baby arrives, see if I don't."

"Don't worry," she returned, a little sharply. "I don't want any orchids."

She went into the bedroom to remove her things.

The married sisters and their husbands now arrived. They had brought all the newspaper clippings and pictures they had been able to collect. There was a great deal of laughter as these were compared to the ones Mrs. Evans already had. Everybody was excited. Envy was forgotten in happy expectation. Bob filled glasses for all but the younger ones. It was arranged by Henry Evans that, as soon as the door opened and Lyla and Jim appeared, a toast was to be made to them. Everyone was a little tremulous excepting the teen-ager, who looked completely unimpressed.

Lyla and Jim were already late. Mrs. Evans had taken the scalloped potatoes from the oven but now she wondered if she had not better put them back.

"I'm going to give Jim a ring," said the father, "and find out what is keeping them."

"Don't be fussy, Dad," said his plain daughter. "They're likely on their way."

"Well, I'll give them ten minutes, then I'll ring."

Before that time had passed the telephone rang.

"Somebody else to congratulate us," Mrs. Evans exclaimed. "I never saw the beat. You answer it this time, Bob."

Willingly Robert took up the receiver. The more congratulations the merrier.

"Hello." He smiled expectantly into the telephone.

He listened for a moment, then the smile left his face.

"Why, Lyla," he said, "you can't do that."

His sisters demanded, "Can't do what?"

"Sh-h," he ordered them, and again listened.

"But Mother's got everything ready," he said loudly. "We're all waiting."

"What's the matter?" cried his mother.

"O.K." he growled into the telephone and banged down the receiver.

They crowded anxiously about him.

"Is Jimmy sick?" Mrs. Evans demanded.

"No, Jimmy's not sick. But some of Lyla's folks are there and Jim and Lyla can't leave. She says they'll be over after supper."

Mrs. Evans flopped into a chair. Her face was blank with disappointment.

"Well, if that wouldn't make your blood boil," exclaimed the pretty sister.

"I knew it'd be like that," the plain one added. "Jim will be dragged just where she wants to go and he won't go anywhere else."

"But I've got the supper ready," wailed Mrs. Evans.

Her son-in-law Bill patted her shoulder. "Don't worry, Ma."

The quiet son-in-law remarked, "There'll be all the more for the rest of us."

"But I made all the things they like," she moaned.

"Let me at the phone," said her husband. "I'll tell that woman a thing or two."

"No, no, we mustn't have any words. Not at a time like this."

"But it's so *mean!*" cried Lizzie.

"Just like that old Lyla," put in the teen-ager.

"What's Lyla done?" demanded the small boy.

"Haven't you got ears?" Bob demanded.

"What time did Lyla say they'd come?" Mrs. Evans asked Bob.

"About nine o'clock. She said they were sorry."

"Sorry!" echoed his sisters scornfully. "They've spoilt everything."

"No, they haven't." Mrs. Evans forced herself to be cheerful. "We'll just enjoy our supper, as though nothing had happened and then, when they come, give them a hearty welcome."

Grumbling a little they obeyed her. They carried their beer

to the table and drank it there. Bill told a funny story and the four wives laughed immoderately, as though forcibly to throw off the shadow that had fallen. Henry Evans began to show off a little, as he liked to do in front of his family. Mrs. Evans, who usually tried to repress him in this, now encouraged him. By the time the meal was finished they were in quite good spirits, even though the orchids at Lyla's place were a constant reminder of the absence of the guests of honor.

While the women cleared away the supper things and Bill had a sparring match with little Ronnie, Henry Evans brought out the bottle of whiskey and poured drinks for the men. The hands of the clock moved with, it seemed, added speed, and before they realized the lateness of the hour, ten o'clock was striking.

Bob said angrily, "What the dickens has happened to Jim and Lyla? Why don't they come?"

"Gosh, it's ten o'clock," added Bill.

The quiet son-in-law muttered under his breath, "They're not coming."

"Not coming!" Bob's voice was sharp with anger. "I'll see whether they're coming or not." He strode to the telephone and dialed Lyla's number. Every face turned expectantly toward him. The women came from the kitchen and gathered about him.

"Is that Lyla?" he demanded. "Oh, tell Jim I want to speak to him." He put his hand over the mouthpiece. "It's some friend of theirs. She's gone to fetch one of them. I can hear a lot of voices. Must be having a party there too. Say, I'll tell that boy a thing or two when I get him on the line." He removed his hand from the mouthpiece.

"Hello! That you, Lyla?" He spoke with false geniality. "Well, we're getting tired of waiting. When are you folks coming over?"

They could hear Lyla's voice, but he interrupted her. "Bring them along. Lots of room here. We'd like to meet them."

Now Lyla was speaking.

Bob's tone changed. He exclaimed roughly, "Send that kid to the phone. I want to tell him he's got to come!"

Again Bob listened, his face flushed and a frown darkening his forehead. Then he groaned — "Oh, my gosh — too tired to come?"

Lyla's voice rattled on. Henry Evans who already had had a little more to drink than was good for him, strode to Bob's side.

"Give me that receiver," he ordered. Bob put it into his hand.

"Now — " Henry rapped out in a staccato tone " — Explain yourself, Lyla. I want to know just why you and Jim haven't turned up tonight."

He listened attentively, standing very erect. His daughters were giggling. Bill was pouring himself another drink of rye. Lyla's voice rattled on and on in the telephone.

Mrs. Evans put in somewhat shakily, "If Jimmy's too tired, tell Lyla it'll be all right."

Her husband did not reply. His attitude was so rigid that everyone in the room became rigid, except the teen-ager, who lolled on the couch examining the soles of her flat-heeled shoes. Ronnie felt that someone was being unkind to his mother and he climbed onto her lap.

Would Lyla never stop talking! Would Henry go right on listening, with that terribly set expression! Presently he did speak.

"Listen," he said, in his most educated voice. "Listen, Lyla, for this is probably the last time I shall ever speak to you. I just want to tell you that, when Jim married you, we — every one of us — felt pretty sick. We thought you'd lead him round by the nose. Now we know it. We don't care what you do. You and he can drive to Banff or to hell for all we care and stay there. Send Jimmy to the phone. If he doesn't come I'll go to your house and tell him and your parents and your friends what I think of you. Tell him to come or he'll be sorry." The last words were almost shouted into the receiver. His family could see how he was trembling.

"Oh, Henry," implored Mrs. Evans, "do be careful what you say. Remember — "

He stopped her with a furious look. Then he said, "Is that you, Jim? Well, aren't you a mean dog — letting your mother get a fine supper for the celebration and never coming to it? If I had you here I'd mop the floor with you. What?"

He listened to Jimmy's mumbling at the other end and then broke out, "We don't want you here nor your wife either. If you came now you'd get a hot reception. You can go your own way, from now on — you sneaking, sniveling, henpecked little louse. As for that bitch Lyla — "

Mrs. Evans was coming toward him, calling out, "Henry — *stop it!*" He slammed the receiver on the hook, strode to the table and poured himself a drink. He stood swaying with it in his hand, glaring belligerently at his family.

Lizzie was unnerved. Tears were trickling down her cheeks. Bob sat scowling at the floor. "I don't like this kind of talk," he said, "in front of my wife."

"Shut up," said his father. "I don't want any lip from you." He drained his glass.

Mrs. Evans came to take the bottle away but he guarded it with his body. "No, you don't!" he said. "I'm going to have a little fun out of this — after all the expense I've been put to."

"What I can't get over," growled Bill, "is them two with a new Buick, starting out on a trip to Banff."

"Who cares what they do?" The pretty daughter made a grimace of disgust.

The plain daughter gave a snort. "Everybody'll be laughing at them. They look and act so silly together."

"I wish they'd take me with them to Banff," said Ronnie.

"You go to your bed," ordered his father, "and don't let me hear another word out of you."

He watched the little boy drag himself reluctantly from the room, then turned his tragic eyes on his wife.

"The trouble is," he said, "that you've spoilt all the children. You made a fool of Jimmy from the start because he was delicate. You've made fools of them all. You've made a fool of me. But I'm not going to put up with any more." He waved his arm derisively at the circle seated about the room. "Look at them!" he said. "What a stupid lot. Look at their faces. Look at the mates they've chosen. Not the kind of people I was brought up with. And more of them coming!" He gave a sardonic jerk of the head toward Lizzie. "More and more of them! Almighty God, I'm sick of everything." He took another drink and walked swaying but still light on his feet, up and down the room. Before he married he had knocked about the world a bit and picked up some choice profanity. This he now released as was his habit when he had too much to drink. Lizzie never had seen him like this before. She began to feel completely unnerved.

"Don't mind what he says," Mrs. Evans counseled her. "He doesn't mean a word of it."

"It's shameful the way he goes on." The pretty daughter used her lipstick, as though to fortify herself.

"What's that?" shouted Evans. "What's that about me going on?"

"I didn't say anything," she muttered, reddening.

"You'd better not. If there's any man in this city could keep his temper better than I have tonight, by God I'd like to meet him!" Another blast of profanity leaped from his trembling lips.

From the undertaker's rooms below there now rose a sound of wailing, as some mourners wept for their dead.

Lizzie got heavily to her feet. "I want to go home," she whimpered. "Ring for a taxi, Bob."

"You bet I will," he muttered, giving his father a resentful look. "And we'll not come back here in a hurry."

Mrs. Evans began to cry.

"Everybody's suffering," remarked the quiet son-in-law.

"It don't mean anything to me," said the teen-ager.

Bob had called a taxi. He now led Lizzie to the bedroom where her coat and hat were. Evans followed them to the door and, while she put on her things, treated them to some more bad language. Bob kept his back turned. As the young couple moved toward the head of the stairs Evans had an idea. He went to the disarranged supper table and found the orchids he had bought for Lyla.

"Here you are, Lizzie." He proffered the flowers with a leer. "Don't say I never gave you orchids."

"I don't want them," she screamed hysterically. "Take them away." She tottered at the head of the stairs.

Bob picked her up in his arms and carried her down. The taxi driver was waiting by the outer door. All was quiet now in the funeral parlor.

Evans followed after Bob and Lizzie, clutching the banisters with one hand, while in the other, at arm's length, he held the orchids.

"Lizzie, Lizzie," he supplicated, "do accept them, with my love and respect."

Lizzie went on crying as Bob, without a look at his father, carried her to the taxi. Evans stood in the doorway alone. The street was quiet and a fine rain was falling. The night air calmed his brain. He remembered he was caretaker of the funeral parlor. He closed the door softly and then went into the silent room, where the dead body of a woman lay in a coffin. Evans turned on the light and stood looking down on the aloof face which showed no sign of suffering. He could hear movement in the room above, and then the sound of his daughters' and their husbands' leaving.

' He stood a little longer, then he noticed the orchids he still carried. He laid them on the folded hands of the dead woman.

He put out the light and slowly climbed the stairs to his own apartment.

His wife was stacking the dishes in the kitchen sink. She did not look at him.

"Has everyone gone?" he asked.

"Yes."

"Kids in bed?"

"Yes."

He came close to her. "Let me help."

"I'm not going to wash dishes tonight. I'm too tired."

"I bet you are. Me too. Tired out."

She did not upbraid him. She put her large kind hand on his arm.

"Get to bed," she said, "or you won't be fit for work to-morrow."

He laid his head on her shoulder and began to cry.

"Twa Kings"

LITTLE George MacQueen stood on the top step of the three that led to his father's bicycle repair shop wearing, pinned on his breast, the large Jubilee medal sent to him all the way from London by his Aunt Aggie. He was so small, his little chest so narrow, and the medal so large that it hit you in the eye the moment you looked at him. And everybody did look at him. No one could help looking at him because his figure, tiny as it was in the deep, dingy doorway, seemed symbolic of noble elation in great achievement.

His mind was, in truth, almost overwhelmed by two emotions, pride and a great pity for those who were not as he was. His eyes glowed with pride, his neck was stiff with it, but his lips wore a pitying smile for the passers-by, none of whom wore Jubilee medals, and particularly for Sandy McKay, his greatest friend, who today was removed from him by a gulf impossible to bridge. Sandy stood across the way in front of his mother's tobacco shop, barefoot and dirty, as he always was, staring in bewildered envy at the friend now so far above him.

The medal had come in a wee sma' box addressed to Geordie himself. It was the first time he had ever got a package by post and shivers of excitement ran along his spine as his mother carefully untied the string and unwrapped the box. Inside, in a nest of cotton wool, lay the medal and a card on which was written — "With love from Aggie." Aggie was Mrs. MacQueen's sister who had been a waitress in a London restaurant for six years, and who came home to Scotland once every year for a week's holiday. She was very fond and proud of her nephew George. She thought he was superior to all other small boys. Often, waiting at table, she felt contemptuous toward the people she served, remembering the superiority of her own family. They were, without exception, clean, neat and industrious. Angus MacQueen, too, had all these virtues and, like his wife and sister-in-law, he was small, pale and even fragile-looking, but he had their spirit and determination and he had worked so hard that last year he had found himself able to afford a second-hand motorcycle which he had bought at a great bargain. Now, on the Sabbath, instead of taking George by the hand and his wife on his arm for a walk on the hills beyond the village, he mounted his motorcycle and, with wife and child in the sidecar, disappeared in a whirl of dust to parts, before now, unexplored. It was glorious.

When the medal had been brought to view and Mrs. Mac-Queen had explained that it was made to celebrate the King's Jubilee, Geordie asked at once:

"Can Ah hae it pinned on me today, Mither?"

"Weel," answered Mrs. MacQueen thoughtfully, "I dinna think that would be quite right. I think it ought tae be kept for the day itsel'." As always, she was anxious to do the right thing.

"But, Mither," declared Geordie vehemently, "Ah want ye tae pit it on me right awa'! Ah want Alec McKay tae see it."

"I think ye'd better wait, Geordie." But she had no strength to oppose him.

"It's ower long to wait. Ah canna."

He had his way. Not only was he allowed to wear the medal but he was allowed to wear his Sunday suit as a fit background for it. He also had his face and hands washed and his hair licked with a wet brush. Ah, but he looked grand when at last he stood outside the shop door, with the medal on his breast and his heart swelling almost more than he could bear! No wonder everyone turned to look at him and Alec McKay's bare toes turned up in envy!

There was trouble the next morning when again he demanded to wear his Sunday suit, his Sunday boots and his red Sunday tie.

"But ye'll ruin yer Sunday claes!" expostulated Mrs. Mac-Queen.

"Na, na, Mither, Ah'll no' ruin them. Ah'll no' be playin' in the mud wi' Sandy. Ah'll juist be standin' by the door for a' the folk tae see." And stand by the door he did all day long with short intervals for rest. He was only six years old and the medal had changed the course of his life. He had his father's support. Angus MacQueen thought that the child should be humored, indeed both parents thought that the child should be humored. They were as proud of him as he was of the medal. He took to asking questions about the King. How big was he? How old was he? When he learned that the King was nearly seventy, he exclaimed:

"Havers! Ah hope he'll last!"

Though he did not explain why or for how long, his mother took it for granted that he meant during his own lifetime. She did say, however:

"It seems queer that a Scots laddie should set sae much store by an English king."

Little Geordie's face was a study in disappointment.

"Ye're no' tellin' me, Mither, that the King is an Englishman!"

"Ay, he is that."

Geordie's face went crimson but he controlled himself. He drew in his chin so that he might the better see his medal. He gained strength from it to bear his disappointment. The next day he came into the kitchen radiant.

"Mither!" he cried, "Ah've juist heerd tell frae Duncan MacTavish that the auld Queen was a Scotswumman! He tuk me intil his ain room and shewed me the medal he had for her Jubilee. It was fine but no' sae big as mine. He telled me how she lived in Balmoral and he has a picture of her and her bairns in a plaid shawl and kilts!"

Duncan MacTavish was a retired schoolmaster who boarded above the provision shop on the corner. He took a great interest in the little boy and had prophesied more than once that he would be a remarkable man. Consequently Mrs. MacQueen thought him a very astute man, though she knew that anyone with an eye in his head could see that her son was born for greatness.

She said, mixing her scones — "Well, I'm glad tae hear that Queen Victoria was a Scotswumman. I hadna heerd tell of it before."

"Ah'm thinkin'," went on George, "that our King taks after his Scots grannie."

"I daursay."

"It 'ud be an awfu' thing if he was a' English, wouldn't it?"

"Ay, it would." She looked tenderly at her little boy, standing straight and proud, with his medal on his chest.

Just as she was taking the scones from the oven he came again to the kitchen.

"Ah maun tak' a wee rest," he said, and seated himself on his little stool by the fire. She looked at him with concern, noticing how pale his face was, how set his mouth.

"Ye'll wear yersel' oot wi' this flummery-dummery!" she declared. "I wish ye'd play aboot wi' the ither bairns."

"Ah canna," he answered. "Nane o' them hae medals. Ah canna play 'til the Jubilee is past."

"Will ye eat a scone, then?"

"Ay. Ah'll eat a scone."

She broke one open steaming hot and spread it with treacle. Fortunately, she thought, his appetite was better than she had ever known it. When he had eaten he went back to the door to show himself.

As he stood motionless he had time for long thoughts. They were concerned almost entirely with the King's Jubilee and his own share in the rejoicings. With each succeeding day his share loomed larger and larger until, at last, it almost equaled that of the Sovereign. They both bore the name of George. They both celebrated their birthdays on the third of June. They were both giving themselves over with Royal magnificence to the celebration of the Jubilee. There was the King in his Palace waiting for the great moment. Here was he, in front of his father's shop, his medal on his breast, the cynosure of all eyes in Garlochry. Sometimes the lads made fun of him, jeering as they passed, even throwing a small stone or two at him. But the effect of this was only to increase his prideful elation. And, at last, the other boys became proud of him, too, and pointed him out to any passing stranger.

"Yon's Geordie MacQueen! He's celebratin' the King's Jubilee."

Each day as Duncan MacTavish passed on the way to get his morning paper he saluted the little boy with — "Guid morning, Your Majesty. And I hope this fine weather holds out for your Jubilee." One day he remarked — "It's a remarkable thing, Geordie, that your surname is MacQueen. You must come by your Royal proclivities honestly."

The little boy did not understand him but he felt for the first time that both his names were associated with the Royal Family. His chest seemed scarcely big enough to contain the swelling of his heart.

Every night he laid his medal on his bed and knelt by it to say his prayers, which now always ended with the words:

"Lord, please gie us a fine day for it. Amen."

Mrs. MacQueen, for her part, would be glad when it was all over and her son was restored to normal again. She was thrown into excited perturbation by a letter from her sister urging that they should all go to London for the celebration. Never in their lives again might they have the chance to see such sights. Little George would remember it to the end of his days.

She was almost afraid to make the suggestion to her husband, so sure was she of disappointment. He was all for careful living and saving up for George's education. But, almost without a moment's hesitation, he threw himself heart and soul into the scheme. Considering the way, he said, Geordie had been impressed by the Jubilee medal, it was their bounden duty to give him the opportunity to be still more impressed by the celebrations in the capital. He had his motorcycle. They would make the journey to London in good time so that they might secure places in the front row on the curb and hold them down throughout the night, as Aggie said. It was his duty to Geordie and he was not a man to shirk his duty.

Geordie was so overwhelmed by the news that he was to see the great procession and the King himself, that he walked around the kitchen in a circle, with a dazed look in his eyes, not knowing what he was doing. But, when he did take it in, his elation reached the point of a high serenity. It was then that he began to feel pity for those who were not as he and the King. One night at supper he said suddenly:

"Fayther, ma Sunday suit's no' guid enough to wear tae the Jubilee. Ah maun hae a kilt. Ah'd like fine tae show the London folk what like a Scot in his kilt looks."

His mother laid down her knife dumbfounded. But Angus MacQueen, after a long look into his son's eyes, said calmly:

"Aye, laddie, ye maun hae a kilt."

"Ah, the pair o' ye!" cried his wife. "Ye'll hae us impover-

ished!" But her eager mind flew to the details of a grand Highland costume with velvet coat and sporran and a bonnet with
ribbons to it.

From that day Geordie's appetite failed him. He could
scarcely sleep for excitement. Luckily there was only a short
time until their departure, barely enough for the acquiring of a
Highland costume, a little on the large side but still becoming.
Oh, how grand the Jubilee medal looked when it was pinned on
the velvet jacket! Geordie's ribs ached from swelling out his
chest. On the last day he did not stand at the door of the shop
for long intervals but, like Royalty, showed himself for only a
few moments at a time to the gathering of children, with a few
grownups, who collected for the spectacle. It was Duncan Mac-
Tavish who encouraged them to cheer Geordie at each reappear-
ance.

The little boy was pale and tired before ever they set out for
London which they did as soon as the shop closed at noon of
Saturday. But still his eyes were bright with courage, though the
thought of going so far from home, which he had never left
before, loomed fearfully in his mind.

Mrs. MacQueen packed a substantial lunch to eat on the way;
the Highland suit was carefully wrapped in clean paper, but
Geordie carried the Jubilee medal in its little box clasped in his
hand. Through the bewildering maze of roads he clasped it. He
held it tighter when they passed through crowded towns, thinking of the folk who might so fiercely snatch the prize from him,
if but once they glimpsed it. All the way his mother held him on
her lap, softening a little for him the jarring and jolting of the
machine.

Under the clear starry sky they sped, their three faces growing whiter and more wan. They had a few hours of restless sleep
in a crowded inn on the highway and at sunrise they were on
their way again. With every mile the traffic became more press-

ing, more raging, more like a flooding river urging toward the sea.

They stopped to drink ginger beer and lemon squash. Ice cream was bought for Geordie. Ellen MacQueen's headache got worse and worse and, at long last, they raced into London.

Aggie had arranged for a place where the motorcycle could be left without charge. The friend with whom she shared a room had gone home for the week end, so Aggie was able to take her relations completely under her wing while they were in London. Neither her sister nor her brother-in-law had been there before, and, now that they were there, it seemed doubtful if they would have the strength to enjoy it, so completely done up were they.

But Aggie made a pot of tea, of a strength that can be only achieved by a Scotswoman, and after three cups apiece of it (Geordie having six lumps of sugar in each of his) they were able to look forward to the Jubilee with eager anticipation.

Mrs. MacQueen and Geordie stretched their weary bodies on the lumpy bed and a quilt was laid on the floor for Angus. Almost instantly he fell into a heavy sleep but Ellen and Geordie felt the vibration of the motorcycle in all their nerves. Their legs twitched, they threw their arms about and moved their heads uneasily on the thin pillows. The air in the room was very close and beyond the grimy panes of the open window a steady roar of traffic came. Through the window Geordie could see a cluster of dark roofs and chimney pots which, after a while, were richly gilded in the sunset.

It seemed to Angus MacQueen that he had scarcely slept when he was wakened by the entrance of Aggie, who had come to tell them that it was time to be off if they were to secure places worthy of their great endeavor. There was just time for another cup of tea and a bite to eat and, much more important, the dressing of Geordie in his Highland costume.

He could scarcely believe that the great moment had come.

He stood trembling with excitement while mother and aunt stripped his clothes from him and exclaimed at his general griminess.

"Ye'd never believe, Aggie, that he was scrubbed from heid tae heel before we left hame! But na wonder he's dairty, puir bairn! Mony a time I thought we'd be smothered wi' the dust."

"Dinna fret, Ellen! I'll gie him a wipe wi' my flannel an' he'll shine like the new medal, won't ye, Geordie?"

The two women stood back from him when he was fully dressed and they felt weak with admiration and possessive love. Angus MacQueen, washing in the water left over from Geordie, felt that no sacrifice was too great for such a son. Geordie looked grand. His kilt hung to perfection. The buttons on the velvet jacket gleamed like lesser stars beside the constellation of the medal. But it was the bonnet, placed jauntily on his fair head, that most truly set him off. His mother's eyes filled with tears as she looked at him. His father took him almost solemnly by the hand as they preceded the two women down the linoleum-covered stairs.

Everyone in the crowded bus stared at Geordie, or so it seemed to the relatives who guarded him. The busman said "Hoot, mon," to him as he collected the fares and more than one person called "Hello, Scottie!" when they saw him. Everyone seemed to be excited and in good humor yet they were all rivals for the best places to view the procession.

Geordie had been disappointed at what he had first seen of London. It had seemed overpoweringly crowded and the houses dingy and dour. But, after they had left bus and tube and had walked through several streets he stood at last before a scene that was beyond all he had imagined. He saw a green park with brilliant flower beds set among the trees. He saw water where white swans calmly sailed, as though the floodlighting was truly sunshine. All this was surrounded by great gleaming buildings each one of which might well be the palace of the King. These were festooned with flags and bunting and all the street was like a fairyland of Venetian masts and banners and little pointed pennants and lights of blue and gold and crimson. He wished there were not quite so many people or that he were taller so that he might drink in all this bewildering beauty. He wished his friends in his own village could see him but, in truth, all his thoughts were confused by the kaleidoscopic movement before his eyes.

The MacQueens would have been nowhere without Aggie. As it was, she was almost distraught for a time with the seeking out of a good place for them. Hundreds of people were there before them stolidly planted on the spots they meant to hold. There seemed no room anywhere but at the back. Then suddenly a big gray-haired woman saw their anxious faces, saw Geordie's Highland kilt and gave a friendly smile to Aggie.

"Come along," she said, "get in here in front of me. You're little and I'm big. There's room for the lot of you." The friend who was with her was not quite so genial but she made way and Aggie and the MacQueens were established in the front row in a position from where they could see the Royal Standard above Buckingham Palace and where nothing could come between them and the sight of the King. The new moon was up in the sky. Aggie gave Geordie a red lollipop on a wooden stick to suck. They prepared to face the long hours of the night.

Again Geordie was an object of interest in his kilt and tartan caught on his shoulder by a gleaming clasp, the bright buckles on his patent leather shoes. Angus MacQueen would have to work many a day to pay for all this finery. He and his wife and Aggie could scarcely take their eyes off the boy. His decorations were more to them than the decorations of all London.

Geordie felt his heart so strong within him that all sense of fatigue was gone. He stood bravely at the curb, conscious of admiring glances, now and again moving his body so that his kilt might swing. But his small vanity was insignificant compared to his stark Northern pride in his fellowship with the King. A golden cord seemed to join him to the Royal form in the Palace.

"Twa Kings," he murmured to himself. "Twa guid Kings."

Men went about selling hot coffee and chocolate and little flags. Aggie offered to buy a flag for him but he graciously refused it.

"Na, thank ye, Aunt," he said. "Ah'll no' wave a flag."

There was much chaffing among the crowd and, now and again, a burst of song. This was led by the strong clear soprano of the stout gray-haired woman. Geordie stared up into her face as she sang. He liked the looks of her. She took his little hand in hers and beat time with it to the song.

Some had brought stools or cushions and sat on these to rest, but for the most part newspapers were spread on the pavement. Aggie had brought some and she and Ellen and Angus sat down on these as the night drew on and Ellen took Geordie on her lap.

He fell into a restless sleep filled with confused dreams of little villages flying past, great human faces looming above, while, in a reddish sky, his medal shone like a sun. His bonnet fell over his eyes, his mouth hung open, his small hands hung limp.

He was wakened by a blast from a bugle. He started up terrified, not knowing where he was.

"It's naething to be frighted of," comforted his mother. "It's juist the bugle fra yon barracks." She sat him up and straightened his bonnet.

"Ah'm no' frighted, Mither," he said, and scrambled to his feet.

The bright sky arched above. The air quivered beneath its brilliance. Geordie saw that his medal was in place. He took off his bonnet and bowed his head. He murmured:

"Thank ye, Lord! Ye've gied us a fine day for it."

Ellen MacQueen rose with difficulty from her cramped position. Indeed she scarcely could have risen had not the stout
woman taken her under the arms and given her a heave. If it
had not been for Geordie she could almost have wished herself
back in Garlochry. But a bun and a drink of hot tea from Aggie's
Thermos put new life in her. She moistened her handkerchief
at her lips and wiped Geordie's face and tweaked and patted the
intricacies of his Highland costume into seemliness. Angus lifted
him onto his shoulder that the newcomers surging up behind
might have a look at him. He said sneeringly out of the side of
his mouth to his wife:

"Ye'd think these Londoners had never seen a Scots laddie
afore."

"I don't suppose they have, puir things," she said complacently.

It was grand for Geordie sitting on his father's shoulder. Even
though Angus was a small man it seemed a long way up. He
could see the greenness of the park, the new leaves fluttering in
the breeze, the Palace with the Royal standard floating above it.
A band marched by playing a Scottish air.

"It's a guid thing," muttered Geordie to himself, "that the auld
Queen was a Scotswumman."

There was always something new to look at, new relays of
policemen, officers trotting by on splendid horses, the purple and
gold-draped stands filling with ticket holders. But the sun came
out hotly, beating down on the patient people, the breeze fell and
the pavement gleamed hot and bright. Ellen and Aggie removed
their coats and appeared in thin blouses. But Geordie's fine
Highland costume made him feel the heat greatly though he
would not acknowledge it or remove his bonnet to cool his head.
Yet to himself once he murmured: "Lord, ye need na hae made
it quite sae fine."

Nothing ruffled the good humor of the stout woman. Again

and again she led the singing, shouting the words of the old wartime songs. Over and over she sang — "Pack Up Your Troubles
in Your Old Kit Bag" and "Tipperary," while the sweat gleamed
on her ruddy face and the sun beat without mercy on her gray
head.

Now the crowd wanted to cheer. They were in the mood for
cheering and when cars passed bearing guests to the Service in
St. Paul's they were cheered as though they were doing something remarkable. Field Marshals, statesmen and rajahs with
their ladies looked severely ahead or exchanged humorous
glances with the crowd, according to their nature.

Then all that the people had waited for began to happen —
music, glittering uniforms, haughtily stepping, shining horses.
Again and again Geordie asked — "Is it the King?"

His father would answer through the cheers — "Na, laddie,
it's one o' the Princes."

The stout woman knew who they all were. She pointed out
each notability by name. She knew all about the little Princesses.

Suddenly she grasped Angus by the arm and said, her voice
quite hoarse from much singing and shouting:

"Here they come! Their Majesties! 'Old 'im up, Mister, so the
King can see 'im an' 'e can see the King!"

He did see the King. He threw all the fervor of the pent-up
emotions of the past weeks into a long penetrating look into the
smiling blue eyes of the gray-bearded man in uniform. And the
King saw him! There was no doubt about it. Everybody said so.
The stout woman looked about truculently as though she dared
anyone in the crowd to deny it.

" 'E looked straight at 'im," she declared, "straight at little
Scottie 'ere, an' smiled. I wouldn't 'ave missed it for anything!"

"Twa Kings," murmured Geordie to himself. "Twa guid
Kings."

It was hours before they were back once more in Aggie's

room. What a lucky thing for them that the store, in the restaurant of which Aggie was a waitress, was closed for the day.
And Aggie, being a waitress, was not nearly so tired as the
others. Again she made Ellen and Geordie lie down on the bed
while she and Angus lay, in different corners, on the floor. But
they were all too excited for sleep. Aggie insisted that they must
not return to Scotland without taking Geordie to the Palace that
night, for it was whispered that Their Majesties might show
themselves on the balcony.

The third journey by underground railway and bus made no
impression on Geordie. He had seen too much, felt too much
already. Like a puppet he moved where he was led. His glazed
eyes looked straight ahead of him seeing only the figure of the
King in his gilt state coach drawn by six white horses. When he
found himself once again in front of the Palace it seemed to him
that he had never left there. But now a vast throng had gathered
in one great block, all gazing intently at the aloof façade of the
Palace. He saw no other children. He was suffocating down
among the legs of men and skirts of women. His father lifted him
onto his shoulder but there was no stout gray-haired woman to
protect them. They were swayed like seaweed in the tide of the
crowd. The crowd sang, shouted, stood stolid, and sang again.
The floodlights blazed. An illumined airplane sailed far above.

Then someone cried out — "There They are!" Geordie, safe
on his perch, saw two figures on the balcony of the Palace. "God
bless the King and Queen! Long live Their Majesties!" Geordie
saw the King vigorously waving his arm. He took off his bonnet
and waved it with all his might. "Ah'm here, too!" he shouted.
"See me!"

The crowd roared itself hoarse. It surged forward toward the
great gates. Geordie saw Aggie sink down out of sight among
the moving feet. His mother screamed and his father put him
into her arms, then rescued Aggie and struggled with her limp

body toward the Victoria Memorial where other fainting women were receiving succor.

Geordie looked at the poor things with mingled pity and contempt. He knew that they were not dead for he saw them reviving.

Soon Aggie recovered her senses and the four made their way toward the underground station. All the rest was a blank to Geordie until he found himself sprawling on his mother's lap in the sidecar of the motorcycle and on the way back to Garlochry.

On and on through the clear bright night they sped, until they reached the open country and the sun rose above peaceful woods. Geordie slept and woke and ate and slept again and still his father bent above the handle bars of the motorcycle, and the day passed and the bright young moon showed herself in the twilit sky.

They were within a few miles of home when a truck, coming round a bend, took more than its greedy share of the road. The truck struck the motorcycle and the three riders were hurled into the ditch in a sort of sandwich, Geordie being between his parents.

Although Angus was at the bottom he was the first to rise to his feet and gather up his wife and son. The motorcycle was demolished. Geordie was unhurt but Ellen had rather a bad cut on her hand to which she paid no heed whatever but clutched Geordie frantically to her, feeling him all over to see that he was sound.

Good fortune followed them. A car directly behind them was driven by a doctor who saw their accident. He bound up Ellen's hand and took the three MacQueens into his own car. He also took the name and number of the truck driver and gave them to the traffic officer who now approached. He said:

"I saw the whole thing. The driver of the truck was entirely to blame. I'll give evidence to that. This poor woman shall get damages and her husband a new motorcycle!"

Deposited in their own home the MacQueens could scarcely believe in their good fortune. They had been to the Jubilee. They doubted if any there had had a better view of the great happenings than they. They were to have a new motorcycle, to say nothing of damages for Ellen. Geordie had been admired almost as though he were Royalty.

Now he stood examining the havoc of his Highland costume. A tear rolled down his cheek. He held the medal in his hand, looking at it dolefully.

"Dinna greet, laddie," comforted his mother. "I'll send the kilt an' a' tae the cleaners an' it'll coom back as braw as ever."

"I ken that," he answered glumly. "But, Mither," he turned a look of reproach on her, "ye need nae ha' bled on the Jubilee medal!"

The Submissive Wife

THEY SAID he bullied her, but that was not quite fair. He loved
her and he was often very kind to her. Yet the other guests in
the little Riviera hotel looked on her as a downtrodden wife and
on him as an exacting and domineering husband. Unfortunately
this too was true. When he trod her down and domineered over
her, he did so unconsciously and often, as he thought, for her
good. He was a good deal older than she and surely he knew
what was best for her. Yet there was not a guest in the small,
intimate dining room who did not either flinch or long to kick
him, when he raised his high-pitched penetrating voice, just as
she was helping herself to something from a dish and exclaimed,
"No, no, Billee — " (her name was Stephanie, but he required
a playful diminutive for her) — "No, no! not that piece! It's a
perfectly pernicious-looking piece. It looks like the breastbone
of a Jabberwocky, doesn't it, Henri?"

The waiter, who never had the slightest notion of what
Colonel Bell meant and thoroughly hated him, would reply
genially, "*Oui, oui, monsieur, vraiment!*"

Mrs. Bell would hesitate painfully, then look appealingly into
his face.

"Which piece do you think?" she would ask in her low,
musical voice.

"This!" he would declare vehemently and, when she had

meekly laid it on her plate, he would flash a look of whimsical triumph into the unresponsive faces of the other guests.

The Bells lived permanently in the hotel. When newcomers arrived, Colonel Bell invariably took them in charge and put them on to the ropes. There was nothing about the Basque country that he did not know — indeed, little about the world.

He told the new arrivals just what to see and how to see it with the least possible expense and fatigue. He told them just what to do and how to do it. And all this in a ruthlessly jocular and facetious tone. He would say, "If you go that way you are likely to break your neck, which, I have no doubt, you would find decidedly unpleasant."

When the guests who had got to know him heard Colonel Bell uttering these pleasantries to newcomers they gave a concerted mental yell of rage. The newcomers hung on his words. Old ladies named him "The Kind Colonel." Young people gathered about him to hear his adventures, which were astonishing.

He had served on every known front in the World War, and many that were unknown. He had seen such courage, such orgies of killing as few could have witnessed and kept their reason. He told of them all with the same determined facetiousness, "It was far from pleasant, I assure you, to see your best friend lying at your feet with his ears cut off, his nose cut off, and his eyes gouged out."

It was difficult at first meeting with him to decide on Colonel Bell's nationality; that is, before he began to talk of himself, which was, of course, almost immediately. He spoke with an accent that was neither Scotch nor Irish but rather like each. It turned out that his mother was the one and his father the other. He had been born in England. Now, after many years of residence in France, he had acquired such French gestures, such Gallic grimaces, that it was not easy at times to believe that he was British. He uttered even trivialities with an emphasis so biting, a stare so intense, that his listeners felt bound to show a profound receptiveness. If this, by any chance, were lacking or diluted, Colonel Bell's light gray eyes turned at once to his wife, who sat always poised ready for this emergency. Her lips parted in a quick inhalation of wonder, her whole face sparkled in response. The Colonel concluded his story in triumph.

It was then that the observant noticed how Mrs. Bell's expression changed to unspeakable weariness. Her lovely golden head drooped, her eyes became heavy with boredoom.

If she had been a plain woman it would have been more bearable, but to see this graceful, charming being in a position so crushing, roused a devil of hate in all the other guests at the hotel.

They were quite unable to help her. Except for conversation at mealtime and a couple of hours each day in the lounge or garden, the Bells kept strictly to themselves. They joined in no excursions, they did not play bridge, they did not bathe in the sea. All attempts to separate them were fruitless.

The Colonel refused all invitations to drive, to go to concert or movie or picnic. He scoffed at all these things as a waste of time for Mrs. Bell and himself. They were all very well for people who were out to kill time, but Mrs. Bell and he had their work cut out for them and dreadfully exacting work it was, but they liked it and were quite willing to lose their health and their eyesight, if need be, in scientific research in connection with it.

No one could find out just what the nature of this work was, though it was known that he was writing a book on it. Some said that it was about sanitary conditions of armies in wartime. Others said it was about vitamins. A few declared that it was concerned with the atom and was driving him mad.

Soon after breakfast the Bells disappeared into their room and remained there till shortly before lunch, when they took a brisk walk. After lunch they again disappeared and were not seen till teatime. By this hour Mrs. Bell looked very pale and dejected, but the tea revived her and in the interval between then and dinner she was almost gay, as though with relief that the dragging day was over.

She was the prettiest woman in the lounge after dinner and the Colonel showed unmistakable pride in the admiring looks she attracted. But he was soon restive and after some last long-winded tragic incident of his past, told with fine whimsical detachment and eloquent French gestures, he would look at her meaningfully. She would speak of the exacting call of their work and they would drift out of the room, leaving behind them at least a dozen incipient murderers and murderesses.

Then Hartley Drewe, a novelist, and his sister Edwina came to the hotel. He was thirty-eight, not yet much known by the public, but his last book had been well received. He and his sister were having their first holiday in years. She was fifteen years older than he and had always looked after him. They both were thin, dark, and distinguished-looking.

Like everyone else they were drawn into Colonel Bell's net. They were his most interesting captures of the season. He pinned them down on their first evening and opened his usual campaign of whimsical advice and derisively tragic anecdote. They gave him a tranquil attention that exhilarated him so much that even the most pessimistic of the other guests in the room were forced to wonder or laughter as he willed. It was only mechanically that he called on the reserves of his wife's sympathy and support. She, on her part, relaxed as she seldom did. She looked less pale when they left the lounge and there was a natural sparkle in her eyes. The Drewes had lifted the weight of her husband's presence from her spirit. She had enjoyed watching Hartley Drewe's quiet, sensitive face, listening to his pleasant, flexible voice.

He was unlike any other man she had met. She liked his sister, too, and felt still more drawn to them when, after several days had passed, they showed none of the distaste for Colonel Bell's company generally so pronounced in any but the most weak-minded guests. On the contrary, the Drewes sought out him (and consequently her) more and more.

The truth was that Hartley Drewe was fascinated by Mrs. Bell. He had never been so fascinated by anyone in his life. From where he sat at mealtime he could just see her lovely drooping head, the sweep of her fair hair from her temple, her creamy pale cheek. He could also see her husband's glittering gray eyes, the never-ceasing movement of his lips as talk poured between them, and his large, gesticulating hands; for some reason he spoke only in French at mealtime and, as his assurance in the language far exceeded his proficiency, it was a constant strain on Mrs. Bell to follow him.

"For pity's sake," whispered his sister to him, "stop staring at those people!"

"I can't stop," he whispered in return.

"You must. You will have people talking."

"But I'm so fascinated, Edwina."

"Try to be fascinated by your food, for a change."

"I can't. It's too bad."

"I am sure that Colonel Bell notices."

"He thinks that I am admiring him."

"That will make him show off all the more and make it harder on her."

Hartley Drewe fixed his eyes on his plate, but his mind remained fixed on the Bells.

On the sands he said to his sister, "Edwina, you *must* take Colonel Bell off somewhere and give me a chance to talk to her. We have been here for ten days now and I have never seen her alone."

His sister looked at him curiously. "I hope you're not planning an affair with her. It would never do."

"Of course I'm not. I'm just tremendously interested in her and terribly sorry for her. I think something ought to be done to liven her up."

"I would call such a proceeding decidedly risky — knowing what I do of Colonel Bell."

"But I'm dying to know what sort of person she would be if she were from under his shadow."

"Look here, Hartley, are you interested in her from the point of view of your work?"

"Yes. I can't get her out of my head. I keep thinking of her as the heroine of a novel. You know, I haven't had a single idea since my last book. Now my imagination is beginning to stir. There's something coming to life in it."

This put a different face on the affair for Edwina. Hartley's work was everything to her. She was fiercely eager for his success. She knew every page of his books. She worked with him, criticized him, supplied the word he lacked, and had put more of her own intelligence into them than his public could know.

"I don't see," she said, "how I'm to go about it."

"Edwina, you darling!" he exclaimed.

She looked a little grim but suffered him to kiss her thin hand which was tanned the color of mahogany.

He said, "You can surely persuade the Colonel to take you on one of those walks he is always talking about. Tell him that I am working and refuse to go."

"But we have told everyone you are resting."

"Tell him I'm quite rested."

"But he never goes anywhere with the other guests."

"He will with you, Edwina."

"If he did — he would insist on bringing her."

"She is not very strong. Suggest a walk so long and rough that she will not be able to take it."

Edwina looked longingly at the blazing blue sea, the white sand and her own bronzed length supine on it, then said:

"All right, I'll have a try."

She did, and succeeded.

The next day she and Colonel Bell set out soon after breakfast, he having explained to each of the other guests in turn that for no one in the world but Miss Drewe would he have undertaken to revisit the ruined monastery in the hills, which he had last seen in such tragic circumstances. As they departed, he called out:

"Well, if you don't see us again, you will know that I simply ran amuck, murdered Miss Drewe, and bashed out my own brains on the floor of the monastery, or something equally unpleasant."

But, in spite of himself, he was elated. Edwina Drewe was a very different companion from Mrs. Bell. She was indeed magnificent. Her long, fine legs never tired. Her eager brain never wearied of absorbing the information, the reminiscences he so lavishly poured out. Her appreciative chuckle never failed his grimly humorous anecdote. It was ten years since he had known a morning to go so fast.

Hartley Drewe found himself more nervous than elated as he sought out Mrs. Bell. Perhaps she would refuse to stir without her husband. Perhaps their isolation was as much her wish as his. But no, he could not believe that — not after seeing her look of almost bewildered relief when her husband agreed to accompany Edwina. He searched the garden and the public rooms of the hotel for her in vain.

He discovered her on the beach, sitting motionless with a book. But she was not reading. Her eyes were on a group of boys and girls paddling about in brightly painted surfboats. She had on a vivid yellow dress he had not seen before.

He shrank from breaking in on her thoughts. Perhaps she wanted speech with no one in this hour of freedom. But he sat down at a short distance and waited for her to look his way.

She soon did. She smiled then and held up her book for him to see. It was a copy of his last novel. He remembered how Colonel Bell had said on their first meeting, "I hear you write novels. I'm afraid that neither my wife nor I have read any of them. We have no time for light reading. Our research work takes all our time."

Mrs. Bell had said, in her low, musical voice, "One of the guests is going to lend me your latest book when she has finished it."

The Colonel had interposed with, "Don't bank on my wife's reading your book, Mr. Drewe. She has no interest in fiction, but she's too polite to say so."

Now Drewe exclaimed, "I hope you are not forcing yourself to read that!"

She answered, "I've been wanting to so much. This is my first chance." And she added loyally, "My husband and I have been very busy."

She opened the book at the first page and bent her eyes on it as though she feared he would doubt her sincerity.

He rose and crossed the sand to where she sat. "May I come between you and this long-deferred pleasure for a little?" he asked.

"You put me in a very bad position," she laughed. "What do you want me to say?"

He dropped to the sand beside her. "It's much too glaring for reading," he said. "Won't you talk to me? We two are deserted this morning."

Before she could stop herself, she exclaimed, "Isn't it wonderful!"

The words were spoken in a tone of almost passionate pleasure. They were scarcely past her lips when she flushed painfully and added, "I really don't know what I am saying this morning. It's so altogether lovely on the sand that it carries me away."

"Yes," he agreed gravely. "It does me, too."

"We don't often idle here like this," she went on. "My husband does not care about it — and our work ties us."

"Of course." He looked into her face, finding it even more sensitive, more fascinating than he had thought.

She looked at him with an almost equal interest. She said tentatively, "I suppose your work is very exacting, too. But in such a different way. It must be wonderful to give one's life to art — to something you love to do."

"I could not do anything else," he returned. "I scarcely think of it as work. It's my very breath."

Again she looked into the book. "I do so want to read it," she said. "I should be reading it now while I have the chance."

"But you haven't the chance!" he exclaimed. "I want you to do something quite different. Something that will please me infinitely more."

She looked at him questioningly.

"I want you to do something active. I'm alone today. Won't you take pity on me and come in for a swim?"

"A swim?" she repeated. "Oh, I never go in now. I used to. But I haven't for years."

"Don't you like it?" he asked, angrily.

"I love it. But, you see, we have very little time for that sort of thing. Very little time for pleasure. Not that I'm not very much interested in our work," she added quickly. "I am, though I get very tired. I'm very tired this morning. It seems ridiculous to be tired on such a morning, but I am."

He said excitedly, "It will rest you to go into the sea. Please do. I'm dying to go and I hate to swim alone."

She was weakening, but she said, "What about your book?"

"Speak of it again," he declared, "and I'll chuck it into the water and make an end of it!"

In less than half an hour they walked across the hot bright sand together wearing their bathing things. In scarcely more time every guest in the hotel knew what had happened and was experiencing a hilarious excitement in the incident. The elderly ladies and gentlemen on the garden seats could scarcely believe their eyes. The young people swimming, splashing, dipping in the waves, were even more astonished. The first amazing thing was to see Mrs. Bell in a bathing costume. The second was to see how marvelous she looked in it. There was beauty in the lines of her slender figure. There was grace in her walk. People had forgotten that a skin could be as white as hers. It was dazzling in the sunshine.

Hartley Drewe felt proud of himself for what he had done when he saw her laughing and splashing like any girl in the cool, greenish sea.

"Can you swim?" he asked.

"I've forgotten."

But she hadn't. She struck out and managed a dozen strokes. Then she stood upright, covered to her armpits, laughing up at him out of a dripping, blue-eyed face. She wore a black rubber cap and a lock of hair escaped from it and clung to her cheek.

"Splendid!" he said. "Do you think you could swim out to that rock, if I helped you?"

"I could swim across the sea," she returned recklessly.

They reached the rock and clambered onto it, isolated, a thousand gently tossing waves surrounding them. They were silent, feeling, now they were alone together, that they did not know what to say.

At last she spoke, with a note of bitterness in her voice.

"To think that all this loveliness is here — all the time!"

He asked quietly, "Is it impossible for you to be free to enjoy it?"

"Quite impossible. My husband hates this sort of thing."

"I don't doubt it. But surely you can escape for an hour or so every day."

She shook her head with childlike emphasis. "He needs me. He can't get on without me. It frets him."

Drewe thought, "I'd like to give him something to fret about."

He said brusquely, "What about yourself? You have your own life to consider."

"You don't understand," she answered, her face troubled. "He can't bear to have me away from him. His work is very important to him. It takes all our time."

Drewe saw that he was making her unhappy. He put all questioning from his mind and gave himself up to filling this hour with pleasure for her and stimulus for himself.

He had magnetism. He had power. He realized that, but never before had he rejoiced in it. He made her forget all but the sea, their brief freedom and himself. She was intoxicated by this so unexpected hour of pure gaiety. For the first time in years she was far from the sound of her husband's voice, from the sight of his false animation, his intense, staring eyes, his gesticulating hands. She looked down into the face of Hartley Drewe as he lay stretched on the rock and saw his closed, black-lashed eyes, his lazily smiling lips, his hands clasped on his bronzed chest.

When Colonel Bell and Edwina returned from their walk they found Mrs. Bell waiting for them by the door. They were late for lunch. But the Colonel seemed not to mind this. He had had a thoroughly good time. He did not even ask his wife what she had been doing all the morning. All through the meal he talked incessantly of his excursion with Edwina, magnifying its little incidents to adventures. He threw facetious remarks from his table to hers. She received them with just the admiring badinage he courted, but later, in a corner of the garden with her brother, she flung herself down on a deck chair and groaned.

"Were you bored?" he asked pleasantly.

"To the bone. Give me two cigarettes. One for each corner of my mouth."

He gave her one and lighted it.

After a few puffs, she said, "The woman's a saint. I should murder him. All the while we were out I kept thinking of the different ways I could do it."

He looked interested. "Did you really?"

"Don't imagine," she returned, "that you'll get rid of him that way." Her face became grave. "He is really devoted to Mrs. Bell. He may bully her, but he dotes on her."

Hartley said, dreamily, "You must take him out again, and again, and again. We had a marvelous time."

Edwina looked at him coldly.

"What does it all mean?" she asked.

"It means that between us we've got to give her a break in this awful routine. She's a lovely woman. She's ground down, made wretched by that brute — say what you will about his adoring her. If you could have seen her splashing in the waves, happy as a child, you would not hesitate."

"I saw myself sweating up the mountain path. You seem to forget that Mrs. Bell lives in this heavenly spot all the year round and that I am here for only a short holiday."

"Edwina, think of the companion she has all the year round! And you have me! and this means so much to me — to my work."

She gave him a tender, yet somewhat cynical smile.

"What is there in this for you?"

"I'm not quite sure, but I believe there is inspiration."

"I wish you could be sure before you have me making a monkey of myself."

"I *am* sure!" he exclaimed, impulsively. "I have not felt as much like work in months. You know I have been pretty depressed lately."

She knew.

"I have never met anyone like her," he went on. "I'd love to make a full-length portrait of her in a book. She inspires me."

"If I could write," said his sister, "I'd like to write about the Colonel. He's a most curious character."

"He doesn't interest me in the least," said Hartley.

Edwina asked, "How can I be sure he will come out with me again?"

"My darling, you have only to ask him. He is in the seventh heaven after this morning's walk. You can do what you like with him. You're as clever as the devil, besides being extraordinarily attractive."

She agreed with him in that, and she never had been able to resist him. The very next afternoon she and Colonel Bell set out on another excursion.

A tremor of excitement ran through the hotel as Hartley Drewe and Mrs. Bell appeared almost immediately after, she wearing the same vivid yellow dress, and got into his car.

As they drove off, he observed, "That's an amazingly becoming dress you have on."

She gave rather a sad smile. "It's not new. I fell in love with it and persuaded my husband to let me buy it. But he really hated it on me, so I gave up wearing it. I thought I'd get a turn out of it now."

"It's providential!" he exclaimed. "That dress was especially designed for my delight."

She felt that he should not say such things to her, but she had not the power to stop him. She found a happiness in his presence that she had never dreamed of experiencing. It was something quite new to her. She leaned back against the padded seat of the car and gave herself up to the joy of the hour.

They motored to a distant beach and bathed where they would not be the focus of curious eyes. They had tea in a gay pavilion overlooking the sea. Brilliant flowers bloomed about them. They were surrounded by laughing, reckless people, of the sort she had never expected to mingle with, nor had she desired to, but now they created an atmosphere suited to her mood. She wanted for this moment to forget her own life, to live as these people lived.

That evening when she was dressing, her husband discovered the bright red patches on her shoulders. She had to confess that she had been in bathing and got sunburned.

He was thoroughly upset to think that she would do such a thing when his back was turned. Nothing would induce him to leave her side for three days. The sunburn was painful, it was disfiguring. He fussed over it continually, making it the subject of countless witticisms in front of the other guests.

The Drewes were thrown back on their own company, and dreary, irritable company it was, so far as Hartley was concerned. Edwina was in despair with him. She said, at last, "We shall have to leave here. There is nothing else for it. You are falling in love with Mrs. Bell."

"Falling in love with her!" he repeated. "Falling in love with her! I *am* in love with her. Head over ears. So now what are you going to do about it?"

"All the more reason for our going away," she answered, calmly.

He looked at her in desperation.

"If I go away where I can't see her, I may never write anything worth while again. When I am with her I feel inspired. Something stirs in me which has not stirred for months. When I am away from her I am a hollow black void, mentally and spiritually."

"You will get over it."

"I may, but I'll never write anything good again. I feel it. I know it."

The result of this conversation was that Colonel Bell once more set forth with Edwina Drewe. The truth was that he was not difficult to persuade after three monotonous days had passed. His wife was listless and heavy-eyed. The weather was glorious, just cool enough for a long tramp. Before he left he made her promise that she would do nothing reckless in his absence. He and Edwina carried their lunch with them.

The hotel was a hotbed of gossip, but all agreed that the Drewes were justified in their scheming to give Stephanie Bell the first good time of her life. The gossip was kindly. It had come out that Mrs. Bell's mother had been an overbearing, managing person and everyone felt that the poor young woman was quite justified in snatching at this unexpected taste of real life.

Some of the guests even thought that she was justified when, three weeks later, she ran away with Hartley Drewe. No one could go on, they said, leading such a life. To others it was a shock. They had been full of sympathy when she was gentle and resigned, but when she became wild and reckless, it was a different matter. They had all seen this spirit of recklessness growing in her, all but Colonel Bell who, for the time being, was completely absorbed by Edwina Drewe's passion for exercise and the information which, she seemed to feel, he alone could give her. Now they saw the Colonel as an injured husband, ghastly pale, distracted, not seeming to know what he said or did.

He was unself-conscious as a child in his grief. He talked to anyone and everyone of his wife's goodness and sweetness, but most of all to Edwina. He had no words of blame for anyone, but went on reiterating the tale of his bewilderment, his devastating loneliness, his undying love.

Edwina left the hotel as soon as she could make her plans, and returned to the cottage she and Hartley occupied on the Cornish coast. She came back to it disappointed and bitter. She had pictured their happy return, Hartley invigorated by his trip abroad, full of new ideas for future work that was to make him famous. Now Hartley had gone to Paris with another man's wife. There would be horrid divorce proceedings. She did not know what her future would be.

One thing was certain. Hartley could not remain away for long. He had not the money. At his request she had sent him all she could lay hands on, but it was not much. She had written a letter telling him that she regretted the part she had played in the affair not only because it had placed him in a bad position socially and financially, but because it had broken a man's heart.

Hartley took her letter so hard that he wrote her in return, advising her to marry the Colonel herself when he was free, if she pitied him so much, and telling her that he had found in his love the inspiration he craved. He would be coming home to work before long.

But Colonel Bell did not bring an action for divorce. Instead he wrote to Stephanie saying that nothing on earth would induce him to break the only bond that held her to him, that if she chose to live with another man it must be as his mistress and not his wife.

Hartley was furious and raged up and down their little hotel room, but Stephanie was too happy to care whose name she bore. She wished they might go on living in Paris forever, exploring out-of-the-way corners, dining in strange restaurants, returning at night from concert or play arm in arm. His quietness and repose were a joy to her. He was never facetious, he never told stories either funny or tragic. He never talked about himself but drew her on and on to lay bare her soul to him, to reveal all her experience, her reactions to her past.

The day came at last when they joined Edwina at the cottage. Stephanie had hoped that Edwina might go somewhere to live by herself. But Hartley was aghast at the idea. He could not possibly get on without her. As far as his work was concerned they were one. Besides, Edwina owned half the cottage and had nowhere else to go. It was such an isolated spot, the people of the near-by hamlet would have no way of finding out that Hartley and Mrs. Bell were not properly married. Indeed, when she saw the place for the first time, she thought she had never seen anything more desolate than the stone cottage set on the top of a treeless cliff with the gray Atlantic, veiled in mist, moving in melancholy rhythm far below.

It was so different from what she had pictured. The Drewes themselves seemed different now that she saw them in their own environment. They seemed colder, quieter, more detached. Hartley was burning with the desire to work, but he burned with a flame that gave out no warmth to her. Edwina watched him as though he were a kettle she had set on to boil.

The outdoors was vast and chill. The indoors cramped and rather damp-smelling. The meals cooked by the servant who came in by the day were well cooked and suitable to the climate, but they were not suited to Mrs. Bell, who had lived in France since a child. The Colonel and she had been particularly fortunate in the little hotel where they had made their home. They had had a variety of food and an abundance of fruit.

She longed childishly for fruit and sunshine in the blowy wet weeks that followed. The Drewes told her that the rain was badly needed, since there had been a drought all the summer, but she did not see how any country could need so much rain.

She hated walking in it and somehow took a cold that

tied her to the house. So Hartley and Edwina had to go on their walks alone. Obviously they did not mind this, for they were splendid walkers and would stride for miles across the downs facing a rain-drenched gale. They came back hungry for their mutton, potatoes, cabbage, and steamed pudding with jam.

Hartley walked all the way to the nearest town to buy flowers and fruit for Stephanie. He brought back a huge bunch of draggled chrysanthemums and a bag of stunted apples, greenish bananas and juiceless oranges. He was apologetic. He said:

"They're the best I could get. You must remember that this is an isolated spot and that Cornish fishermen do not run to flowers and fruit in winter."

"But why do you live here?" she exclaimed.

"Because I love it," he answered abruptly. "Don't you love it?"

"No. I think it's a crushing place."

She was sorry she had said that, after his effort to please her, but the words had come out almost without her volition.

He answered coldly, "I'm afraid it's the best I can offer you for some time."

"But we could live very cheaply in Spain."

"I couldn't possibly work there."

She began to feel that his art was everything to him and that she was only an incident in his life. Often she sat speechless and depressed while he and Edwina discussed his work completely absorbed. More and more she disliked Edwina's possessive air toward Hartley, her complete and intimate knowledge of all he did. Edwina read all his letters, she typed all he wrote, not once but several times. She never seemed tired or bored or depressed.

Stephanie was, most of the time, all three. She was horrified to find that she disliked Hartley's books. She had read little fiction and that mostly Continental. His rather grim stories of the Cornish coast were positively uninteresting and even repellent to her. Yet, she had to force herself to seem to like them, to talk intelligently and admiringly of them to him. Of his new novel he spoke only to Edwina.

One morning Stephanie had drifted into the kitchen to talk to the servant. She was a fisherman's wife and she had never been more than ten miles from home. Yet she was always cheery and full of enjoyment of what life brought to her. As they talked their voices grew louder. At some remark of Stephanie's the woman broke into a laugh.

A moment later the door was flung open and Edwina stood there, white and angry.

"Do you suppose," she exclaimed, "that Hartley can write when there is such a horrible noise going on? He's distracted. He doesn't know what he is doing. He is put off his work for the rest of the day."

Stephanie followed Edwina to the dining room.

"Hartley should never have married," she said.

Edwina turned her dark eyes on her.

"Married?" she repeated.

From that day Stephanie began to brood on her position. She began to feel that her unhappiness was her punishment for leading a wrong life. She pictured things as growing from bad to worse, here on this rain-soaked, sea-beaten cliff. She saw herself as cast off by Hartley, scorned by Edwina, alone in the world. Through the long months of winter she had one cold after another — not bad ones, but severe enough to keep her indoors.

Hartley was getting on wonderfully with his book and she never again interrupted his work.

But one morning at the end of March, she wrote a simple line and addressed it to Colonel Bell. It read, "What would you say if I were to suggest returning to you?"

She was always first to hear the postman's knock. Two

days later her answer came. It was a telegram in these words: COLONEL BELL DIED LAST WEEK AND WAS BURIED HERE.

Stephanie carried the telegram straight to the desk where Hartley worked. She was too excited to think of his feelings. She laid the paper in front of him.

"He is dead," she said, in a tense voice.

Hartley read, then raised a face all alight to hers. He got up and snatched her into his arms.

"My darling," he exclaimed. "You are free! We can marry at once! And, good Lord, what a strange coincidence! I have this moment finished my book! We'll get married and spend our second honeymoon on the Riviera!"

The Broken Fan

THE CAPTAIN and the other officers of the transatlantic liner did everything in their power to make the passengers forget the sea. They instituted golf tournaments which took place on a ridiculous little mat on the promenade deck. They arranged tennis tournaments on the sports deck, and bridge tournaments for the glassed-in lounge. At night all the different groups collected in the ballroom to watch the horse racing. And after the horse racing came the dance. The efforts of the captain and the crew were so effectual that the sea, lapping and curling, pressing and withdrawing about the sides of the vessel, was almost entirely ignored. The waves seemed to be curious about the passengers, rearing their heads as though to peer up at them, but the passengers were not curious about the sea. Even those who had their luncheon carried to them on deck scarcely seemed to notice the great fluctuating expanse about them. The wine and cold viands on their trays held their attention while they lasted, and when, drowsy with repletion, they settled comfortably under their rugs, novels or books of travel in their hands, it required the passing of Mrs. Friedland and Mr. Wolfe to stir them to interest.

These two never failed to arouse their curiosity. From the first day out to the day of landing the sight of their two figures slowly pacing the length of the promenade deck produced a ripple of curiosity in the rows of swathed, reclining figures.

Mrs. Friedland and Mr. Wolfe seemed to be as unconscious of the interest or lack of interest they created as the sea itself. His massive shoulders slightly bent, he looked down into her face, apparently oblivious of the other passengers. Phrases, uttered in his sonorous voice, were caught by young girls and passed from one to the other. Nothing audible came from her lips, though they moved smilingly, while her full black eyes were raised unwaveringly to his face. Each day her short figure, which moved with the toddling walk of a woman who has spent her life in French heels on polished floors, appeared in fresh and luxurious creations of milliner and costumier. She must have carried an immense amount of luggage with her, for those wraps of mink, of seal, of squirrel and velvet could have been packed into no moderate space. She occupied the most expensive suite on the ship. With her was a tall, inscrutable young companion.

When these two, in company with Mr. Wolfe, took their places at dinner, their table was the center of interest for the other diners. No other table showed such an array of wineglasses. There were no such diamonds and emeralds as hers. About her the wine steward and a group of waiters seemed constantly to be hovering. It was to her that the ingenious and beautiful confections of the chef were first exhibited. She clasped her hands delightedly before a pair of rearing steeds or a dolphin bearing a cupid on his back. Hers was the first helping from the heart of intricate flowers formed of many-colored jellies. She tipped with the recklessness of vanity. Her present to the orchestra after they had given a concert almost equaled the combined contributions of the rest of the audience. In the dining saloon it was obvious that it was to her the orchestra played. She would lift her heavy-lidded eyes to the musicians' gallery and raise her wineglass with

an imperial gesture if the piece pleased her. If it did not please
her she signified her disapproval by the ancient gesture of the
down-turned thumb, and that selection was not played again
during the voyage.

But, indeed, her eyes seldom left the face of her lover. She had
made up her mind that he was to be her last lover, and she was
giving to him the final fierceness of her passion. He was forty and
she was nearer sixty than fifty.

Lest anyone should retain some disturbing memory of the sea
at the end of the voyage, the ship's officers arranged a fancy-dress
dance for the last night out which was to surpass all previous
festivities. Costumes were displayed on a table in front of the
shop where French embroideries and bizarre dolls were for sale.
One might hire an elaborate crinoline dress or a simple domino.
Young girls stood in a laughing row before the table, perching
fantastic caps on their heads, trying the effect of various costumes. Elderly gentlemen chose the gay dress of clown or harle-
quin.

Neither Mrs. Friedland nor Mr. Wolfe took part in this. Like
a few others of the passengers they had brought their costumes
with them.

That night the air turned suddenly warm. A sweet-smelling
breeze came to them from the shore of Spain. This added to the
feeling of hilarity on board the ship. The windows of the ballroom were opened wide. The music of the dance was carried out
by the breeze into the dark vastness towards the coast of Morocco. Surrounding the space for dancing many small tables were
crowded, about which were gathered those who were not in
costume and those dancers who rested, drinking champagne and
smoking.

With calculated theatrical effect Mrs. Friedland entered late,
elaborately dressed as a favorite of the harem in a costume of
green and silver. Beneath the spangled veil her masklike face

looked out with something of the nervous impassivity of a liz-
ard's. Her full black eyes, her painted mouth, scorned those
about her, even while inviting their admiration. Above her
towered Wolfe, as a rajah, turbaned, jeweled, always smiling
down into her face.

Their entry was so spectacular, their costumes so superb, that
a small thunder of applause greeted them. Mrs. Friedland's impassivity melted into a smile of happiness. As the noise and
energy of the evening increased she became more and more
elated, gaily drinking champagne with a little group to whom
previously she had barely spoken, even dancing with one of the
men, commanding Wolfe to find another partner.

Electric vibrations excited the nerves of the swiftly intermin-
gling throng. Beneath their feet was the ceaseless quiver of the
motor; from above beat the searching light of the electroliers.
The musicians played in an impassioned crescendo. Innumerable
pretty toys were offered on trays by the stewards to excite and to
be broken. Fantastic whistles shrieked above the violins, brilliant
melon-shaped balloons were struck from hand to hand, white
balls, light as thistledown, flew from gilded racquet to racquet.
A girl with blackened face was dancing a Charleston, surrounded
by a group rhythmically striking their palms together. A youthful
couple, she in vivid scarlet, he dressed as an Apache, whirled,
with their bodies flattened together as one, until they seemed as
impersonal and sexless as insects.

A group of five whose features suggested that they were of
Jewish extraction were gathered about a table, drinking and
smoking rose-tipped cigarettes. They were all young, four of
them married couples, the fifth a younger sister of one of the
women. The two wives were pretty, with plump, boneless shoulders like white velvet. Their husbands, who had not long ago
been bridegrooms, were flushed with wine. It was not possible
for them to keep from caressing the shoulders and arms of their

wives or, at least, holding their red-tipped finger ends. The young
girl of the group was an exquisitely colored blonde, with deep
gold hair, violet eyes, and a mouth like a budding flower. She
stood beside the table, a reel of scarlet paper ribbon in her
hands. Mrs. Friedland, gliding past, noticed, with a feeling of
shock, that the girl wore a costume of the harem, white, filmy,
surrounding her seductive blond beauty like a cloud.

It was not the first time that Mrs. Friedland had noticed this
particular face. It had peered up at her, with flattering curiosity,
above a fur collar when she took her walks on deck. She had
seen it, smiling against the shoulder of a man, at other dances.
She had noticed it as one passing notices carelessly the beauty of
a flower. Now it rose before her as a menace. She felt a con-
traction of pain in the nerves, followed by a violent anger
that the girl had chosen a costume so similar to her own, out-
shining her.

With a graceful movement the girl threw a loop of the ribbon
at Wolfe's towering head. It caught his turban and slid to his
bare throat. Those near by laughed, applauding her dexterity.
She took a quick step forward and threw another strand of ribbon. This caught them both, and, as they glided away, she followed them, half shyly, half boldly, entangling them more and
more in the bright ribbon. Wolfe pressed Mrs. Friedland closer
to him. He exclaimed:

"She is determined that we shall never separate."

Mrs. Friedland gave a joyous laugh. Her anger, her fear left
her. She felt a passionate delight in being thus enmeshed with
him. She felt the warm pressure of his hands, heard his grave
laugh above her head. She had a sudden melancholy wish that
these ribbons were of iron.

The whirling Apache and his partner spun swiftly between
them and the girl, severing the ribbons. Other dancers surged
through the space. A few of the colored strands clung to them,

the others falling to the floor, already strewn with ribbon and broken toys.

He found a seat for her and sat down beside her. She gave a happy sigh of relaxation. Then, looking across his shoulder, she saw that the seat to which he had brought her was beside the group of which that girl was one. She darted a swift glance at him, and saw his eyes, beneath the jewel of his turban, fixed on the girl's face. His lips were curved in their accustomed lazy smile. A tremor of fresh anger shook Mrs. Friedland's nerves. She raised her fan, hiding her mouth behind it. It was a brilliant green Oriental fan with fragile ivory sticks, carved in a design of lotus flowers. He was saying:

"Are you happy? Do you find it amusing?"

The fan against her lips, she murmured:

"Yes. I'm a little tired."

He did not answer. He was watching the two married couples, who had risen from the table and were about to join the dancers.

The girl was left alone, her arms, pearl-white beneath the filmy veil, extended along the table, her fingers curving about the stem of an untouched glass of champagne. Her sister had said something sharp to her. Her feelings were hurt. Her lip quivered, she winked rapidly.

Wolfe, always so assiduous in his attentions, so careful never to admire any other woman, seemed suddenly thrown off his guard. He turned his face full on Mrs. Friedland, a beaming smile softening its rather battered features.

"Isn't she," he breathed, "the most adorable thing?"

Mrs. Friedland let her fan fall to her lap, and showed her face, a white, smiling mask.

"Yes," she returned. "I've been noticing her for some time."

He offered her a cigarette from the jeweled case she had given him. She shook her head.

"Shall I order something to drink?"

This time it was she who did not answer. She was struggling with the devil of jealousy which possessed her.

He repeated the question.

"Not now — I have one of my dizzy spells. You know I get them. I think I'll go to my room and lie down for a quarter of an hour. There is something, too, that I want to tell Miss Pearce."

She got to her feet, looking straight ahead of her, seeing nothing.

His eyes darkened with solicitude. "Oh, my dear, I'm so very sorry!" He rose quickly and took her arm. "I'll go with you."

He steered her carefully into the passage, supported her down the stairway. At her door she stopped.

"You are not to come in with me. You are to go back."

He protested. He would go in and get her spirits of ammonia, sit with her until she felt better.

"No," she insisted; "I would rather be alone for a few minutes. Go up and ask that attractive child to dance with you. She was looking so lonely. Then, after that, come back for me."

She stood inside her door listening to his retreating footsteps. Through a crack she watched his broad, fantastically garbed figure disappear.

The companion's businesslike voice came from the next room.

"Is that you, Mrs. Friedland? Do you want something?"

"No, I don't want anything. I'm going back directly."

"Is it a nice party?"

"Delightful. You made a mistake in not coming."

Her voice was harsh with the effort of steadying it. She pressed her forehead against the cool woodwork of the door and felt a deep vibration from the heart of the ship, as though it were in sympathy with her. She gave a little moan.

She returned along the passage and up the crimson-carpeted stairway. She stole on to the promenade deck, from where she

could see into the ballroom. From there came a delirious mingling of voices and music. It was getting very late. The deck was
deserted, its appearance of loneliness increased by the long row
of folded chairs and the pale glimmer of the silver urn on a tea
wagon in a corner. Very cautiously she approached a window.
For a space her eyes were dazzled by the brilliance of the lights
and the whirling, many-colored costumes of the dancers; then
she distinguished his head above the others, on the far side of
the room. Her heart beat chokingly as her gaze followed him
along the outer edge of the crowd and saw him draw near, a girl
in his arms.

The music stopped as they were almost opposite the window.
Wolfe did not take his arm from the girl's waist as he led her to a
sofa. He was smiling as though he were conscious of no other
presence in the room save hers. The girl looked up at him, wistful
and tremulous no longer, but calm and seductive. In spirit they
were clasped in each other's arms, giving and returning fierce
kisses. Mrs. Friedland saw that, and her heart was wrung with
an anguish she had not thought possible to her. She would have
liked to kill him where he stood. She pictured him lying dead in
his silken robe, like some stealthy, marauding animal. She would
have liked to kill the girl before his eyes, snatching his sleek,
white prey from him. She was of mixed races, and their different
characteristics in this moment of tragic emotion clamored within
her. She was bewildered. She turned from the window and moved
gropingly to the side of the ship. She could not bear the sight of
them together. She had wished that the paper ribbons the girl
had thrown about them had been iron, that they might be bound
together for ever. Now she realized that the bonds that held him
to her were weaker even than paper, evanescent as wreaths of
mist. She set her teeth, thinking of all she had done for him, how
she had met him in South America, ill, disgruntled by his failure
in his profession of civil engineer, craving travel and luxury. She

had given him these, given him herself, the passion, the bitterness of her love. That look in his eyes which had stirred her to her depths she had seen him give tonight to a girl he had met for the first time. She felt herself dishonored. Never again, oh, never again, would she let him touch her!

The sweet breeze from the shore of Spain came to her across the water. A flounce of foam was thrown from the side of the ship and spread delicate as lace into the darkness. Again she felt the deep vibration from the heart of the ship, this time against her breast. The ship and the sea were in sympathy with her; they understood her, while to the world and to Wolfe, her lover, she was an enigma not worth solving.

She would end it all! Though she could not kill him where he stood, she would give him a stab, slanting though it might be, by her death. She pictured his horrified face — for he was tender-hearted — when it was found that she was not on the ship, had drowned herself. And she would have peace. And the understanding of the sea.

A great strength surged through her in her resolution. This was the solution of her life which she had been seeking for years. To throw it away. To give it to the sea, as was fitting, for her forbears had been mariners. She would call the steward, send him for Wolfe, and when Wolfe came she would not be there.

A theatrical desire to leave something of herself on the deck, something that should smite him cruelly with remorse, came to her.

Her fan. That was it. Her beautiful green fan — of the color of jealousy! He should find it on the deck, with all its ivory sticks broken, where the steward had last seen her standing, white and distraught. It would be a message that he could not help understanding.

She would call a steward now, tell him to send Wolfe to her, and while the message was being given she would break the fan. Wolfe, rushing to the side of the ship, might even see her in a terrifying glimpse, one white arm in its filmy drapery out-thrown against the foam. She must not hesitate. She must do it while the courage of jealousy, of despair, upheld her. She could not go on with life, could not hold Wolfe to her. It was impossible.

She went swiftly, her veil floating about her, to the door of the corridor. A steward was passing. She said, thickly:

"Send — send — I mean — bring — a glass of Benedictine to me, on the deck. I am faint."

He glanced with curiosity at the ashen mask of her face. "Yes, madame."

He turned away.

She swept back to the darkness of the deck. Her heart had failed her. She must have a few moments more. She would drink the Benedictine, and that would renew her courage. One's life could not be taken with such careless swiftness. It was too cruel. A glass of Benedictine. A farewell drink to her soul. She paced up and down the deck, the mixed races within her crying out their memories of the past. Vividly she saw scenes from her childhood in Athens, in Bucharest, in Paris. She saw scenes from her married life with Friedland, who had given her luxury, given her power that had brought her to nothing but this. She could bear her life no longer.

The steward appeared before her with the glass on a little tray. She took it from him, avoiding his eyes, and turned away.

A shaft of light from a window awoke a dark gleam in the liqueur. She drank it and set the empty glass on the tea wagon.

What was she going to do next? Her eyes moved blankly from the bright squares of the window to the black expanse of the sea. She felt confused. Timidly she moved toward a window and looked in. The delirious medley of music and voices had ceased. The orchestra was playing a slow, rhythmic waltz full of sensuous melancholy. There was only one pair of dancers on the floor. This was Wolfe and the girl. The others had become onlookers, while they moved rhythmically, as one body, oblivious to all but themselves.

It was enough. She could do it now. One by one she snapped the ivory sticks of the fan. It lay like a broken-winged tropical bird in her hands. Clutching it, she moved steadily to the door of the corridor and beckoned to the steward.

"Go to Mr. Wolfe," she said, "the tall gentleman dancing. Tell him to come to me. At once."

She was outside the window at the moment when the music stopped and the steward reached Wolfe's side. She saw his startled look, saw him withdraw quickly from the girl — waited for no more. She was shaking from head to foot. She rushed to the side of the ship. In a moment he would be here, tall, full of life and strength, her lover, so soon to be shocked by the tragedy of her death.

She felt that deep tremor of the ship. Far below she saw the curling half circle of the foam, like an opening fan.

She dropped her fan to the deck. There, on that spot, he should find it.

The sweet wind from the shore of Spain strengthened. It beat across the sea with its message of spring, of life in a lovely land. The ship quivered, full of life, as though eager to reach the port. Her hands clutched the cool moist wood of the side. It vibrated under her fingers, full of strong, subdued movement. The waves curled and uncurled, throwing up their foam. The wind blew against her body, caressing it.

She saw Wolfe's figure framed a moment in the doorway, then he strode eagerly down the deck towards her. His face was in darkness, but his figure was that of her moving, breathing lover, full of life. Behind that silk robe was the deep chest from which came the voice that she loved.

He drew near. There was not a second to lose. She bent, and snatched up the fan.

"What is it?" he asked, his voice full with anxiety. She ran to him and pressed herself against his body.

"Oh, sweetheart, I am so upset!" she sobbed. "See! I have broken my darling fan!"

Patient Miss Peel

SHE FELT VERY TRANQUIL this morning, as she sat by the window of her bedroom, tucked up in her comfortable chair with everything she could possibly need close at hand. She felt stronger too, ready for any of the tiny adventures that come the way of the convalescent. She was grateful for all her mercies during this long period of helplessness following a dislocated hip. She had had a few faithful friends who had come regularly to see her, she had an excellent radio, many new books and an almost perfect maid. Her house, just outside one of the prettiest New England villages, was surrounded by fine trees and shrubs. It was secluded but not lonely.

She saw her friend, Virginia Ward, coming down the street and through the gate. Virginia was one of the faithful few who had helped to make her illness bearable. She was carrying a bunch of marigolds and something in a basket. What a dear she was!

The front doorbell rang. Steps hastened along the hall. The door opened and shut. Mrs. Ward came into the room.

"How well you're looking!" was her greeting. "You'll soon be up and about again."

They talked about Miss Peel's progress and Mrs. Ward remarked for the hundredth time, "What a blessing it is that you have Eileen! Really, she has kept the place in perfect order. She always seems to be on the spot to answer the bell. And she's so good-looking and cheerful."

"No one," declared Miss Peel, "will ever know what a comfort that girl has been to me. I realize that I'm terribly fussy about my belongings but no matter how I fuss she never gets impatient. If I make her bring up my best coffeepot, to show how she is keeping the silver, or insist on her cleaning out rooms that never are used, she is always smiling and cheerful."

"She keeps the blinds down, except in this room. It makes the house look gloomy but certainly the summer's sun has faded nothing."

Miss Peel gave a sigh of satisfaction. "I can scarcely wait," she said, "to go downstairs. My doctor says I'll be able to in a week."

"I'm so sorry I'm going away on a visit," said Virginia Ward. "I'll not be here to see your first excursions. I'll be away for a month."

"Everybody seems to be going away!" exclaimed Miss Peel, a little petulantly. "You and the Frazers and the minister and Jane Walton."

"Never mind. The time will soon pass. You'll be doing something fresh every day."

When she was gone Miss Peel sat, just pleasantly tired, making her plans for the month to come. She would not be lonely, even though all her friends were away. Even though her old friend, Dr. Trevor, was off for his August vacation and was leaving a stranger to take his place. She would have her beloved house, her cherished belongings, to herself, to get acquainted with all over again, to put in even better order than before, with Eileen's help.

Eileen came into the room carrying a glass of milk and some biscuits on a small tray. Beyond the edge of the snow-white doily the shining silver rim of the tray was visible. Eileen smiled down at Miss Peel, the reassuring, almost maternal smile that had been the invalid's support in the long months of confinement. How young she was, to have such an old head on her shoulders! It scarcely seemed right. She had had no childhood and had been the eldest of nine in an Irish hamlet. They had come to America seven years ago and in that time Eileen had become thoroughly Americanized in dress and speech. She always wore an air of happy youthful assurance. So Miss Peel thought, as she looked up into the smiling face.

"Thank you, Eileen," she murmured, taking the milk.

"Is there anything else you'd like, ma'am?"

"No. I'll just be quiet for a little. Then I'll ring for you and you can help me to have a toddle about the room."

"Sure, I will. I wonder how long it will be before the doctor lets you come down the stairs." The girl's lovely amber-colored eyes had a solicitous, even anxious look in them.

"I'm afraid it will be ten days or even more. I must be very careful."

"Yes. We've got to see that there ain't no more bones broken."

Miss Peel sipped her milk.

"Eileen, do you remember to scald out the garbage can every day? We can't be too careful of flies and decayed matter this time of year."

"Oh, sure. I never forget."

"How long is it since you defrosted the frigidaire?"

"I done it yesterday."

"This is the day for the fresh butter. Have you scalded the butter container?"

"Sure. I scalded that just before I came up with the milk."

"Have you watered the house plants?"

"Yeh. They're looking grand."

"Do you keep on the watch for moth millers?"

"Yeh. I killed one yesterday."

"Goodness! Where?"

"It had just flew into the kitchen from outdoors."

"Then," said Miss Peel sharply, "the screen door must have been left open."

Eileen smiled tenderly down at her.

"No, ma'am. The moth had a ride on my shoulder as I carried in the milk bottles. But I finished him with the flat of my hand." Suddenly her voice had sounded soft and Irish.

Sitting alone again, Miss Peel thought, for the hundredth time, what a miracle of good fortune it had been that she had engaged Eileen quite casually at an employment bureau just a fortnight before her accident. She had barely got her into her own ways when she had had to leave everything to the care of the girl — all her precious belongings that had been under this roof for three generations. She had not even thought very well of Eileen at the first. But how the girl had risen to the emergency! And she would be rewarded.

Miss Peel often amused herself by thinking of the nice things she would do for Eileen. It seemed a sin that such a beautiful girl should be lost in a kitchen. What if she had some special talent? Miss Peel had heard her singing very sweetly in a distant part of the house.

It was surprising how strong she felt. She was sure that the doctor underestimated her strength. She wanted very much to get out of her chair and walk about the room, all by herself. She was tired of ringing bells, of being waited on. She had a feeling that the mother instinct was so strong in Eileen that she enjoyed making a baby of her.

Well, she wasn't going to be coddled any longer. She threw aside the rug that lay across her knees and supporting herself by the arms of the chair, rose to her feet.

She had not yet been about the room alone. Now, with something of the feelings of an adventurous child, she explored every corner. She opened drawers and fingered their contents. She took out a gay scarf which she would give Eileen that day.

She opened the door into the passage and looked out. How odd her own house seemed, as though it scarcely belonged to her! But how clean the stair carpet was and how shining the panes in the window! The window looked onto the back garden where the young Swede who came once a week was weeding the flower border. He looked very strong and virile with his sleeves rolled up and the muscles showing on his round arms. Miss Peel had an idea that Eileen spent a good deal of time with him on the day he came to work. But what could you expect? She was young. She was human. Yes, there she was, going across the grass to him, her apron fluttering in the breeze!

Miss Peel simply could not resist going down the stairs. She said to herself, "I must not go down the stairs. The doctor would be very angry." Then, as though against her will, she found herself going down, very carefully, a step at a time.

At the bottom she stopped to admire the picture of the clipper in full sail that had once belonged to her great-grandfather. He had been a tough old sea dog and she was not very proud of him, but she had always admired the lovely ship.

She thought she would go into the living room and rest a little. Then she would ring for Eileen and get her to help her up the stairs.

Softly she opened the door of the room and looked in. The blinds were down and the room was almost dark. She could scarcely see the furniture but a strange, unearthly, moldy smell filled her nostrils. She felt so mystified by it and by the half-discerned aspect of the room that she felt she must be dreaming.

She groped her way to a window and put up the blind. Sunlight came pouring in.

But its brilliance only made her feel more dazed than before, more certain that she was under some nightmarish delusion. Yet she could see by the dim reflection in the mirror above the man-telpiece that she was there in the flesh. The pain in her injured hip was real enough. She sat down in one of the two straight-backed chairs, which had been her great-grandmother's, to rest and clear her head. By degrees she became calmer and was able to take in the condition of the room, to realize that she was wide awake and that what she saw was the result of months of the most brutal neglect.

It was obvious that, in those long months of her confinement, no broom or brush had ever touched the rugs or floor. They were thick with dust. The window at the far end had been left open and the roadside dust had poured in. Rain had draggled her most prized curtains. Wind had beaten them to sodden faded rags. She sprang up and hobbled to the table beside the window. On it stood two old family silhouettes, in their original frames, and beside them lay the hundred-and-fifty-year-old Bible of the Peel family. All were ruined.

She made little moaning sounds and braced herself with her hands on the table. She had not known that a room could be so treated. Surely nothing like this had ever happened to a woman before! On top of all she had been through, to have had her trust so outraged, to have been so hoodwinked by an unscrupulous hussy of a girl, was enough to kill her.

She must know the worst. She must see the dining room.

Slowly, to conserve her strength, she walked, looking straight ahead of her, into the hall, crossed it, and opened the door of the dining room. Here too the blinds were down but there was not quite such a smell of mold and damp. She put them up and surveyed the room, prepared, as she thought, for the worst.

But the living room had not prepared her for the dirt and disorder here. Evidently Eileen made free use of this room. A pair of muddy shoes, run over at the heels, were in the middle of the rug, which was gray with dust and bore a large stain from an overturned coffeepot. The beautiful mahogany table was strewn with dirty dishes above which a cloud of flies buzzed. On the sideboard stood the silver, tarnished almost beyond recognition. Among it was a bundle wrapped in a soiled towel. She opened it and discovered the best silver teapot, shining and bright, ready to be taken upstairs for her inspection.

She was quite calm now. Her legs were not trembling any more and the pain in her hip was gone. But a new rage, icy and fierce, rose in her when she saw a pair of coarse socks, a man's socks, lying among the silver, a ball of yarn beside them, waiting to be darned. She was about to hurl them to the floor when she heard voices in the kitchen.

She left the socks where they were and hurriedly drew down the blinds. She opened the door of the pantry and stepped inside closing it softly behind her. She all but screamed when a mouse, nibbling a piece of cheese, squeaked in fright and darted out of her way. She sank onto a stool and bent forward to listen.

A man's voice, in a heavy Swedish accent, was saying, "Eileen, Eileen, vich iss de cream?"

"There, on the table, you big baby."

The swing door between the dining room and kitchen was thrown open and Miss Peel heard the two enter. She smelt sausages and heard dishes being set on the table. No heatproof mats under them either! She heard coffee gurgling from the pot into their cups. She heard the man gulping his, smacking his lips in satisfaction, making animal noises over the sausages. With his mouth full he said:

"So, de old girl's gettin' better."

"Gee, you never saw the like how she's gaining. She'll be able to come down here in two weeks."

The man chuckled. "Where'll you be den, eh?"

"Not here, you bet. She can get someone else to clean up. What'd she take me for? Powerful Katrinka? Expecting me to cook and clean and wait on her, hand and foot! Say, she's one of the sort would make a slave of you, if you'd let her. She near drove me crazy at first with her fussing but I found out how to manage her!"

"You bet you did! And you've given me a good time, baby."

Hugs and kisses, revolting in their energy, sickened Miss Peel in her hiding place. Yet she was able to control herself. She even opened the door a hair's breadth and had a glimpse of the pair locked in a heavy-breathing embrace.

When they were gone Miss Peel crept softly up the stairs, helping herself by the banisters. When she reached the top she was almost exhausted. She was just able to totter to her chair and fall into it.

Her one thought now was that she must conceal her agitation from Eileen. She pretended to be dozing the first time she came into the room. The next time she told Eileen that she thought she had overdone it that morning. She was very tired and feared that it would be necessary to go more slowly. She confessed that she had walked twice round the room alone.

How solicitous Eileen was! She scolded Miss Peel in that motherly way of hers. She put her back in bed. She brought her a hot-water bottle. She made her sip a little brandy. Miss Peel would as soon a serpent had touched her but she set her teeth and smiled wanly. She looked up at the girl's round milk-white throat and had a sudden fierce desire to throttle her.

Indeed her feelings during the following week often surprised herself by their savagery. She imagined all sorts of things she would like to do to Eileen. She grimly remembered her great-grandfather, the sea captain, and wondered if after all she might not have inherited some traits from him. But she concealed her feelings under a timid, docile mask. She took little walks about the room, leaning heavily on Eileen's arm. But, when the girl was safely downstairs, she walked strongly up and down, stretching her arms, gaining strength every hour, her rage never lessening. In fact it so increased that she knew she could no longer conceal it. One night she could not sleep for it. She lay tossing on the bed thinking of her cherished belongings that Eileen had ruined by brutal neglect.

She arose at five. She put on her warm woolen dressing gown and went to the bedroom that had once been her father's. From a drawer she took a leather case containing a brace of heavy pistols. She removed one of these, saw that it was loaded and grasping it in her hand walked steadily along the passage to Eileen's door. She opened the door and went in.

The light was still faint. She could just make out Eileen's features relaxed in deep sleep, one round white arm thrown out across the pillow. She bent over her and touched her bare arm with the cold metal of the pistol. Eileen gave a start and cried out in her sleep. Then she opened her eyes and stared up at Miss Peel.

"Goodness' sakes," she cried. "Are you sick, ma'am? You ought to have rung your bell!" She sat upright. "Say, your hand felt like ice."

"It was not my hand, Eileen," said Miss Peel. "It was this."

She held the pistol up before her. It pointed just above Eileen's head.

Eileen turned a greenish color. "Yes," she said in a whisper, knowing from stories told her by her mother that you must humor crazy people. You mustn't let them know you're afraid of them. She remembered in a flash how Miss Peel had seemed different the last week. She'd seemed broody like an old hen. "Yes," she whispered, "them things are cold. You'd better give it to me and I'll take care of it for you."

"No," said Miss Peel. "I'm just going to carry it about with me while I watch you work. I want you to get up now and begin your day's work. You have a lot to do, so you'd better hurry."

Eileen scrambled out of bed. She picked up her clothes from the chair and edged toward the door. Miss Peel pointed the pistol at the space between Eileen and the door.

"I advise you not to try to get away," she said. "If you do just what you are told I won't harm you but there's no knowing what I'll do if I'm crossed."

She sat down on the chair and looked with cold authority at Eileen. Trembling from head to foot the girl began to put on her clothes. By the time she was dressed she was a little less terrified. It was just like something out of the movies. Gee, she'd land the old woman in the asylum, once she'd got away from here!

She began to feel like a heroine. She said, in a soothing tone, "I'll make you some breakfast. Then you'll sure feel better and you'll give me the gun to keep for you, won't you?"

Miss Peel did not answer. She followed Eileen down the stairs. The girl had a mind to make a dash for it and try to reach the outside but she knew the door was locked. No, she'd just have to humor Miss Peel and wait her chance. She set about preparing breakfast.

"It's terrible early for you, ma'am, ain't it?"

"Yes," agreed Miss Peel, "but there's a lot to be done."

She directed Eileen to boil two eggs and to carry both breakfasts on a tray into the dining room.

"Och!" cried Eileen, throwing up her hands and becoming suddenly very Irish. "The room's not fit fur you at all, dear Miss Peel! I'm in the middle of house-cleaning it."

"Don't worry," said Miss Peel. "I saw it a week ago."

Eileen's jaw dropped.

"A week ago! And how could you see it a week ago?"

"I came downstairs," answered Miss Peel, polishing the pistol on her sleeve, "and went over all the rooms."

"So that's why you were broody!"

"Yes. And that's why you're going to work like the devil till you have everything in order again." Such language on the lips of Miss Peel shocked Eileen almost as much as the sight of the pistol in her hands. Trembling from head to foot she set down the tray. Obsequiously she turned and began to sidle out of the room.

"Don't go," rapped out Miss Peel. "You'll have your meals with me for the present."

But Eileen had no appetite. Never had food been so tasteless to her. She sat, trying to get it down, while tears ran over her cheeks and her fascinated eyes were fixed on the heavy pistol lying beside Miss Peel's plate. Miss Peel ate with relish.

When she had finished she said, in a commanding voice, "Now get your cleaning cloths. There are plenty of them. And a pail of hot water and cleaning powder and soap. You will do this room first so we shall have a decent place to eat in."

She went behind Eileen to the kitchen and stood close beside her while she filled the pail and collected the cleaning things. Eileen kept thinking, "She's crazy. She's crazy. I've got to watch my chance. The minute she turns her back I've got to get out and give one screech fur the p'leece."

But Miss Peel did not turn her back. She never took her eyes off Eileen. When they were back in the dining room she seated herself in an armchair and rapped out her directions in a voice that made Eileen tremble. The girl was soft from lazy living. By the time the floor, the windows, the woodwork were cleaned, the sweat was pouring down her face. She had been working hard for four hours. It was half past ten.

The milkman had come and gone unnoticed but Eileen listened hard for the grocer's man. That was her chance. She would give a yell and get behind him. He was strong. He would hold Miss Peel while she ran for the police. Miss Peel seemed to read her thoughts. She said:

"When the grocer's man comes you are to go and stand in that

far corner, with your face to the wall. If you look round or make
any kind of noise it will be the worse for you. I am a very dangerous woman when I'm roused. You know that, don't you?"

"Yes, ma'am."

In a short while the grocer's man came. They heard him march
into the kitchen and begin to thump the parcels on the table.
Miss Peel gave Eileen a look. She jumped up and stood in the
corner as directed. Miss Peel opened the door and looked out
at him.

"Thank you," she said.

He was a young Negro. He stared at her, smiling.

"You better, hey?" he said.

"Yes. I'm quite well again. It's a good thing, because my maid
had to go to her family for a couple of weeks."

He laughed. "I guess you won't notice that much. She ain't no
good, that girl. She's as lazy as they make them."

"Yes," agreed Miss Peel, "she's not much good."

"Well, Ah'm sure glad you's better."

He was gone.

"Now, get to work," ordered Miss Peel.

Pail after pail of water was turned black by the dirt. Over and
over again things were washed, scoured, polished. The vacuum
cleaner was brought into service.

They had lunch, sitting opposite each other in awful silence.
But this time Eileen was ravenous. She devoured slice after slice
of bread and cheese. Her hair hung in damp locks into her eyes.
She was an unpleasant sight but Miss Peel never faltered in her
purpose.

Soon after lunch, while Eileen was washing a great pile of
dishes in the kitchen, the telephone rang. A flicker passed over
Eileen's face. She would make a dash for freedom when Miss
Peel answered the phone. But the cold voice commanded:

"Go into the corner. Stand with your face to the wall."

Eileen obeyed.

Miss Peel answered the phone. "Yes? Oh, hello, Myriam. . . . Yes, I'm getting on wonderfully. . . . So you are going away too! All my friends are going away. . . . Oh, I'll be all right. . . . Yes, I'm feeling stronger every hour. . . . Yes, she's been wonderful. She's having a little rest now. . . . Yes, I'm sure she needs it. . . . No, you mustn't worry about me. . . . Have a good time."

The receiver was hung up. Before leaving the phone Miss Peel rang up the butcher and the grocer and ordered supplies. She looked almost cheerful as she returned to the attack.

The afternoon wore on in ceaseless labor on the part of Eileen, ceaseless vigilance on the part of Miss Peel. No speck of dirt escaped her eye. Over and over again the worst spots were washed till they shone. The one thing she ignored was Eileen's sighing in weariness. Heartfelt groans as the girl's knees grew sore and her knuckles raw were seemingly unheard. She herself was tireless, sitting upright on her chair, watching her belongings regain something of their onetime brightness. But no amount of rubbing removed the stain from the carpet or the marks of hot dishes and wet tumblers from the mahogany table.

When night came all Eileen thought of was getting to bed. Never in her life had she done such a day's work. She ached in every joint. If she had to spend another day like this it would kill her, she was sure. But tomorrow was the day the gardener came. Miss Peel would never be able to deceive him. He would march into the kitchen as soon as he arrived, like he always did. Eileen was too tired to think.

Miss Peel directed Eileen to make herself a bed on the couch in her room. This was not a new experience, for the girl had slept there in the first days after Miss Peel's accident. Tears of pity for herself filled Eileen's eyes as she remembered how kind and gentle she had been then to Miss Peel. But the older woman seemed to have forgotten all that. There was no sign of relenting in her set face.

"Good night," she said, as Eileen pulled the bedclothes over her head. "I hope you have a good sleep. You'll need all your strength tomorrow."

The only answer was a smothered sob.

Eileen slept like a log. Miss Peel had to shake her by the shoulders to wake her. Sun was pouring in at the windows. The clock was striking eight. Eileen stretched and yawned, hardly knowing where she was. She felt as though she had been beaten, her muscles were so sore. Her pretty face, rosy from sleep, peered up at Miss Peel over the edge of the sheet. Then she remembered all.

She dived under the covers.

"I won't get up!" she sobbed. "I won't! I won't!"

The curve of one bare elbow was visible. Against it she felt the ice-cold barrel of the pistol.

"Get up," commanded Miss Peel. "Dress."

Eileen leaped out of bed and began to pull off her night-gown.

"I won't dress," she sobbed. "I won't, I won't!"

But she dragged on her clothes as fast as she could. When they were in the kitchen she peered out of the window to see if the gardener had arrived.

"You need not look for him," said Miss Peel. "I phoned him from my room while you were still asleep and told him I'd not need him for several weeks. I told him you were off on a holiday. I don't enjoy lying but, when anyone has acted as you have, other people are forced into wrongdoing as a consequence. Put on the kettle."

Work on the dining room continued all that day. The next day the kitchen — through which it was almost impossible to walk because of the accumulation of dirty utensils, cartons, empty tins and rubbish of all sorts — was attacked. By night Eileen could scarcely move. She blubbered, sniffled, sobbed and choked, as she scrubbed.

The next morning, as Miss Peel was telephoning her doctor to tell him that it was quite unnecessary for him to call, Eileen made a rush for the pistol and wrenched it from Miss Peel's hand. They struggled. There was an explosion. The bullet went into the wall behind Miss Peel's head. They were almost equally terrified. But now Miss Peel had possession of the pistol. She pointed it at Eileen.

"Put up your hands!" she ordered.

Eileen put them up.

"Now," continued Miss Peel, ghastly pale but able to control her voice, "if I have any more trouble with you I'll march you straight off to the police station and say that you fired at me. I want you to swear that you will obey me."

"I swear I will," said Eileen faintly.

The work of cleansing went on. Heavy rain set in and the isolation of the two was complete. Silver and brass were polished till they shone again. China was washed, windows cleaned. The study and the living room, the pantry and the cellar, each in its turn regained its order and brightness. Every now and again a day was taken for going over that part of the house which Eileen had kept in order, so that it might remain so. A fortnight passed.

Surely, in that time, Eileen had lost ten pounds. Miss Peel too did not look the woman she had. But her will never failed her. When she looked at objects that had been hopelessly injured by Eileen's callous neglect, she turned the screw a little harder and squeezed a couple of hours extra work out of her.

It was now plain sailing so far as the work was concerned. Either the girl's spirit was broken or she actually began to take an interest in putting the place in order again. She was healthy and strong as a young animal and when she gave up rebelling against her fate, she worked, ate and slept with a serenity that matched her mistress's inflexibility.

In the third week she actually began to sing at her work. The rains had ceased. The weather had turned bright and cool. She was washing the linoleum on the kitchen floor with good sweeping strokes. Suddenly she burst into an old Irish song. Her voice was as sweet and fresh as a May morning. Miss Peel remembered how she had always enjoyed Eileen's singing. She looked down at her almost kindly.

But the strain had told on Miss Peel. The sitting alert hour after hour through the long days, her eyes on Eileen, had become too much for her. She realized that, when all was in order, she must have complete relaxation for a while. Even now she found herself nodding in her chair. She woke with a start and found Eileen's eyes on her. Their expression was speculative, almost amused.

"Well, Eileen," said Miss Peel, "this begins to look like the house of a Christian once more."

"Sure, it does, ma'am," agreed Eileen, sitting on her heels and speaking confidentially. "And we've had a time of it, haven't we?"

"We certainly have. . . . Eileen, there is a fly over there. Get the swatter quickly and kill it. No, give me the swatter. I'll kill it."

She took the fly swatter and moved quickly across the highly polished floor. Her feet slipped. She fell heavily. Eileen screamed and ran to her. The shadow of the big Swedish gardener fell across the room.

"Vot's de matter?" he asked.

"It's the missus falling again. Gosh, ain't it awful? You carry her upstairs for me."

Miss Peel was light. With very little effort he carried her up the polished stairs and laid her on her immaculate bed.

A few days later Miss Peel's friend, Virginia Ward, came to see her. She was full of anxiety and solicitude. She bent over Miss Peel, as she lay in bed, and kissed her.

"You poor darling," she said. "I've never known anything so cruel as that you should have fallen and injured your hip a second time. To think that you will have to lie here, for months, till it is mended! What a blessing it is that you have Eileen! She looked so kind and capable when she let me in. She took me all over the downstairs and showed me what perfect order it is in. She is a treasure, isn't she?"

"Yes," agreed Miss Peel, with her patient smile, "Eileen and I understand each other thoroughly."

A Word for Coffey

I was *talking with a seafaring man beside the harbor of St. John. He had been loading kegs of nails on a little schooner, but he must have been his own master, for in the middle of the afternoon he sat down on a keg and told me the story of Bill Coffey.*

Coffey was about as bad an old man as I've ever seen. You couldn't look at his face without knowing that he'd lived an awful tough life. He'd a kind of a devilish look like one of them gargoyle faces, and he'd a triumphant look too, as though he was glad of all he'd done and only wished it might have been worse.

He'd been born in Ireland, but he'd knocked all over the world since he was a little feller, and one country was no more to him than another. But I always think that him being born in Ireland accounted for the queer thing he did at the last. For the Irish are a queer race and no mistake. Once they get an idea in their heads they get kind of possessed by it.

Coffey had been a splendid seaman in his day, neat, and smart, and strong as a horse. But if there was trouble on board he was certain to be in it, fighting, mutiny, bloodshed — why, he'd even been on a pirate ship once in his young days. He'd bit the ear off one man, and the thumb half off another, and he'd killed a Portugee, though somehow he'd not swung for it. But I'm telling about his death and not his life. I just wanted to show you what sort of rum old codger he was.

It happened that I sailed with him on his last voyage. I was only about twenty then, but he was getting oldish. We'd sailed from Colón, and as we were coming out of the gulf we were caught on the edge of a hurricane. We were kept mighty busy, and in the midst of it a great comber came along and struck Coffey and sent him flying into the sea. He was up forward at the time. Then a backwash caught him as he landed in the water and sent him back on the ship, this time aft on the starboard deck. When we got to him he was cursing enough to raise your hair, but he didn't seem much hurt.

But some time after, a sort of paralysis took him, and he was done for as far as work was concerned. He'd taken a fancy to me, and he thought he'd like to spend the rest of his days in the house that I called home. That was a boardinghouse kept by my aunt by marriage, a Mrs. McKay. She was Irish, too, and a kinder woman never lived, though she was so religious.

It did make me feel funny to come home after a voyage and find Coffey sitting up at my aunt's table in a clean white neckercher, looking at respectable as he could with that face. My aunt was a grand cook, and he knew when he was well off. And she was glad to have him, for he kept her best room permanent; and I never let on to her what sort of a life he'd led.

He was able with the help of his sticks to walk at a terrible slow pace to the dock, and there you might see him, unless it was raining cats and dogs, day in and day out, telling queer yarns to anyone that would listen to them, and looking like some battered old hulk cast up on the rocks by a storm.

Tourists liked to take pictures of him, and he'd pose for 'em with one eyebrow cocked and his chin sunk in his neckercher, looking what they called "picturesque"; but if they could have heard the remarks he made about them when they'd gone! He seemed as stuffed full of hate as the hold of a privateer full of loot.

But he was always very civil and respectful to my aunt. She was a fine, clear-skinned woman with a steady gray eye that could give any man look for look, and put him straight in his place, if need be. He took an odd fancy to her only child, little Alfred, a boy of nine. If Alfred had been a bad young one, I could have understood it better. I'd have thought Coffey'd found an apt pupil to train in the ways of wickedness. But Alfred was as religious as his mother, with her big, steady gray eyes, only he was sallow, and delicate from birth.

Sometimes Coffey would bring him along to the dock, and you never saw such a queer pair of companions, Coffey rolling along like an old tub in the trough and Alfred trotting alongside, grasping hold of Coffey's stick, which was carved to represent a sea gull's head with the beak open. He'd sit quiet as a mouse while Coffey spun a yarn, his eyes fixed on the sea with a look that used to make me wonder if he'd live to be a man. But he was a human boy in lots of ways, too, for he was desperate proud of Coffey's liking for him, and I've seen him swagger across his mother's kitchen with his hands in his pockets, fairly crowing, "Mr. Coffey's sigly" — Alfred had adenoids and never could say the letter k — "and I'm sigly. We gets along fine."

When Coffey got down on his seat, it was hard for him to get up again. We used to take him by the arms and heave him into a standing position, young Alfred pushing from behind; and once we got him up on his pins, he'd stand rocking like a bent old oak in the wind till he could get up strength to navigate.

That last year he was with us, I was away all winter on a long voyage, and when I got back I saw a great change in Coffey. It wasn't so much that he'd failed in body as that he'd an

anxious, yearning look in the eyes that I'd never seen there
before. He'd always had that triumphant look I've spoke of, as
though he didn't regret anything he'd ever done.

It soon came out what the change was. The fear of death had
taken hold of him. And not only death, but the terror of the
hereafter. That winter had been a terrible one of cold and fog.
He'd hardly had his nose out of doors, and, sitting in the house
by the fire with no one but Alfred to talk to, religion had got in
its work on him. Alfred was subject to bronchitis, and he was
out of school all winter, and I guess the only fun he had was in
talking about repentance and hell-fire with Coffey. Though he
couldn't go to school, he managed to get to Sunday school, and
my aunt told me how the old man would watch for him to come
back, with his hairy old face pressed to the pane, glaring up the
street for the first sign of that little codger and, when he saw
him, shouting to her: "Ship ahoy, there! Open the door for
Alfred!"

And Alfred would be pretty sure to have some new horror
to add to the old man's misery, and he'd spin texts off like a
regular preacher and expound the lesson of the day with his eyes
shining like stars, his mother said, and Coffey shaking in his old
carpet slippers.

"Well, I call it a shame," I said, "to scare the poor old sinner
in his latter days like this, for it isn't as though anything on earth
could save him after the way he's carried on and all."

"Alfred can save him," said my aunt. "And you just see if he
doesn't!"

I tried to get Coffey's thoughts into different channels, but it
wasn't any use.

I took him down to the dock the first fine spring day, with a
grand breeze blowing off Fundy, and the gulls sailing overhead.
I fetched up a few cronies he used to like to yarn and cuss with,
and I filled up his pipe with my own tobacco, but it wasn't any

use. It was Alfred's first day at school since winter, and Coffey kept muttering, to himself more than to us: "It'll be too much for the child. . . . He ain't fit for it. . . . I wish he'd just run along out and come down here where he'd get the sea breeze."

And the odd thing was, Alfred did appear before very long, trotting down the wharf on his spindling little legs, and his hair flying in the wind.

"Oh, Mr. Coffey!" he says, leaning against Coffey's shoulder. "I was took bad in school, and teacher had to let me out, and mother said I could come down here to you where I'd get the good air. And all the way I ran I kept saying to myself" — he put his mouth to Coffey's ear and whispered. Coffey's jaw dropped, and he clutched the boy to him, and it seemed as though a sudden tremor ran through him.

After that Alfred was never away from his side. They'd give each other queer, secret looks, and when they were alone — and we left them together mostly then — Alfred was always talking, talking, with his little, shining white face turned up to Coffey's grim old mug, and his two hands spread out on his little thin knees.

One day when there was half a gale blowing, the two had taken shelter behind a pile of bales, and when I came up behind them they didn't hear me but went right on talking. Coffey's gums were showing in a fearful kind of smile, and he was saying: "Ye know well, Alfred, that I've lived a bad life, and now, with the fear of death and eternal punishment on me, I get no wink of slape at all. Ye see I'm afraid to go to slape for fear the life'll just slip out o' me, and me not knowing it, and I'd wake up before the Judgment Seat."

"You must just resign your soul to the Lord, Mr. Coffey," Alfred says.

"Och, that's just what gets me," groaned Coffey, "for He'd

have the weasand out of it in a jiffy. Alfred, you must never forget that you're to put in a good word for old Coffey, if the time comes when we stand before the Throne together. You've promised me, mind. And He'd believe you even if you did lay it on a little thick about me goodness, Alfred darlin'."

"I'll put in a word for you, never fear, Mr. Coffey," pipes Alfred, eating gumdrops out of a bag Coffey'd bought him.

Tears were trickling down poor Coffey's cheeks. "Now what would ye say, Alfred, supposin' you an' me — just the two of us — was stood before the Throne this minute — me all shiverin' in me nakedness, an' Him settin' there ferninst us with His long white beard, an' the eyes of Him like two searchlights — what would ye say, Alfred? Ye'd stand up for Coffey, wouldn't ye?"

Alfred took the gumdrop out of his mouth and stared up in the old man's face. He spoke clear and solemn: "I'd — I'd — up an' say to God, 'Be aisy on Coffey, God. He ain't so bad as he looks.' "

"Good — good — " gasps Coffey. "Go on, Alfred. That's the talk. You're a marvel."

" 'He ain't so bad as he looks,' " Alfred repeats, still more solemn. " 'He's terr'ble pious in all his goin's and comin's. He pays his board on the tick o' the clock. There ain't a whiter soul in our street — 'ceptin' me own. Be aisy on him, Lord.' "

"It's great," gasps Coffey. "Say it again!"

The wind and the waves suddenly set up a great noise and drowned the rest of their talk. I sneaked away feeling very queer.

One night I heard a shuffling noise in the passage outside my door. Someone seemed to be dragging himself along and breathing very heavy. I hopped out of bed and softly opened my door just wide enough to peek out.

There was the old man in his nightshirt in the passage, carrying a candle at such a slant that the grease was dribbling all over his hand. He shuffled along to Alfred's door and went in. I was after him in a minute, keeping very quiet so as not to awaken the other lodgers.

He was standing over Alfred's bed, staring down at the little shrimp and drawing deep sighs as though his heart was heavy as lead.

I laid my hand on his arm. "What's the trouble, Coffey?" I whispered.

"Och, I'm feared," he says, "that the wee lad's goin' to get away on me."

"Get away?" I asked. "Get away where?"

"Out of this world," he says with a terrible groan. "Into the next. He's as wake as a kitten, and this life's too much for him. Look ye, Tom, the day he gives up the ghost I give up the ghost too, for I can't risk facin' the Wrath alone."

Well, there's no use in talking to anyone that's as crazy as that. I led him back to his bed and covered him up like a baby and blew out his candle. Next morning I told my aunt that I thought she ought to get rid of him. He might set the house on fire prowling around at night, or do some mischief to little Alfred. But she said, nonsense, that he doted on the child, and there was a chance he'd leave him his money.

"Oh, that's it, is it?" I said. "Well, if you knew where that money came from, Aunt Mary, you mightn't want Alfred to touch it."

"There's no money," she says, "so dirty that it can't be put to a good use."

The end came about three weeks later. Coffey all this time had been like a man moving in a dream. His eyes had a glazed stare, and he and Alfred were always passing that queer, secret look to and fro between them, like a bad coin they couldn't get rid of.

It was a wild sort of evening in April. The sky was flaming

red, and the waves that tumbled up against the pier were as green as those jade stones you see sometimes. The gulls were flying low and crying the loudest I've ever heard. I'd just strolled down after tea to look at the weather, and I was talking to a West Indian sailor, when I saw Coffey and Alfred walking hand in hand, looking in each other's faces and smiling. Well, I thought, where is this thing going to end? And I forgot for a minute what I was saying to the West Indian. . . . He was facing the harbor, and suddenly his face changed and then he gave a yell.

"What's wrong?" I asked.

"The old man," he said. "He grabs the kid in his arms and jumps into the water."

We both started on a run to the end of the pier. It was a quiet time, and there seemed no one about to help. There was no sign of Coffey or Alfred. I've never been as scared in my life. The things Coffey had said about the boy pleading for him at the Judgment Seat came back like fire in my brain, and I gibbered and shook like an idiot. Thank goodness, two men in a motorboat came along, and I and the West Indian got in, and a second later we saw the two rise not far off, bouncing about in the green waves like toys.

It was the West Indian that leaped out and held them up till we could get all three aboard. Coffey's arms were clasped around Alfred like a vise, and he had on the triumphant grin he'd used to wear when I first knew him. He was as dead as a doornail.

But Alfred was not dead. We had only worked with him a few minutes when he showed signs of life. When he was breathing regular I took him in my arms, wrapped him in my pea jacket, and ran with him to my aunt's house, only a block away. We got him to bed and sent for the doctor.

Alfred lay on his little bed like a dead child. His mother was sobbing at the foot while she chafed his feet, when the doctor came in. He was a large, noble figure of a man, with a full white beard spread out on his chest, and a shining white forehead above heavy brows and piercing blue eyes. You could almost understand how Alfred came to think he was God, but at the time, following all the other excitement, it gave my aunt and me a terrible turn.

The doctor felt his pulse and lifted his eyelid and looked in his eye. Suddenly both Alfred's eyes flew wide open, and he glared up into the doctor's face. Then he doubled up his skinny little body as though he was galvanized by fear. And then he seemed to gather all the life that was in him for one big effort, and he scrambled to his knees. The blanket we had around him slid off, and there he was, stark naked, with his heart jumping against his ribs like a fish in a net. He folded his two hands as if in prayer, and he began to plead for Coffey as he'd often promised to do before the Judgment Seat.

"Please God — I want to say a word for Coffey — be aisy on him — he's not so bad as he looks — not so bad as he looks — he does be a terr'ble pious old feller — please wash away his sins — like you've washed away mine — and — oh, God, I'm awful cold!"

Of course the doctor didn't know what the child meant, but he was properly startled, for Alfred looked like a little saint, and he gabbled like one possessed. We couldn't do anything with him till the doctor made him certain that Coffey was forgiven and washed whiter than snow.

That rascally old fellow had planned the whole thing some time before, for he'd made a will leaving all his money to my aunt and stating that a suitable monument was to be raised and inscribed to Alfred and him.

Well, we put up a nice headstone to him, though he didn't deserve it, and my aunt was able, because of the money, to give up taking lodgers and live private, except for me, and send Alfred to college for a grand education. He's almost through for the ministry.

The Widow Cruse

MR. UNSWORTH was an impressive figure when he took his morning walks. He was a retired merchant who had conducted a successful business for many years with the utmost probity. The dignity and honor of his past was reflected in his bearing. It was proud without being lofty, magnanimous without being benign, interested without being curious. In short, it was exactly right for a prosperous retired merchant with a well-furnished house, a capable housekeeper, and unimpaired health.

Although not curious he was interested, in varying degrees, in all he saw in his walks. That autumn, as the air grew crisper, he walked farther afield, head well up, sniffing the frosty air, for he was feeling exceptionally fit. It interested him to penetrate into the poorer streets, where the lives of the people were lived more openly than in his own region. He watched the children at play, the women cleaning their doorsteps or buying vegetables from carts. His tall spare figure, well-cut gray clothes, and close-clipped white whiskers became a familiar sight on several of these streets.

He would have liked very much to give pennies to the children, but he was afraid that they would follow him and become a nuisance. He liked best to stroll quietly around, seeing all, and attracting as little attention as possible.

In one street there was a certain house which interested him

more than any of the others. It interested him first because of
the brightness of its windows, the whiteness of the curtains, and
the fact that a flowering plant showed between them. More than
ever it interested him when he had seen Mrs. Cruse. She was so
neat, so very thin, and so terribly anxious. One need not look
at her the second time to know that she had had a hard life,
had coped with almost intolerable things, and was in the stress
of a struggle at that moment. Her best room — that is, the front
room on the ground floor — had always the sign To Let on it.
The To Let card had appeared first in the lower right-hand
corner of the window. Then it had been moved to the lower
left-hand corner. Now it hung suspended from a cord in the
middle. By such maneuvers Mrs. Cruse tried to draw the attention of passers-by to her vacant room.

When Mr. Unsworth had first observed the window, the curtains had hung in straight folds with only a narrow space between, through which the flowering plant might be glimpsed. In
three weeks they were looped back by white cords affording a
complete view of the plant. By another fortnight they were drawn
back so far that the curious (for Mr. Unsworth was becoming
curious) could distinctly see the glittering outline of the brass
bed within. A most attractive room, considering the locality,
thought Mr. Unsworth and could not understand why the room
was not taken. Still, the street was spattered with To Let cards
and all prospective tenants were, of course, not so discriminating
as himself. But he was distinctly disappointed when the card
disappeared from a neighboring window, which was far from
clean and backed by soiled Nottingham-lace curtains. He stalked
down the street feeling angry and hurt for Mrs. Cruse.

A fortnight passed before he had another of his brief glimpses
of her standing in her doorway. This time she was scrutinizing
the wares of a peddler. Mr. Unsworth walked very slowly, not
pretending to hide from himself the fact that he was terribly

curious about what Mrs. Cruse was examining. Even from the pavement he could see the look of wild longing in her eyes. It was a longing definitely mixed with worry. She could not afford what she wanted to buy. In her hands she held a length of wide pink satin ribbon. Mr. Unsworth drew in a quick breath. To think that a tall, very thin woman whose hair was going gray should be yearning for broad pink satin ribbon and not be able to buy it! He could not believe that such a ribbon would become her, but her longing for it was more touching to him than the longing for finery of a young girl. He had a fierce desire to go back and buy the ribbon for her, but the cool judgment of a long life in business restrained him. Nothing could restrain him from turning at the nearest corner and retracing his steps.

As he neared Mrs. Cruse's house he saw the peddler snap the fastening of his box and turn away with a pleased look. He saw Mrs. Cruse disappearing into the passage with the ribbon in her hand! Again he drew a quick breath, this time of relief, for he wanted her to have the ribbon. At the same time he felt worried that she should spend money so unwisely with a vacant room on her hands.

The next morning was one of snow and sleet. His housekeeper advised him, considering that he had a slight cold already, to remain in the house by the fire. But his interest in Mrs. Cruse's front room, which had developed into vigorous curiosity, would not be denied. Instead of his silk neckerchief he put on a woolen one. He took a glass of sherry. He selected a heavier walking stick and went forth. He had a feeling of determination somewhere in the back of his head though he could not have told why.

The mixture of snow and sleet blurred Mrs. Cruse's house so that he was right upon it before he saw what he did see in the window. This was the snowy-white curtains well drawn back and each one tied with a loop of broad pink satin ribbon. The poor woman! Oh, the poor woman! This was what she had been spending her scanty means for — to lure, to entice the eyes of passers-by to her vacant room. If Mr. Unsworth had not a lump in his throat as he splashed on down the street through sleet and snow, he had something that made him swallow hard. He had always been kind. Now suddenly he was becoming tender-hearted. Living alone has this effect on some natures and the very reverse on others.

The sleet and snow did their work, combined with the east wind. Mr. Unsworth was not out of doors again for a fortnight and when he did go his legs felt too shaky to carry him as far as the mean street where Mrs. Cruse lived. Days passed before he again approached the window where the card hung. He had hoped against hope that it would be gone, that the room would be taken, but it was not so. The card still hung there, the curtains were still drawn back by the ribbon loops, but a new bait was displayed. Between the curtains on a table stood a blue glass vase which held six pink carnations. Not paper ones — Mr. Unsworth could tell that by the way their heads were beginning to droop. "Well, well," he said aloud, hitting with his stick at a bit of orange peel on the pavement, "this beats all. Why is it that she can't let that room?"

Four other To Let cards had disappeared from windows in the same block and still hers stared out at him every time he passed. But she was not to be daunted. He was filled with admiration for her pluck. She would have made a good business-man, he thought. When the pink carnations died, red ones took their place. When they in their turn wilted, a tiny Jerusalem cherry tree appeared, for it was now the Christmas season and they were on the market.

The cherry tree made the window very gay. Surely it would do the trick, thought Mr. Unsworth, swinging his stick in anticipation as he neared the house. But it did not. If Mr. Unsworth had been more familiar with the business of letting rooms he would have realized that at this time of year people were settled in for the winter and shrank from any change before spring.

Six days before Christmas he met Mrs. Cruse face to face on the street. She wore rusty widow's weeds and looked very respectable. There was a look of anxiety in her eyes, though their natural expression was rather piercing, as though she was beginning to realize that life was a stone wall against which she might beat in vain. Yet her chin was held at an aggressive angle, for if she was discouraged the world must not know. She gave him a quick glance as they passed and a flicker of recognition brightened her eyes. She had often seen him from her window.

Mr. Unsworth was reasonably sure that she had lodgers already in the house (he had seen her buy vegetables in fairly large quantities from the huckster and when she passed him she carried a large paper bag from the top of which appeared the round shining face of a bun), but he passed the house at a time of day when they would be at their work. The only other occupant of the house he had seen was a youth of nineteen who, he judged, was the widow's son — old enough to be holding down a steady job, but in these days, Mr. Unsworth remembered, steady jobs were not easy to get. Still the youth impressed him as being indolent from the way he lounged along the street and entered the door with a cigarette always hanging in the corner of his mouth. Just the sort of youth to sponge on a brave struggling mother, Mr. Unsworth thought.

He was so very comfortable himself, so contented with his lot as Christmas Day drew near, that the thought of this gallant widow and her unlet room seemed to him unnecessarily cruel. He tried to think of some way in which he might help her. He thought of sending her money in an envelope, a nameless gift. It was a good idea but not good enough. What the woman wanted was to let her room and, even if he sent her a sum equal to three months' rent, the room would still be vacant. What she wanted was a lodger, and the problem was how to provide her with one.

The solution came three days before Christmas at five o'clock in the morning. He had been enjoying a wakeful spell. Enjoying it because he had slept soundly throughout the night, had woken refreshed and pleasantly conscious of the armor his downy blankets provided against the cold and of the silky smoothness of his sheets. It was still pitch dark, but a near-by clock had just sounded the hour in its tower. Like an inspiration, almost at the moment of waking, the thought came to Mr. Unsworth that he would rent the widow's room for himself. She should have no more tossing about in the early morning wondering how she should make ends meet, for he was sure she often did this.

Taking the room would not necessarily mean occupying it. He would tell her that he was engaged on some literary work which required a quiet he could not get in his own house. All he would need to do would be to spend an hour in the room every morning and, considering the interest, bordering on curiosity, which he felt toward Mrs. Cruse, that would be no hardship. It might even be a benefit to him because, if he had an hour's rest at this point in his morning walk, he might easily do another mile or so before luncheon. He could scarcely wait for morning to come. He had not felt this peculiar sort of excitement since he was a young man, this feeling of straining toward the day with eagerness. Why, he could almost go back further and say he had not felt like this since he was a boy.

Yet when he stood on Mrs. Cruse's doorstep with the knocker in his hand his courage almost forsook him. Why was he there? Was he making a fool of himself? Would the widow, with her piercing gray eyes, see at once that he was a sham and resent his intrusion? On the whole, he thought, with the knocker in one hand and his chin in the other and his stick dangling from his wrist, it might be better to send her a present of money and keep the personal touch out of the case.

While he stood so the door opened and the youth stood before him, hat on the side of his head and cigarette in the corner of his mouth. He stared in a moment's surprise, then said: "Did you want to see the room?"

"Yes, I should like to see the room." Driven to speak, Mr. Unsworth spoke in a full, resonant tone.

"Ma!" called out the boy over his shoulder, "there's a gent here wants to see the room."

The two males stood taking each other in with rather hostile glances while Mrs. Cruse changed into a clean apron, wiped her nose on a corner of the soiled one and tucked in a loose strand of hair.

"Dear me, Jack," she said hurrying down the passage, "why didn't you ask the gentleman in? Come right in, sir, and I'll show it to you."

A moment later Mr. Unsworth was standing in the very room he had seen so often from the outside, alone with the woman whose worries had given him such anxious thought. The room was smaller and dingier than he had expected, but it was very clean and there was a gas grate. He explained, every word ringing false in his own ears, what he wanted.

"You mean to say that you won't be sleeping here?"

"No. I shall only require the room for a short time each day."

"Well, you have to pay the regular rent for it just the same, sleep or no sleep." She eyed him aggressively.

"Oh, I quite understand that."

"And you understand about the gas?"

"Yes. I put a shilling in the slot and the gas comes."

She looked at him searchingly. "What about meals? My other lodgers take breakfast and dinner. I don't like letting my rooms just for lodgings. It don't pay so well. You needn't be afraid of my cooking. I could feed you up so you wouldn't look the thin man you do."

Mr. Unsworth was embarrassed. He was proud of his slender figure. And she was not at all what he had expected. He began to see how she might easily intimidate a prospective lodger. There was nothing pathetic or ingratiating about her.

"I am willing to pay the full board," he said.

"Full board!" she exclaimed. "And never eat a meal? You must have more money than brains! Or perhaps — " the suspicion in her eyes deepened. Was this handsome gentleman possibly insane? She looked toward the door wondering if her son had gone out.

Mr. Unsworth spoke with dignity. "I shall occasionally require a meal but, as I cannot tell you definitely just when, I feel that it is only fair to pay for them all."

"And you mean to say you'll take the room? I'm very particular, you must know. I like a gentleman to be tidy and respectable and not get ink on the furniture if he's a writer. I had one writing gentleman before and he was a terror. Left owing three months' board, too."

"I'm not like that," said Mr. Unsworth, heavily. "I'm willing to pay in advance and, if I do any damage, I'm willing to pay for that, too."

He took the room and paid a month's board and lodging in advance. As he walked down the street he was sure that Mrs. Cruse was peering after him between the curtains, not so much elated by his munificence as suspicious of his strangeness. Certainly it had been very different from what he had expected. He had expected to leave the house in a glow of well-doing, but what he felt was embarrassment and a little alarm. He had let himself in for a certain responsibility and he must play up to it and that under the penetrating gaze of Mrs. Cruse.

He had said that he would not take possession of the room

until the new year. So ten days intervened in which he might reflect on what he had done and have the satisfaction of knowing that the widow was in funds. He ate a hearty lunch and thanked his stars that he had not engaged to take any of his meals away from home.

He had his Christmas dinner where he always had it, at the house of his late partner who, like himself, was retired. He was a Mr. Robertson, a widower of long standing, who had lately taken a bride twenty years younger than himself. Mr. Unsworth had always enjoyed his quiet Christmas dinner with his old partner, but this year he rather dreaded it. The new Mrs. Robertson made him feel old-fashioned, seemed to put him definitely on the shelf. At the Christmas dinner she was even more intimidating than she had been before. There were only the three present, whereas formerly Mr. Robertson had always collected a couple of other old cronies.

Mrs. Robertson was very plain but you forgot all about her looks when she talked. The talk came from her in short explosive bursts while she leaned toward you showing her teeth and savagely watching for the effect of her words upon you. She laid herself out to fascinate, to astonish the two elderly men. Her husband had grown moderately used to her, though she depressed him, but the effect of these explosions of talk on Mr. Unsworth was devastating. If he chewed he could not tell what she said, so he bolted his food, his eyes fixed in apprehension on her face. She did not leave them to enjoy their wine and cigars in peace, but sat between them exploding in the face of first one and then the other. Everything she told them about had been great fun. Everyone was so amusing. She had roared with laughter. By the time the evening was over Mr. Unsworth hated her with a slow, concentrated hatred. He wondered what poor old Robertson had been thinking of when he married her. She had made little of the present he had taken her, though he had spent a good deal of thought and money on it. She had passed the latter part of the evening, however, in showing him trivial gifts from friends of hers with an explosion of appreciation for each.

Never again, vowed Mr. Unsworth, slumped in his easy chair at home, never again! For the first time in his life he felt old, a back number. He thanked God he was not in Robertson's shoes or, worse still, Robertson's bed.

The failure of his Christmas dinner turned his thoughts back to Mrs. Cruse. How was she getting on? Was the expression of her mouth less baffled, of her eyes less piercing?

He thought they were when she opened the door to him on the morning after New Year's Eve. She smiled severely yet pleasantly at him as he stood there, a dispatch case in his hand, like a student arriving for an examination.

"So you've come?" she said.

"Yes, I've come. Didn't you expect me?"

"I never expect anything in this world," she returned, "until I see it." Then she added grimly, "Except trouble."

She had placed a table with a chair beside it and an ash tray on it in the middle of the room. He set his dispatch case beside the ash tray and hung his hat and coat on a hook on the door.

"If you'll give me a bob," she said, "I'll start the fire for you. It's bitter cold here, being shut up so long."

Mr. Unsworth produced the shilling. There was a rattle, a spurt, then a clear steady flame sent warmth into the chill damp of the room. Mr. Unsworth seated himself at the table, took out his writing materials and tried not to look like a fool.

"If you want anything," Mrs. Cruse said from the doorway, "just come into the passage and shout. I'm always in the kitchen below."

"Oh, please don't trouble about me." He spoke anxiously. "I shan't want anything and when I've done I'll let myself out."

She came back into the room and he was surprised to see an

apologetic yet mischievous twist to her mouth. She said, "You haven't missed anything out of the room, have you?"

He looked vaguely about. "No-o. It looks just the same to me."

"Well, I took the pink satin loops off the window curtains. I thought as you was only going to be here for a part of the day you wouldn't mind. And they'll come in handy when the room's vacant again. It was them that caught *your* eye, wasn't it?"

"It was," he replied firmly. "And seeing that they led me to take the room I think I have a perfect right to enjoy them while I'm here. So will you please just tie them on again?"

He did not know why he had said this, but it was probably a desire to get nearer to Mrs. Cruse, to keep her from going away quite so soon, leaving him alone with his blank paper.

She gave an astonished look, then without a word marched upstairs and returned with the pink ribbon. She looped back the curtains carefully, then said, "Now, I hope you're satisfied!"

He saw that she had got quite red and that it became her, turning her eyes from gray to blue-gray and making her face look less worn. He was pleased with himself, for all along he had felt that she had the upper hand and now he felt that he had it. He took up his pen with gusto and wrote the date at the top of a page.

He thought about the "writing fellow" who had preceded him in the room. He wondered what he had written here and whether it had been of any value. Not much, he judged, or he would have been able to pay his board. Though, of course, there had been times when quite famous things had not brought in any money. He liked to think that the writing fellow had done good writing here and that he had succeeded him. Strange if he should turn to writing at his age and make a name for himself. . . .

An hour passed and he began to think that he might safely go. If he went very quietly Mrs. Cruse might not know how short his stay had been. He must ask her for a latchkey so that he might come and go at will. He rose and stretched himself and turned off the gas. The small room had become insufferably close. There was a knock at the door. Mrs. Cruse entered carrying a tray. She said: "I brought you a cup of cocoa and a hot scone. It don't seem quite fair that you should be paying for a lot of food you don't get and you with so little flesh to speak of."

Mr. Unsworth was positively frightened at being forced to eat in the middle of the morning. He also felt huffy at this second reference to his slightness.

"You're not very fat yourself," he retorted gruffly.

"Me!" she cried. "The way I work and the way I worry, I've cause to be thin. If you worked and worried the way I do I shouldn't wonder if you was a skeleton!"

Mr. Unsworth peered at the scones. There were three of them split open and buttered, and a small dish of blackberry jam as well as the jug of cocoa.

"Thank you very much." He waited for her to go, thinking how he might put the scones in his pocket and empty the cocoa out of the window. But she did not move. She said:

"I don't suppose you'll mind if I sit down while you eat. Then I can take the tray back with me."

There was no help for it. He set to work doggedly on the scones and was surprised to find how easy they were to eat. They were as light as feathers, so hot as to melt the butter, and the jam and cocoa were excellent. He made a clean sweep of the tray.

"I expect you feel a little more comfortable now," observed Mrs. Cruse complacently. "I certainly do myself. I couldn't bear the thought of taking all that money and giving nothing in return but the room."

She got his topcoat and helped him on with it. She followed him to the front door talking about the weather and the price of coal. When he asked for a latchkey, she said that the last gent had lost the extra key and that she was always about in the mornings and didn't mind a bit letting him in and out.

Mr. Unsworth took a brisk walk before returning home. He was surprised to find himself able to eat his usual lunch without discomfort. He had feared that his housekeeper would worry about him. He was pleased with himself. He gave a little grunt of satisfaction as he remembered how he had made Mrs. Cruse return the pink satin loops to the curtains. He had got the upper hand of her, had made her blush — and how it had become her! Behind her defiant, baffled look she was a nice woman. A kind, sweet woman he was sure, who deserved a better deal in the game of life than she had got.

Promptly at eleven o'clock the next day he was installed in his workroom, as he now called it. He had provided himself with a new volume of biography so that he might pass the time with profit. However, he kept one ear cocked for the approach of Mrs. Cruse from the basement. When he heard her he closed the book and began energetically to write. This time she brought him cocoa, a slice of plain bread and butter, and a piece of raspberry tart. He was glad to see her and began to eat and drink without protest.

"You're not getting on very well, are you?" she said, seating herself on the edge of the bed and eying the scant lines he had written.

"The work I do," he replied, taking a large bite, "requires a great deal of thought."

"Ah!" Mrs. Cruse looked sympathetic. "That's what keeps you thin. It's thoughts — worrying thoughts — that keep me thin."

"You have a lot of responsibility, certainly."

"Yes. I have three boarders besides yourself. Mr. Boyle, he's a vet. Mr. Cohen, he's in the clothing business. And Miss Rogers, she's a milliner. They're all reliable, but there they are — waiting with their mouths open to be fed!"

"Yes, indeed," agreed Mr. Unsworth, attacking the raspberry tart which was the most delicious he had ever tasted. "Feeding a household is a great responsibility."

"Then there's my Jack. He's a good boy, but he never knows his own mind. He's only got one vice. And that's correspondence courses. I'm always having to foot the bill for a new one. He thought he'd be a draftsman and took a course for it. But he got discouraged and thought he'd be a motor mechanic and took a course for that. Next it was some sort of plumbing. I shan't be surprised if the next course he takes is one in undertaking. If he does that, he can have his mother for his first subject. It's beyond bearing."

"You shouldn't give in to him. You should be firm," admonished Mr. Unsworth, finishing his piece of tart.

"I try to. I do, indeed. But what's a poor woman against a grown man? And he was such a delicate child! If only his father were living . . ."

Mr. Unsworth's kind face grew still kinder. He nodded sympathetically.

"*There* was a man to depend on! Weighed fourteen stone six and he wasn't tall, either. I always think you can depend on fat. If there's anything I miss in my present life it's fat." She stared at Mr. Unsworth.

He tried to puff himself out. Tried not to look thin and undependable, but was conscious of not succeeding.

Mrs. Cruse went on — "There's Mr. Boyle — he's big and rawboned — North of Ireland. There's Mr. Cohen — he's small and dapper, not an ounce to spare. Then there's Miss Rogers — mostly hair and eyes. And now there's you!"

They talked on and on. Before Mr. Unsworth knew it his lunch hour was upon him. He had no time for an extra walk in

which to get up an appetite but found that he had an appetite
without it. A new interest in life made his circulation quicker.
He was eager for tomorrow to arrive.

It became the usual thing for Mrs. Cruse and him to have a
long talk while he ate his little morning repast. One day he became so interested in telling her of his early vicissitudes, for they
had reached the stage of mutual confidences, that it was too late
for him to go home for lunch.

"You'd better have your lunch here then," said Mrs. Cruse.
"It's your right. You pay for it. You can have it here any day
you want." She looked at him kindly.

He said that he was shy about meeting strangers.

"There's no one here but myself. None of them comes home
until night."

She produced an omelette, some cold meat, and fried potatoes.
They sat at one end of the long table in the basement dining
room with an oil heater blazing away beside them and an en-
largement of Mr. Cruse's fat face beaming at them from the
wall.

After that Mr. Unsworth took his lunch with Mrs. Cruse more
often than not. He explained to his housekeeper that business in
the city was claiming his attention. Every morning he set off
jauntily from his house, dispatch case in hand, moving straight
as an arrow to the widow's house. Once or twice Jack joined
them at lunch, seeming to quail under Mr. Unsworth's stern
glance.

The inevitable day came when Mr. Unsworth appeared at the
evening meal and was introduced to the other boarders. He had
shrunk from it for weeks, yet had been goaded to it by his overpowering curiosity to see the entire household. Mrs. Cruse had
talked so much about them, so intimately described their idio-
syncrasies that he felt he must see them.

He would not have believed it possible that he could feel so much at home among them. They were just as Mrs. Cruse had described them, only more human. They accepted him with respect but without embarrassment. Mrs. Cruse sat at one end of the table, Jack at the other, Mr. Boyle and Mr. Cohen on one side, Mr. Unsworth and Miss Rogers on the other. This nearness to Miss Rogers was a new and wonderful experience for Mr. Unsworth. She was fragile, she was pretty, she had a soft voice and eyelashes so long that it was hard to keep from staring at them. She was thirty-two, but she was so innocent and gentle that she seemed more like eighteen to Mr. Unsworth. It was even more terrible to think of her battling against the world alone than to think of Mrs. Cruse battling.

From this time on Mr. Unsworth became divided into two men — the man dominated by Mrs. Cruse and the man dominated by his housekeeper. As the one grew, the other shrank until, at last, the man who returned to his housekeeper was no more than a husk, a shadow of his former self. The other man, the one whose blood was beginning to move quickly in his veins, soon learned that Miss Rogers's Christian name was Peggy. He began to loiter with her in the passage after dinner, bending his distinguished head under the flickering gas jet the better to see her face.

She told him of the difficulties of the millinery business. How because of the cool damp summer she had not sold off the season's hats and still had a number on hand. He wished that he might buy them from her but could think of no plan to make such a purchase plausible. He worried about the leftover hats considerably after he went to bed, but when he fell asleep he dreamed of her eyelashes and that they were tickling his cheek.

"Oh," she exclaimed one day, "I feel as though I had known you for ages! I tell you all my troubles. I don't know what I should do without you."

"And I don't know what I should do without you," he replied. And he did not know whether to be glad or sorry that they were under the gas jet because something inside him was impelling him to kiss her.

His advance toward intimacy with Mr. Cohen was not so pleasant. Mr. Cohen was in financial difficulties and was behind with his board.

"He'll go off without paying just like the writing gent did, as sure as my name's Lily!" cried Mrs. Cruse.

Mr. Unsworth got no thrill out of knowing that her name was Lily, yet he felt more and more drawn to her and he began to worry about Mr. Cohen and his unpaid board. It would be terrible if he went off as the "writing gent" had done.

One night after dinner he asked Mr. Cohen to stop a minute in the basement dining room, that he wanted a word with him. He stood looking down with troubled eyes into Mr. Cohen's sallow, animated face.

"Yes?" said Mr. Cohen eagerly. "You would like something in the clothing line? I have a nice suit of a chocolate-brown that would just fit you."

"All I want," replied Mr. Unsworth, "is that you should pay your board! Mrs. Cruse is a widow. Life is uphill going for her. I don't think you should take advantage of her."

Mr. Cohen did not question Mr. Unsworth's right to champion Mrs. Cruse. He had a simplicity of nature that made him accept life as he found it. "Me take advantage of any lady! Never! I will pay my bill in full next Saturday night."

But Saturday night came and went and he did not pay the bill. Mr. Unsworth tackled him again, this time on the stairway. Mr. Cohen looked as though he were going to faint. "How can I pay?" he exclaimed, "with things so dead in the clothing business? I'm at my wit's end to meet my creditors! If only I could sell a couple of good suits this week I could pay her. . . ."

Mr. Unsworth said heavily, "I need two good suits. I will go to your shop tomorrow and see what you have."

He went, and bought the chocolate-brown suit. He carried it to Mrs. Cruse's house and laid it in the chest of drawers in his room for he dared not let his housekeeper see it. He ordered also a black suit to be made to his measurements. He paid for it in advance. On Saturday night Mr. Cohen settled his bill.

Mrs. Cruse's gratitude to him touched him deeply. Again he had the pleasure of seeing her face warmed by a becoming flush. A strongly protective feeling was roused in him, but he continued to dream about Miss Rogers's eyelashes. He wanted very much to take her to a concert, for he discovered that she was fond of good music, but he could not yet make up his mind to ask her.

Mr. Cohen and he were now firm friends, but he was still a little standoffish with Mr. Boyle. He was an Irishman and Mr. Unsworth distrusted him. Then one evening Mr. Boyle invited him up to his room. He had a bottle of Scotch there and gave Mr. Unsworth a drink. He told Mr. Unsworth a funny story. It was the first really coarse story that Mr. Unsworth had ever consented to listen to. He not only listened but laughed heartily. He searched his mind for a funny story in return but could not find one.

They talked until so late and Mr. Unsworth took so much Scotch that he decided to spend the night in his room at Mrs. Cruse's. This was the first of many nights. His housekeeper would have been greatly worried by his absorption in his financial affairs (for he continued to pacify her with lies) had not his physical condition been so good. He was actually putting on flesh.

The oftener he went to Mr. Boyle's room the better he liked him. He began to imitate his hearty, horsy manner. One night, over a bottle of Scotch, Mr. Boyle confessed to him that it was his ambition to buy a partnership in the veterinary establishment in which he was an assistant, but he lacked the necessary funds. Mr. Unsworth immediately offered to lend him the amount required, at a low interest. Mr. Boyle did not flush becomingly as Mrs. Cruse had. He became purple with gratitude. Mr. Unsworth thought he might be going to have a stroke.

But, though he had many interests, the chief one was Miss Rogers. When he sat in his room, his writing materials before him, pretending to work, he would write "Peggy" again and again over the sheet. At last he reached the point of writing "Peggy Unsworth," and had to snatch up the paper and crumple it when he heard Mrs. Cruse coming.

By the time spring was well established he had taken Miss Rogers to several concerts and was seriously thinking of leading her to the altar. She was growing prettier all the time and was affecting a tender shade of green in her dress, with touches of pink.

One evening in early June, when the front door stood open and the shouts of children came in on the balmy air, he opened the door of his room and went up the stairs with the purpose of finding her. His mind was made up. He would ask her to be his wife.

In the passage above he saw a figure that looked like Mr. Boyle at the first glance. At the second, he saw that it was too broad for Mr. Boyle. At the third, he discovered that it was two figures clinging together — Mr. Boyle and Miss Rogers hugging each other. He crept softly down the stairs.

He went into his own room and shut the door behind him. For the first time he locked it and threw the key with a clang on the table. He sat down, staring blankly before him, seeing only those two figures clinging together. He broke into a sweat caused by the chill of his disappointment meeting with the heat of his anger. He was not so angry at the two on the landing as at himself, for he had made the embrace possible by his loan to Mr. Boyle. His own character was so honorable that the thought that Mr. Boyle might hug Miss Rogers without intending to marry her never entered his head. Mingled with his disappointment and anger was a strong relief that he had never given himself away, that Peggy had never found out that he cared for her other than as a friend.

He had become calm by the time the two appeared at his door arm in arm.

"You are the first one to know!" cried Miss Rogers smiling up at him from under her eyelashes, and the thought crossed his mind that they had lately been tickling the cheek of Mr. Boyle.

"If it hadn't been for your loan God knows when we could have got married," said Boyle, wringing his hand.

"Are you going to be married soon?"

"Right away!" shouted Mr. Boyle, grinning at his fiancée. "And if Mrs. Cruse will have us as a married couple, we're going to stay on here."

Mrs. Cruse would and they did. As the bride had no male relations Mr. Unsworth gave her away and, strangely enough, when the day of the wedding came he was glad he was not in Mr. Boyle's shoes. She was too young for him. He was better off as he was.

Mrs. Cruse gave them the wedding breakfast. Mr. Cohen, who had no religious convictions, was best man. Mrs. Cruse had bought a new dress for the occasion. Without warning she had laid aside her weeds and appeared in bright blue with flowers in her hat. Mr. Unsworth was pleased with her appearance. She was putting on flesh.

When the Boyles settled down as a married couple in the house, turning Mr. Boyle's bedroom into a den, things were more pleasant than ever. They were like one family. When the warm summer evenings came Mr. Unsworth would hire a taxi and take Mrs. Cruse for rides around the parks and into the country. Her only worry now was Jack. He wanted another correspondence course. He wanted a course in short-story writing. He could stay at home beside his mother and write stories that would bring in a lot of money.

"He's such a good boy," sobbed Mrs. Cruse, sitting on the foot of Mr. Unsworth's bed while he drank his cocoa, "yet he worries me to death! With all his courses he never earns a penny. If only his father were living it would be different! He never raised a finger against Jack, but he'd just give him a look and Jack would quail. That's the way with a fleshy man. His presence is commanding and a look from him means more than an hour's harangue from a thin one!"

"I will see what I can do with Jack," said Mr. Unsworth, swelling himself out.

He climbed the two flights of stairs to Jack's attic room. The youth was sitting in his shirt sleeves perusing booklets on the subject of the short-story course.

Mr. Unsworth eyed him sternly and said, "Now, Jack, let us hear no more about this short-story business. You've had courses enough and none of them has led to anything. You don't want to sponge on your mother, do you?"

"I ain't goin' to sponge on her! I'm goin' to learn to write short stories and make lots of money."

"Nonsense! From what I hear not one short story out of a hundred is accepted. And besides, what would you write about?"

"Well, I could write about the Boyles."

"They wouldn't like it. They'd probably leave. No, the thing you must do is to get a real job, go to work and help your mother."

"You just leave me to look after my own affairs, please! I don't want any interference from you. Who do you think you are? Do you think you're my boss?"

"Yes, I do!" He sat down beside Jack and talked to him long and not unkindly. He saw that Jack quailed before him and he felt proud. The next morning he took him to the warehouse of a friend and got him a situation. The warehouse was on the river-bank where Jack could watch the boats pass. He was quite docile and had given up the idea of the correspondence course after pocketing the substantial bribe Mr. Unsworth had given him.

Mr. Unsworth said nothing to Mrs. Cruse about the bribe. All she knew was that he had got the upper hand of Jack and had put him into a situation.

"Well," she said, her face flushing in the becoming way it had, "I couldn't have believed that I'd depend so on a thin man!"

That night Mr. Cruse appeared to Mr. Unsworth in a dream. He was dressed in black and looked stout and commanding. He handed Mr. Unsworth a carving knife with a smile that was almost a smirk. He uttered the words "before you can say knife," and disappeared.

Mr. Unsworth was somewhat worried by this dream. What was its portent? Did the departed Mr. Cruse resent interference in the affairs of his son and his widow? What was the significance of a carving knife in a dream? What was the meaning of the cryptic words? What was going to happen before you could say knife? He brought up the subject at the dinner table. General opinion was not encouraging. A knife in a dream might mean anything from suicide to murder, at the very least the severance of a tie.

He was worried a good deal by the dream, but soon a deeper worry drove it completely from his mind. The autumn brought with it heavy financial losses. Two companies in which the greater part of his money was invested failed almost simultaneously. If he had not been so absorbed by the doings at Mrs. Cruse's he would almost certainly have had warning of the coming crash. As it was he was unprepared for the blow and for several days his mind felt numb and he could only sit in his rented room and brood. He could not bear to be in his own house or to face the reproachful looks of his housekeeper for, with woman's intuition, she had divined that, instead of being immersed in his affairs, he had been neglecting them. She had watched him develop into a different sort of man and nothing that happened to him could now surprise her.

His one comfort was Mrs. Cruse. Of course, he did not tell her the extent of his losses, but she knew that he was harassed by money matters and she laid herself out to cheer him. She made new dishes to tempt his appetite and the strange thing was that the more despondent he became the hungrier he grew. His digestion seemed impervious to worry when he ate the food prepared by her. Yet, in his own house, everything now disagreed with him.

When he and his lawyer had surveyed the wreck of his fortune he found that he had just enough income left to support him at Mrs. Cruse's for the rest of his days. He sold his furniture, disposed of the lease of his house and settled down in the room which now had become his home. He brought a few of his best-loved possessions with him so that he was able to make himself very comfortable.

By the time a month had passed in this new life his spirits had become as good as ever. In fact he had a sense of relief that he had washed his hands of his old responsibilities. The weather had become abominable, as it does so often in November, and now he could sit comfortably by his gas fire till bedtime. The returning home at night had always tired him.

Nothing could have come about more naturally than his proposal to Mrs. Cruse. He watched the desire to marry her approach him, but he did not try to escape. He wondered if she too saw the approach of a crisis. All she did was to talk and talk to him. She told him so many of her past troubles that his own dwindled to insignificance. She comforted him with cheering words. Then one day she exclaimed:

"Oh, if I only were a fleshy woman, I could be a greater support to you in your trial! I do think there's nothing like flesh to lean on. . . ."

"I ask for nothing better than you to lean on," said Mr. Unsworth, putting his arm about her just where her apron tied, "and you will make me very happy if you will lean on me."

There was no reason for delay. They were married as soon as the license could be got.

By the time Christmas came they wondered how they had ever got along without each other. It was hard to say which was the more devoted couple, they or the Boyles. Jack was getting along well in his situation and had a girl of his own.

It had been arranged that the Christmas dinner was to be their wedding feast. All the household was in a state of happy anticipation. Mr. Boyle, who, as a partner in the veterinary concern, had got a car for use in his work, had driven into the country and bought a magnificent turkey, young but extraordinarily large and fat. Mrs. Unsworth, as she must now be called, had made delicious mince pies and one of the handsomest plum puddings ever seen. Mr. Cohen had provided the punch. Mrs. Boyle had herself trimmed the windows and the picture of the late Mr. Cruse with holly and evergreens, though her husband was a little anxious about her standing on chairs in her present delicate condition. Jack had brought his pretty, plump, black-eyed girl to dinner.

Mr. Unsworth, looking handsome and dignified, sat before the still intact turkey glistening in its own rich juice. He looked around the board in a glow of satisfaction. Life had been kind to him, he thought. How little he had thought when he had rented the room out of pity for Mrs. Cruse that he would be a happy husband in that very house. His wife, wearing her wedding dress of maroon silk, was smiling at him from her end of the table. That becoming flush was now almost always in her cheeks. He suddenly noticed that her cheeks were quite plump. He looked at Mr. Cohen and saw that he was filling out. Jack, too, was no longer the thin youth he had been. His girl showed dimples wherever dimples have the habit of appearing. Even Mr. Boyle was looking less rawboned. As for Mrs. Boyle . . . but her roundness was of that touching transitory kind not to be described in cold words.

The carving fork was there but not the knife.

"Lily," he said, "you have forgotten the carving knife."

She sprang up agilely and fetched it from the kitchen. "Dear me, how stupid of me! I was just putting a good edge to it and then Peggy called me and I forgot to bring it."

She put it in his hand and he was surprised to notice how full and firm his own hand looked. There was no doubt about it, he was getting stout!

He was about to plunge the knife into the yielding bird when his eyes were drawn to the portrait of Mr. Cruse. A smile that was almost a smirk broadened the face above the triple chin. This was the face of Mr. Unsworth's dream. The dream came back with astonishing clarity. He saw now what the shade of Mr. Cruse had meant. The knife it had been offering him was a carving knife. Its message had been, "Before you can say knife you will be married to Mrs. Cruse." The ghost had been a kindly one. The words of fair omen, "Before you can say knife. . . ."

Knife suspended in hand he looked up into the pictured face of Mr. Cruse, framed in holly, and grinned in good-fellowship.

Quartet

B<small>EHRENS HESITATED</small> at the corner of the Via Parthenope and
the Via Santa Lucia, wondering whether or not he should take
a carriage to his destination. The moment his hesitation was noticed by the drivers who stood laughing and talking together on
the seaward side of the street, the group broke up and the members of it hurried toward him, beseeching and commanding him
to ride in the particular carriage of each.

He looked from one healthy, sunburned face to another, not
understanding a word they said. He wished he had not hesitated,
for it was a fine January morning, exhilarating for a long walk.
He shook his head doubtfully, and half turned away, but two of
the drivers followed him, one on either side, inviting him to take
various expeditions.

He found himself beside the carriage of one of them, who,
with a wide gesture, implored him to enter, shook out and displayed proudly a ragged, woolly rug for covering his knees.

Behrens had just put a foot on the step when his eye fell on
the horse, its drooping head, its wretched side through which the
bones seemed ready to protrude. Seeing his expression, the other
driver caught him by the arm and pointed triumphantly to his
own horse farther along the street.

"Very fine horse!" he exclaimed, unexpectedly in English.
"Very fine. Fat. Round. Go very fast. The very best horse in

Napoli!" He drew Behrens toward his carriage. "Very fine carriage, too. Very beautiful. *Molto bello!*"

There was no doubt about it, this horse, of a bright chestnut, was sleek and well cared for, able to work; while the other poor beast had little endurance left in him. Behrens chose the chestnut.

When Behrens had seated himself, a bitter altercation began between the two drivers. The first seemed to have half a mind to carry Behrens by force to his carriage. The second sought to climb to his seat, but the other pressed his body between, waving his whip and letting loose all his Neapolitan vitality in curses.

Behrens, rather anxiously, awaited an exchange of blows. Seeing the flash of their eyes and teeth, he felt that even a thrust from a knife would not be surprising. He had a mind to alight from the other side of the carriage, but miraculously, the dispute ended, the second driver gave the first a halfhearted push on the chest, got onto the seat, and cracked his whip. The first strolled back to his companions, his rage apparently subsiding into tolerance. A moment later he was again laughing and talking in the sunshine.

Above the blueness of the bay was the blue arch of the sky. From Vesuvius rose a golden feather that spread and hung plumelike against the sky. Capri lifted a bronze shoulder from the sea. From behind the Castello dell'Ovo a racing skiff rowed by eight youths darted into the open, their bare arms shining in the sun. They uttered a rhythmic musical singsong as they pulled. It was all delightful, Behrens thought.

He planted his stick between his feet, clasped his hands on it, his eyes obediently following the pointed whip of the driver, but his mind not taking in the descriptions in broken English of the buildings. He was thinking: "All of this is perfectly natural to Alice. By now none of these things looks strange to her. This is her home, and she's absolutely used to it. Loves it, I suppose."

Everything he saw he tried to see not as a tourist, a stranger, but as Alice, who was now accustomed to its foreignness. A little band of blind musicians was playing by the roadside. Extraordinarily sweet, wistful music, Behrens thought. He fished out a coin and threw it on the small tin plate one of them held out. The blind man bowed, smiled, but at that instant a bicyclist, passing between, knocked the dish from his hand and the coin to the road. Behrens gave a "Tck!" of compassion and craned his neck as the carriage rolled on to see whether the man had recovered the coin. He could see him on hands and knees groping for it. His comrades had begun a fresh tune. Behrens sighed.

His eye was now caught by a friar of some sort, whose bare red heels showed at every step beneath his rough habit. His tonsured head gleamed; his face had an expression of inscrutable patience. Meeting him were two tiny children in white fur coats unbelievably short above slender bare legs. Their nurse, wheeling a perambulator, wore a black velvet skirt, a yellow lace-trimmed apron, and a fringed scarlet shawl. Her gleaming black hair was massed beneath a tortoise-shell comb. The friar passed them without seeming to see them. "And all this strangeness," thought Behrens, "is as natural to Alice now as Massachusetts once was."

They turned into the shadowed intricacies of the side streets. The driver continued to point out objects of interest, and Behrens suddenly remembered that he had never told the man where he wanted to go. He leaned forward and touched him on the arm.

"Please drive," he said in his slow, rather heavy voice, "to the villa of Count Rombarra."

Even as he heard his own voice saying the name, it seemed unbelievable that he should be going to see Alice. Six years since he had seen her, and that on the day of her marriage to Rombarra. How exquisite she had looked that day! Beautiful, with the pride and happiness of a freshly opened flower. And it was Rombarra who had brought that happiness, not he! He had never been able to stir her to anything warmer than a feeling of placid friendship for him. He was an old story. A great disadvantage it was to be neighbors and all that, if you suddenly fell in love with a girl and wanted to impress her. He had been able to make no impression in that way; it had taken Rombarra with his Latin fire to do that. Well, he was going to see her now, after six years, and, thank goodness, he had got over it and would be able to make a friendly call without any humiliating embarrassment on his side.

A young woman was letting down a basket by a rope from a balcony, and a man was waiting with silvery little fish to put into it. In a doorway an old woman was cooking apples over a charcoal fire. The air was full of unfamiliar sounds. It was all strange and exhilarating to Behrens. After all these years of hard work and colorless surroundings, he felt as though he were experiencing a new birth. In this ancient place he felt his own newness as ludicrous, even pathetic.

If only he had someone, as naïvely impressed as himself, as companion! Supposing that he and Alice were making this trip together for the first time. On the voyage over and in the hotel he had met several couples abroad for the first time, laughing together, getting mixed over the foreign money together, experiencing this new birth together. But, he remembered, it would not have been new to Alice, after all, for she had been to Europe twice as a young girl. Strange that he should have forgotten, when it had been on one of those trips that she had met Rombarra.

A street rose on his right, ascending in a flight of sunswept stone steps. One above another were the stands of the flower sellers, mingling the colors of carnations, roses, violets, and heliotrope. A small boy ran from the nearest stand, holding a bunch of violets toward Behrens.

Behrens shook his head. No, he could not take violets to Alice. Rombarra might not like it. He felt sure that Rombarra of the sloe eyes and chiseled features would not like it. But the boy thrust the nosegay onto Behrens' knees, running alongside and holding up his little brown paw for money. Behrens could not resist him. He found a five-lire piece and put it into the hand.

They were on the heights, the old city spread out below. It looked immense, crowding about that blue bay. A great, rather frightening foreign city for a young girl like Alice to have come to. The driver had alighted and was awaiting his fare. Behrens paid him and entered the gate, glancing curiously about the terraced garden with its urns, its statues and trickling fountain. Apparently without reason his heart began to pound heavily; his lips became dry; and he found no moisture on his tongue to moisten them. He rang the bell, wishing very much that he was not carrying the little nosegay of flowers. Still, if Alice were alone, if, perhaps, Rombarra were busy with his own affairs somewhere, it would be all right. Alice might like to have the flowers, for the sake of old times, her old life.

He was shown into a vast, high-ceilinged room, furnished with quite wonderful antique pieces, Behrens supposed. But he thought, standing there, his heart still thumping, that he should have hated to live with them. One would have the feeling always that they would look exactly the same five hundred years hence, when one's bones were only a handful of dust.

And the penetrating chill of the room! He shivered in his handsome gray tweed coat. He heard steps, voices. Alice and her husband and her little girl of four (Behrens had forgotten about the child) came into the room. They shook hands. Rombarra's long, cool finger touched Behrens's without enthusiasm. Alice's hand was hot and dry, Behrens noticed, and her fingers seemed to curl almost feverishly about his. Her eyes smiled up at him beautiful as ever, more beautiful — or perhaps he had forgotten just how lovely she was.

Behrens thought, with a sudden pang, that Rombarra was a much more suitable mate for her physically than he would have been. Romarra was wearing the romantically dashing uniform of an officer of the cavalry. Alice explained, in her voice that had exactly the same soft, precise quality as of old, that they had just returned from the Horse Show, where her husband had been riding. He was very fond of horses and had done remarkably well in the show. Behrens congratulated him, and the Italian smiled, showing a rim of perfect teeth.

Behrens wondered, with sudden misgiving, if Rombarra understood English. But, surely, after six years of marriage with Alice, he would have learned to speak her native tongue. Behrens knew that he himself, slow though he was, would have learned to speak Arabic, had it been the language of Alice. He said, in halting French, to Rombarra:

"I was congratulating you on your success in the Horse Show."

It was as though he had touched an electric button. Rombarra's face became brilliant. He began to talk swiftly and eagerly in French. Behrens could not understand a word, and murmured so, apologetically, to Alice.

"Oh, it does not matter," she said. "I want you to come and sit down by me. It's so wonderful seeing you again after all these years."

Behrens sat down near her. He felt intensely embarrassed, for Rombarra's intelligent eyes were fixed on his face, not with the look of suspicion that Behrens had half anticipated, but with a look which seemed to say: "Come, now! Let us talk about horses. I can see that you are fond of them and so am I. Let us talk about them."

Behrens said to Alice:

"Please explain to your husband how stupid I am. I knew my French was very bad, but I didn't realize how little I have of it."

"It does not matter," she repeated. "And he understood quite well that you were congratulating him."

"But what was he saying to me?"

"Really, I did not notice. I was thinking only of you — how strange and wonderful to see you here." She was sitting on the edge of the sofa, poised in an attitude that suggested recklessness — Behrens thought that she looked like a bird just about to fly upward. Behind her stood a tall bureau, inlaid with ivory, on the top of which was a nude female figure in alabaster in an attitude of gentle resignation. The contrast between this figure and Alice was so great that Behrens's eyes and mind were held by it for a space and he missed what Alice next said.

She had drawn her little girl beside her, and he now heard her say:

"You knew I had a child? Her name is Félicité. She was born in the first year of our marriage or, you may be sure, I should never have called her that."

Behrens was startled and bewildered. Why had Alice spoken so? And in front of her husband, even though he understood little English? Was it possible that Alice was not happy?

He covered his discomfort by picking up the little girl and putting her on his knee. He placed the nosegay of violets in her hands, glad to be rid of it.

"Flowers," he said emphatically, hoping that in this case he would be understood. "I brought them for you."

The child took them, laughed, and held them to her face. She jigged her little body happily on his knee.

"Children always loved you," Alice said; then spoke to the child in Italian.

"*Grazie, signor,*" murmured Félicité. She threw herself back against Behrens, laughing roguishly. She had never lain against such an enormous, comfortable body before, and was delighted by its proportions.

Behrens, looking down at her, felt a deep and tender thrill pass through him. Alice's child! And he had once hoped that Alice's child would be his also. He bent his head and pressed his lips against her hair.

"You little darling!" he murmured. He had never known anything so delicious as the feel of this supple, exquisite little body in his arms. He wondered if Rombarra loved her as he would have done.

When he raised his eyes, they looked straight into those of Rombarra, who was leaning forward, an expression of gratification on his handsome face. They smiled across the child.

"*Bellissima bambina!*" cried Behrens, reckless of what a few words of Italian might bring forth.

Again the Neapolitan's face was illuminated, but this time there was added to its brightness a tender pride that touched Behrens. Rombarra broke into a flood of musical Italian which ended in a pointed question.

Behrens turned ruefully to Alice. "Whatever does he say?" he implored.

"He is asking you if you have any children of your own."

Behrens shook his head. "*Non, non,*" he said. "*Je n'en ai pas.*"

At once Rombarra obligingly turned to French.

"But," exclaimed Behrens desperately, "how can I talk to him? The moment I say a word or two in Italian or French, he says so much that he frightens me! Doesn't he know any English at all, after — after all these years?"

"No," returned Alice in a cool, clear voice. "He is far too narrow-minded, too stupid, to learn English."

Behrens could scarcely credit his senses. Alice, sitting there poised on that sofa, with the reckless air of a bird about to fly straight upward, calling her husband narrow-minded and stupid before his face, to Behrens, whom she had not seen for six years!

"For God's sake, be careful!" he said.

"Oh, there's no danger. He doesn't know a word of English. He probably thinks we are saying how well he looks in his uniform." She smiled serenely at her husband. He put another question to Behrens, who, following Alice's remark, had glanced involuntarily at the uniform.

"What does he say?" asked Behrens miserably, knotting his forehead.

"He wants to know if you, too, are in the army."

"No, I am not," replied Behrens firmly and distinctly. "I am a stockbroker." He gazed into Rombarra's eyes, beseeching him to understand. He was trying to tell Rombarra not only that he was a stockbroker, but that he was an unwilling participant in this dreadful situation. For surely, though the count could not understand English, he must feel the impact of those appalling words beating about him. Behrens was afraid of Alice, afraid of what she would say or do next. She seemed capable of anything.

She said: "He looks clever, doesn't he? With those intense eyes and that smile. But he's only clever at lovemaking. He's jealous of me. He wouldn't let me have you here without his being present, but he's absolutely unmoral himself. Before we had been married two years I found out that he had been unfaithful to me time and again!"

She spoke composedly, her eyes, with a pleasant, friendly light in them, on Behrens's face. She had leaned back, and her graceful arms were extended along the back of the sofa. To Behrens their curve seemed like the outline of half-spread wings. His forehead was flushed crimson. He stared straight at Rombarra, striving, with that stare, to build a wall around him, to protect him.

The little girl struggled to her feet and ran to her father, holding up the nosegay for him to smell. Rombarra began to talk rapidly and caressingly to her.

Behrens got out, in a muffled tone: "For the love of God, Alice! Don't talk like that. I simply can't bear it. I'll have to get out. Isn't it possible for me to see you alone?"

"No, no! It would be too dangerous. Besides, what would be the good? He appears to be friendly to you, but you don't understand him. He is sly, and he can be violent."

Behrens had an odd sensation of floating; there was a singing sound in his ears. He wondered if he might be going to have a stroke. He experienced, too, a feeling of deep self-pity. How cruel of Alice to create such a ghastly situation as this! He had suffered so much because of her in the past. He had come here feeling that that was all over. He had been reasonably sure of himself, prepared for a meeting that might revive a little the old pain, but that would establish a new picture of Alice in his memory — an Alice dignified, happy in her husband and child, with perhaps an affectionate backward glance for the old life in which he had had a part. His hands trembled. He tried to speak, but even his English seemed to desert him now. He turned a troubled gaze on her.

Her voice went out, not cool and even now, but staccato, with little gasps, as though at any moment she might lose control of herself:

"Of course, you were the only one I ever really loved, David. It was just that I was carried off my feet by Gaetano. You seemed so commonplace, so terribly uninteresting beside him. I thought that life with you would be intolerably dull, and now — if you only knew — how beautiful you look to me, sitting there! If you knew how I am longing to put my arms around you, and kiss you and kiss you!"

If Rombarra felt nothing strange in the atmosphere of the

room, the child certainly did. She got from her father's knee, with a strange look of excitement, and began to run round and about the three, tearing the nosegay into pieces and scattering the violets over the marble floor. Rombarra laughed at her, clapping his hands together.

Alice bent and picked up the violets that had fallen at her feet. "I shall always keep these," she said. "The nosegay was really intended for me, wasn't it, David? Do you remember how we used to hunt for the first violets together, under last year's dead leaves? Do you remember, David?"

He nodded, gulping. "I'm not likely to forget, Alice."

At the sound of his wife's name Rombarra turned his head sharply toward them with an intense and significant gesture.

The child began to run about over the flowers, trampling them with her little feet. When she passed Behrens she threw back her head and looked up at him with a defiant and challenging gaze.

Behrens muttered: "Why do you stay with him? Why do you bear it?"

"There's the child. He would never give her up. You see what he is like with her."

"You will endure it, then? After — this meeting? All you have said today?"

"Yes — I will endure it. And I'm sorry for having made you suffer, David. But I wanted you to know. And I wanted to be unfaithful to him — he's been so unfaithful to me. And I have been unfaithful — before his very eyes. Can you understand?"

The little girl ran suddenly to her mother's knee. Alice took her up and held her close. "I must not fail Félicité," she said.

Félicité stared across at Behrens as though suddenly resentful of his presence. Rombarra regarded his wife and child with satisfaction, then turned toward Behrens with a questioning smile. Behrens rose to go.

He thought he would take advantage of the foreign custom

and touch Alice's hand with his lips. It would be their last kiss. As their flesh touched he had the feeling that he was kissing the hand of a stranger. This was not the Alice he had known. He was afraid of her, and he longed to be away.

As the two men shook hands, Behrens said in his broken French: "It has been very pleasant meeting you."

This time the Italian made no attempt to respond, but he gave Behrens's hand a quick, almost sympathetic grip, and his eyes still held that look of questioning.

Behrens passed the columns and urns of the sunlit garden, and, as he reached the gate, he turned and looked back at the villa. He had felt that he was being observed. Now he saw that the three had come out on a small iron balcony. They were watching his departure, the child linking Alice and Rombarra together.

Behrens raised his hat. They waved to him. With a great sigh of relief, he strode swiftly down the street, hidden from their view now by a row of tall palms.

A Boy in the House

I

LINDLEY HAD DECIDED that this was the very sort of place he
had been looking for. Here was a seclusion he had not thought
to find possible within his means, not in these days of senseless
noise and ant-hill confusion. Even if he had rented a cottage in
a tiny village, what might not his neighbors have been? Did a
village exist without its burden of motor traffic? But here would
be peace. Here was true remoteness, and that only a stone's
throw from a highway. Here he would write the book he had
been longing for ten years to write. Those years when he was im-
prisoned in the civil service.

A small legacy had made it possible for him to be independent for a year, or even more, if he were careful. Through
a chance acquaintance he had heard of the two sisters who
owned the house. He had come to see it and had taken part of
it on a year's lease. When he had been told that only a part was
to be let, he had all but refused even to inspect it, but once having seen it he had made his decision and was now entrenched
in a silence that might be matched, he thought, only in a desert.

He recalled what the chance acquaintance had told him of the
sisters. "Rather eccentric," he had said, "and as Victorian as
crinolines. I remember their old father. He certainly was a Tar-
tar. Kept his wife and daughters subdued, if ever a man did.

Once they lived in fine style but he lost most of his money in bad investments. I guess it made him bitter. Anyhow these two women have had a hard time. They've sold most of their good antique furniture. I've bought some of it myself. They live absolutely secluded. You couldn't find a quieter place in Ontario."

Now he was settled with his few belongings, in his part of the house. He had his own front door, leading into a narrow hall, out of which mounted the white-spindled stairway to the rooms above. To the right of the front door was a large, sparsely furnished room. A handsome walnut table dominated it. Here he would write. He wondered how he would feel about that tall pier glass, with its heavily gilded ornate frame. He would see his own reflection in it, every time he raised his eyes from the paper. Of course he could place his back to the mirror, but in that case he would cut himself off from the view through the open window of long grass moving gently in the breeze and old lilac trees heavily in bloom. Lindley almost trembled in anticipation of the moment when he would sit down to write in this room. But, on this second day of living here, he was still too restless to begin work. It crossed his mind that perhaps he would be better off writing in one of the upstairs rooms. He went up the stairs, covered by a worn brown carpet, and examined the three bedrooms. He would sleep in the largest, the one with the mahogany four-poster and the marble-topped dressing table and wash stand, with the huge ewer and basin and intimidating slop bowl. The floor was bare and the clean pine boards unpainted. The walls were of pale-gray plaster, a lovely room for sleeping and dreaming.

Of the other two, one was small and unattractive, the other looked out on an enormous cedar tree, still wet from last night's rain. The sweet scent of it came through the open window. He remembered his stuffy room in the lodginghouse in the city, the monotony of his work in an accountant's office, and his heart sang for joy. He realized now why he could not yet settle himself down to work. He was simply too happy. In another day or two he would become tranquil. Then he would choose a room for his work, sharpen his pencils, take out paper and lose himself as he longed to do.

Slowly, in a kind of haze, he descended the stairs. At the foot he stood still, staring at the door which connected his part of the house with that part occupied by the sisters. It had been locked, they said, ever since their father had died and they had decided that the house was too large for their needs. Mrs. Morton, the younger sister, had added, with her genial smile, that they somehow felt safer with that door locked. From what? he wondered. Perhaps from the ghost of that disagreeable old man who had dominated their lives. Standing there, with bent head, he tried to recall what else his acquaintance had told him of their lives. Oh, yes, Miss Lydia Dove had been a beauty who had considered no man she had ever met worthy to become her husband. Mrs. Morton had at twenty-six married the son of a neighbor who had left her widowed and without means. Only a year later, she had returned to this house and her father's tyranny.

On the other side of the door there was dead silence. What did the two women do to pass the time? Lindley wondered. He rather wished the door were not there. It was a reminder of the existence of other people in the house, and the very silence on the other side of it had strange significance. He was but newly transplanted, he thought, from the noise of the city, and it would take him a day or two to get used to this seclusion.

Suddenly, from the other side of the door, a sound came, the sonorous tones of a clock striking the hour of six. Lindley smiled. It was just the right sort of sound — unhurried, tranquil. Yet it told of the passing of another day.

His front door stood open. He saw that the shadows of the

trees were lengthening on the now motionless grass. A small bird began its evening song. He thought he would take a stroll through the grounds before he prepared his supper.

Outdoors it was warmer than inside. He took off his jacket and hung it over his arm. He went along the drive which was almost overgrown by tall grass and buttercups toward the gate. The front of the property was occupied by an ugly red-brick house and its well-kept lawn. It had been built by a retired grocer who had bought the land old Mr. Dove had been forced to sell when his investments failed. Passing motorists never suspected that another house lay behind. In truth almost everybody had forgotten it, excepting the grocer who lay in wait to buy it, when poverty should force its sale. Mrs. Morton herself did all the shopping. With her shopping bag on her arm she slipped through the narrow gate, walked the two miles into the village and returned, looking hot and tired, the bag bulging with provisions for the week.

Now Lindley saw her coming along the drive and wondered whether or not he should turn to meet her. He did not want to create an atmosphere of such intimacy with these two women that they would expect a friendly chat at every encounter. On the other hand he did not want to appear unfriendly, and his writer's curiosity made him wonder about them. What were they really like? Were they resigned to their isolation or embittered by it? Well, the least he could do was to offer to carry the heavy bag for her which must have doubled its weight with the miles. She did not see him coming till he was quite near. Then the look of pleased surprise and the return of his smile told him that the encounter was welcome. She gave up the bag with a sigh of relief and stretched her arm. It was a short plump arm, Lindley noticed, and her figure was short and strongly made. She must have been an attractive young woman, with those shining gray eyes, that full-lipped, smiling mouth. But now she was obviously near to sixty and her face had coarsened. She took pride in her appearance however. Her beige linen jacket and skirt were immaculately laundered. Her gloves were freshly white and her thick hair, strongly streaked by gray, was swept neatly back, beneath her small black hat. She glanced up at him with a look that was almost flirtatious.

"How nice," she said, "to be met by a gentleman, and a gallant gentleman who will carry your bag for you."

She had a pleasant contralto voice.

"I suppose," he said, "it was pretty warm in the town. Surely these things should have been delivered for you." He was so incurably kindhearted that he pictured himself going to the shops with her, carrying that ugly cretonne bag.

She relieved him of that fear. "Oh, I don't mind it at all," she said. "In fact I like it. It makes a little break — and I'm very strong." She straightened her shoulders and stepped out briskly. "My sister will be wondering what has kept me," she added. "You know how it is with people who never go out. The time seems much longer to them." She spoke as though she herself went out a good deal.

At her own door, which opened into the dining room of the house, he left her, but not before he had a glimpse of her sister hovering inside. He heard her greeting, high-pitched and querulous. "Why, Elsie, whatever in the world have you been doing? I expected you an hour ago. Was that Mr. Lindley who was with you?"

He did not hear Mrs. Morton's answer. He turned away and went along the path that led past the back of the house, past the empty stable that looked ready to tumble down, past the empty poultry house which was indeed tumbling down, and followed the path toward the lake. This soon lost itself in the long grass out of which rose a few fruit trees whose gnarled branches still produced fairy-white blooms but whose fruit was the succor of

worms. The grass waved gently and he noticed a few white narcissi blooming among it, the remnant of what had once been a
flower garden. He picked four of them and held them to his nostrils and inhaled their sweet, languishing scent.

He came at last to the steep bank, below which lay the lake,
stretching like a pale blue sea to the pale horizon. He knew that
the two sisters had been born in this house and he pictured
them as little girls paddling on the sandy beach or sailing tiny
boats. He pictured them as young women, walking here with
their friends and lovers, feeling free, when they were here, of
their father's tyranny. Their mother, Mrs. Morton had told him,
had died when they were children. Did they ever come here now,
he wondered. Probably not, for Miss Lydia had been ill and
still was weak and Mrs. Morton's energies must be conserved
for the housework.

"If I keep on thinking about these old girls," he reflected, a
bit grimly, "I shall be dragging them into my book. . . . But I
needn't worry. As soon as it is begun I shall never give them
another thought."

He remembered his evening meal and retraced his steps. The
shadows were longer and darker. He saw some white birds sailing in the blue sea of the sky and realized that they were gulls.
The scent of the narcissi he carried rose to his nostrils. Suddenly
he wondered if he should have picked them. He avoided the
open door of the sisters' part of the house and from the opposite
direction went into his own.

He had no kitchen and the arrangement was that, at certain
hours which had been specified, he would have the use of theirs.
At these times the two women disappeared, leaving the kitchen
and dining room to him. He had a cupboard to himself where
he kept his provisions and few dishes and utensils. Now he put
the flowers into a small vase he had found and carried them up
to his bedroom. They shone out like pale stars against the gray

plaster of the walls. They took possession of the emptiness of the room. He stood looking at them for a bit before he went downstairs.

The kitchen was empty and a fire was burning in the wood stove. He took bacon and liver from their brown paper wrappers and laid a fraction of each in the frying pan. Soon they were sizzling. He went into the dining room and set a place for himself at one end of the table. Before long he was sitting there, happily munching, a pot of coffee ready at his elbow. His attention was drawn to the open piano, of which, up to this moment, he had been scarcely conscious. Which of the sisters had played on it? he wondered. Probably Miss Dove and he could imagine the die-away pieces. He wondered why the piano should be here in the dining room, then remembered that this was now the sisters' living room. The piano stood near the door which opened into his part of the house.

He was clearing the table when he heard steps coming down an uncarpeted stair. So, there were two stairways in the house. No — *three,* for he had noticed a short stairway leading from the kitchen to a room above it.

Mrs. Morton came into the room, not abruptly but hesitating on the threshold. She looked refreshed and her rather full mouth wore an almost shy smile.

"I waited," she said, "till I heard you moving about. I hope you're getting on all right with your meals."

"Oh, fine, thank you."

"It seems hard for a gentleman to have to look after himself."

"I enjoy it. You see I came here to be alone." He must emphasize that, he thought, or she might bother him with her chatter.

"Yes, indeed, I know," she said hastily. She took another step into the room. "I do hope you're getting on with your writing."

"Well — I've not actually begun. I begin tomorrow morning. You have to get used to a place, you know."

"It must be wonderful to be a young man — and writing a book."

"I'm older than you think," he laughed. "And the book will probably be a failure — if it's ever published."

"I can't imagine your failing at anything." She showed open admiration in her shining gray eyes.

"I wish I felt that way about myself."

"But you must. It's splendid to do what you want to and to succeed. I was ambitious once."

He sighed and set the coffeepot again on the table, giving her his attention.

"I wanted to be a really good musician. I used to practice a great deal, on this piano. But then I fell in love and married and everything was changed."

"Girls generally give up their music when they marry, don't they?"

"Not I," she denied quickly. "I loved it too well. I've always kept up my practicing."

He could not hide the consternation that swept the mild interest from his face. Was his seclusion to be shattered by piano practice?

Mrs. Morton gave him a wide, reassuring smile. "Please don't worry about finger exercises or anything of that sort. But I've been wondering if it would bother you if I played in the evening. Perhaps at the time when you take your walk. You see," she hurried on, "my sister is used to hearing me play at that hour. It's soothing to her and she hasn't had much pleasure since her illness. Of course, I shouldn't like to bother you."

She looked apologetic, even pathetic, standing there in the doorway. He felt ashamed of his overbearing position in the house. The two women seemed so defenseless.

"Why certainly," he agreed. "We can easily arrange a time."
He looked at the piano. Every note from it would be audible
in his part of the house. "What about from seven to . . ." he
hesitated to set either too long or too short a period.

"Never longer than an hour," she exclaimed. "Usually less.
And I don't play very loudly. But you see how it is. My sister
looks forward to it."

"And I shall, too, I'm sure," he couldn't stop himself from
exclaiming, while, at the same moment, he cursed his imbecilic
good nature. What sort of torture might not the woman put
him to?

"I should have spoken of this when I rented you the place, I
know," she said, almost humbly. "But I couldn't bring myself to.
I so badly wanted you to come. You are just the sort of quiet
gentleman — "

"Oh, I'm quiet all right." He smiled and picked up the coffeepot. "But not so quiet that I don't like a little music in the evening. So please go ahead."

She did, that very evening, but waited till she saw him out
of hearing, walking toward the lake. There was a large boulder
there which he liked to sit on, looking out across the calm expanse of the water. Strangely shaped clouds were edged with fire
by the aftermath of the sunset. He heard the distant voices of
boys at play and, in his mind's eye, saw a white sheet of paper
with the first words of his book written on it. A shiver of something between apprehension and exultation passed over him.
In twelve hours he would begin his book.

When he drew near the house it was dusk. Out of the long
grass the white narcissi showed like stars. Their faint scent came
to him for an instant but was soon drowned in the heavier scent
of lilac. The door of the sisters' living room stood open and
Lindley heard the sound of the piano. Mrs. Morton was playing
one of Mendelssohn's "Songs Without Words," playing it with

feeling and great sentimentality. It was what he had expected, only better. She really had skill.

Lindley had a desire to see the performer — and her audience. The two windows of the room were shaded by a trumpet vine. He moved close to them and peered through the glossy new leaves. It was as though he were in the room with them. The light fell from an oil lamp hanging from the ceiling. It was of china and decorated with glass prisms. In its kind light the two women were transformed. He saw that the elder, Miss Dove, had once been beautiful. She must have looked like a Dresden-china shepherdess, with her sloping shoulders, delicate hands and exquisite features. She now sat, leaning forward, drinking in the music, her large blue eyes dreamy with delight. Mrs. Morton too was transfigured. She had now begun to play "The Hunting Song" with much spirit. Her countenance took on a look of pride and power. Her hands poised above the keyboard, swooped like amorous birds and, at last, came to rest.

Lindley went round to his own side of the house and stood for a space in the doorway, drinking in the deepening dusk in the garden, the almost palpable stillness, for the music had now ceased. He felt deep relief at the thought that he was not to be annoyed by bad piano playing. In truth he rather liked the thought of those two women cherishing their love of music through the years of adversity. He tried to remember all his acquaintance had told him of their past but, at the time, it had seemed important only in the light of their willingness to let him part of their house. He did, however, recall that Mrs. Morton's husband had been a handsome young fellow but that her father considered him "fast" and had forbidden the marriage and the pair had eloped. Later, when she had been forced to return home, a widow, he had made her pay for her disobedience.

* * *

There was a gentle rain in the night and the morning was moist and mildly sunny. Growing things were pushing up, unfolding, with urgency, as though there were no time to waste. In tune with the morning Lindley laid out his paper, sat himself down at the uncompromising marble-topped table, and wrote the title of his book at the top of the page. The opening sentences had long been in his mind. Now he wrote them, with almost precise care, and looked at them. They looked somehow different from what he had expected and he sat staring at them, with a feeling of wonder.

Half an hour passed and he still sat there. He found that he had smoked two cigarettes without realizing it. He got up and paced the room. Outside a woodpecker was tapping on the trunk of the old cedar. He could see its small head, its thin muscular neck in energetic movement. As soon as it stopped that noise he would sit down and get to work.

In the next hour he wrote two pages and had nothing more left in him. He felt exhausted but a glad exhilaration possessed him. With a kind of tender solicitude, as for a newborn weakling he laid the manuscript in his writing case. A manuscript of two and a half pages.

I I

He saw Mrs. Morton in the small garden patch that was given over to vegetables. She was digging with a spade and looked hot and breathless. He stood, hidden by a thick screen of lilacs, watching her. If he did the decent thing he would go to her, take the spade from her hand, and himself prepare the ground. But he could not set about digging the moment he had finished his own work. And, if he began by helping her, he would have to go on helping her. He saw that the plot was already overgrown by weeds. The place was badly neglected. The dozen fowls that lived in the leaky stable, laid their eggs in the manger and perched on the shafts and seat of the old victoria.

Miss Dove appeared from the direction of the house. She wore an ugly woolen jacket over her print dress and a sunbonnet, the like of which Lindley had not seen since he was a child. She walked feebly, leaning on a stick. It was hard to believe she was the woman he had seen through the window last night.

Mrs. Morton went on working harder than ever, apparently unconscious of the fragile figure approaching. The elder sister laid a transparent hand on the handle of the spade. "Stop that digging, Elsie," she commanded. "It's too hard for you. Why, you might have a stroke, getting overheated like this."

Mrs. Morton pushed back the thick hair from her forehead with the back of her hand and leaned on the spade. "We've got to have salad," she said.

"Well, hire a man to dig the beds."

"I can't afford it."

"We had a man for three days last year."

"I can't afford it this year." And she returned to her digging.

The stubborn repetition of words, the dogged lines of the thickset figure seemed to enrage Miss Dove. "*You* can't afford! *You* can't afford!" she cried. "Who do you think you are? Sole mistress here? Let me tell you, my girl, if I want a man hired, I'll hire him without help or hindrance from you."

"You talk like a crazy woman," grunted Mrs. Morton, her breast heaving. "Move out of my way, please." She tossed a clod of earth dangerously near to Miss Dove's feet, whose voice now rose to a scream.

"A crazy woman! A crazy woman, eh? Oh, how dare you say such things, Elsie? And to me, just able to be out of bed."

"We had peace when you were in bed."

"Peace! Peace! Yes, we had peace, while I lay abed, and you

conducted yourself as though you owned the estate. You have sold most of my father's furniture — "

Mrs. Morton interrupted furiously — "I sold it to buy medicine — to pay doctors' bills."

"You throw my illness up to me! My God, what next!"

They became incoherent, screaming at one another.

It was a frightful quarrel. Lydia leant on her stick as though but for it she would have fallen. Elsie raised her spade in one moment of rage and menaced her sister with it.

Lindley had not the power to remove himself from the scene. He stood rooted, hidden by foliage, till it was over and Miss Dove tottered away and Mrs. Morton again thrust her spade into the earth. He felt shaken. These two aging women, living so remotely, relics of such a decorous age, to let themselves go like that. This seclusion that he so valued. What was he to do? Go to Mrs. Morton and complain? Or, without explanation, say that it was necessary for him to move to another place? He strode through the long grass, past the old fruit trees that had dropped their bloom into the grass, to the peace of the lake. He sat on the boulder and considered what he should do. He lighted his pipe, consciously drawing serenity from it.

Lindley had come from a peaceable family of Scottish origin. He could not remember ever having heard a row in his own home — nor even bickering. Such a scene as he had witnessed was completely outside his experience. He shunned the thought of another, yet in a strange way, his creative impulses were stirred by it. He put it from his mind and his thoughts, with avidity, turned to his novel.

An hour passed. He sat with the empty bowl of his pipe cradled in his hand, his imagination moving among his own creations. When at last he returned to the house he had made up his mind that he would remain there. No matter where he went he would probably meet with some disadvantages. He need overhear no further quarrels between the sisters if he kept out of their way, and this he would do.

It was not difficult in the three days that followed. He avoided the sisters and it was plain that they were avoiding each other. In his comings and goings through kitchen and dining room he never heard them exchange a word. There was no music in the evenings. The deep silence was only broken by the singing of a small bird or the hoarse crow of the old rooster. Lindley finished the first chapter of his book.

But on the fourth day he heard them speaking in quiet tones together. He had just come into the kitchen to put away some groceries he had bought in the village. He stood as though stricken immovable and listened. The cat, perched on the window sill, ceased washing its face and appeared to listen also. Mrs. Morton was saying:

"You know, Lyddy, I have been thinking that we might get a little Home boy. He could do the rough work. Then we could teach him to wash the dishes and lay the table, and he would be company for you when I have to go into the village. What do you say?"

She spoke deferentially, laying the matter before her elder.

There was astonishment in Lydia's voice when she spoke. "What an idea, Elsie!"

"I think it is a good one. It would cost nothing but his food, and we could make that up by growing more vegetables and keeping more poultry." The deference in her voice increased to humility. "I do hope you'll consent to it, Lyddy. I'm sure it's a good idea."

Lydia answered thoughtfully, "If we could get a nice obedient little boy . . ."

"Oh, I'd insist on that. I'd tell them we are just two women alone."

A note of eagerness made Lydia's voice young. "A boy like

that would be company for me when you had tea with one of your friends. You don't get out nearly often enough, Elsie."

She moved nearer the door, close to which Lindley had stood listening. He busied himself putting his groceries in the cupboard. His ears tingled with shame. He had been deliberately listening to the private conversation of these two women. He could not have believed such a thing possible to him. But this was a matter so vital to his privacy. A young boy in the house. It might mean noise and racketing about. Well, he wouldn't stand that. He'd promptly complain. If they consulted him he would warn them of the dangers of a boy about the place. He might be a pernicious little rascal — lazy, impudent and noisy.

But they did not consult him. He saw nothing of them till the afternoon of the next day when he came face to face with Miss Dove in what the sisters called the pleasure grounds. She was dragging a quite large dead branch that had fallen from an elm tree, through the long grass. She was breathless and her delicate face was flushed a deep pink. Lindley rushed to help her.

"Miss Dove — " he took the branch from her hands — "you shouldn't do this. It's too heavy for you."

She gave a gay little laugh. "Oh, I'm getting so strong all of a sudden, Mr. Lindley. And I thought I'd tidy up the pleasure grounds while my sister is in the city. She went off early this morning, you know."

"She did?" He looked into her face, trying to keep his own face innocent.

"Yes. You'll never believe it when I tell you. She went to get a little boy — a little Home boy — to help with the work."

"Well," he said slowly, "I think that's a very good idea." He walked beside her, dragging the branch toward the house. "Provided, of course, that the boy is the right sort."

"Oh, my sister will see to that. She will accept no other. If a nice little boy is on hand she will bring him back with her tonight."

"Tonight? But Miss Dove, those things take some time to arrange."

She smiled complacently. "Not with us. We are acquainted with the head of the Home. We were people of importance once, Mr. Lindley, though of course we're nobodies now." She led the way to the back of the house and pointed with an almost regal gesture to the woodpile. "Will you just lay the branch beside the pile, Mr. Lindley. When the little boy arrives he can break it up for kindling."

The sun shone full on her face framed in the sunbonnet. Lindley noticed the delicate fineness of her skin, the long white lids above the clear blue eyes. Her hands had been exquisite. As though conscious of admiration in his eyes, Miss Dove said, almost abruptly:

"Come into the house a moment, Mr. Lindley. I should like to show you photographs of Elsie and myself when we were girls."

He followed her half unwilling, yet fascinated by the change in her. Now that Mrs. Morton was out of the way Miss Dove moved with a renewed vitality. It was as though Mrs. Morton took the strength from her, made her uncertain and querulous.

From a cabinet she took a heavy old photograph album. It had heavy gilt clasps and, inset on its fine leather cover, an oval porcelain medallion of a sentimentally draped female head with upturned eyes. With an almost girlish gesture Miss Dove pulled off her sunbonnet and threw it on a chair. She sat down on the sofa and made Lindley sit beside her.

"Look," she said impressively, "there is my father, Mr. Dove. You can see what a fine-looking man he was. And such a gentleman, though he had a violent temper at times." She seemed to quail at the recollection of it, after all the years.

Lindley looked and saw a masculine Mrs. Morton, with side whiskers and smooth-shaven pugnacious lips.

"And this is my mother. I am supposed to resemble her, though I never was so beautiful. And here I am in my twenties. You can judge for yourself."

Lindley found mother and daughter equally lovely and elegant. "You can see by our dresses, Mr. Lindley, how different everything was with us then." She showed him a picture of Mrs. Morton as a young woman. "Elsie had the loveliest naturally curly hair and *such* eyelashes! But she was always so *dreadfully* jealous of me, poor Elsie." Lindley was shown photos of the sisters at various stages of childhood, Lydia always exquisite, ethereal; Elsie stocky, curly-headed, pugnacious. He was told anecdotes to illustrate the aristocratic connections of the Dove family. The grandfather clock struck the hour. Miss Dove rose in consternation.

"Five o'clock! Good gracious, Elsie will be here with the little boy before I know it."

Lindley stood up, glad to be allowed to go. Already the habit of aloneness was growing on him. He wanted to go back to his own part of the house, to the dark companionship of the cedar tree, to the cool stretch of the marble-topped table at which he wrote.

"I must be laying the table." Miss Dove removed the red cloth from it with a nervous hand. "It will be the first time I have laid it since my illness and I'm just wondering where I ought to put the little boy to eat. The proper place, of course, is the kitchen but — "

Lindley spoke from the open doorway. "Supposing he doesn't come, Miss Dove."

"Oh, he'll come. I have every confidence in Elsie. She'll choose just the right boy and bring him with her. Do you know what I have a mind to do? I've a mind to put him at this little table in the corner. I could keep my eye on him there and it wouldn't be quite so lonely for him as in the kitchen. A little strange boy might feel very lonely at the first, and after all he's to be a sort of companion."

"A very nice idea," agreed Lindley smiling.

He escaped.

I I I

In his own writing room he went straight to the drawer where he kept his manuscript, drew open the drawer and looked down at the slender accumulation of pages, as though to assure himself that nothing had happened to them. He sat down in the twilight coolness of the room and lighted his pipe. His visit with Lydia Dove occupied his mind unreasonably. He could not forget her or the old photograph album or the small table to be set in the corner for the boy. He should not have given these trifles more than a passing thought but their images filled the silent room, almost with an air of foreboding.

He heard the town bus bumping over the grass-grown drive to the door. He heard voices, the thud of a trunk as it was set down. The bus drove off. He allowed what he thought was ample time for the sisters and the boy to dispose of their meal, then went round to the kitchen to prepare his own. He had a strange feeling of shyness, as though this small new presence had upset the balance of the house.

He discovered that he had come too soon, that in the dining room the meal had not been finished. He was about to leave when Mrs. Morton bustled out from the supper table. She looked excited, almost triumphant.

"Oh, Mr. Lindley," she cried, "do come and see our little boy." She realized then that Lindley was being kept waiting. "I'm so sorry — dear me, I'm afraid you are being dreadfully put out."

Lindley gave her his pleasant smile. "Don't worry about me. I shall be all right if I don't eat for an hour." He stepped into the dining room. "What about you? I expect you had a tiring trip."

She pushed her fingers under her roll of thick hair to liven it. Little drops of sweat showed on her forehead. "What a time!" she said. "The crowd, the dirt, and dreadful people eating oranges. But I accomplished my mission and that's the main thing." She moved to one side so that Lindley might see the small table at which the boy was sitting. "Stand up, Eddy, and bow to Mr. Lindley."

The boy did as he was told with a broad, childish smile. He was thirteen years old but no taller than a well-grown boy of eleven. His face was round and chubby, and he had agate-brown eyes and rough light-brown hair. He wore a half-amused, half-dazed expression. The situation in which he now found himself was unmatched in his experience. He sat down again and stared round-eyed at the room, at Miss Dove, at the tables laid with white cloths and silver. The carved Victorian furniture, the pictures with gilt frames seemed to fill him with awe. There was something innocent and alone about him that touched Lindley. He spoke to him kindly, hoping he would get on well. The boy appeared too shy to answer.

"Go ahead with your tea, Eddy," Mrs. Morton ordered with kind peremptoriness.

He picked up a cake and began to munch it.

"Do sit down on the sofa, Mr. Lindley," Lydia Dove exclaimed suddenly, in an afterglow of their recent intimacy. "We shall be finished in a moment and the room made ready for you." She spoke in a high-flown tone, as though to impress the boy with their grand way of living. Mrs. Morton looked surprised but not ill pleased. Lindley himself felt an objection to any continuation of the intimacy but did not know how to refuse.

He sat down rather stiffly on the haircloth sofa. Mrs. Morton continued to talk about the discomforts of the journey. The boy stared at her, listening, but, when she looked at him, respectfully lowered his eyes. Soon the light meal was finished.

"Now, Eddy," she ordered, "you must carry the dishes to the kitchen. You may as well begin to learn things at once."

The boy rose uncertainly to his feet.

"Our table first," directed Mrs. Morton.

He picked up the plate of cut bread and moved slowly with it to the kitchen. Lindley noticed then that he dragged his left foot.

Miss Dove exclaimed in a sibilant whisper, "Why, Elsie, he limps! Was that a good idea? A *lame* boy?"

Elsie spoke rapidly, with a triumphant note in her voice. "Because he comes much cheaper, can't you see? He'd been on a farm but they'd sent him back because he wasn't fit for rough farmwork. I guess the superintendent was at his wit's end to know what to do with him and then I came along and when he heard of all the advantages and the bit of light work — "

The boy was now back in the room.

The three grownups sat watching him as he cleared the table. Since the coming of the boy, Lindley felt himself drawn into the watching circle of the family. He was expected to say something. So, when the boy had again gone into the kitchen he said, "He looks healthy."

Mrs. Morton beamed. "Perfectly. Such lovely round cheeks and bright eyes. He's almost beautiful, isn't he?"

"Oh, Elsie, don't say such ridiculous things."

"And his keep will amount to very little."

Lindley could see that the boy knew they were talking about him. He gave embarrassed sidelong glances at them as he passed, carrying out the dishes. His advent into the house had deeply moved Lydia Dove. There had been no young creature there since she and Elsie had been children. Now she was quivering and apprehensive of what the change might mean to them and, at the same time, she felt a strange deep delight. The novelty of the situation put new life into her. She jumped up, weakly active, directing the boy where to put things, counting the silver spoons as she laid them in a drawer, as though she feared he might already be pilfering.

The boy began to feel more at ease. He limped hurriedly, stepping on the side of one foot, to do Miss Dove's bidding. When he set the silver teapot on the sideboard he moved backward a step to admire it. For the first time he spoke.

"I say, what a pretty teapot!"

His voice was a clear cool treble, very distinct, with a Cockney *oi* sound in it. He had appeared shy but now he spoke with cool familiarity. Lindley noticed how small and undernourished his body was, in spite of his round cheeks. Lindley had the quality of pity and now it rose, strong and protective toward the boy. Yet there was nothing he could do for him.

"It's a shame to keep you waiting like this, Mr. Lindley," said Mrs. Morton. She was brushing the crumbs off the table into an old-fashioned crumb tray. "But the table is ready for you now and I see that my sister has Eddy at work, washing the dishes."

Lindley fidgeted about the room waiting. He was now very hungry and beginning to feel himself put upon. He had not bargained for such intimacy with the sisters. However he murmured some polite words and waited doggedly for the moment when he would have the place to himself. He could see the boy standing by the kitchen table, one shoulder a little higher than the other, his lame leg relaxed. He had taken off his jacket and his suspenders crossed over thin shoulder blades. His childish hands and wrists were plunged into the dishwater. He kept talking to Miss Dove and once his treble laugh rang out.

Mrs. Morton now also went to the kitchen. The sisters took turns in giving him orders, as though with a delightful sense of returning prosperity. Lindley heard Lydia Dove say, "If you are a good boy, you will find I am an indulgent mistress." Obviously she was letting him know at the first what was her position in the house.

"Oh, I'm used to doing what I'm told," he answered. "And the work here'll just suit me. You two ladies can sit down from now on and watch me make things nice and comfortable for you. I'll bet you'll be wondering in a little while how you ever got on without me." He was full of Cockney assurance. Yet he was scarcely bold, just ingenuously pleased with himself and them.

They seemed to have forgotten Lindley's existence and he resigned himself half sulkily to wait till they had shown Eddy the ropes and retired to their own rooms. He told himself that, from now on, he would retreat into his own life and endure no infringement of his seclusion.

At last Mrs. Morton came back into the dining room. "I'm going to send Eddy to his bed," she said briskly. "But first I have to help him upstairs with his trunk. The busman just dumped it down by the door."

"Let me help him," Lindley offered. He followed her through the open door and saw the old-fashioned battered tin trunk standing on end on the flagstones. It was now almost dark. A tree toad sent his plaintive trill among the blossoms. The air felt pleasantly cool to Lindley's forehead. His irritation passed and his natural gentleness returned. The boy now joined them and grasped the rope that bound the trunk, in his small hands.

"I can do it. I can carry it up alone." It was as though his disability had made him boastful.

"Nonsense." Lindley took hold of the rope also.

"Oh, how kind of you, Mr. Lindley. Look, Lydia, Mr. Lindley is giving a hand with the trunk. Isn't that kind of him?"

The steep and narrow back stairs led up from the kitchen.

Mrs. Morton had lighted a small oil lamp and placed it in a bracket on the wall, at the top of the stairs. It sent a dusky light into the cavern below and discovered the worn and greasy wall-paper above.

Lindley went up first and maneuvered to keep the weight of the trunk from the boy, whose feet made an uncertain clatter on the bare steps. His face, upturned toward the light, had a sin-gularly appealing quality for Lindley. At the moment he looked beautiful, and the straight lock of hair that stood upright on his crown added a touch of the ridiculous without lessening the beauty.

"All right?" asked Lindley, smiling, as they set down the trunk in the little room where the ceiling sloped to the edge of the bed and the only light came through the leaves of the vine that covered the window and through the open door from the lamp.

"Fine." The boy spoke a little breathlessly. He sat down on the trunk and gave it a slap with his palm. "This 'ere box," he said, "holds everything I owns in the world."

A little Robinson Crusoe, thought Lindley, washed up on a strange shore. He said, "A mighty good box, too. All your treasures in it, eh?"

"Just one treasure." He gave a shy smile. "The rest is clothes. The Home bought me new ones when I came over."

Lindley's eyes were on a scar on the boy's forehead which gave an odd bend to one of his eyebrows.

Eddy tapped it with his finger tips. "Noticing my scar, ain't you? That's where my stepmother throwed a pair of scissors at me when I was seven. She nearly blinded me, she did."

Lindley gave an exclamation of sympathy.

"Ah, she was wot you might call a devil, she was. Often she'd turn me out in the streets in the rain. She'd pull my hair — 'ole 'andfuls out, mind you."

"And your father, would he stand for that?"

The boy gave a reminiscent chuckle. "He took his belt to her. The buckle end too. But it didn't do any good. She wouldn't let me be, so he had to put me in the Home. He's fond of me, my daddy is. He's a sailor. I'd be a sailor too, if it wasn't for my foot. You can't nip up among the rigging — not wiv a foot like this."

He contemplated it with a look that was an odd mixture of ruefulness and pride.

"Were you born with it?" Lindley asked and at once regretted the abruptness of the question. Because he was a child and poor and alone was no excuse.

But Eddy was obviously pleased to talk of his handicap. "It was a bit twisted from the time a neighbor's little gal dropped me when I was a babe in arms but the hurt I got after I came to Canada was the worst. The Home sent me to a old farmer and he set me doing work only fit for a boy twice my size. One day we were shifting logs and I dropped my end of the log and it fell on my foot and pretty near mashed it. Mr. Wilson from the Home came and took me back and they put me in 'orspital and I had a operation. Want to see the scar?" All this was brought out eagerly in his clear child's voice, the *-ings* clearly enunciated and with the *oi* sound marked. He did not wait for an answer but drew up his foot and pulled off his shoe and sock. The small white foot was ridged by a jagged red scar. The sight of him sitting on the battered tin trunk displaying the scarred foot was touching to Lindley. All he could find to say was, "Well, you'll not be overworked here."

Mrs. Morton's voice came from the bottom of the stairs. "Is anything wrong? Can I help?"

"Nothing is wrong," Lindley answered. "We shall be right down."

The female voice came back with a dominant ring. "Eddy is not to come down again. He's to go to bed."

"I say," the boy exclaimed, "mayn't I go out and explore a bit?"

"No. You must go to bed. You must rest and be ready for work in the morning."

"Just as you say, ma'am," the boy sang out. He shrugged his thin shoulders and threw Lindley a mischievous look. He sat resigned on his trunk.

The feeble and mysterious light from the oil lamp falling across the small figure lent it an air of mystery. Out of nowhere the boy seemed to have come, and where might his journeying lead him? Lindley thought of the emphasis placed by psychiatrists on the craving by children for a feeling of security. But this bit of flotsam had none, yet sat on his one possession, the little tin trunk, smiling serenely and clasping his maimed foot.

"Well — good night, Eddy." Lindley left the room and began to grope his way down the stairs.

He heard Lydia Dove say, "Elsie, do you think you did well to give him an egg? If we start him off eating just the same as we do, he may get forward — forget he is a servant lad."

"Sh-h." Mrs. Morton heard Lindley approaching.

The sisters came close to him in the kitchen. "Don't you think he is a nice little boy? And so biddable. . . . I think I did well, don't you, Mr. Lindley? I think Elsie has made a good choice, Mr. Lindley." They were pleased with the boy and with each other.

Soon the kitchen and dining room were clear of all but Lindley and he thankfully set about the preparation of his own meal. As he sat alone, eating it in silence, no sound came from the other rooms but from outdoors the continued trilling of the tree toad, and once the mournful cry of an owl. The sweet springtime scent of the moist earth mingled with the rather musty smell that penetrated this part of the house. Lindley spent little time over his meal and the washing-up of the dishes took scarcely a quarter of an hour. While he did this he could hear movements in the room above, the boy settling in beneath the sloping roof, the faint dragging sound of his maimed foot.

Back in his own rooms Lindley relaxed in the one comfortable armchair, with his pipe. Deliberately he drove the two women and the boy from his thoughts. His mind remained blank till, one by one, the characters of his book moved into it. He watched them. He listened to them. They became more real to him than any living being. At last he took his manuscript from its drawer and began to write.

It was long past midnight when he went to bed. He slept late, though brokenly, his mind filled with grotesque images, made up of the happenings of the day before, mingled with unearthly pictures of great confusion, all of these in a somber gray twilight. But in his dreams the characters of his books remained aloof from him.

When he went round to the kitchen to prepare his breakfast he found it and the dining room deserted. Soon he was again at his table writing and it was noon before he went into the grounds for his usual stroll. He avoided the vegetable garden, where he could see Mrs. Morton and the boy at work, and walked through the long, gently waving grass toward the lake. He had a glimpse of Miss Dove again dragging a dead branch toward the woodpile and he kept out of her way for fear she would expect him to help her. If she chose to overdo herself, why — let her. If she was a silly old woman it was not his concern. He could see that she wore a kind of woolen hood, with a broad-brimmed straw hat tied over it.

He sat on his boulder by the lake till he realized that it was time to get his lunch. These mealtimes of his occurred with irritating frequency and, by the arrangement he had made, he was more or less bound to take them regularly. He saw that the boy was alone in the garden and, in spite of himself, Lindley felt drawn to go and speak to him. He was at his side before the boy raised his eyes.

Obviously he had been playing with the spade, making a sort of castle in the earth, like a child at the seashore. He made no attempt to hide it, and when he saw Lindley smiled cheerfully at him.

"You can't work all the time, can you, sir? You got to have a little fun, haven't you?"

Lindley was not going to commit himself. "Been gardening, eh? What have you planted?"

"Lettuce and radishes. And we're going to have peas and beans and spinach and squash. Mrs. Morton knows all about gardening, she does. But she never used to work, not till they lost their money. They used to keep a gardener and a cook and a housemaid. They lived in grand style till they lost all their money. *Now* they've only *me*." His treble laugh rang out, as though in exultation over his new position of power. "I shall look after them. I can turn my hand to anything."

"But you're only playing now, aren't you?" Lindley pointed with his stick to the small erection in the seed bed.

Eddy flattened it out with his spade. "I was just having a bit of fun. Are you going to tell on me?"

"Certainly not." He felt he was putting himself on Eddy's side, against his employers, so he added, "Not this time."

He realized that he did not know how to talk to boys, never having had anything to do with them. Nevertheless he was fascinated by Eddy, by his energetic movements, his childish hands, his tousled light-brown hair and the charming proportions of his slender body. There was something fascinating in Eddy's agate-brown eyes. When he left him he glanced back over his shoulder and saw that those eyes followed him, with a gentle and speculative look.

I V

In the days that followed, the thought of Eddy occurred persistently to him. It flashed in and out, between him and his work. He would raise his eyes from the page and fancy, for a captivating instant, that the boy was sitting on the straight-backed chair near the door, as he had seen him on that first evening in the dining room. He asked himself whether Eddy was different from other boys or whether the fascination lay in his being thrown, as it were, into the midst of this strange household. He decided that Eddy was quite different. In spite of his commonplace clothes, his sordid beginnings, there was something delicately aristocratic about him. He had an almost patronizing way of looking at one. When he was at work in the garden, he would turn his head to follow Lindley with that speculative look when he passed. But Lindley, in those first days, kept strictly to himself. The sisters appeared also to avoid him, as though to make up for the previous infringement of his privacy. Life flowed quietly, in increasing summerlike heat, and Lindley's pile of manuscript grew thicker. He would work until he was exhausted, then walk to the lake, where, sitting on his boulder or stretched out on the long grass he would try to hide himself, to find the peace from his own imagination which the artist craves.

One afternoon there was a series of thunderstorms and then, at sundown, when every dripping leaf and blade was glistening and the birds had burst into songs of joy, a tap came on Lindley's outer door. It was the first time this had happened since his coming, and the sound of it came as a shock to the quiet rooms.

When Lindley opened the door he discovered Eddy standing there. He looked freshly washed and had a pleased air.

"Mrs. Morton sent me" — he was important in the message — "to see if it will be all right if she plays the piano a bit this evening." There was the *oi* sound in the treble voice.

Lindley remembered then that there had been no music since the boy's coming. Certainly he had not wished to keep the two women from that pleasure.

"Why, of course — of course. I hope she will. Please tell her so."

Eddy looked past Lindley into the writing room.

"I say, you look jolly comfortable here. You live here all by yourself? Is that the table where you write?"

He limped quickly into the room and ran his hand over the marble top of the table. "It must be fine to have a table like this and write books on it. Why, look — " he broke into delighted laughter — "you've been drawing pictures on it! Sea gulls — and good ones too. My word, how pretty."

"I amuse myself when I'm thinking, by making pictures."

Eddy slid into his chair, put an elbow on the table and propped his head on his hand. With an imaginary pencil in his fingers he pretended to write. He glanced up roguishly at Lindley, then compressing his lips, applied himself to the pretense of writing.

Lindley came close to him, looking down, with an almost tremulous sensitivity, on the boyish figure that seemed too small for the large chair. Lindley longed to touch him, to find out if this fascination the boy had for him would vanish at the touch, but he refrained. Eddy again raised his eyes to Lindley's face and this time they exchanged a look, in which Lindley thought he discovered in the boy's dusky eyes some understanding of his own emotion.

Lydia Dove's voice came from outside. "Eddy! Eddy! Whatever are you doing? Why don't you come?"

The boy raised his shoulders in a gesture of despair. "That one's always after me. What can a fella do? If Mrs. Morton wants me one place, Miss Dove wants me t'other. She's right after me, she is." He got up and went toward the door, then hesitated. "Could I come in to see you again?"

"Yes." Lindley busied himself with some papers. "But not for a few days. I'm pretty busy."

It was dark when Mrs. Morton began to play the piano and she had lighted the candles in the two silver candlesticks that stood on it. Lindley saw this as he strolled past the open windows. She was playing the "Blue Danube" and he pictured her as a young girl sitting at that same piano, putting all her romantic soul into that same waltz. He pictured Lydia, fair as a lily, her wide skirts spread on the sofa, one of her admirers on the ottoman at her feet, reveling in the fervent strains. He stood listening till the music ended. Then, in the quiet, he heard the plaintive drip of raindrops from the lilacs.

He had a sudden longing to go into the room and sit there in that atmosphere of the past, among the sequestered ruins of the sisters' lives. He lingered and, after a little, Mrs. Morton appeared in the doorway.

"Is that you, Mr. Lindley?" she called.

He came forward. "I hope I haven't startled you. I was just hanging about, enjoying the music."

She gave her wide, eager smile. "Really enjoying it?"

"Very much. You play beautifully."

Lydia Dove called from the room — "Ask Mr. Lindley to come in and sit down, Elsie."

"Will you? We should like to have you." Mrs. Morton gave him an inviting look. Indeed it was almost coy.

Lindley was conscious of great weariness. He would be less tired, he thought, when he got deeper into his book. Now it would rest his nerves to sit in the dim light, listen to the music, in the presence of those two so remote from the world. He thanked her and went in. Lydia Dove invited him, with an imperious smile, to sit on the sofa beside her. She wore an air of almost gaiety and again he was able to picture her early beauty.

Mrs. Morton seated herself at the piano, waving her hands gently above the keys, as though to limber up her wrists, then dropping them to the keyboard. It was then that Lindley discovered the boy sitting on the straight-backed chair, just inside the door that led to the kitchen. He was sitting on his hands and watching Mrs. Morton with eager attention. When she began to play Ethelbert Nevin's "Narcissus" a rapt look came into his beautiful eyes. It was on him that Lindley fixed his own gaze, scarcely conscious of the music, just drinking in, with spiritual thirst, the details of the young figure. It was as though he were inventing the boy, to satisfy some longing deep in himself. He turned his eyes to see if Lydia were also fascinated by Eddy's beauty but she was gazing at the ceiling, as though she saw herself dancing there.

Mrs. Morton went on playing, one piece after another, some of which Lindley hadn't heard since childhood, others which must have come from a forgotten album. When at last her hands came to rest and she swung round on the stool with a gratified smile at her audience Lindley rose at once. He heard himself thanking her, heard her asking him to come again. Then she turned to the boy.

"Eddy, you must go straight to bed. Remember there's work to do in the morning." Then, with an air of gentle familiarity, she asked, "Did you enjoy the music?"

His eyes became luminous. "Oh, yes, ma'am. It was wonderful. Thank you, ma'am."

He limped off to bed. Mrs. Morton looked after him with an indulgent smile. "Such a nice little boy, isn't he, Mr. Lindley?"

Lydia Dove spoke from the sofa. "I'm afraid you're going to

spoil him, Elsie. You will make so much of him he will forget he's just a little servant lad."

"Nonsense, Lydia. Don't you think that is nonsense, Mr. Lindley?"

Lindley, by agreeing with Elsie and smiling at Lydia, tried to please both of them.

"And you're sure it won't annoy you if I play a little in the evenings?"

"Quite sure."

"And you'll come again and sit with us?"

"I'd love to."

He escaped and went as usual to sit on his boulder by the lake. Between heavy clouds the moonlight fell on the dark expanse of moving water where glimmering foam showed the breaking of the waves. Lindley's weariness had left him. He felt refreshed and a strange youthfulness possessed him. He had a longing for adventure and he thought that, when his book was finished, he would, by hook or crook, get to some foreign land for a time.

He heard a movement of small stones on the shore below as though someone were walking there. Peering down he made out a small figure in the moonlight. He saw that it was Eddy and that he was moving erratically, as though stalking something. One arm was raised in a gesture of defiance and something bright shone in that hand. Lindley went to the edge of the steep bank, down which a flight of broken wooden steps led to the shore. He crept down them, keeping the boy in sight and, at the bottom, he hid himself among the scrub that grew there. It was sticky in its spring growth and a sweet smell came from it. About it the shore was sandy and Eddy was standing near him on this sandy surface. The waves made a muffled roaring as they curved and broke.

Eddy brandished the knife and his treble voice rose above the sound of the waves in a melodramatic kind of snarl. "They don't think anything of ripping a fella up with a knife like this. He'd bleed like a stuck pig, I can tell you. My word, how he'd bleed! You'd better be careful or I'll do it to you."

Lindley stepped out of the scrub. "What's that you say?"

The boy cried out in terror and dropped the knife, which in an instant Lindley had in his hand. He caught Eddy by the shoulder and held him fast. The feel of that thin shoulder went through him in a nervous exultation. He was fascinated by the boy's smallness and weakness.

"Ah, Mr. Lindley, don't take me knife away," Eddy gasped.

"What were you up to?" Lindley frowned down at him.

"Just having a bit of fun."

"Mighty queer fun."

"Didn't you ever pretend when you were a boy?"

Lindley freed him and closed his own fingers about the handle of the knife. It was warm from Eddy's grasp.

"Where did you get it?" he asked.

"My father gave it to me. I've never been parted from it — not since he put it in me 'and. He's fond of me, my dad is. Someday I hope I'll come acrost him again."

Lindley doubtfully toyed with the knife. A queer present for a father to give his child. He could picture the man — a drunken sailor, with a brawling wife. But Eddy was proud of him. His eyes shone with pride. "My dad said to me, 'You keep this knife always, Eddy, but don't use it unless you're forced to.'"

"Good advice," said Lindley, running his thumb along the edge of the blade. "But I'm going to keep it for you while you're here."

"No — no — please, Mr. Lindley, don't take my knife from me! It's all I have. I didn't mean any harm. I was only playing."

"You were talking in a very queer way — and you were

brandishing this. Have you ever seen a knife used? In a fight,
I mean."

A lull came in the onward wash of the waves. Though Eddy
spoke low Lindley could hear him. "There was a sailor killed
his wife with one of these in the house where I lived, when I
was a little shaver in London. He'd come home from a voyage
and found another chap with his wife. He ripped her clean up
and gave the other chap a nasty gash too. Lord, it was a sight
you'd not forget. It makes my blood run cold now to think of it.
Please give me back my knife, sir. I promise I'll hide it away in
my trunk."

But Lindley would not relent, even though the boy's pale
cheeks were wet with tears and he poured out broken plead-
ings. Lindley dropped the knife into his jacket pocket and turned
and climbed the steps. The feel of the knife in his pocket gave
him a sense of power, as though he owned the boy. But — whatever way you looked at it, they shared a secret. The boy's most
precious possession would be hidden in Lindley's room. When
he reached his part of the house that lay in deep darkness, he
lighted his lamp and looked about for somewhere to hide the
knife.

He chose the bottom drawer of the chest of drawers in his
bedroom and laid the knife beneath clean pyjamas. It was early
but he thought he would go to bed, so that he could rise early
and begin his work. Morning, for him, was the best time for
writing and night the time for losing himself in his imaginings.
He undressed and got into bed. It was still cool enough at night
for a blanket. But, before he beckoned to the characters of his
book, he let his mind pass through the dividing door of the
house and seek, in the darkness, for the rooms of the three occu-
pants of the other half. He pictured all three asleep — though
Lydia Dove he could not picture as entirely unconscious. She
would move restlessly on her pillows — she had told him that

she used three enormous down ones — trying to find oblivion. Yet pictures from the past would torment her, or some irritating act of her sister's, for it was easy to see that Mrs. Morton irritated her. As for Elsie Morton he was sure she slept like a log, her thickset body relaxed, her lips parted.

And the boy. Cast on his bed like a helpless drowned creature, perhaps clutching the pillows in his hands and crying for the treasure that had been taken from him. But what a little savage he had seemed on the shore. Still, that was nothing — he had been staging a show for an imaginary audience, a group of gaping boys who would look on him as a dangerous fellow. Perhaps he was dangerous, or might become so, if he were angered. It was better to keep the knife away from him. Why, if those two women knew he owned such a thing, they might well feel panic. Possibly it was well for them that they had a protector in the house.

Lindley played with strange thoughts about Eddy. After all, he had come from a dark and fearful environment. He had risen like a flower from a dung heap. Lindley's mind, in the darkness, insisted more and more on Eddy's beauty, the fine hair that needed cutting and waved so gracefully about his ears, the smooth white forehead, where the scar from the stepmother's scissors showed as a cruel indentation — or was that story a fabrication? The limpid, long-lashed eyes, the slender body with the maimed foot.

V

The following day Eddy followed him as he went for his stroll after writing.

"Mr. Lindley," he called out, "please, sir!" With a little skip, he caught up to Lindley, who turned to him with a defensive frown.

"My knife, please. Could I have my knife?"

There was something so tender about Eddy, standing there, a little lopsided, so like a child begging for his toy to be returned to him, that Lindley had an impulse to tell him where the knife was hidden and to go himself and retrieve it. Then the scowling and the growling of the night before came between him and the boy's pleading face.

"I am going to keep that knife for a while," he said, and he spoke quite gently. "I'll give it to you when I leave."

The boy showed dismay, but not because of the knife. "Are you leaving, sir?" What a well-mannered, innocent little boy, compared to the small ruffian of the lake shore!

"When I finish my book."

"And how long will it take to finish?"

"I don't know."

Eddy laughed outright in skepticism. "Don't know? W'y — how many pages has it?"

"I don't know."

He laughed again. "I say, do you know what it's about?"

"Sometimes I wonder if I do."

A loud call for Eddy came from the kitchen doorway.

"There goes Mrs. Morton." He raised pathetic eyes to Lindley. "I've no sooner done a job for one of 'em, than t'other one's after me. And they never wants anything done the same way. My word, they're terrors to scrap with one another." He grinned up at Lindley in enjoyment of the squabbles.

Lindley did not want to discuss the two women with Eddy, but he was curious, for he had hoped things were now peaceable between them. Miss Dove's health was so much improved. She no longer tottered when she walked and she now used the old red walking stick which had been her father's, rather as a weapon than a support, poking it into the flower border after garter snakes, shaking it at little boys who came to steal cherries, and pointing the way down the road to beggars who dared stop at the gate. As the days went on she began to waylay Lindley to complain of the boy. He was always wasting his time. He was deceitful, pretending he was at work but running off to play by the lake. Last night he had not fed the hens. They had gone to perch supperless. A weasel had crept in by the coop door he had left open and killed two chicks. Miss Dove would walk quite strongly beside Lindley, pouring out her complaints of the boy.

Lindley began to avoid her, moving away among the trees when he saw her coming. This was easy because she invariably wore a bright red shawl no matter how warm the weather.

Mrs. Morton too complained of the boy's idleness. "Have you noticed, Mr. Lindley, how often he leaves his work? Not that I want to overwork the child. But I do like to see the little jobs I set him finished before he runs off."

Lindley murmured absently, "Of course. Of course."

"I hope he doesn't annoy you in any way."

"Annoy me? Oh, no."

"I thought I saw him going round to your side of the house. I don't want him to be a bother." Her voice took on an odd possessive tone. "You do think he's a nice little boy, don't you? I like him so much. It will be years and years before he is grown up."

"Well," Lindley looked down at the ground, "I've scarcely noticed him."

"Then he hasn't bothered you. I'm so glad."

But, when it came to canning fruit, Mrs. Morton could not complain of Eddy's idleness. The strawberry bed, the two cherry trees, the tangle of raspberry canes, were in turn stripped of their fruit. It was bottled in the kitchen and filled the house with its sweet odor. Mrs. Morton and Eddy worked side by side. This was the sort of work he liked — not digging or weeding or cleaning floors. Lindley could see how the happy intimacy grew day by day. She talked of past grandeurs and present trials and Eddy listened in awe, sympathized or laughed aloud at her little jokes. She looked cheerful and full of vigor. Eddy ate fresh fruit and bottled fruit, grew round-cheeked and self-important. He would greet Lindley as though he were the owner of the property and Lindley his respected tenant.

Lindley grew more deeply absorbed in his book, yet he was not satisfied with the turn it was taking. Into the tragedy he was building, a strange grotesqueness had entered. He found that, in describing one of his characters, he had described Miss Dove, wearing her red hood and carrying her red walking stick. Between his eyes and the page, Eddy's face, with the white scar on the forehead, kept reappearing.

Every now and again he went to the dining room in the evening to hear Mrs. Morton play on the piano. It was a peaceful time for all four of them. Lindley soon became familiar with Mrs. Morton's repertory. Eddy before long had learned the names of the pieces. He would leave his little chair by the door and come and lean against the piano, gazing rapt into Mrs. Morton's face. Only Lydia Dove was outside the circle. She sat on the sofa aloof yet watchful.

One evening, when Mrs. Morton was playing a love song of Schumann's, Eddy came so close to her that he touched her right hand on the keyboard. With a sweeping gesture she motioned him to move away. It was as though her sister had been waiting for this signal. She leapt up, ran to Eddy and caught him by the shoulders. She dragged him back to his chair and literally threw him on to it. He shuffled unresisting before her onslaught. As for Lydia Dove, she appeared exhausted by the effort and sank back on the sofa panting, her hand to her breast. Mrs. Morton played the piece to the end. When it was finished she put her elbows on the keyboard and buried her face in her hands. Lindley did not wait to see them recover their equanimity but slipped quietly from the room and found his way, through the darkness, to his own door. He made up his mind that he would not again go to hear Mrs. Morton play. As he had left the room he had given a glance to Eddy, sitting with folded arms on his chair by the door. He had had an odd smile on his lips. He appeared unruffled.

This was an unusual hour for Lindley to write, but now he had the desire to wrestle with the characters who, that morning, had shown him unfamiliar and grotesque faces. He worked till past midnight. When at last he went to bed it was two hours before he slept and, when he did, he dreamt that the dividing door between the two parts of the house was open and could not be closed, even though he struggled with great strength against it. The dream made such an impression on him that, coming downstairs the next morning, he half expected to see the door ajar. But no — its tall pale panels rose in front of him, inscrutable as ever.

He went round to the kitchen to prepare his breakfast. It was very quiet there, the way cleared as usual for his activities. He made his coffee and stood by the outer door, waiting for it to simmer. It was a hot, bright summer day, when the sky in its blueness seemed a tangible jewel-like substance.

Suddenly Mrs. Morton's voice came, full and strong, from one of the inner rooms beyond the dining room.

"You're getting too well. That's what's the matter with you. We had peace when you were ailing but now you're into everything. You're getting too well, I tell you!"

Lydia's voice rose in a shriek. "Too well! Too well, am I? You had rather I were on the flat of my back. Ungrateful girl!"

"Ungrateful? I'd like to know what I have to be grateful for? Grateful for your interference? Grateful for your silly pretentious ways?"

In a confused babble their recriminations were hurled back

and forth. Lindley felt frightened by their vehemence. He decided he would not eat breakfast in that room but carry his pot of coffee to his own seclusion. A combined scream of rage from the two women almost made him drop it. He was hurrying round the corner of the house when he all but ran into Eddy. He was standing just outside the dining-room door, lounging against its frame, listening. His small face wore an expression of the keenest enjoyment.

"Aren't they terrors?" he asked, in his clear sweet treble. "I like to hear them fight."

He looked grandly conscious of his masculinity and power. But it was shocking to Lindley that he should so take him into his confidence. He made no answer but strode on toward his own rooms. Eddy trotted alongside, with his quick, uneven step. He looked up into Lindley's eyes. "What Mrs. Morton says I'm to do, Miss Dove says I'm not to. If Miss Dove says yes, Mrs. Morton says no." A smile that to Lindley showed more malice than mere mischief, bent his lips. "I keep them going, you know."

"You shouldn't tell me this," Lindley said repressively. He moved more quickly and the coffee slopped.

"Oh, see what you've done, you naughty boy," shrilled Eddy, imitating Lydia Dove. Then, seeing the expression on Lindley's face, he threw himself on the grass and rolled over in his mirth.

Lindley set down the pot of coffee on the doorstep. He lifted Eddy sharply to his feet. "You ought to be ashamed," he said with severity. "These ladies are very kind to you. You should be grateful."

Eddy showed a contrition that Lindley felt to be spurious. "Oh, I am grateful. Reely, sir, I am. Only I likes to see them fight. They're grand at it. I didn't teach them. They've been at it all their lives. Miss Lydia, she says Mrs. Morton always was jealous of her being a beauty and Mrs. Morton says Miss Lydia has always been a boss cat. From the time she was a little girl Miss Lydia has tried to boss her — but she won't stand it, she won't. And now she's got me on her side. I'm all for Mrs. Morton."

Lindley was astounded. "They talk to you about each other?"

"Do they? Why, it'd make your hair rise up the things they say."

Lindley picked up the coffeepot and went into his study. Eddy limped after him. Lindley wanted to tell him to go but could not make up his mind. He did not want to hear about the sisters' quarreling. He clung, with a feeling almost of desperation, to the seclusion this place had promised. He could not blame Eddy for creating a situation which had existed long before he was born. Yet he could not help concluding that the boy was playing them off against each other. As if to confirm this Eddy said, "There's an old pink teapot Miss Lydia don't want used. Says I'll break it. So yesterday I asks Mrs. Morton if she wouldn't like me to carry her tea to her bedroom in it for she'd a headache and she says Miss Lydia wouldn't like it and I asks her if she has to do what Miss Lydia says and she says no and to bring the tea in that pot and I did and Miss Lydia missed it off that shelf and I says Mrs. Morton would have that pot and Miss Lydia says I'll see if she will and she goes right up to the bedroom and they had a real good row and Miss Lydia snatched up the pot and carried it down to the kitchen but when she was washing it she dropped it and broke it to bits. I saved one of them it was so pretty. Look." He took a broken piece of pink luster, with a bird on it, from his pocket and displayed it on his palm, a small palm, pink from dishwashing.

On an impulse Lindley put an arm about the boy's shoulders. "Try to keep the peace, Eddy. It would help me with my book."

The boy raised astonished eyes. "Help you with your book? How?"

"I need quiet or I can't think."

A bright smile lighted Eddy's face. "I'd do anything for you, sir. I say, where do you keep my knife? Could I have just one peep at it to see if it's safe."

"It's safe enough. Don't worry."

"But I'd like to see it. I miss it cruel."

"You be a good boy and I will give you back your knife. But now I must be alone."

"Will you show me your book one day?"

"Yes." He propelled the boy firmly through the door.

V I

As the summer progressed, so did the book. Its characters became more real to him than the three who led their strange lives in the other half of the house. He avoided them. He no longer went in the evenings to listen to Mrs. Morton's playing. But sometimes he would light his pipe and sit on the stairs near the door that led to the dining room. From there he could hear the romantic strains, now sweetly sentimental, now vivacious, and could picture Mrs. Morton and her audience of two.

In July the heat became intolerable outdoors but so well was the house built and so shaded by a dense growth of trees were Lindley's rooms that they were always cool. The marble-topped table on which Lindley wrote became disfigured by the many sketches he had made on it — waves beating on rocks, grotesque faces leering through clouds — unsuccessful attempts to portray a small boy with a twisted foot.

At night Lindley would take his lonely walks, sometimes far along the country road, sometimes to the murmuring vastness of the lake. One night, as he sat there on his boulder, he heard the sound of boys' voices and a sudden splashing of water. There was bright moonlight and, running through it in the wavelets, he saw Eddy and two other small boys. These were brothers who lived in a cottage near by. Mrs. Morton had told Eddy that he was to keep away from these boys but Lindley guessed that he often stole off to play with them. And who could blame him? He spent his days in the company of women who long ago had forgotten how to play, and whose lives were an endless conflict.

The boys raced into the water, their naked bodies gleaming like wet gold in the moonlight. They looked unearthly beautiful. Their ugly clothes thrown off like dark cocoons, they had emerged airy, graceful, free as birds. In and out of the water they dashed, splashing each other, rolling on the narrow strip of sand, in an ecstasy of happiness, like young animals. Lindley watched them with delight, his eyes always resting on Eddy's agile little body. The handicap of his lameness was forgotten. He was graceful as a fish in his play.

Lindley was startled to discover that someone else was watching them. There was a cedar tree to his left and beyond it a strip of rough ground where clumps of black-eyed Susan were already in flower and Michaelmas daisies soon would be. In this space stood Mrs. Morton, watching the boys in fascination. Her strong-featured face was clear in the moonlight. It was transfigured by an extraordinary expression of longing that softened it to a strange girlishness. Lindley felt that she longed to run down the steps into the lake and dance and leap and play with the boys. From his concealed place he watched her, half ashamed to see the change in her. He had been delighting in the play of the boys, he thought, with the appreciation of the artist but there was something sensuous in Mrs. Morton's face.

Then, in a sudden irritation, either at them or at herself, she called sharply, "Eddy, Eddy, come up here this minute!"

The boys were on the sand but at her cry they ran startled into the water up to their armpits and then turned and stared, half timidly, half belligerently.

Mrs. Morton called again, "Eddy, Eddy, do you hear me?"

"Yes, ma'am. Coming." He splashed his way out of the moon-lit water, crossed the strip of sand, the ridge of shingle, and began composedly to climb the bank.

She turned away while he drew on his clothes, then impulsively turned back and threw her arm about his shoulders. "Why, you're damp, Eddy, you haven't dried yourself."

He snuggled against her. "I was hurrying. I'd rather be wet than keep you waiting. 'Cause you're so kind to me. Gosh, the water was nice. I shouldn't be surprised if you'd like a swim yourself." There was a shrewdness in his voice, as though he had guessed her thoughts. She looked down into his face. They were young together. Lindley followed at a distance, watching them return to the house as two culprits instead of one. He heard Lydia Dove meet them in a fury. She had been searching for a white hen which Eddy had left roaming at large. In catching the hen she had pulled out its tail feathers. Didn't Eddy care if weasels killed all the hens? Hadn't Eddy any sense of duty? Didn't Eddy realize he was a little servant lad? Didn't Elsie realize she was making a fool of him?

Mrs. Morton fiercely told her to go into the house and mind her business.

Avoiding all three Lindley went to his own door. From that night on he was conscious of the bond between Mrs. Morton and Eddy, he saw them so often together. The house was divided. Eddy was always on her side, against Lydia. Lydia grew more and more exacting with the boy. She gave him no peace. No longer would she allow him inside the room when Mrs. Morton played the piano and sang. Lindley found him stretched on the wet grass beneath the dining-room window listening. The time of heavy dews had come. The contralto voice was singing the refrain, "Tender and true, adieu, adieu." The piano throbbed out a heartbreaking accompaniment.

Eddy raised eyes full of tears. "Oh, Mr. Lindley," he said, "isn't it sad?"

Lindley bent over him. "Are you unhappy, Eddy?"

"Miss Lydia, she's terrible. I can't do nothink to please her."

"Eddy, you must try. You know that you make trouble between the two ladies."

The boy scrambled to his feet. Lindley was returning to his room. He did not want the boy to follow him. "Shouldn't you like to stay and listen to the music?"

"It's over. I heard her close the piano."

"Well — good night, Eddy." Lindley turned away with a decisive stride. But he heard Eddy following him. He followed him into his own room where the marble top of the table was clear in the moonlight. Eddy leaned across it and looked up with slanting eyes at Lindley.

"Why do you write a book, Mr. Lindley?"

"Because it's the one thing in the world I want to do — to write a good book."

"Does it feel good to do it?"

"Sometimes."

"And when it's done will people read it?"

"Lots of people, I hope."

"I've never read a book."

"No? Have you ever owned a book?"

"Never." The strange beauty of his eyes, the fragile virility of his body, his lameness, were unbearably poignant to Lindley. At that moment he longed to possess Eddy's future, to protect him, to pour out the love of a lonely heart on him — but he had barely enough means for himself and that for only a short while. This strange interlude, this isolation with this oddly assorted trio, would soon end. He would never see one of them again. Eddy appeared as though dimly conscious of Lindley's thoughts. A long look passed between them.

Eddy pointed with his thumb over his shoulder to the other side of the house. "We're none of us happy, in there. We used to be but not now. Miss Lydia acts like she hates me but when Mrs. Morton goes to the village she treats me the best she knows how. She gives me presents, like this here" — he drew a short silver chain from his pocket. "It's a watch chain and when I own a watch I'm to wear it. She tells me not to mention it to Mrs. Morton. Isn't it funny?" With a puzzled knitting of the brows he caressed the chain. "She'll make me sit near her in the garden while she drinks her tea. But — " his child's smile lighted his face — "it's Mrs. Morton I like. Us two have our own secrets. Mrs. Morton thinks a lot of me, she does."

The heat, the sultriness of August, did not depress Lindley. He was getting on with his book. The characters in it stood between him and the rest of the world. The partition dividing the house seemed to grow more impenetrable. Few sounds came through. Like a criminal Lindley skulked about the grounds avoiding human contact. He prepared and ate his meals hurriedly for fear he would have to engage in conversation with the sisters. The boy he avoided most of all, because of his almost overpowering attraction for him.

One afternoon, in the brilliance of sunset he was strolling through the orchard whose worm-poisoned fruit was already beginning to fall, when from the stable he heard Eddy's voice raised in the same bragging tones he had used on that night by the lake. Lindley moved closer to the stable from where the voice came, clear and high.

"Ah, you should have seen the body. Ripped clean open it was. Lord — what a sight! It makes my blood run cold to think of it."

Now Lindley was in the stable doorway. From the broken floor there was a short ladder which led to the loft. Up this he saw Lydia Dove scrambling. She moved with great agility. A

wide-brimmed straw hat was worn over her cap. She had doubtless come here to search for eggs.

"Miss Dove," Lindley called. "Don't go up."

She did not hear him and now he sprang up the ladder after
her. Eddy and the two neighboring boys were up there, knee-
deep in the moldy hay. Eddy was brandishing the knife and so
hallucinated was he by his own visions that she was grappling
with him before he saw her. The top rung of the feeble ladder
broke with Lindley. He barely escaped falling to the floor below. By the time he had clambered up, she had torn the knife
from Eddy and in her turn brandished it. His twisted foot
turned beneath him and he fell at her feet. She leaned over him,
the knife poised, the delicate veins in her wrist showing blue.
The neighbor's boys, squealing with fright, scrambled pell-mell
down the ladder. Eddy rolled over, trying to bury himself in the
hay.

"You're nothing but a young murderer," screamed Lydia
Dove. "A young murderer! Oh, to think that we should shelter
the scum of London in our home! Where did you get that
knife?"

"My father gave it to me, he did," sobbed the boy, "and I
ain't a murderer. No more than you. You give me that knife,
d'you hear?" He glared up at her out of the hay like a young
animal.

Lindley strode forward, picked him up and set him on his
feet. He spoke soothingly to Lydia Dove. But she was past being
soothed. "I shall have you thrown into prison, my lad, if you
threaten me," she screamed. Threats and lamentations poured
from her. She scarcely knew what she was saying.

Now Mrs. Morton's stocky figure appeared at the top of the
ladder. She moved to Eddy's side. A cold intense fury shone
from her gray eyes. "Go down out of here, Lydia," she commanded. "You're acting like a madwoman."

"Mad," shrieked her sister. "How dare you use such a word

to me? But, if I do lose my reason, it will be because you and your villainous young protégé have driven me to it."

"Come, Mr. Lindley — come, Eddy" — Mrs. Morton was making a great effort at self-control — "leave her to herself." She put her arm about the boy's shoulders and drew him toward the ladder. "I've seen her this way before."

Miss Dove stood erect, glaring after the three as they descended the ladder. She was a grotesque and even a frightening figure. Below, in the stable, Mrs. Morton asked, in a choking voice, "How did you come by that knife, Eddy?"

"My daddy gave it to me," he whimpered, "just to play with. I didn't mean no 'arm with it nohow."

"You must never have it again. You'll drive Miss Lydia mad. Oh, why does she carry on so? I can't bear it — with our responsibilities and the mortgages and all." Tears rained down her cheeks.

Eddy hung on her arm. "But you'll not send me away, will you? I shan't ask for the knife again. Only let me stay, please, please — "

"You are all I have to lean on," sobbed Mrs. Morton. "You must try to be a little man and help me bear things." She turned, as though in despair, to Lindley. "My sister is getting so — so strange."

"Do you think," asked Lindley, "that we should leave her up there alone?"

"It's the only thing to do," Mrs. Morton spoke with passionate conviction. "So long as anyone is near her, she'll go on making an exhibition of herself. Oh dear, if you knew what I have to bear!"

"I'll look after you, ma'am," Eddy declared. "I'll make you a pot of tea right now."

They turned in the direction of the house.

Lindley, looking after them, saw how excited and elated the

boy was. His arms were rigid at his sides, his hands clenched. He looked ready to martyr himself for Mrs. Morton. But what of the knife? He must have gone to Lindley's apartment and searched till he found it. He had shown no embarrassment at Lindley's discovery of his duplicity. Still, he looked on the knife as his own property and probably thought Lindley had no right to confiscate it.

Lindley, of a sudden, felt very sorry for himself. He had come to this remote spot for peace and what had he found? A turmoil of emotion that every so often sought to entangle him. He picked up a switch and gave vent to his feelings by whipping the nettles that clustered about the stable. What he needed was exercise, he thought. All his days he had lived a sedentary life.

He looked up to see Miss Dove standing in the doorway of the stable, and felt both foolish and irritated at being caught in beating the nettles. She, however, looked remarkably calm. She spoke with restraint.

"You can see how dangerous it was to bring such a boy into our house. I have warned my sister time and again that he is a bad boy."

"But you liked him at the first, didn't you?"

"I thought him harmless. Now I find he's vicious."

"I think he was only showing off in front of the other boys."

"Well, he'll show off with this no more. I shall hide it in my clothes cupboard and tell him I've buried it in the hay. Let him hunt for it there." Now she straightened herself and added with great dignity: "I am sorry, Mr. Lindley, that you had to witness such a painful scene."

"If I can help you, in any way — " he stammered.

"Thank you." She gave him a bow that was a mixture of graciousness and hauteur. She might have looked ludicrous, her hat and cap having fallen off and her silvery hair blowing loose, but she did not. She looked much more composed than had Mrs. Morton, who had looked ill.

As usual there was calm after the storm. Lindley heard nothing of the other three till twilight, when Eddy appeared at his door.

"Well?" Lindley asked brusquely.

Darker than twilight the child's appealing eyes were raised to Lindley's. "I came and took me knife, sir," he said, like a small child answering a question in class.

"So I saw."

"I 'ad to 'ave it."

"Well, you've lost it again — this time for good."

Eddy's face darkened in anger. "She ought to be in a madhouse, that she ought. For very little more I'd stick it into her. It's *my* knife what my dad gave me."

Lindley darted down the steps and grasped the boy and shook him. "Be careful what you say. What I should do is to take you back to the Home."

The boy was as pliable in his hands as a kitten. He put his fists to his eyes and pressed back the tears. "I didn't mean that, sir," he whimpered. "It's just a way of talking. I wouldn't harm Miss Dove." He gave a ridiculous little hiccup of distress.

Lindley relaxed his hold but still kept his hands on the boy. A strange vibration of sympathy and understanding passed between them. Lindley felt shaken. He had been putting too much of himself into his book. His nerves were suffering. He would throw off all thought of these warring women who, he felt, would willingly have dragged him into their struggles. As for the boy, he had better be in a place where there was more work and less dissension. Lindley made no attempt to put thoughts of Eddy from his mind. He knew that was not possible. He watched him disappear among the trees and then sat down on his own doorstep, lighted his pipe and gave himself up to brooding on him.

Perhaps he should tell Mrs. Morton what Eddy had said, take it upon himself to escort him back to the Home. But he was too deeply immersed in his book, too indolent to do anything but muse on the affair which already, in the sultry August air, had taken on the quality of a dream.

Lindley had never experienced a sultriness equal to this. As usual after an outbreak between the sisters, there was a reconciliation but their hostility was like a fire banked by ashes ready to flare into flames at the first breath. A feeling of dark expectancy hung about their part of the house.

V I I

A strange smell became noticeable in the lower rooms. A disgusting smell as of something decaying. They traced it at last to the old woodshed behind the kitchen. Rubbish had been accumulating there for the past forty years. Never in that time had it been cleared out. Half the shed was well floored but the other half was of damp moldy earth. On this part the rubbish had collected, sinking, as the years passed, into an indistinguishable mass of boxes, rags, bags, bundles, papers, sweepings. Here the cat reared her families, here bats clung to the rafters, spiders hung their webs undisturbed.

Now it must be cleaned. For the first time in months Lydia and Elsie agreed about a piece of work. It must be done. Something was decaying there.

On a Monday morning Eddy began work. The sisters stood by, handkerchiefs to their noses, to direct him. He was very self-important, very excited. He was a man engaged on a difficult job, these two weak females standing by in wonder. He heaved incredible loads. He dragged the most amazing things from the litter. Smells didn't worry him. Lindley, looking in to see what was going on, wondered at the fierce ardor with which he attacked the ancient mass. The shed was almost as vile as the stable of Augeas. By Friday all the rubbish had been carried to a bare spot near the vegetable garden, and that night Eddy was given his reward — a great bonfire. The two boys from the cottage were allowed to come to it. They brought potatoes which they roasted in the hot ashes and Eddy filched a chunk of butter from the crock in the cellar. They ran about, eating hot potatoes, the melted butter trickling down their wrists, yelling like wild Indians.

Lydia and Elsie were excited, fearful of the danger of fire from the flaming mass, thrilled by the strange glamour cast by the blaze on the familiar scene. They stood side by side, motionless, like two quaint china figures. Lindley stood alone in the shadow watching with brooding eyes.

It had been a strange week. Things had been unearthed which had in turn produced sighs or merriment. There was the silver sugar spoon lost thirty years ago, now discovered black with tarnish, thrown out doubtless by a maid when shaking the table-cloth. There was a pair of buttoned boots, there were ancient whalebone stays, in which a family of mice had made their nest, far below the prowling cat. Now all was reduced to clean ashes.

On Saturday morning Eddy swept the floor of the shed. It was now immaculate. The odor of decay had fled and at Lindley's suggestion, a bottle of disinfectant was sprinkled about. Eddy had found a forgotten well in a corner of the shed, the water of which was surprisingly cold. He was like an explorer who has made a great discovery.

"Look — taste," he had cried, holding out a dipperful of the water to Lindley.

"It is probably not fit to drink. Better throw it out."

"It's good. I've been drinking it all the week." He would have taken another drink of it on the spot but Lindley took the dipper from him and emptied it.

When he was preparing his own meals, Eddy would come into the kitchen with, "Please, sir, come and 'ave a look at the shed, will you? It looks so nice." And Lindley would follow him and admire.

Eddy no longer ate his meals in the dining room, for Lydia Dove could not endure the sight of him there. He ate from a corner of the kitchen table or sitting on the doorstep with the plate on his knees.

But, on the Sunday after that week, Lindley saw the three standing together beneath the trees. They smiled as though on happy terms and Eddy wore a new white shirt and blue tie. He had a bold confident look, as though he felt himself capable of great things, as though he wondered how the sisters ever got on without him. Lindley, with his contemplative eyes on the three, felt more apprehension than relief. He had lost all hope of continued serenity among them.

And it was as he feared. The passing weeks saw the boy doing less and less. An idle young wastrel, Lydia called him, and even Elsie was out of all patience with him. Evidently the cleaning of the shed was to be his first and last great labor. Lindley found him, in the midst of dishwashing, sitting on the kitchen doorstep, the dish towel across his knees, staring blankly before him. Again he found him leaning heavily on his broom, with the same look of seeing nothing, and a few days later saw him scrape the food from his plate into the dish of scraps.

"What's the matter, Eddy?" he asked. "Aren't you well?"

"Oh, I'm well enough, sir. Just a bit tired."

A few days later he came from the lake, dripping wet and with a bleeding lip. Mrs. Morton told Lindley about it the next morning. She looked really worried. "It was those horrid boys from the cottage," she said. "He got into a fight with them and they ducked him in the lake. My sister is furious and has gone to the boys' father to complain. She threatens to have them jailed."

"Where is Eddy?"

"I put him to bed and he's still there."

"I'll go up and see him."

But, as Lindley was about to go up the stairs, Eddy appeared. His jacket and trousers were crumpled and damp, his hair long and tousled.

Mrs. Morton went close to examine him. "Dear me, your lip is quite swollen. You must keep away from those nasty boys. Get yourself some breakfast now. I've saved porridge in the saucepan. Do try to look a little brighter, Eddy. He has no reason to look so dull, has he, Mr. Lindley?"

Lindley pulled at his own lip, wondering about the boy.

"It's hard enough on me," she went on, "having Miss Lydia behave as she does, without your getting queer."

Eddy leaned against the side of the door and stared blankly into the garden, his small hands jammed into his pockets.

"I ain't queer," he said. "I'm sick."

"Sick? Where are you sick?"

"I ache."

"Well, you were fighting, you know. And that ducking, too. What a mess your clothes are in." She laid a hand on his sleeve. "Why, you're quite damp. When you have eaten your porridge, you must go out and sit in the sun and get thoroughly dry. I shall not ask you to work today."

He scowled. "I couldn't do it if you did ask me. I ache."

"Well, eat your porridge and you'll feel better."

"I tell you I won't eat," he shouted. "I'm sick."

He picked up a kitchen chair and set it outside the door, on the flagstones. He sat down on it and tilted it back against the wall. The warm sun fell on him. He looked cold.

"Really, that boy is a trial." Mrs. Morton looked sorry for herself. "He's not nearly so nice as he was. But I'm fond of him, Mr. Lindley. I'm very fond of him."

"I expect all boys are a trial at times."

"Of course. And here are you waiting to get your breakfast. Dear me, I do hope you're not annoyed with us." She bustled off.

An excessive apology, Lindley thought, for a very small annoyance, considering the extreme ones he had suffered. He was at a point in his book when what he wanted was to be let severely alone. Yesterday he had torn up all he had written that day. He ate his bacon glumly and, after washing his few dishes, was about to depart through the outer door of the dining room when he saw Miss Dove passing. He waited, so that he should not encounter her. She was wearing her wide-brimmed straw hat and red woolen spencer, and carrying the red walking stick.

Lindley heard her say, "What an idle little servant lad. Sleeping in the middle of the morning."

"Don't poke me with your stick," Eddy shouted. "I ain't idle. I'm sick."

"Sick? Not a bit of it. You're idle. Spoilt. My sister spoils you. She encourages you to idle your time away and be saucy to me. Don't you know that you're here to work?"

Eddy's voice sounded hysterical. "Work! Don't I work? Look at that there shed. That's wot's the matter with me, I do believe. I worked too 'ard, I did."

From somewhere in the garden Mrs. Morton came on the scene. "Let the boy alone, Lydia. I told him to sit there and dry himself."

Lydia's voice rose in that maddening way. "*You* told him! *You* told him. I am nobody here. It is always you who give orders. Now *I* say he shall do his work or go back to the Home."

The two buzzed about him like angry bees.

Desperate, Lindley dashed through the door, and fled to his part of the house. There was silence and peace there but it was some time before he could compose his thoughts to writing.

The air had become very humid. Silence had descended on the birds but the air vibrated to the sound of the cicadas. The earth was parched to hardness and on its dry surface lively ant hills appeared. Lindley spent a solitary day but toward evening Mrs. Morton waylaid him in the shrubbery.

Lindley turned to face her, his expression one of mingled defense and solicitude.

"Oh, Mr. Lindley," she began, rather breathlessly, "I do so hate to trouble you — "

"Please don't feel that you're a trouble. Is it Eddy?"

"Yes. Will you come and look at him? I'm wondering if I should call a doctor tomorrow morning."

Lindley wheeled and began to stride toward the kitchen. She hurried breathless at his side. He heard her saying, "My sister too. Oh, I'm so worried. She is driving me to desperation. I've never known her so bad as this. Between the two — " her voice trailed off to the strangled sound of a sob.

"I'm very sorry." Lindley stopped. He curbed his longing to escape. "Perhaps it might be well for the doctor to see her too."

She was eager to lean on him, to lean on any male. "That's a good idea. I'm sure it's a good idea."

Lindley climbed the short, dark stairway to Eddy's room. The boy was lying on his back. He had thrown his pillow to the floor and his arms were flung above his head on the mattress. His breast was bare and it moved quickly with his heavy breathing. At first he did not see Lindley but kept his eyes on the moving shadows of leaves against the window. Lindley spoke and the boy raised his heavy lids and regarded him out of glazed and feverish eyes. Then he smiled in pleasure.

"Hello, Mr. Lindley," he said. "Did you come all this way to see me?"

"Yes, Eddy. Mrs. Morton tells me you're not feeling very well."

"No, sir, I ain't. I'm awful hot. But Mrs. Morton, she's kind. She brought me a whole jug of ice water. Look." On a chair by the bed stood the glass jug nearly emptied. "Feel my head, sir, how 'ot it is."

Lindley laid his hand on the child's forehead, burning beneath the tousled hair. "You're certainly feverish, Eddy. We shall have the doctor to you tomorrow. He'll fix you up."

Eddy smiled, gratified by his importance. Then he threw himself to a new position. Its childish grace and pathos went to Lindley's heart. His heart ached for the boy.

Eddy muttered, in a voice made rough by the dryness of his mouth, "It's the faces. They won't let me be. Sometimes it's my dad's face, when he'd been drinking — sometimes it's my stepmother's looking like when she fired the scissors at me — then it's my little stepsister's face, as big as a pumpkin, with a comforter in 'er mouth. Sometimes it's just crazy faces grinning at me. Sometimes they goes and I'm like I was in a ship at sea. You don't think I'm going daffy, like Miss Dove, do you? She says she sees queer things."

"You'll be all right, old fellow." Lindley took a washcloth from a nail on the wall and wet it with iced water from the jug. He laid it on Eddy's forehead.

A look of sheer bliss calmed the boy's troubled face. "Oh, how good that feels. Oh, how good." He closed his eyes in bliss.

Lindley stood looking down on him, on his helplessness, his aloneness, with the old pang of longing. Then the boy opened his eyes. He raised them to Lindley's face in gratitude, their dark depths shining below the white cloth, and, with a feverish hand, caught Lindley's hand and pressed it to his lips. "Oh, Mr. Lindley," he murmured, "I do love you."

A rush of love for the sick boy swept through all Lindley's

being. He bent over him, gathered him into his arms and held him close. He felt the heat of him, smelt the fever.

"Am I going to get better, sir?" whispered Eddy.

"Of course you are." Lindley laid him down. He took the cloth from his head, wet it, and again laid it on his forehead.

Below he met Mrs. Morton. "What do you think of him?" she asked anxiously.

"I'm afraid he's pretty ill."

"I've telephoned the doctor. I'm so worried. He can't come tonight but he'll come first thing in the morning. There seems no end to the worries I have and now there'll be another doctor's bill."

"I'll pay it," said Lindley and hurried away before she could thank him.

V I I I

In his cool, sequestered room he sat down and lighted his pipe. There was a gentle stirring of air among the trees. He could see their branches moving as though they communicated with each other, in vague touchings and caresses. It was just light enough for him to see a bat pass the window. He took out his manuscript and laid it on the table. It was a first book. It might be treated tolerantly by reviewers but would it sell? Would it make enough for him to live on while he wrote his next?

But he could not keep his mind on the book. Eddy's eyes, large and luminous, kept coming between him and it, Eddy's feverish lips against his hand, the feel of Eddy's slender body in his arms.

Darkness came and still he sat brooding, motionless in his chair. It became black outdoors and two owls were answering each other. Then a great golden-red full moon showed behind the trees and there was a different world. Lindley rose, feeling rather stiff, and went to the window.

At that moment a piercing shriek struck his eardrums and echoed through the house.

Galvanized by fear Lindley ran to the door which separated the two parts of the house. It rose tall and pale, just touched by the moonlight that came through the narrow glass windows on either side of the front door. As he laid his hand on the door-knob, another scream rang through the house, like a wilder echo of the first. Then followed a shrill shout in Eddy's voice. Lindley shook the doorknob, then put his shoulder to the door and threw his weight against it, but it would not give. He ran through his own door and round the house to the dining room. There was silence in the house.

He stood in the middle of the room, his heart thumping horribly and strained his ears to hear any sound. There was only the ticking of the clock which was exaggerated to persistent blows on steel. That and the thudding of his heart against his ribs. . . . There was no light in the room save the moonlight, but in the passage beyond it, there was a hanging oil lamp still lighted and its light fell on the pale face of the grandfather clock. Lindley went to the foot of the staircase that led from this passage and called out:

"Mrs. Morton, are you all right?"

There was no answer. He waited, then called again. There was only his own voice, loud and with a strange crackling sound in it. He called Miss Dove's name.

Then, as though shot from a bolt and full of fear, he sprang up the stairs two steps at a time. He never had been in this part of the house before. There were several rooms up here and in two of them he could see lights, for their doors were open. Again he called out the names of the sisters, and again no answer. Hideous visions of what might be inside held him transfixed for a space. Then he went into the nearest room.

It was empty. The enormous moon seemed to hang in the

window. A dress he had seen Mrs. Morton wear that day hung across the back of a chair. The bedcovers had been turned down but the pillow was undented. . . . He turned, his fear increasing in him and hurried to the other lighted room. It too was empty but the bed was disturbed and Lydia Dove's clothes were scattered about. An old-fashioned wardrobe stood open and clothes from it were thrown out, as though there had been a search for something. After those terrible screams the silence was almost equally frightening.

Lindley took the lamp from the dressing table and explored the other rooms. One was quite empty of furniture but smelt of apples. He could make them out, spread on the floor. The other room was partly furnished and smelt of must. Lindley searched for a door that might lead to Eddy's bedroom, but there was none. He set down the lamp from his shaking hand and ran down the stairs, through dining room and kitchen and up the steep short flight to the boy's room. It too was empty.

All of Lindley's senses were tonight abnormally acute. His eyes took in every detail of these untidy rooms. Now the smell of the disinfectant came to his nostrils. His ears were acute for the faintest sound but there was none. The house was empty.

Downstairs again and the creak of his own footsteps. He went through the black door, past the shed where the smell of the disinfectant could still be noticed. He stood hesitating, in the orange moonlight, not knowing which way to turn. He felt dazed and found that he had walked in a circle. Then he heard someone crying, a faint strangled sound of crying, from the direction of the lake.

It was so bright he could see the separate blades of grass like tiny metal spears. On the path, halfway to the stable, he found a woolen bedroom slipper. It had been shuffled about in until it was broad and shapeless. The sight of the homely object, lying there alone, moved him to an excess of apprehension.

He ran on, past the stable, through the gnarled apple trees where still a few apples hung. Near the shining golden carpet of the lake he saw two — no, three — figures: Mrs. Morton, half dressed, wringing her hands and crying hysterically, Eddy, bending over Miss Dove, who lay sprawled, a strange figure in her long white nightdress. As Lindley drew near, Mrs. Morton sank in a grotesque heap, her face against her knees.

The boy straightened himself. "It's Miss Lydia, sir. She's dead. Look. It's my knife, in her breast." His eyes were large and luminous, not terrified.

Lindley looked. Unearthly white and fragile in the moonlight, the red stain on her nightdress was spreading and her hands had torn at the tough grass.

"Why did I do it?" sobbed Mrs. Morton hoarsely. "Oh, why did I do it? Oh, God help me!"

Lindley, feeling sick, felt for Miss Dove's heart.

"She's dead all right," said the boy. "There's no need to feel. It's stopped."

Mrs. Morton threw herself on the ground but her wild eyes looked up. "She came at me in my bedroom, Mr. Lindley. I ran and she chased me through the house and down here. Then I had to face her and I took the knife from her. I don't remember doing it. I don't remember. But they'll put me in a madhouse. Oh, save me, Mr. Lindley. Save me!"

She raised herself to her knees and crept to Lindley's feet and clasped his legs. She nearly dragged him off his feet.

The boy stood up straight and white, with glittering feverish eyes. "Don't be scared, ma'am. I'll say I did it. They'd never hang a child, would they, Mr. Lindley?"

"You can't do that." Lindley spoke roughly. He felt an equal horror for the two women. Now he saw this terrible event as the natural outcome of all he had witnessed in this place. He would not let Eddy suffer for it.

But Mrs. Morton snatched at the hope. Still on her knees she moved clumsily, like some bulky animal, to Eddy, and clasped him to her. Ignoring Lindley, she gasped hoarsely, "Oh, Eddy, darling — if only you would do that! I've been kind to you, haven't I? You know what I've had to put up with . . . how she's driven me to desperation. Eddy, I'll say you were delirious. . . . You do look very strange. . . . I'll say she attacked me with the knife and that you did it, in your delirium, to save me. Oh — my God, I hear men coming!"

They could be seen, clambering up the steep bank from the shore, the black humps of their bodies lumbering up like prehistoric animals out of the lake. From the neighboring cottages they had heard the voices, the cry of Lydia Dove as the knife pierced her.

"Oh, Mr. Lindley, don't say anything to harm me, I beg of you," implored Mrs. Morton.

Eddy moved between her and the running men. "Don't you worry, ma'am. I'll look after you. They'll never hang a kid like me."

"Never! Oh, how can I reward you, Eddy? Why, there was that other boy, not long ago — he killed his own father — his father — and the boy was older than you — they didn't hang him. . . ."

The last words were lost in the shouts of the men. The three principals in the tragedy were surrounded. Mrs. Morton again sank to the grass, burying her face in her hands. But the men were looking at Lydia.

"Good God, the old lady's dead," exclaimed one.

The father of Eddy's playfellows shouted, "Grab that boy! He done it. That's his knife. My kids told me weeks ago about that knife. He was threatening to use it on somebody then. I thought it was just boys' foolery."

"You did wrong not to tell," said another man, "and this is what's come of it."

"But the boy is very ill," sobbed Mrs. Morton. "I don't think he knows what he did. I'm sure he doesn't."

"You can tell that to the police," said one of the men. "Somebody go and telephone." A man ran off, full of self-importance.

The first man put his arm about Mrs. Morton. "Let me help you back to the house, ma'am. You fellows guard that young murderer."

The two laid heavy hands on the child's shoulders.

"Do you confess you did this murder?" asked one.

"Yes, sir," the clear treble voice piped up, full of assurance. "I killed her all right. She ran at Mrs. Morton with my knife and I took it from her and killed her with it."

"How did she come to have your knife?"

"She pinched it one day in the loft and hid it."

"And you killed her?"

"Yes, sir." Eddy stood up, straight as a young sapling, eager, it seemed, to martyr himself for Mrs. Morton.

"He's ill," Lindley said hoarsely. "He's delirious."

"He don't sound delirious to me."

"I killed her," Eddy reiterated, in a thin sharp voice.

Mrs. Morton held up her hands as though calling on Heaven to witness. "He did it to save me," she cried. "My sister was going to kill me. She's often threatened me."

"That she has. I've heard 'er." Eddy put up his chest and stiffened his neck in defiance.

"What did she say?" a man asked.

"She said — 'I'll kill you yet — see if I don't.' "

"You heard her, more than once?"

"Sure I did."

"Did she say that tonight?"

"She went after her with the knife."

"Eddy!" Lindley said hoarsely. "Look at me."

Eddy raised his eyes to Lindley's face. In their dark depths Lindley saw both terror and resolution. "I won't let you do this," he said, and turned to the men. "It's impossible. The boy couldn't do it."

"He says he did," growled one. "He is old enough to know."

"I'm thirteen," said Eddy. "I've seen murder and I done this one."

Mrs. Morton began her wild crying again. Her face was terrible. She tottered to Lindley and clung to him. "Oh, Mr. Lindley," she repeated, over and over. His mouth became parched, his throat constricted. He lost the power to speak, and could only let things take their course, while he soothed her and the fit of crying passed. One of the men took off his jacket and covered Miss Dove. The group stood waiting for the constable, the low-hung, deep-colored full moon hanging above them. Those standing became equally stricken by silence as the one lying prostrate.

Silence flowed up over Eddy like a wave. His body drooped under the hands of the men. He sagged and fell.

Lindley was kneeling at his side. "I'll carry him to the house," he said. "He's a very sick boy."

"I don't think we can allow that," one of the men said importantly. "We've got to wait for the constable."

"It'd be all right," said another, "if you go with them. You can help the lady to the house. I'll wait here."

Mrs. Morton said, with her hand on her throat, "I must be here when the constable arrives. I must tell him at once just how it happened. Someone must be here who *knows* how it happened."

With a bitter look at her Lindley took Eddy into his arms. "If you want to watch the boy, come along with me," he said to one of the men. "I'm taking him to the house."

"I guess that'll be all right." The man spoke grudgingly, as though in authority.

Lindley strode away from them. They and Mrs. Morton were

strangely unreal to him. The only reality was Eddy, whose tousled head and whose face, with half-closed, glazed eyes, lay against his shoulder. Eddy was not unconscious. He said, in his clear high voice, "They'd never hang a kid like me, would they, sir?"

"Of course not." Lindley put his cheek to the boy's burning face. He strode on through the long grass sweet-smelling and wet with dew. "You're a brave boy, Eddy."

"Yes, I think I am. It takes a good deal to scare me. But I'm awful scared of hanging. You don't think they'll hang me, do you, Mr. Lindley?"

"Eddy, you're not to do this," burst out Lindley, in a protective fury. "I won't let you."

The boy's voice became sharp. "But I *will*. You can't stop me. Mrs. Morton and me, we've got it all fixed up."

He was growing excited. He struggled in Lindley's arms. He looked terribly ill in that bright moonlight. "All I want," he reiterated, "is not to be strung up."

Lindley held him close. He could feel the rapid beating of Eddy's heart. "You shall not be hurt. Leave it all to me."

"Don't you say I didn't do it, Mr. Lindley, because I'll swear I did and Mrs. Morton she'll swear I did. Even if they hang me — "

"Put that out of your mind," Lindley ordered him harshly. In his agitation he stumbled and all but fell.

Eddy clung to him. "Where are we?" he whimpered. "Where are you taking me?"

"To your bed."

He heard the constable's car coming in from the road. He stood among the shrubs till it passed. Then he turned in at the kitchen door and climbed the stairs to Eddy's room. He laid him on the bed. There again was the great ruddy moon hanging outside the small-paned window.

"My head aches," moaned Eddy. "I'm awful sick."

Lindley went downstairs and got ice from the icebox. He laid cold cloths on the boy's head and sat down beside him. The look of gratitude in Eddy's eyes hurt him. He longed for morning and the doctor.

After a time there were strange noises in the house. He guessed that Miss Dove's body was being carried in. She would be quiet now, acquiescent in all that was done to her, she who had been so domineering, so restless. There would be no more quarreling between the sisters. What hundreds of encounters they must have had in their life together! He pictured them, Mrs. Morton's face heavy with anger, Miss Dove's incensed to a fragile flame. But they were unreal to him. The only reality was the boy, lying there — the victim, yes, the victim of their violence. The boy had witnessed dreadful scenes between them and now he was brought to this.

The constable came stumping up the stairs, carrying a small oil lamp. Its light was ridiculous against the splendor of the moonlight, but it was reflected in Eddy's feverish eyes. The constable spoke loudly, as though to a deaf person.

"I arrest you for the murder of Miss Lydia Dove. Anything you say now will be held against you." He turned to Lindley. "Is he able to come with me, do you think?"

"No. He's very ill."

"He looks mighty sick and small too. D'you think he had the strength to do it?"

"I did it all right, sir," piped Eddy. "I've wanted to, ever since she took my knife."

"Your knife?"

"Yes. The one my dad gave me, over home. She swiped it."

Lindley put in, "Look here, constable, I want you to come out into the passage with me."

Eddy sat up in the bed, his face ablaze with purpose. "Don't you do it, constable. This Mr. Lindley, he's sorry for me. He thinks I'm just a kid. He doesn't know that I think nuffing about doin' an old lady in when I'm roused. You just ask Mrs. Morton. She'll tell you. I'm a dangerous fella, I am."

The constable stared at Eddy uncertainly. He said, "The kid seems delirious — clean off his head. Well — I've put him under arrest. Do you guarantee to guard him till morning, sir?"

"I'll guard him," Lindley said grimly.

The constable looked Eddy over. He had boys of his own. "This is a mighty sad case," he said.

Lindley took the man by the arm and spoke low into his ear. "This child didn't do it. He's got to be protected. He has some crazy notion . . ."

Eddy sprang from the bed as though galvanized. He pushed Lindley with all his strength. He shouted:

"Don't you mix yourself up in this, Mr. Lindley! The constable, 'e knows how to make a arrest wivout you 'elping him."

"He's delirious all right," said the constable. "I guess I'd better go."

Lindley picked up Eddy and put him back on the bed. He lay passive now, his glittering eyes fixed on the men. A smile bent his lips. When the constable had gone he hugged himself, as though in an excess of pride in his own importance.

"I *did* want to kill her, Mr. Lindley," he laughed. "I really did and now I've done it!" He rolled on the bed laughing or crying, Lindley could not tell which.

Under the sloping roof, he spent the long night with the boy, feeling nearer to him than he ever had to anyone since he himself was a boy. Sometimes Eddy's mind was quite clear. At other times he was confused and seemed scarcely to know where he was.

"Mr. Lindley," he said once, "this is pretty bad for your book, I bet. I bet you'll be too tired to write tomorrow. How many pages have you written? Is it a funny book, an adventure book or a sad book? Will you sell it yourself? How much will it cost?"

He never waited for an answer but just rambled on, seeming not to hear clearly what Lindley said. But always he sought for the comfort of Lindley's hands. Sometimes he would catch one of them in his and put his dry lips against it. Toward morning his mind became more confused. He would cry out, — "There's my dad! Stop him before he gets away!" Then he would think he was on a ship in a rough sea, and cling to the sides of the cot and cry out in fear.

"Oh, Mr. Lindley, hang on — hang on! Gosh, what waves!"

"You're all right, Eddy." Lindley would steady him with his hands.

"But 'ow this old boat rocks! My dad wouldn't sail on such a boat. I wish we could get off, Mr. Lindley."

"We shall. We'll soon be there."

"Where?"

"On shore."

"In Canada?"

"Yes."

Suddenly the boy screamed in terror. "I see a body in the water! It's Miss Dove. Oh, I say, Mister, I want to get off this boat!"

Again and again Lindley soothed him, gave him cool drinks. That little room became the whole world to them, a world of pain and fear, and a desperate clinging together.

I X

The moon was gone, the interminable night was gone and the gray flat daylight came in at the window. The boy had fallen asleep and Lindley, in his chair, had dozed. He was so weary, so stiff, that when Mrs. Morton came into the room he had trouble getting to his feet. He gave her a searching look. She appeared ten years older, her eyes sunken and the lines in her face greatly deepened. But she had tidied her hair and put on a fresh blouse. She leant over the bed.

"What sort of a night did he have?" She was obviously straining for self-control. Her hands were clenched and she breathed as though climbing the stairs had been an effort.

"Very miserable," answered Lindley coldly.

Eddy opened his eyes. He looked up at them dazed, then passed his tongue over his lips, which had a black line on them, before he asked, "Is that you, ma'am?"

"Yes, Eddy. Can you eat some breakfast? Some bread and milk?" Her voice trembled as though she were very old and weak.

He shook his head. "No. I'm just thirsty." Then he sat up in bed and threw the question at her, like a shot from a pistol. "You did run my knife into Miss Lydia, didn't you?"

As though she had indeed been struck, Mrs. Morton fell to her knees by the bed and raised her face to the boy's. "You know what you promised, Eddy! To save me. I won't let them hurt you — I swear." She was almost unintelligible.

He answered, with the old cocky self-assurance. "Course I remember now. I thought I'd been dreaming. Don't you be afraid, ma'am. But — " his anxious eyes sought Lindley's — "you're sure they won't hang me, Mr. Lindley? I'd be awful scared of that."

"They won't hang you," Lindley answered through his clenched teeth. He was filled with repulsion for Mrs. Morton, as she fondled the boy's hand.

The doctor had heard of the murder and he came early. Eddy greeted him with a strange delirious account of the murder, repeating over and over again that he had stabbed Miss Dove because she tried to kill Mrs. Morton and he liked Mrs. Morton and he didn't like Miss Dove and did the doctor think they'd hang a kid like him?

The doctor listened, his calm physician's face unresponsive, his deft hands moving over the boy's body. "Quiet now — quiet now," he said once or twice, and held the stethoscope to his ears. A load was being lifted from Lindley. He drew a deep breath, as he felt it shift from his shoulders to the doctor's. He now noticed the wind rustling the vines and a patter of raindrops on the low roof. He pressed a thumb and middle finger to his throbbing temples.

He heard Eddy reiterate his dreadful question and the doctor's reassuring answer, as though the boy had asked, "Do you think they'll thrash me?"

The doctor turned to Lindley and said, in a whisper, — "It's typhoid. I must get him into the hospital."

Eddy overheard. " 'Ospital!" he cried. "Oh, I am glad. They treat you fine there. Ain't you going to let them arrest me then, Doctor?"

"Don't you worry." The doctor began to roll him up in a blanket.

"Do you want me to go with you?" Lindley asked of the doctor, a sudden longing to escape from Eddy gripping him. "If I can be of use . . ."

"Thanks — but my son is with me. He drives the car. I shall carry this little fellow." He gathered Eddy into his arms. The boy was now just a sausage-shaped bundle. His eyes were closed. "I think he's dropped off," the doctor said. He hesitated in the doorway. "I've known these sisters for many years. Lydia Dove was a mental case and nothing that could happen here would seem impossible but — I'm sorry this boy is mixed up in it."

Lindley got out, "If he didn't do it. If it was Mrs. Morton — what would happen?"

"Well — it would be prison or an asylum — depending on the evidence, and the jury. Have you any evidence? Were you there when it happened?"

"No. Miss Dove was dead when I got there."

Miss Dove was still in the house. Still she was in the house. As still as death. . . . Eddy was gone. Lindley and Mrs. Morton alone lived there. A few old friends came to see Mrs. Morton and condole with her. Everyone said what a shock her sister's dreadful death had been to her. She looked so ill. Curious people found their way into the grounds to stare at the house. Lindley remained shut away in his own apartment. The strange thing was that he was able to write. Never before had the flow of his imagination been so strong. Weary as he was, he worked all morning and again at night. Only by work could he control his mind. The boy's small figure, his head with its tumbled light-brown hair, bobbed like a cork in the maelstrom of Lindley's thoughts. Sometimes he would fancy he heard that quick, uneven step coming in at the door. Sometimes those luminous eyes looked up at him from the page.

The weeks passed in a kind of dream. The inquest, which Lindley was forced to attend as a witness, was over. Through the doctor he heard of Eddy's struggle for life, his improvement and his recovery. "He is a good patient. All the nurses are fond of him. It's a great pity he got into this trouble at the start of his life. The worst is that he shows no contrition. He takes great pride in having saved Mrs. Morton's life."

Several times Lindley made up his mind to go and see the boy, when he was stronger. He would have it out with him, force him to give up this insane idea of protecting Mrs. Morton. But then Mrs. Morton's tortured face would confront him — prison or an asylum. It would mean the end of her life. He thought of her playing Mendelssohn's "Songs Without Words." Sometimes her eyes, when they met his, had an anguished appeal in them but more often a growing confidence brightened them. Lindley's power of pity was such that, even while he shrank from the sight of her, he felt compassion to see the gray-haired woman hard at work rebuilding her life. She still was looking ill and Lindley could see that she was worrying about the time when Eddy would be well enough to appear before a magistrate. Lindley wondered what she did with herself all day, with no boy to order about and no Miss Dove to quarrel with. She told him she slept badly of nights.

Once a week she went to see Eddy and each time, on her return, sought out Lindley to tell him of the boy's improvement. Always she ended by saying, "He's such a nice little boy — in many ways. I've grown quite fond of him." She plainly showed that she did not want Lindley to go to the hospital. "Now that he's convalescent the quieter he is kept the better, so the nurses tell me. I really think it might excite him if you went." There was something almost pious in her attitude as she crossed her hands on her stomach.

Lindley, ever more deeply immersed in his book, found it easy to be persuaded. He wanted to free himself of the boy, wanted to feel that he was less real than the characters in his book.

The time came for the trial and Lindley tore himself from his work to attend it as a witness. Eddy looked ridiculously small and young. Mrs. Morton looked as though she might be about to collapse, but her voice was strong and vibrant as she told of her sister's mental deterioration, of her attack on her, that early autumn night, of how the boy had struggled with Miss Dove, torn the knife from her grasp and plunged it into her heart. She used just those words. The judge expressed wonder that so small a boy could have overcome a woman in such frenzy.

"But I was stronger then, your Lordship," piped up Eddy,

the look of readiness to martyr himself bright on his face. "I killed her all right with the knife my dad gave me."

Lindley testified that he had not come on the scene till after the crime was committed, but he had known Miss Dove to be in a hysterical and violent condition. Had Mr. Lindley seen the knife before that night? Yes. He had once taken it from the boy. What had the boy been doing with the knife when Mr. Lindley took it from him? He had been playing with it — showing off. What had Mr. Lindley done with the knife? He had put it in a drawer in his own room, but the boy had found it and regained possession of it. And later Miss Dove had taken the knife from the boy? Yes, she had.

Then Lindley told of the cleaning of the shed, of the boy's gradual sickening and of what he believed to be his state of semi-delirium, on the night of the murder. All the while he kept his eyes averted from Eddy and from Mrs. Morton.

The doctor's testimony was entirely in Eddy's favor. Eddy had been in a high fever when he first called to see him. He would not be surprised if the child had been quite delirious when the deed was done. The doctor stressed the word child and, in contrast to Lindley, his eyes frequently rested on Mrs. Morton.

Eddy Lennard was sent to a boys' reformatory to remain there till he was eighteen years of age. He would be taught a trade. The general opinion was that Mrs. Morton had been most magnanimous in her evidence. She had stressed the growing harshness of Miss Dove to the boy and his devotion to herself. She did not want his young life to be blighted by this evil beginning. Nevertheless people thought it had been dangerous for those two women living alone to take the Home boy into their house.

The trial was brief and, when it was over, Lindley hastened from the courthouse and made his way, against a gale that made him bend and grip his hat, to the back of the building.

Without hindrance he entered a narrow hall and saw four people sitting on a bench with a policeman on guard. Two were young men, handcuffed, waiting to be taken to the penitentiary. One was a ramshackle-looking female. The fourth was Eddy. The policeman stopped Lindley. "You can't come in here without a permit," he growled.

"I just want a word with the boy. Please let me."

"It's against the law."

"But he's just a child. He's been ill. I only ask two minutes' talk with him."

Eddy sprang up and came to Lindley's side.

"Oh, hello, Mr. Lindley. I'm glad you came to see me."

He looked very fragile and tidier than Lindley had ever seen him. His hands were white and clean, with the cleanliness of the hospital. He clasped them about Lindley's arm. Lindley had forgotten how clear and sweet was his voice.

"They're not going to hang me," he said on a joyful note. "It's just going to be a reformatory."

"I know." Lindley's eyes devoured Eddy's changed looks — his pallor, his fragility. He said, "I told you not to be afraid, Eddy, that they wouldn't — "

"Sure you did, Mr. Lindley, but I was scared. I heard of a boy who was hanged for stealing a sheep."

"But that was more than a hundred years ago. . . . Eddy!"

"Yes, sir."

"When you come out . . ."

"Oh, yes, sir. I'll look you up. I shall be eighteen then, grown up."

A burly man entered the passage from outside.

"Where's the boy for the reformatory?" he demanded.

"Here," answered the policeman. Eddy drew away from Lindley and stood erect, with a stiffening of the neck, a look of resolution.

The burly man stared down at him, as though in discomfiture. "*That!*" he ejaculated. "Whew!"

Eddy pushed out his chest and looked the man in the eyes. "I'm your party," he said, with his old Cockney assurance.

"Well, come along with you. I've no time to waste."

"You'd better put the bracelets on him," remarked one of the handcuffed young men, and the ramshackle woman, for apparently no reason, burst into tears.

"Good-by, Mr. Lindley," Eddy called out.

Lindley twisted his face into what he hoped looked like a cheerful smile, then, with a sick heart, turned homeward.

For a week after the trial Lindley was unable to work. He sat alone in his room brooding. Before his heavy eyes he saw enacted again one scene after another. That scene in the thick orange-colored moonlight by the lake . . . the night in Eddy's room . . . Miss Dove's funeral, with Mrs. Morton audibly weeping by the grave . . . the inquest . . . the trial, which came to seem more and more grotesque, so that when he thought of it he would hear himself laughing — that sliver of a boy and all those grown-up people — and he innocent!

Lindley's emotions were divided between love for the boy and hate for Mrs. Morton. In those days Eddy became a symbol to him of all he longed for. He wanted to possess Eddy's future, to invent him, as he might a character in his book. He wanted to go in strength and tear him from that house of correction. He wanted to take Mrs. Morton by force and throw her into such a one. He saw her, day by day, regaining her composure, beginning to look her old energetic self. She was very thoughtful in keeping out of his way. Once, however, she spoke to him in a warm, sympathetic tone. "Little did I dream, Mr. Lindley, when I promised you perfect quiet for your writing, that such terrible things would happen. But now all will be different." She turned away and then added, "But he was a nice little boy, wasn't he?"

A nice little boy! But *was* he? And, in truth, *what* was he? A child from a strange past, cast up by the sea of chance on this distant shore. Yet how vividly were pictures of him woven into Lindley's mind — bathing in the lake with the neighbor's boys, washing dishes in the kitchen with his childish arms immersed in the soapy water, swaggering and threatening an imaginary opponent with his knife, clinging to his cot in his delirium. His life was so short, he lived passionately in the present. Lindley, his mind crowded by memories, relived scenes of the past, lived in the creation of his book, while Eddy, with only a handful of memories, and some of these terrifying, must rejoice more and suffer more in the happenings of the moment.

The weather turned suddenly frosty. Lindley found it difficult to keep warm in his rooms. But the cold stimulated him, refreshed his weary mind. Again he threw himself into his work. So absorbed did he become, it seemed that a beneficent veil had been drawn between him and the disturbing events of the autumn. Winter came early with snow transforming the grounds to a thick white silence. The alighting of a bird on the cedar tree outside his window would loose a fine spray of glittering snow. More and more Lindley turned his thoughts inward on himself and his book, pushing Eddy outside by force of will. It would have been easier for him had the boy not been lame. Still that young halting step came to haunt him at times, making him turn his head, with a quickening of the heart, to make sure he was alone.

At Christmas Lindley *was* alone in the house, for Mrs. Morton had been invited to spend a week with another widow, an old girlhood friend. He was pleased when she told him of the proposed visit, while commiserating with him at being left alone in that season. He wanted to be alone. She told him she had sent a little present to Eddy at the reformatory and written him a letter. She looked quite pleased with herself. When she left him Lindley was muttering beneath his breath, "Murderess." He was alarmed by the vehemence of his antagonism to her. He would find himself thinking of things he might say to her, like — "How do you feel about going off on a holiday while that poor boy is spending his Christmas in a reformatory?" or — "You are fortunate in finding such a protector as Eddy," or even — "Look as smug as you like, guilt is sticking out all over you."

Then he would picture her in a penitentiary or shut away in a madhouse and his heart would soften in compassion — but not for long. Soon the bitterness of what she and her sister had done to the boy's life would begin to ferment in him again, like a bitter yeast.

Yet, when she was gone and he left alone, he felt desolate in that house. Suddenly it seemed full of sounds — Eddy's step, the tapping of Miss Dove's stick, the playing of the piano. He tried to think of a Christmas present for Eddy and remembered how he had heard him wish for a toy airplane. The following day he took the bus into the small town and found a shop where stationery and toys were sold. The airplanes were rather shoddy, he thought, probably they would be put out of order in the first flight, but Eddy was not critical and the gift would show that he was remembered. He bought one and as he carried it back to his rooms he pictured the child's look of glad surprise when he opened the package.

But when Lindley had it boxed and neatly wrapped he found that he could not remember Eddy's surname. Of late his memory had been playing him tricks. Now, try as he would, he could not unearth that name. God knew, he had heard it uttered pompously enough in the courtroom!

Then he recalled having seen Eddy carve it on the wall of the shed, after the work of cleaning was done. He hastened through the deep snow to the shed and found the name staring at him from the frost-gray wall — Edwin Lennard! It was like Eddy's hand stretched out to touch him.

He climbed the stairs from the kitchen to Eddy's room and stood looking down on the cot where he had watched over him and which was now only a bare mattress. The little room was bitterly cold. Probably Eddy was more comfortable in the reformatory. Lindley went back to his own room and his writing. He wondered what his life would have been if those people in the other half of the house had never entered it. He would never be the same again after those long months under that roof. He made up his mind then that when his book was finished he would go to the reformatory to see Eddy.

When his book was finished! He took the pile of manuscript from its drawer and weighed it in his hands, as though he might discover from its weight its value. Well — good or worthless — he had a feeling of pride in the sheer bulk of his principal achievement. The mere writing of five hundred pages of manuscript required a great deal of effort. If its yellowing pages ended in a forgotten cupboard, he would, at the least, have had one year of doing what he wanted to do. Perhaps it would make his name known, make him independent of the civil service. Bright visions would then float before his mind — of himself in foreign lands, and he would, for the time, forget all about the boy.

In truth, as the weeks went on, through the inexorable winter months, he thought of him less and less. He thought only of his book. He became afraid to go for a walk lest, in his absence, the house might be burned down and his manuscript destroyed.

Then one morning he discovered small footprints in the snow leading to the kitchen door, then away from it toward the lake — a boy's footprints. He followed them, walking faster and faster, breaking through the thick crust of the snow, till he ran, shouting Eddy's name. When he reached the frozen lake, with its hummocks like Eskimo igloos, he saw climbing up one of them the boy from the cottage who used to play with Eddy. Lindley retraced his steps, with a feeling of profound disappointment. Yet, he asked himself, what would he have done with the child, had he been there? He should have been forced to return him to the reformatory. He could not keep him. He was powerless to help him.

When Mrs. Morton returned after Christmas she brought with her the friend she had been staying with, who was now going to make her home here. The friend was fat and cheerfully bustling and, in spite of himself, Lindley found her presence comforting, though he told himself he hated both women. She had not been in the house a week when Mrs. Morton again began to play the piano in the evenings.

On the first occasion Lindley could scarcely credit what he thought of as her coarse-grained stupidity. He had been about to light his pipe but he let the match go out and, with the bowl of the pipe in his hand, went to the dividing door. She was playing some chords and an exercise to limber her fingers. Then she broke into "The Skaters' Waltz," with almost girlish gaiety. Lindley pictured Lydia Dove languishing gracefully on the sofa, breathing the atmosphere of her beautiful young womanhood. But he knew that the fat newcomer was ensconced in the rocking chair, rocking cheerfully in time to the waltz.

These two women appeared completely happy. The friend had means, which meant that Mrs. Morton was now much more comfortable financially. She began once more to look the picture of health. But she still wore deep black, in mourning for her sister.

X

The day came when Lindley had finished his book. It was February and a blizzard was blowing. He could not go out for the exercise he needed, but paced restlessly up and down the room, now uplifted on a wave of hope, now filled with an almost tremulous questioning of the future. He longed to speak to someone — someone who could, even remotely, understand his emotion. Again and again he took up the last page of the manuscript and read the final paragraph, and laid it down again.

He must tell someone.

He opened the outer door and was met by the blast of biting snowflakes. He turned up the collar of his jacket and, slamming the door behind him, ran round to the kitchen. When he opened that door and appeared before Mrs. Morton she was frying two pork chops over the coal fire. Her cheeks were rosy from heat. She looked a little startled at his bursting in on her like this.

"Oh, Mrs. Morton," he got out, feeling suddenly rather shamefaced, "I've — finished my book!"

For a moment she looked blank, as though she had forgotten all about his book. Then she gave her wide, genial smile. "Oh, how very nice for you, Mr. Lindley. You must be very happy." She had a long-bladed kitchen knife in her hand, with which she was to turn over the chops. He stood staring at the hand that held the knife — a strong, capable hand. . . . She laid it down and held out both hands to him. "I *am* so pleased. Dear me, it seems a long time since you began it. The time has just flown."

He could not help himself. He took her hands and held them a moment. He could hear the creak of the rocking chair in the dining room.

"And I suppose that now you will be leaving. I shall be sorry to lose you."

"Thank you," he muttered and withdrew his hands.

"You once spoke of wanting to travel. Perhaps you'll do that now."

"I can't afford it — yet. But I shall be giving up my rooms at the end of the month."

"But — Mr. Lindley, I think we arranged for a month's notice."

"True. I had forgotten. A month from today then."

She pressed her hand to her forehead. "How I dislike these business details."

"It was very stupid of me to forget."

Smoke began to rise from the sizzling chops.

Embarrassed, feeling rather foolish, Lindley apologized for his untimely visit. She scarcely heard him. The air was filled with blue smoke.

How hollow, how empty, seemed his apartment, now that the characters that lived for him had closed the door of creation in his face. Now they stood alone, independent of him. But he felt better for that brief excursion through the blizzard. He mixed himself a glass of whiskey and water, lighted his pipe and began to make plans. An hour passed.

A tapping came on the door which divided the house. It was the second time this had happened since his coming (the first had been Eddy). He strode to the door and apprehensively called out:

"Anything wrong?"

"Oh, no, Mr. Lindley. But I'm wondering if — now your book's finished — you'd mind if I'd play the piano more often. My friend is fond of music and this sort of weather makes things pretty quiet."

"Please go ahead and play . . . play whenever you wish," Lindley called back. "It won't trouble me at all."

In a few minutes the sound of the piano came to him. With startling clarity he pictured Eddy, sitting on his hands, in the little chair by the kitchen door, listening enthralled, his attitude striking in its innocence and grace. Lindley stood transfixed, absorbing the vision, his compassion for the child welling up into an almost angry desire to see the boy — not at some vague date, but now. He would have liked to forget Eddy. He would be free of him, as he was now free of the characters in his book. But the urgency was there. He must see him once more, find out if there was anything he could do for him.

The remainder of the day was spent by Lindley in dreamlike uncertainty. The gale and snowstorm continued. He spent an hour in weary, yet delicious, relaxation, making plans. Then, restless and full of nervous energy, he paced the floor, driven by a confusion of thoughts. If only he had someone to talk to — someone who would understand. Off and on, throughout the day, he heard the piano.

The following morning was bright and calm. Lindley wrapped his manuscript and took it into town to a typist. It was like leaving a part of himself in the hands of an unfeeling stranger. On his return he began the task of tidying his papers, destroying unwanted notes, answering long-neglected letters. He came upon Eddy's childish scrawl, thanking him for the plane. He had ended it with the words: "Love to all. Yours respectfully, Eddy."

For the next month Lindley went each week to retrieve that portion of his manuscript which had been typed, along with the typescript. The task of polishing and revision kept him busy till the next visit to town.

In these days Mrs. Morton never met him without inquiring brightly how the work was progressing. But he had the feeling that she scarcely listened to his answer. She was full of plans for spring — long-delayed repairs on the house were to be made. She had let Lindley's apartment to a gentleman, "rather a mental case but so nice and quite harmless," and his male nurse, at double the present rent. Probably she would be glad to be rid of him and of the memories evoked by his presence.

The day came when he posted his novel to a publisher and, inside the hour, boarded a train to take him to the reformatory.

During the train journey he had a feeling of exhilaration. The burden, the long strain of his book, was lifted from him. He was on his way to see someone who, he realized with a flash of astonishment, meant more to him than any other human being. He had been singularly free of human ties and had cherished that freedom. Now he found himself eager to forge afresh the bond between himself and Eddy.

Yet Eddy was a prisoner and would be for more than four years longer. And at the end of that time what would the boy have become? Possibly a hardened young reprobate. As Lindley left the train and hired a taxi for the reformatory, he felt an increasing apprehension. Perhaps even these few months would have changed Eddy. Better perhaps to have kept the memory of what he had been.

He told the driver to wait for him and walked slowly toward the large, bare building that stood at the end of a long, bare driveway. The building was not exactly grim, but impersonal. The young trees which had been planted about it had done nothing to alter this, but stood as though in youthful helplessness. Why were we planted here? they seemed to say — we can do nothing to change the character of this pile of bricks and mortar.

It was a day of March wind and high white clouds. Last year's grass was flat in the pale sunshine. A group of older boys were digging a drain in the soaking clay. A band of crows flew low above this upturned earth but were fearful to come to rest. Their loud cries echoed against the flat front of the building. There was a great bareness about the place.

Lindley was shown into a hall, with a linoleum-covered floor and the smell of disinfectant and many boys. He waited here for a while and then was taken to the superintendent's room. His geniality was as impersonal as the building. He looked up Eddy's name in a file, fluttering the leaves nervously with long gray fingers. When he read the notes on Eddy he compressed his lips and looked hard at Lindley.

"A very serious case," he said, in a flat voice.

"How is he getting on?"

"Very well, I believe. I don't have any complaints of his behavior. Not now. At first he was inclined to boast to the other boys of what he had done but, when we found out, we put a stop to that."

"Oh." Lindley hesitated and then asked, "How do you put a stop to things?"

"Well, generally by cutting privileges. But sometimes — not often — we use the strap."

"I see." Lindley was picturing Eddy under the strap.

"He's a pretty well-behaved boy," went on the superintendent. "He has an unusually good singing voice. Best voice we've ever had here, the teacher says."

"I've noticed his speaking voice but I didn't know he could sing."

"Neither did he — not till we discovered it. That's what we do here. Find out the boys' capabilities."

"Perhaps there's a future for him in his voice." Lindley was eagerly thinking of how he might pay for singing lessons for Eddy, how he would become a great singer.

"Of course, his voice may be worth nothing after it changes."

"Of course," agreed Lindley, the light gone out of his face.

The superintendent made no difficulty over Lindley's seeing the boy. With that same genial, yet detached air, he summoned a pimply-faced young man and told him to send Edwin Lennard to that room. He then returned with absorption to the reports he was studying. Lindley listened, his ears straining for the sound of that uneven footfall. He kept his eyes on the door, and all the anger and pain he had suffered for Eddy now showed in his face. He was afraid to see what change might have taken place in him, for in spite of his beginnings Eddy had had a look of un-sullied innocence in his face. Would not the very fact of being a prisoner have changed him? A prisoner. Even though they boasted of doors not locked, of boys who might run away if they chose, where could a child like Eddy run to? A little crim-inal — a little murderer — and I, thought Lindley, helped to bring him to this — because I did nothing. If a degraded Eddy comes in by that door I shall never feel the same again.

Suddenly the step was coming; eager, unaccompanied, it moved nearer. The door opened and he stood there.

"Come in and close the door after you." The superintend-ent's voice was now genially authoritative. His order obeyed, the typed pages again claimed him.

Eddy's eyes and Lindley's met and, for an instant, each saw reflected that scene by the lake. It rose tangible and solid be-tween them. Eddy was the first to be able to push its power and its terror away. He came a step closer and now Lindley saw him clearly.

He gave his wide, child's smile. "Oh, hello, Mr. Lindley." He appeared to be not at all abashed by the presence of the superintendent.

Lindley thought, "Why, he's grown — " then discovered that he looked taller chiefly because he was thinner. His head ap-peared smaller, for his thick, untidy, light-brown hair had been cropped short. But it was the beauty of the luminous eyes in that small, pale face which held Lindley. He felt, for a moment, overpowered by the strength of this attraction. After a period of calm, almost of forgetfulness, a crisis of emotion again struck him. He could not speak but forced his lips to a smile.

"It's mighty kind of you to come and see me," Eddy was say-ing. "It's like old times."

The superintendent raised his eyes from his papers and lis-tened.

"We used to have good times, didn't we?" Eddy went on. "Do you remember how Mrs. Morton used to play the piano in the evenings? Does she ever play now?"

"Yes, sometimes."

Eddy looked pleased. "And how glad Miss Dove was when I found the silver spoon in the old shed?"

Miss Dove! How could he utter that name? But he spoke it with no embarrassment and its gentle syllable fell like an explosion on the quiet air.

"I remember."

"Do you ever see the boys I used to play with?"

"Once in a long while. We've been very quiet."

Eddy nodded gravely. "Since Miss Dove and me are gone, of course."

There was silence for a space. The man at the desk returned to his papers. Eddy gazed tranquilly at Lindley who longed desperately to pick him up and run with him out of that building. All sounds echoed there, a sound of distant hammering beat through the passages and against the greenish drab of the walls.

A knock echoed on the door. The same young man who had admitted Lindley, now entered and went to the superintendent with an air of bearing momentous news. The two conferred in a whisper, then the superintendent rose.

"I'm going to leave you alone with Eddy for a little," he said, showing his dark strong teeth in a genial smile. "It's not customary but you are an unusual visitor. I read in the papers, at the time of the — er — inquiry, that you are a writer."

"Yes."

"Books?"

"Well — I hope so."

The pimply-faced young man began to hiccup quite violently. The superintendent gave him an admonishing look which seemed only to make him worse. The two then marched in step, to the music of hiccups, toward the door.

When it had closed behind them Eddy hugged himself in the way Lindley so well remembered. He gave his clear, high laugh.

"Sh-h — " exclaimed Lindley.

"Old Hiccups we call him," chuckled Eddy. "Every time anything goes wrong he begins to hiccup and as there's always some-fing going wrong he's always at it."

"Tell me — what is it like here?" Lindley demanded.

"Not so bad, sir, when you get used to it. Not so bad as hanging, sir. I'm glad they didn't do that to me."

Color mounted to Lindley's forehead. How could the boy still harp on hanging? It was shocking. In anger and compassion he looked down into the upturned childish face. He sought for something to say which would change his thoughts and stammered, "That airplane I sent you — did it fly all right?"

"It lasted through Christmas Day, sir."

After another silence Lindley said, "I'm told you sing in the choir."

Eddy put up his chest and the back of his neck stiffened. "I have the best voice what's ever been in the school, sir. And another thing." He came close and spoke low. "I'm the youngest murderer they've ever had, sir. There was one fellow — he was fifteen and he'd shot another boy. That was a long while ago. But *I killed an old lady with a knife!* What do you s'pose they did with my knife, Mr. Lindley? My dad gave it to me and I'd like to have it back when I get out."

Lindley interrupted him harshly. "You didn't kill her, Eddy. Why lie about it to me?"

"If it wasn't for that, sir, I'd be nobody here. Just one of the kids. But they looks up to me."

"You are here to be reformed, Eddy," Lindley said bitterly.

Eddy chuckled. "Reformed my eye!"

Lindley caught him by the arm and looked sternly down into his eyes. "Do you mean you don't want to be good?"

The bravado faded from his face. Eddy's lips quivered. "Yes, I do want to be good, Mr. Lindley. Like I was when you and Miss Dove and Mrs. Morton and me all lived together and you were writing your book. Did you get it finished?"

"Yes. It is finished."

"Shall you go about peddling it from door to door? My word, I'd like to help you do that."

"If it's made into a book it will be sold in the shops."

"How much will it cost?"

"Two or three dollars."

"For a *book?* Whew! You *will* be rich."

"It depends on how many people will buy it."

"I'd say it depends on how many people have that much money."

"Eddy."

"Yes, sir."

"If I make some money — in the next few years — I'd like to do something for you — have you taught."

Eddy stared. "But I'm being taught *here,* sir. I'm to learn a trade."

"I don't mean a trade. I mean — well, what would you say to music?"

Eddy brought his hands together with a clap of delight. "To play in a band? Oh, I'd like that!"

"No. I meant to learn to be a singer."

"A *crooner,* eh? That'd be better still." Again his high, clear laugh rang out. "They make tons of money, don't they?"

"No. I mean to sing *good* music."

"Like Mrs. Morton played?"

"Well — yes."

"Could I be with you?"

What hopes was he putting into the boy's mind? After five years in this place what might he be? Probably a good-for-nothing — with no talent worth developing! The reasonable thing would be to let him learn his trade, with no expectations beyond it, but Lindley could not be reasonable when his emotions were stirred. Even if Eddy's voice, after it changed, were not worth spending money on, he could not believe that Eddy himself would ever be worthless — not with that look in his eyes — not after what he had done for Mrs. Morton.

He put his arm about the boy's shoulders and pressed him for a moment against his side. He said:

"Yes. You will be with me."

Eddy's eyes blazed with resolve and eagerness.

"I will be good," he said. "I'll work hard and I'll not brag to the boys about being — you know what. My word, I wish that four and a half years would hurry up."

Lindley, clinging to the years, said, "Not too fast. You will learn a trade and grow up in that time."

"But — if I'm going to be a musician — I don't need a trade."

"It's well to know how to use your hands."

"Just the same I wish the time would pass. I'm awful lonely here — without you and Mrs. Morton and Miss Dove." His cockiness deserted him. A spasm crossed his face as though he were going to cry.

That would be terrible. To ward it off Lindley asked, "Is there anything I can send you, Eddy? Are presents allowed?"

Eddy controlled himself. With the swiftness of a child's change of mood his face brightened. He thought a moment, standing on one leg and gently swinging the lame one. Then he said, "What I'd like best is your book when it gets printed. I've never owned a book."

"You shall have it."

"And, please sir, will you write in it? I saw books of Mrs.

Morton's and Miss Dove's that were written in. Write — 'To Edwin Lennard, with kind regards, from Mr. Lindley.' Will you do that?"

"I will," said Lindley, a little unsteadily.

The flat, hollow sound of footsteps was heard and the superintendent came into the room. He glanced at the clock.

"I'm afraid visiting time is up," he said, as though addressing the clock.

"I'll come again. I'll write." Lindley grasped Eddy's hand which felt surprisingly small and cold and rough. Now he wanted to leave as quickly as possible — to be free of this place.

A bell began to clang.

"It is the dinner bell." The superintendent withdrew his eyes, as though with difficulty, from the clock and fixed them on Eddy.

Lindley mumbled a good-by and was invited to come another time at a more convenient hour and see the boys at work. The superintendent went with him as far as the door. Lindley could hear Eddy's footsteps, hastening in a jog trot, down the hall.

Now he was outside, in the free air. His taxi was waiting. The boys who were digging the drain had disappeared. The crows were settled on the freshly turned earth. A breath, a feeling, as of Lindley's own childhood came to him. He raised his face to the swiftly moving clouds and drank the wind and freedom.

BY PETER DE VRIES

NO BUT I SAW THE MOVIE

THE TUNNEL OF LOVE

The Tunnel of Love

THE
TUNNEL
OF LOVE

by
PETER DE VRIES

Little, Brown and Company · Boston

LIBRARY OF CONGRESS CATALOG CARD NO. 54–6879

Published May 1954
Reprinted May 1954
Reprinted June 1954 (**twice**)
Reprinted July 1954
Reprinted September 1954
Reprinted October 1954

Parts of chapters 6, 11, 13, 15 and 17 of this
novel have appeared, in somewhat different
form, in *The New Yorker*.

Published simultaneously in Canada
by Little, Brown & Company (Canada) Limited

PRINTED IN THE UNITED STATES OF AMERICA

Virtues are forced upon us by our impudent crimes.

T. S. ELIOT

The Tunnel of Love

One

I DON'T know whether you've ever been interviewed by an adoption agency on behalf of friends bent on acquiring a child, or if you have, whether any doubts were in order concerning the qualifications of either of the prospective parents, or of yourself to judge, for that matter, and whether in that case you were realistic with the agency or romantic. I don't know, either, what you would have done had you been in my shoes that Saturday afternoon the caseworker called to ask if I wished to offer any opinion on Augie Poole as paternal timber. "In my shoes" is a loose metaphor, for when she arrived I was not in them. I was stretched out flat in bed with symptoms for which no organic cause could be found.

This in itself was answer enough. I tried to guard its significance from my wife, who didn't know the half of what I knew and who only said to me, "Get up, lazybones," as she pulled the slipping bedclothes off the floor or otherwise tidied up the premises for the approaching visitor. Her hands were not hyssop, neither was there meat and drink in them. Lazybones indeed! How I should have liked to deserve that charge rather than the one implicit in my prostration. A lazy man would simply have got up and gone through the motions of giving a reference, whereas some vestige of moral fiber in me caused me to malinger. The burden I bore was a complex one, involving both

Augie and myself in a mess of matters quite intimately plaited. The Augie part of the hazard consisted in my knowing him, not only better than my wife did, but better than his own did. The ordeal under which I lay was one for which the name of the imminent caseworker struck me as abysmally apt: It was Mrs. Mash. That was enough to throw cold water on anything.

My wife, at length, began to look as if she would like to throw some on me. However, she called Dr. Vancouver when I finally convinced her how punk I felt. He arrived an hour later.

My symptoms were soon rehearsed: sore throat, heavy feeling in my chest, and feverishness. Dr. Vancouver took my temperature and found it normal. Then he examined my throat, peering down it gingerly and with great care not to get himself breathed on, for he is an awful hypochondriac. "There's nothing in your throat," he said. He chucked me under the chops with his fingertips. "Perfectly O.K. Let's have a look at your chest." I loosened my pajama coat, and he tappped my trunk in several places, holding his head averted. He tested it next with a stethoscope, telling me to look well away when I coughed. "I can't find a thing anywhere," he said at last.

I watched the jaws of his alligator bag close on the stethoscope. He walked over to a chair in the far corner and sat down. Dr. Vancouver is a bald man with a ruddy complexion (like most hypochondriacs he is in perfectly satisfactory health) and a jutting nose. He has a double chin, except that he has none to begin with, which makes him rather all wattles from the mouth down. He crossed his legs and regarded me the length of the room, with such a bedside manner as the distance between us afforded. By habit he was hygienic even with patients from whom he was unlikely to catch anything.

"Has anything been troubling you?" he asked. "Some situation you want to avoid?"

"Not that I know of," I said, reaching to my nightstand for a pack of cigarettes.

"The human system is the greatest counterfeiting machine in the world. I mean in its ability to simulate symptoms. You say this feverish feeling, it's as if the underside of your skin was tender. That's a perfect description of fever, but remember you have the benefit of previous fevers to go by. Are you sure there isn't a difficult situation you don't want to face? Something you want to get out of?"

"I just want to get out of bed," I said. Let him make what he wanted of it. I could take myself with a grain of salt any time there was a necessity, which was more than could be said for anybody else in this room. It was peaceful in here and I wanted him to go away. He irked me. He was dressed to the nines in the kind of country "togs" you saw all over Avalon, Connecticut (where this was), with a pullover sweater under a jacket of barleycorn tweed, pebble-grain brogans, and no doubt a tartan cap on the hall tree, as though he had come on horseback to see me and not in his air-conditioned Buick.

Sitting up, I leaned back against the headboard. "I feel kind of faint," I said.

"That's from the rapid breathing just now when I examined your chest. Please cover your mouth when you cough."

"Why make such bones about someone there's nothing organically wrong with?" I put to him.

"That's not the point," he answered irritably. "It's no more than you'd ask of a person sitting next to you in a bus."

Not wanting him to go away angry — and sick as a dog as I was — I started to crack jokes. "I've always suspected that feeling of well-being of mine was completely psychosomatic," I said with a rather charming smile. "That underneath I was riddled with complaints."

Vancouver opened his black bag again and rummaged in it. "I try to combine the old and the new, what's good in each," he said tersely.

"I know." I appeared to have wounded him. Feeling, therefore, that I should redouble my efforts to make amends, I went on: "That's the way to be — eclectic. So why don't you give me some sulfa and molasses?"

This had the peculiar effect of making him freeze up altogether. It's hard to understand the resistance of some people to humor, which is after all only laughing at our little troubles and differences. Dr. Vancouver addressed my wife. "I'll give you some pills for him to take. And see that he gargles every hour or so with either aspirin or salt water — I don't care which. You've got the week end to rest him up in, so if he has got a slight cold or grippiness that ought to take care of it. If he doesn't feel any better by the first of the week, give me a call then."

My wife saw him out. There was a huggermugger at the front door of which I caught only the repeated word "him." Once I thought I heard "humor" in front of it. My wife returned. She stood in the bedroom doorway. Her hands still were not hyssop, neither was there meat and drink in them, though I had demonstrably eaten nothing since the night before. "You might get up and have a bite," she said. "You ought to take one of the pills now, and I'll fix you either the aspirin or the salt water to gargle with. Which would you like?"

"Suit yourself," I said "It makes no difference to me." I closed my eyes and went on: "I'll gargle on the hour. That way it'll be easier to remember when to do it again. For you as well as me." My plan was to humor her before she did that to me.

"You don't have to gargle for me, or take the pills either. Doc says you're malingering."

"Is that serious?"

"It could be."

"How long will I have to stay in bed?"

"It's twelve o'clock. Mrs. Mash will be here in two hours."

I turned over from supine to prone. I lay for some time after my wife left, thinking, through the hum of a vacuum cleaner, about Augie. To begin with, how did he himself feel about pressing a deposition out of me, knowing what I knew? You assumed it was basically Isolde, his wife, who wished to adopt a child, though he protested he wanted one just as bad. But even if he didn't, Isolde's wanting one was enough, for he was devoted to her. I knew he liked me too, with perhaps a special amused affection for the wholesome advices with which (speaking of the fate of having met him at all) I had tried to brief him on our community after he and Isolde had moved into it. Such as, "If you get mixed up with *that* crowd you'll spend every night of your life at some damned party." Such homilies performed the function served by the inverted directions which used to appear on those wine bricks manufactured during prohibition: "Caution, do not immerse in water as it will turn to wine."

My wife and I were — to undertake as systematically as possible the task of putting the sinner in that perspective that is required by charity no less than by narrative — neighbors of the Pooles as well as friends. That made everything twice as ticklish: People are allegedly forever parting friends, but how can you part neighbors? From the time we and the Pooles first met to the morning I turned over from supine to prone was three years. Augie had in that period touched me for sums of which I had lost count; but the fact that I could estimate them as upwards of two hundred dollars can be taken both as a measure of my friendship for him and my anxiety at the thought of his acquiring additional pecuniary strain. After all I had mouths of my own to feed. I never expected to get any of my departed tens and twenties back: I saw them as gone in a flutter of jockey silks. Now, Augie was not a "sporting" type — not a bit; he understood perfectly that I was paraphrasing Shakespeare when, catching him out with a *Turf Guide* after a period of professed reform, I flung out something about a man who could "post with such dexterity to racing sheets." The effect on him could not have been more tonic than it was. No, Augie's interest in the sport was part of your intellectual's colloquial underside. A kind of fine self-consciousness made him lapse into some convenient dialect or other every time he put the bite on me. "Man, Ah ain't just flat — Ah is concave," he would say by way of preamble, or, "Divil a penny it is I've got on me this day. Is it a sawbuck you could be helping me out with?" He strove by these means to give my every fresh financial nick and scratch a quality of gay inconsequence, or nothing to worry about.

Of course it would be straining at a gnat to deny Augie Poole his "character" on the ground of thriftlessness alone. It was the trouble I had swallowing camels that undid me as a witness. My situation was not unlike that of the marriage guest who must, if he know any just cause etc., speak now or forever hold his peace. That I could do neither of these accounted for my being still in a horizontal position when Mrs. Mash arrived, and for my astonishing behavior when she walked unexpectedly into the bedroom.

My wife had worked herself into a state of suspicion by the time the doorbell rang. "You know something you're not telling me," she said. "I insist you do. Is it about Augie?" I shook my head. "Is it money? Is he head over heels in gambling debts?" I shook my head. "Is it that he doesn't really want a family?" I shook my head. "Has he fallen in love with another woman?" I closed my eyes like a wearied saint.

"Mrs. Mash is here. Go answer the door."

She did. "Surely you can get up for a minute," she said as she went. "The woman coming all the way from Haversham and all. . . ."

I heard the front door open and a voice say, "I'm Mrs. Mash from the Crib." There was an exchange of greetings and then, our children being dispersed among neighbors, the women spent an unmolested hour in the living room. The data fell softly and steadily from my wife's lips. "Isolde Poole is really a swell sort. Fine with kids from what I can judge . . . took care of mine several times . . . seem to like her . . . nice roomy house and all. . . . Oh, about three years . . . income? . . . Well, my husband knows more than I about the Mr. Poole side of it."

I crept out of bed and stood with my ear to the crack of the closed door. Suddenly I heard my wife say in answer to something of Mrs. Mash's, "I don't see why not . . . not that sick . . . your head in the door anyway."

I popped back between the sheets just in time. I lay with my eyes shut tight, like bars against which my caged conscience fluttered, when the door opened. My wife said, "He's not asleep. This is Mrs. Mash. She has only a question or two to ask you, and I think it would be a shame to have her make a special trip. *She'll have to see you sometime.*"

"I can — "

"Nonsense, Mrs. Mash. Come in."

My eyes blinked open. "Oh, hello," I said, in a very husky voice. "You'd be Mrs. Mash."

Mrs. Mash was a tall woman with a mouth like a mail slot and eyes the color of soy sauce. She stole apologetically in with the assurance that the merest word was all she wanted from me concerning Augie.

"They tell me you know him well. What say, do you think he has the makings of a solid citizen and a good father?" she put to me humorously.

A peal of cracked laughter broke from my lips, and then, sitting bolt upright, I pointed helplessly at my throat, from which no further sound issued. Not a peep. Mrs. Mash looked inquiringly at my wife. I sat gesticulating for some seconds, my legs plowing the covers in my effort to recover the power of speech, which had indeed quite fled. My wife burst into tears and left the room, followed by Mrs. Mash who marched out pad and pencil in hand.

At five o'clock that afternoon my vocal chords were still dead as a doornail. And I responded to my wife's hysterical displays by snatching up a sheet of paper and scribbling on it:

Now stop this, damn it! Can spill beans about Augie in ten words, but that not fair to him. Or to me — I deeply involved too. Only fair way is to tell all from the beginning. Will do so at earliest possible moment. This throat condition like when people victims of stick-up or frightened in some other way. Voice back in few hours. Now pull yourself together. This is no way to act in front of children.

Two

WHEN I try to analyze Augie Poole, I generally get about as far as recalling a movie I once saw about a man who could dive but not swim. Having tumbled adroitly through an aerial sequence, the man would be fished, threshing and coughing, out of the water by servants and friends before he drowned. Augie is something like that in his knack for the fancier turns of life, with little or no sense of its rudiments. I remember the first time he and Isolde had dinner at my house. We were eating at a table set with some imported place mats of which my wife was especially proud — Oriental mats, I think, with some kind of cryptic figure in the center. Twirling his fork between courses, Augie peered at his, lifting a plate to do so, and said, "I do believe these are prayer rugs." Augie knows about as much anthropology as whoever it was wove the mats, but that's not the point; the point is he could just as easily have said, "I love your prayer rugs." As it was, his pedantic flourish left enough doubt in the minds of his hosts so that their eating off the mats any more was out (even if they said grace). My wife answered with a mock mock wail, "Oh, and I was so fond of them — whatever can people like us do with prayer rugs?" Isolde said, "Shoot craps," and turned her beautiful China blue eyes on her husband like two gun barrels.

I began purely as a spectator of Augie's affairs. But I became so rapidly drawn into them, and was in the end so narrowly grazed by the absurd calamity which crowned them — of which the business that rendered me mute before Mrs. Mash was not even yet the last — that I felt a little like the Kansas farmer must have felt who saw his neighbor's house picked up and deposited elsewhere by a cyclone which then, crossing the farmer's own premises, swiveled his cap around on his head, leaving the peak behind. No more of that for me.

We met the Pooles not in Avalon where we all live but forty miles away at a New York cocktail party, as befits Eastern commuting culture — those numberless intact globules of metropolitan life that float on the surfaces of numberless New Jersey, New York State and even New England country-town populations. My first glimpse of Augie at this party is sharply chased on my memory. Reedy and handsome in chalk stripes, he stood talking about Kierkegaard with gestures perfected at El Morocco, waving his drink so it just didn't spill. Near him was an exquisite creature with a face like tinted Dresden, sipping a Martini. I have always prided myself on a gift for spotting people's vocations by circumstantial evidence. When I see a girl bent on standing at right angles to herself — a heel against an instep to form a T with the feet, or her chin lined up along her shoulder as though she's slightly out of touch with herself — I know we have a model striking the photographic poses of her trade. The Dresden beauty was so patently a magazine manikin to my practiced eye that I was interested to hear the hostess say at my elbow, "That's Isolde Brown, the actress." As we watched, the object of our regard broke into animated conversation. Isolde Brown's smile was a plagiarism. It gave me no trouble. Joan Fontaine. Of course. The sort of half-smile, a one-cheek smile, the lips just parted. . . .

"And that's her husband over there — Augie Poole," the hostess said.

"Is he in advertising?"

"He's a cartoonist. Why, he must send his cartoons in to you, come to think of it." This was not my day, but what my hostess was referring to was *The Townsman*, a weekly whose picture jokes happens to be my editorial responsibility (to take care of the occupations for the moment). "I don't seem to place the name," I answered, not making the slight mental effort that would have spared me so much embarrassment later. I was mesmerized by the virtuosity that went into Isolde Brown's small talk.

"They've just moved out to Avalon, so you must come meet them," the hostess said, taking my hand.

I permitted myself to be towed across the room, reflecting on the basic connection between modeling and acting, the latter being but a series of successful postures, etc. I was soon at Isolde Brown's side, hearing her introduced as Mrs. Poole. "Tell him your story about Helmholz," the hostess said, after the presentation, and was off in a gasp of taffeta. Helmholz was a half-baked theatrical character who was then in the news in connection with a fashionable gambling raid. "I'll tell you about Helmholz," Isolde said, settling herself in an unoccupied chair and patting the ottoman for me. The woman she had been talking to had twisted off through the crowd, leaving us together.

In the press of a cocktail party everyone is in bas-relief. Friends lose a dimension; their talk, nervously disbursed for quick consumption, becomes all surface in a way that curiously drains them of characterization. Familiarity is undone — even one's wife appears at times a chattering alien. With strangers the trick is reversed. Having nothing previous to go by, you take at face value what account they give of themselves, and out of small details erect a character, for whatever it may be worth in accuracy. Quite quickly I had a full-blown version of Isolde Brown, which took a lot of checking up on later. For the moment, I could but let her represent herself as she would.

"Helmholz," she began, running the ball of a forefinger around the rim of her glass, "is a fool, sure. But then perhaps ambition makes fools of us all, at one time or another."

I have by no means yet lost the capacity for wonder, and I hung on her words, which her pretty mouth fashioned with a somewhat overprecise diction, like shapes turned out by a cookie cutter. And for the benefit, no doubt, of any producer who might be within earshot.

"I went to see him about, oh, seven years ago, when he was a producer, or trying to be. He said he wanted to know how well I could project an emotion without saying anything. So he gave me an assignment from real life. He wanted me to go to the Empire State Building and be rejected."

"He wanted you to go to the Empire State Building and be rejected?" I said softly.

She nodded, drinking. "The Observatory. That was before they had the high fence around the roof, and they were more careful about jumpers. At the window where you had to get your ticket, they watched for people who seemed moody or preoccupied. Anyone who answered that description, no ticket. That was my exercise — to be refused a ticket. If I couldn't convince the people at the ticket window that I was brooding about something, Helmholz said, how could I convince an audience in the theater?"

"This isn't what they call the Boleslavski Method, is it?" I inquired.

"The Stanislavski? No. Oh, I forgot to tell you — he wore felt slippers in his office."

"And did you do it?" I asked, flabbergasted by an image of a girl shuffling up to a ticket window to register anxiety with a mouth that reminded me of nothing but that fine old-fashioned simile about snow in a rose.

She tipped the dregs of her Martini into it. She was a moment chewing the olive — business, as they call it in the theater. I relieved her of the glass and set it on a table with a little craftsmanship of my own.

"I left Helmholz's office at one o'clock that afternoon. Two hours later, Helmholz got a phone call from a distracted girl who said she had not only been stopped at the ticket window but had been taken to the police station. I was there now, I told him hysterically, and would he hurry over in God's name and straighten this thing out. Well, I was calling from a phone booth in the drugstore downstairs of his office. His office was on the second floor. I hurried out of the drugstore and met him as he came running down the stairs, felt slippers and all, and sort of clawing his way into his overcoat. 'How was that for an imitation of a woman in distress?' I asked him. 'Did I convince you?' His eyes went so." She lowered her lids in a graphic rendition of reptilian menace. "I never got an interview with him again, let alone an audition."

I was curious about one thing. "Did you do this with your tongue in your cheek or were you serious about it the way he was?" I asked.

"Hm? Well, Helmholz never did put on a play. His only plays were the plays he made for the gals. I don't even know whether he had a script then. Oh well, so it was no loss. Poor old ham," she said sympathetically, and again I saw the derivative smile.

Well, any number can play at that game, and while waiting to fall asleep that night I gave her her head as Joan Fontaine, playing myself the man Helmholz could never be. The action of many of my daydreams took place at an imaginary lodge I have on a remote promontory of the Maine coast, which I call Moot Point. "Because of some legal kink in the deed," I told her, sucking in my cheeks in the manner of Clark Gable. We were strangers who had collided on the beach in a sudden downpour, and now she sat in the cottage propped among my hypothetical cushions, after a hot shower and dressed in my pajamas, which were way too big for her. I emerged from the bath myself wearing the terry-cloth "blotter" robe also essential to this scene, my neck scarved in additional toweling, and as I shuffled off in matching mules to the kitchen to brew some tea I drew taut the cord and said, "I probably don't own the place at all."

Sipping the steaming oolong we got better acquainted.

"I like to take absurdly long walks in the rain," she told me about herself. "And I like Pogo and Edna Millay and those crazy puzzle shops along Sixth Avenue. I love those foolish little flower carts in the Village. And I like men who don't worry about deeds to things, and smoke a pipe held together with adhesive tape." The eyelashes swept downward and there was the half-smile, with perhaps a touch of some winsome and muted early wildness. "Oh, and deep woods and the smell of pine. I love pine."

"I love yew."

"We mustn't."

She was soon unmasked as an aspiring actress who had con-

trived the encounter on the beach, knowing I was a noted producer holing in at my Maine retreat to read scripts. I had her
recite to me in pear-shaped tones. Later we went to town and
bought tone-shaped pears. Oh, we were silly like that for a
month or more, silly and insanely lazy, knowing the hard work
ahead, for I had decided to undertake her debut. More than
merely talented, she had drawn me out of a husk of misanthropy
into the sun and the fun again. . . .

This was among the reveries with which I detained myself
in the days following the party, during which I wondered when
I would see her again, of which I naturally had every expectation. Three weeks passed without my running into either her
or Augie, whom I had met at the party long enough to shake
hands with, and I forgot about them. I saw their house, once,
for though it turned out to be on our road it wasn't on the way
to the station I commuted from. Then one afternoon as my
train was rolling into the Avalon station I caught sight of Isolde
swaying in the aisle. She flashed a smile of recognition down
the length of the coach, over a shoulder draped with a scarf of
crimson wool. That evening, my wife being dug in at the
telephone, I settled down with an after-dinner bottle of beer
and was soon far away at Moot Point, deep in divagations of a
worldlier order than previously. Then, I had arisen to breakfast
from a couch on which I had all night humorously revolved in
search of a comfortable position, for I had given the girl my
bed. This time it was another story, and she expected to be
made an honest woman.

"Yes, I've given a lot of thought to marriage — that's why
I'm single," I said, striding out to the porch and pitching my
cigar into the disreputable sea.

Friends have noticed — or at least I have noticed — a resemblance between my diction and that of George Sanders. There is the same closed-mouth delivery, the same urbane sense of everything being murmured. These and a knowledgeable fatigue, a sort of offhand *Weltschmerz*, together with features at once fleshy and sensitive, complete the similarity, which is marked enough for purposes of meditation.

"You're trying to make me hate you because you think I'm just grateful to you for making me a star," she said in a later scene, as the surf of applause beat undiminishing against the dressing-room door. "But I don't want this — now — I want us. Oh, Bruce, we'll go where we can hear the larks again."

"Larks, my dear, should be had, not heard. Take another bow now, and I'll see you at the party."

But the chit had proved unquenchable. Now she had followed me here to Connecticut where all along I'd had a wife I'd never admitted. Presently the two must meet — all three of us. What a nasty mess, to be tidied out of whatever faith and courage and plain sense we had between us —

I had been aware of my factual wife hanging up a real-life phone, then of the phone having rung again. "Swell, we'd love to," I heard her say, and hang up again.

She came into the living room where I was nursing my lager.

"That was Mrs. Poole. You remember — we met them at the Crandons' cocktail party," she said. "It seems they live up the road in the old Shively place."

"Oh, yes." I slid up in my chair and got a grip on my glass of beer. I was a bit startled, I must say. "What did she want?" I asked, picking up my drink.

"She wants us to take in a movie with them. Come on. Get up and put a tie on. It's that mystery we both want to see. Snap out of it. I'll call Mrs. Goodbread and see if she can sit."

❨ 18 ❩

Three

I HAD chance enough to be of service, though I didn't know it yet. Not, to be sure, to make a star of Isolde, but to edit into printability the cartoons her husband kept turning out and sending to *The Townsman* — the more Herculean of the two challenges you may be sure. They knew about my magazine connection, but I still hadn't tumbled about Augie's name: some stopcock in charge of my peace of mind held the recognition back. They had the grace not to bring the matter up deliberately and nothing was mentioned after the movie, when we dropped into a bar for a drink.

Isolde had on the bright wool scarf above which, and beneath hair the color of ripe wheat, her smile played, ionizing my stream of consciousness. Augie had on a brown tweed coat and a turtle-neck sweater, which gave him a vaguely profligate air. They were a handsome couple all right in their casual splendor. Spattered brogans completed their accommodation to the country. I felt like a hick in my banker's gray flannel and tie that went well with it.

Trying to keep an ice cube submerged in a Tom Collins with two straws, Isolde asked: "How many children do you have?"

"Four," I answered sheepishly.

"Jesus," Augie said ambiguously. Isolde looked at him as,

Fontaine all forgot, a smile split her face like a coconut. "We'd like to have some. Ever so much."

She had, as the philharmonic commentators say of horns and woodwinds, stated the theme of our relationship; but it passed undetected, as a musical motif will slip by the unapprised listener. The talk went from this to that, and we parted with the Pooles asking us to dinner the following Friday. We could make it.

When we arrived, Isolde let us in. She was wearing raspberry-colored slacks and a white peasant blouse, and blowing at an errant strand of hair, for she had been busy in the kitchen. Augie hove into view, wearing a denim coat and a silk scarf knotted with the proper casualness, even a touch of contempt. He was suavely stirring a shaker of Martinis, which he had just poured out of a bottle of Heublein's ready-made. We were ushered into a large living room through which cats slightly less in size than lynxes freely charged. There was a slight lawn of hairs on things in general, and I reflected how under another code of honor I might be permitted to invert the cushion on which I was invited to sit. I furtively did this, as a matter of fact, when the host and hostess were momentarily out of the room, to find more of the same on the underside. It's not a grudge I don't hold against my own house, reading dog for cat. The room soared to "original" beams, and on its lower levels illustrated its owners' allegiance to forthright fabrics and affirmative hues: there were large bright comfortable chairs almost haphazardly disposed, patternless drapes of the coarse, pleasant family known as homespun, scatter rugs offering splashes of further candid color. A heretical hooked rug or two were the effect of people not conscious of antiques but oblivious to them. Isolde flew between the kitchen and the living room, shading the oven flame in the one, the volume of a phonograph going in the other.

During cocktails, Augie told a story that I remember. "When Stephen Douglas was a young man debating in the political campaigns in Illinois," he said, "there was always a sort of lanky boy sitting in the front row, in one of the best seats. Grownups resented it, because seats were at a premium when Douglas spoke. But when they wanted to put him out, Douglas protested. He asked the boy why he came to the debates so regularly. And the boy said, 'Because some day I hope to be up there on the platform myself.' 'That's fine,' Douglas said. 'What's your name, my boy?' And the boy said, 'Abe.' 'Abe what?' Douglas asked him. And the boy answered, 'Abe Feldspar.'"

"Dinner!" Isolde called. It was a casserole of chicken cooked in red wine, and superb. But while we were eating it, fate chose to move in with his ruffian tactics.

The winds of conversation swung around, from God remembers where, to the subject of cartooning, and a question was put to me that, for some reason I can't fathom, I am constantly being asked. "Is it true that cartoonists draw themselves?" I answered that a lot of them did and that a few of them drew their wives, (but had drawn them before they'd met them). "Not friend Poole," Isolde said, laughing in her husband's direction. "Thank God. I'd hate to think there were any popeyes like that in this family. Maybe a popeyed girl jilted him once."

That was when the stopcock opened. "Good God," I said. "A. Poole. I'm sorry I never tumbled. I'll be damned."

"That's all right," Augie said, picking a shred of cork from his wine with a corner of his napkin, as though he were taking something out of somebody's eye.

Of course it wasn't. The identification was anything but a happy one. The "popeyes" I had now suddenly connected with my visual memory of the signature, A. Poole, were rejected regularly with letters bearing my own. That was half the story. The other half was that the ideas in them were swell. Poole was a third-rate artist in whom a first-rate gagman was trying to claw his way out, or rather that I was trying to claw my way to. For years *The Townsman's* editors had been trying to buy his ideas to send on to our good cartoonists, many of whom were indifferent jokesmiths and often becalmed at their drawing boards on that account. But he wouldn't sell. He went on doggedly resolved to prove the reverse of our view — that the gagman we saw was a cocoon out of which an artist would one day burst. "Thank you, I don't think I'll release this idea. I'll take another crack at a finish and maybe this time . . ." How choked my files were with letters beginning like that. How choked his own must be with my end of the correspondence. And how choked I was on this chicken.

Sensing that her wonderful food had turned to gall, Isolde laid a hand on my wrist and said, "We won't talk shop tonight, will we?"

"Hell, yawl so grim about?" Augie said. "Mean why get so grim? Miro, Klee, Saroyan, they all tell us to relax." However, he was wiping his palms on the sides of his pants.

"I wish I knew what this was all about," my wife said.

"I send my work to your husband's office. They don't want the pictures, only the ideas."

"Oh, that goes on all the time, don't let that upset you. There's one artist he gets off the *train* wailing about. It's been going on for years and this man never *will* . . ." The pressure of my foot on hers brought her up short. "What's that cartoonist's name again, dear?"

"Spittlefield," I said, fetching up for some reason with the name of my stationer. I very nearly said Feldspar. My wife said, "Oh, yes. Well, that's the way it goes."

"Yes," I sighed, "that's the way it goes." I reflected what a damn sight better this conversation would have gone at Moot Point, and made no secret to myself of wishing I was up there now.

"I keep thinking of myself as an artist," Augie went on. "They prefer to think of me as a gagman. Right?" The query came at me across the table like a fast Ping-pong shot.

"The best," I answered with a grin, "of our time."

Isolde put her napkin down. "Leave us repair to the living room," she said.

Coffee had the quality of religious proceedings, despite its being accompanied by a crème brûlée so delicious it was almost obscene. There were silences in which cups lowered on saucers sounded like pistol shots. When Augie was standing over a coffee table some time later pouring brandies and I was hovering in his neighborhood, I bent down and said in his ear, "I'm sorry I called you the greatest gagman of our time."

"Oh, that's all right," he said. "That's quite all right. Christola."

"It's just not constitutional," Isolde protested from elsewhere in the room, where she and my wife were perusing an architectural organ together. "All this shop talkety-talk. We'll have no more."

"Where do you work, Augie?" I asked, calling him that for the first time.

He pointed a thumb over his shoulder. "Old barn back there."

"I'd like to see your studio." I knew what the impulse that had made me say that was. That's the impulse to swallow something hot to get rid of it.

"Better put on your overcoats if you're going to stay in there and chin-chin," Isolde said. I knew what that impulse was too. She thought that now was the time to have Augie lay it on the line with me once and for all, and ask, "All right. Why don't you buy any of my stuff? What's the matter?" So we could get on with the business of becoming friends.

Augie and I bundled into our overcoats, rather in the mood of men being egged out of them to have a fight.

"Shall we take our drinks?" I suggested.

"Take the bottle," Augie said.

Playing the beam of a flashlight behind him like a movie usher, Augie led the way across a long yard, past a disused chicken coop to a red barn. "You haven't had any roughs in the last few weeks," I said, to show I wasn't afraid of him, and springing round a decayed poultry crate. "Done got me involved fixing this place up," he answered in the same tone. He opened a door in the barn, snapped a switch, and led the way up a steep stair to a freshly paneled loft with large windows the length of one side, and a wood stove about which hovered the odor of defunct fires. The room had the comprehensive disorder of a junkyard. Files and tables inclined toward one another, papers lay about like a compost, pictures in varying stages covered everything including the walls. At one end was a drawing board on which was a captionless sketch of a goat in a vacant lot eating a copy of Duncan Hines's restaurant guide.

Augie dropped into an armchair, after a sidelong glance at me taking this in, and waved me hospitably toward a ruptured daybed. It was like an icebox in there. He sat with his overcoat spread open, but I buttoned mine to the chin. We lit cigarettes, and between the plumes our breath made and the tobacco smoke we blew in one another's direction we all but obscured each other from view, which was just as well for we were both twitching with anxiety.

"What shall we talk about?" Augie said, setting the flashlight on a table, still turned on. "The king of Spain's daughter?"

I finished off my brandy and he did the same with his. We refilled our glasses from the bottle which I had carried over in my overcoat pocket. Augie took a sheaf of drawings from the table and began to shuffle through them. "How about a stroll down Memory Lane. Remember this?" He thrust a picture at me.

I remembered it very well. It showed a woman patient peering furtively down into the street from the window of a psychiatrist's office, with a pistol in her hand. The psychiatrist was asking, "What makes you think your first analyst is following you, Mrs. Meyerbeer?" I smiled and said, "Yes." It was one of the first ideas I had tried to wangle away from him. He'd worked over it at least twenty times, always ending up with something too unfunny for tears. Since then he had become if anything more wooden still, out of his drive to "perfect" himself. He handed me a picture showing an artist's studio, inexpressibly squalid, in which a gloved visitor was saying to a painter in rags, "Boris, I wish to God I could get you out of your ivory tower." The editorial mouths had watered in vain for that idea too. Done by the right cartoonist, it might have made a memorable piece of social satire. Now it was another souvenir of a joint frustration, moldering in the attic of a man in an ivory tower of his own.

"Why do you keep sending my stuff back?" Augie asked abruptly.

"Well, I mean hell." My knees came together in a spasm of cold. Dared I say, "Because it's as stiff as a new shoe and will never be anything else" — to be cruelly kind? I said, after a pull on my brandy, "We don't set ourselves up as critics. We just feel whether a thing is right for us or not."

"My stuff isn't right for anywhere else," was his rebuttal to this. I have found only one thing richer in *non sequiturs* than a woman's logic, and that is the logic of an artist about his own work.

"The thing you ought to try to do is loosen up a little," I said. This was, after all, the terminology of his own trade. "Tightness," "stiffness," these were a curse all cartoonists were rightly in horror of. I knew an artist so bedeviled by them that he went to every expedient including, so help me, that of working for a few weeks on transcontinental trains in hopes that the motion of the cars would rock his line free.

"Oh, the joke business!" I groaned. Augie chose that moment to drop all the papers he was holding to the floor with a smack, and didn't hear what I said, so I had to regroan it. I felt a spring in the daybed twang under one haunch. I threw a look toward the stairway.

"Do you think I should give up?" Augie asked, pouring another drink. "Is that your opinion?"

"No editor has the right to say that. I'll just say I've given up myself," I answered with a laugh, handing him back his fine jokes. He saw me roll an eye around the remodeled interior and guessed my thought. "Isolde has a grandmother with money," he said. "She bought this house for her. For us. I didn't marry Isolde for her money, but it's because she had money that I could marry her. Mean the money problem is the artist's perennial one."

"Of course," I said.

Augie brought his hand down on a nearby cabinet with what was neither quite a caress nor altogether a blow. "Well, if I ever get pinched enough to have to sell my ideas, it's nice to know there's gold in them thar hills."

"There sure are. Is." I sneezed and added: "Thousands of dollars."

"Shall we join the ladies?"

"If you like."

I was a time getting to sleep *that* night. In bed, I saw our new friends as having a last cigarette before putting out the lights, talking their guests over with special emphasis on my critical level as illustrated in the frozen loft. Isolde's moving to the suburbs would imply a surrender of her own career, never, I gathered, a very hopeful one, and a consequent deepening of her interest in her husband's. So I couldn't help thinking of them as talking things over, maybe in the kitchen as they did the dishes — another couple huddled together over the blundering wheel of fortune. A wave of pathos washed my fretfulness away, but I did wonder whether business and friendship must be mixed in yet another case, and whether to the detriment of either or both. Had my chances of wooing A. Poole's jokes away from him brightened or declined? But it was too trying a reality to rehearse long at this tired hour. And since I can't count sheep, because I keep trying to guess their sex as they jump over the fence, I was soon again in the land of revery. More wish-fulfillment. I imagined Augie to possess a talent of the first order, which I discovered and nursed into stardom as that of "one of the finest comic artists of our time" (*New York Herald Tribune*), to the undying gratitude of Isolde, and, what was more, the satisfaction of Hugh Blair, my volcanic editor in chief.

Four

THE next time I heard from Augie it was to find the goat eating Duncan Hines on my desk. Which picture was soon again restored to his possession. With the novelty of our not this time beseeching him for the gag.

It was later that same week that my wife got a phone call from Isolde that was to prove important in the lives of all four of us.

It was early evening. Our family were all in bed without the house having in the least retired. My wife lay in hers reading a book in which she was using a bus transfer for a marker, a fact which obscurely vexed me, and whistling tunelessly through her teeth, a grievance on which my hold was firmer. What a greater cumulative toll the small irritations of life take than its major woes; if instead of the thousand perennial gnats a man could pay in one good snakebite! My wife's name, I'm afraid, is Aurora. Since her majority she has gone as Audrey, which she regards as short for it though I take it to be an outright substitution. A woman's name ought ideally to steal over one, and not come up like thunder out of China 'cross the Bay. Our four children are Phoebe, Marco, Ralph and Maude, and some of them were discussing the names they were going to change to when such alterations were within their legal reach. A dog, a hound rich in separate strains, was down in the basement, asleep in a bisected cello. His name was Nebuchadnezzar, and though he was in no position to oppose it there were times when his dark eyes seemed to me liquid with reproach. I felt foolish myself every time I called him.

"We need more air in here," my wife said, turning a page. "And while you're up, get me a small brandy."

She is the soul of service by day, but at night is partial to being waited on. I'd be more willing to consider her whim my law if she didn't tend to regard it as such herself. And tonight it was my own whim to see how long it would take her to prop her request with a complaint about her physical condition; I knew all her gambits and was ready with a stock of medical repartee. Also, I wanted to show her that taking an executive tone with me was not in itself enough.

"My back is stiff as a board," she said presently.

"In through here?" I laid a hand on the small of mine.

"Yes."

"It's supposed to be stiff as a board there. That's called the lumbar region."

The caprices devised for my marital hours had of course both the rewards and the risks of actual testing that could never affect those at Moot Point. At the same time, I was trying to garnish the passing years with some of the prepared glitter of Moot Point, and so my surprise can be imagined when she scowled at me from her bed and lowered her book to her stomach. "I wish you'd have just one of these cricks of mine. Like this afternoon when I sat down a minute to play the piano, all of a sudden I got a twinge down my whole back."

"Possibly you struck a spinal chord."

I bounced over on my side, away from her, and laughed till the bed shook. She would purchase my services dearly! Of course we had some of the stresses you will find in any normal household, and she elected to have no share in the scene, nicely as it was going. I sensed from her silence that she was looking over at me with a slow burn. Those were more or less our positions when the telephone rang.

She was out of bed like a hound over a stile, no sore back now. I heard from her greeting that it was Isolde, and the two of them were soon dug in — something about babies but I couldn't make head or tail out of it. I fetched her robe and mules to the telephone, also the brandy as requested, and then made a patrol check of the children's two rooms.

First that of the girls — Maude, aged twelve, who believed in a monarchical form of government, and Phoebe, four. Maude asked me about everlasting life, but Phoebe goaded me about her name, which was definitely in her craw. I feel rather touchy about the name, having argued for it against my wife when she was pregnant and too drained by the object of the dispute to wage it with much spirit; now here was the child itself carrying on the fight against me. Phoebe had early divined that her name had comic value, also that it had been my idea; so it was that I came home, evenings, to find libelous profiles of myself on the walls, salt to have been discerned in the sugar bowl, and my studs and cuff links wedged into pots of cold cream by a child with a knack for improvisation. "I'll change it to Eleanor," she said as I left the bedroom after turning out the light there the third time. "Go ahead — and be like everyone else," I said.

I crossed the corridor to the boys' room. Something in the arrangement of details struck my eye as screwy. Ralph was standing in a corner trying, of all things, to fall asleep like a horse. I whisked him smartly out of his "stall" and back into bed. "I never heard of anything so asinine in my life," I said. "Horses can sleep standing up because they have four legs." I turned on Marco as a nine-year-old who should be more responsible in keeping his eye on a brother of five.

"Maybe I've got other things to think about," Marco said from his bed, his blue eyes bland in an oppressively circular face. "Whoever heard of a name like — ?"

"That's enough of that," I said with lethal moderation.

"Well, whoever heard of anybody with a name like Marco?"

"Your name is Marco and I've heard of you," I said, borrowing a retort from a Two Black Crows routine of the twenties. I was sick and tired of the fuss about names around here. "Did you have anything else on your mind, that you couldn't see your brother was standing in the corner like a horse without a blanket on?"

"Yes. I was thinking about the arithmetic problem Maude told us. I bet you can't do it. The poor mother has eight children and five and a half apples for supper. How does she divide them?"

"That's better. Don't fuss about your name just because Phoebe does. That's being a copy cat. Learn to have a mind of your own."

"I have. I'm going to change my name to Art as soon as I can."

"Learn independence now. Remember, the child is father of the man."

"What did you say?"

"I don't chew my cabbage twice," I said, wasting no urbanity on the likes of him.

I settled myself in bed with a highball this time, and a book selected from the headboard behind me.

As I was reading or drinking, I have forgotten which, something told me to move my eye and glance under a desk in the corner. I did. A rat, looking like Andy Gump, was watching me. He had an aspect of alert but forlorn protest, as though disclaiming the tradition against him. I drew back my book and let fly at him. He flowed along the wainscoting like a blob of rather dirty quicksilver and disappeared into the closet. I grabbed three or four more books from the headboard and hurled them into the closet, frightening myself half to death; then having given the rat ample time to clear out if he had an exit in there, I went after him. I scrabbled among shoes on the closet floor and found no rat but an arch-shaped hole in the far corner. I wedged the toe of a slipper well into it, retrieved and straightened the books, and hopped back into bed. I was glad when the bedroom door opened and Audrey reappeared, about ten minutes later.

Her face wore the expression that goes with News — the smiling, briefly hoarded relish of the female courier.

"Well?"

"The Pooles want to adopt a baby." She shook off her robe and got into bed. "What are you smiling about? I don't think that's very nice."

"Well, I mean they just moved out here and all," I said, grinning uncontrollably.

"That's why they moved out to the country." Then: "Isolde called to ask us a favor — or rather to tip us off. They gave our name as a reference to the agency."

I slid up to a sitting position. "But we hardly know them," I said.

"We're practically the only people they do know out here. And getting a character reference won't be the only thing the caseworker will come to see us for."

"What else will she want?"

Audrey sipped from her brandy, which she had carried from

the phone, and set it down on her nightstand. "Since we're friends as well as neighbors of the Pooles, with children of our own which theirs will probably play with and all, why, we're part of the applicants' environmental picture. The welfare agency will want a look at us."

"I see," I said, glancing into the closet. I didn't like the turn the conversation was taking, and gave it one of my own. "The main thing the agency will want to find out from us is, do we think the Pooles would make good parents? Just offhand, what would your opinion be?"

She pored over her nails, as she habitually does in a state of thought. I asked presently:

"Are you of two minds about them?"

"Yes and no."

I asked her to explain what that meant, and she said she meant yes for one of the aspirant parents, no as regarded the other.

"Exactly my opinion!" I said. I was eager to compare notes. "I wonder if we've passed and flunked the same people."

"I'll tell you what I think," Audrey said.

It's not a point on which anyone has been successfully sententious, to my knowledge, but I think women's reputation for intuition is based on the speed of their judgments rather than their accuracy. They're no more acute than men in their evaluations but neither are they any less so, which leaves them with some balance in their favor. Penetrating façades gives them more pleasure than seeing frailty in perspective, hence their "I told you I was right about him" is more familiar after someone has discredited himself than after he has brought himself distinction. Women, to their credit, never spare themselves in reversing their own appraisals, under fresh evidence, and their verdicts, if my wife is any gauge, can be astonishing. I remember an epithet with which she officially changed her mind about an acquaintance who fancied herself a sensitive aesthetic type far above distaff chores. Audrey had gone along with this slant, but after disillusionment had crept in, her revised estimate ran: "She's a bitch and a sadist and a good housekeeper."

Well, it turned out we differed about the Pooles right off. I spotted Isolde for "nice, but probably not very practical," and Augie as having "a lot more to him," despite his kinks and quirks, his slightly jazzed-up literacy. "It's just the other way around," Audrey said. "She's basically a sound girl, with all that actress fluff on top. She's serious about canning things this summer. In the short time they've been here she's gotten a line on the best adopting agencies — made work of it. No, that girl's O.K. Augie now. He's got something wrong with him that I can't put my finger on. Something in his, well, beams and timbers. It's as if I can *hear* termites in there that I can't see. It's very frustrating."

"You've got to admit Augie knows more. Has a lot more depth."

"Only on the surface. Deep down, he's shallow."

"Deep down he's *shallow!*" I exclaimed, scarcely able to conceal my delight. These are the word sequences for which I live. I liked a man being shallow at bottom even better than I had her recent "Winter sports leave me cold," and "Penicillin is a drug on the market." Such effects are a kind of specialty of hers, effortlessly come by you might say, which I had detected early in our union. The first, "When I woke up and found I had the flu, I was sick," I had pricked up my ears at on our honeymoon. Topsoil in Connecticut is far from dirt cheap. There is literally no end to them. She was surely the first to feel that anybody who goes to a psychiatrist ought to have his head examined. I don't think she suspects how dear these convolutions are to me, nor that I keep a mental file or "collection" of them. Well, anyhow, to get back to the argument. Her last words were: "Watch."

That was the long-range program; the immediate order of business was to get to sleep. An hour later, I was lying in the dark with my hands laced under my head, thinking about what the caseworker might be told. Audrey's bed gave a sharp creak as she raised her head alertly. "Do I hear a mouse?" she asked.

"No," I said, my lips curled in a faintly ironic smile, which of course she could not see for it was pitch dark. And which was not of long duration, for I thought: How will I handle *that* problem? Could Nebuchadnezzar be banked on to any extent? He had a terrier ingredient in him, to judge from the zeal with which he worried slippers through the house, but the question remained whether the instinct could be brought to bear on a more cunning adversary.

I was about to drop off when something popped Marco's arithmetic problem into my head. What was it the poor mother had had? Eight children and five and a half apples. Well, let's see, eight times five would be forty, so if she cut the apples into eighths she would have forty slices to divide, or five slices for each child. But what about the half left over? She could divide that into eight pieces, of course, but that sounded too simple; the problem must be to find a way of cutting the apples into slices of *equal* size — otherwise what would be the sense of putting it in an arithmetic book? Let's see now, how did the poor mother work it out? Oh, the hell with it, I told myself — go to sleep.

I settled resolutely on one side, kneading the pillow under my head. I tried to get my mind on the rat again, but the way back wasn't easy. Problems and puzzles have a way of getting their hooks into me. Give me farmers with acreage to parcel among their sons and canoes with distances to travel upstream and I am soon out of my wits. I lay stark awake. What composer was it — was it Mozart — who as a small child would torment his father by stealing downstairs at night, striking an unresolved chord on the clavichord, and sneaking back up to bed again, leaving the old man to toss and turn till he had left his own bed and gone down and resolved it? No connection. Yes, there is. The raveled sleeve of sleep. He who has children gives hostages to fortune. The Pooles want children and this is very laudable of them, for could they not just as easily go on spending all their money selfishly on themselves? Isolde's grandmother's money, rather. Would the agency ask me about Augie's finances? Would he ever be self-supporting? It was tough for the head of a family to make both ends meet. The poor mother has eight children —

I threw the covers back and got out of bed. I turned the light on over the desk. I sat down, drew pencil and paper to me, and started in. Now, the thing I must do is find a common denominator for eight and five and a half. Of course. Then I'd as good as have it. I was scratching away when Audrey stirred sleepily. "What are you doing?" she asked.

"Going over some figures."

She dropped off again. But presently the same inquiry was mumbled. "Just something I want to do before I forget," I answered. "You go to sleep."

Then for the third time: "What are you doing?"

"Nothing."

It was true enough. Even finding a common denominator and letting the poor mother divide accordingly would not, I guessed, be the answer; for the suspicion now began to gnaw me that the whole thing was a riddle, with a pun or something for an answer. A hell of a thing to get into in the dead of night. I might lie here fussing till daybreak, unless I "gave up." I gave up.

I snapped the light off and picked my way down the hall, flicking on a succession of others, to the boys' room. I shook Marco awake.

"In that problem, you remember, what did the poor mother do?" I asked him.

He uttered a startled cry.

"Shh!" I said. "You'll wake the others. It's just Daddy. You forgot to tell me the answer — you know, about the five apples and eight and a half children. I mean the eight children and five and a half farmers," I whispered in his ear. "Daddy gives up."

"Leave me alone," he said.

I saw that he would be no good to me. I recalled it was Maude he'd gotten the problem from, so I went into the girls' room and shook her awake. "That problem about the mother and the apples," I said. "You remember. What did the poor mother do?" She muttered something in protest and turned away on her side. I shook her by both shoulders. "What did the poor mother do?" I demanded.

"Made applesauce."

Climbing back into my bed — for what I trusted would be the last time that night — I wondered how Augie would have done as paterfamilias, given tonight as a sample, say. Then the reverse suggested itself: what would the agency have thought of me? A heavy drowsiness began to overtake me. That, I mused, was one of the fortunate advantages of having children the normal way — nobody was around to say whether you should. With such comfort as I could extract from that thought, I fell asleep.

Five

WHEN the caseworker arrived I was making faces at my children to show that I ought to have them. Funny faces, eyes crossed, cheeks squished in, that were great sport. I had been watching for the caseworker from the picture window, and managed to time a tableau of sorts for her benefit on the above lines, when her car turned off the road and came up the gravel drive to the house.

It was now some five weeks since Isolde's call forewarning us of her and three since the caseworker herself had called to make this appointment. This wasn't the Mrs. Mash before whom I was stricken dumb but a predecessor back in the relatively azure days when I didn't know anything much about Augie. It was two o'clock of a Saturday afternoon in mid-April. The children had been bathed, brushed and scrubbed till they looked sullen but simonized, for was it not avowedly among our objects to pass muster with the welfare people ourselves? There was not a member of the family who wasn't dressed in his best from the hide out.

It had not been easy. The day had begun portentously, with a contagious crossness among the children building by noon to that kind of uproar that sometimes seizes pet shops. Phoebe had awoken in a vile humor; she was going to kill Ralph, cut the fringes off the rugs, go to Egypt. She and her mother were at the breakfast table together when I sat down there. I flapped out my napkin and said brightly to Phoebe, "Eating your breakfast?" No answer, and I picked up my orange juice. My wife checked me with a shake of her head. "Phoebe, your father asked you something," she said. Continued silence. The girl's no good till she's had her milk, and then is nothing to brag about. "Maybe you didn't hear him. He will say it again." She gave me a sign to repeat.

"Eating your breakfast?" I said, with somewhat synthetic spirit. Still no reply. I lifted my orange juice and again my hand was stayed with a look. "Phoebe, your father asked you a question," my wife said sternly now. "Must everything stop till you're civil?"

"Forget it," I said, anxious to get on to my breakfast. "It's a rhetorical question, just a remark really. I don't mind."

"But I do," my wife said, with a look which said she was surprised that I could not see when an issue should be made of a thing. "Now, Phoebe," she continued to the girl, "we'll give you one more chance to be polite. If you aren't, I'm afraid we'll have to do something about it." She cued me with another nod. I took it from where I'd sat down. Flapping my napkin out once more, I said with a threadbare smile, "Eating your breakfast are you, Phoebe?"

We both watched her. There was a short silence. Then, somewhat darkly into her cereal, she said, "Yes."

I fell to, and my wife returned to the paper she'd been reading. The next order of business made more sense.

"You're not eating your breakfast!" we both observed to the tot, who was shoving her cereal about in its bowl. At that moment Ralph came in clutching a stuffed horse and revealed plans to spend the day in the MacPhersons' barn, which were promptly countered with the reminder that we had an important visitor coming today, and that cleanliness was of the essence. I dilated on the prevalence of this theme in nature. "Look at the cat," I said, pointing to one of the Pooles' eunuchs, which we had on loan to see if it could help eradicate the rats. "Cats are the healthiest animals in the world. And why? Have you ever noticed how they're always licking themselves?"

"Yes," Phoebe said, "it's a filthy habit." Showing that she can make breakfast conversation when she wants to.

When Maude and Marco arrived we were discussing why cats don't come when you call them, the way dogs do. Now, at one stage in the getting-acquainted scene of my Moot Point fantasies — where the girl is wearing my pajamas and sipping hot tea after the thundershower which had driven us to refuge there, you will remember — at one juncture she tells me that she is fond of cats. I reply with a sort of quip which struck me as apropos of what we were talking about here at the breakfast table. So I threw it into the family discussion.

"Cats are merely live bric-a-brac," I said. My wife gave me a shake of the head to tell me not to confuse the children. I returned to my coffee. Maude tried to call the cat: "Here, Figaro! Here, Figaro!" — with no results. Marco piped up, "Maybe he's another one who doesn't like his — "

"That's enough of that!" I said. I stamped my foot, starting the oil furnace. "Children today are let speak their piece about everything," I complained to my wife. "They're pampered and indulged and kowtowed to. Back in the great pioneer times of our country, people had names like Cotton and Increase. Those were the days of stamina."

In the midst of minding all the children while my wife cleaned the house that morning (with no help, the cleaning woman being sick), I took time out to deal with the rats. I had seen no more since that evening, but my wife had sighted "something" running behind the Bendix in the basement. I went down there toward noon with a broom and a BB gun, and with bicycle clips fastened around the ankles of my pants. After clattering about behind boxes and barrels, flushing nothing, to my considerable relief, I got Nebuchadnezzar aside as I had before. I took him to our bedroom closet. I got down on all fours and showed him the hole there. Then, pointing alternately to that and to the picture of a rat on a box of poison, I went through a series of sounds and motions, which would elude reproduction here, by means of which I tried to drive home the fact that, rather than the footwear which it was his wont to chew, here was his rightful foe, whose challenge was his birthright and whose prompt and faithful dispatch was essential to the preservation of my esteem. Then I wedged back into the hole the beer coaster with which I had been keeping it stopped up.

By this time the children were boiling to some sort of climax. They had been listening to records under the supervision of Maude, the oldest, who had set their backs up by insisting the music played be "good." She had going the Magic Fire music from *Die Walküre*, the story of which I had related to her. "There's the fire," she explained to the circle gathered round on the floor. "Hear the crackle of the flames." She said this so prissily that I could not resist telling her, "No, that is needle scratch." This put her out of sorts with the enterprise as such, and she began to practice a piano piece of her own with the phonograph still going. Above the whine of the vacuum, this was an interesting phonic experience. It seemed as good a time as any to give the girls the shampoos which had been decreed.

I obtained some rather unique effects. In calling out instructions for rinsing, my wife told me to use the juice of half a lemon for each, diluted in a little water. Pouring this over the head was the penultimate step — I got that. But I understood her to have said a cup of lemon juice for each. In addition, nobody said anything about straining the juice (though I did flick the pips out with a spoon), and the resulting pulp in the tresses was more than a simple rinsing could handle, and my wife had to wash the girls' hair all over again. It wasn't till I was drying their locks with an electric blower that I noticed the resemblance to clotted straw, and turned them over to their mother. I stood in the bathroom doorway as she lathered the heads anew, doing my best to keep up everyone's spirits.

"I should think you could spare me at least this," my wife said, "with my back. Yesterday I got another of those twinges driving to Bridgeport. But driving the car," she puzzled. "Must be some nerve."

"Possibly involving the motor area. What," I went on, leaning against the doorjamb with my hands in my pockets, "did you go to Bridgeport for?"

"See about musical instruments — where you're not much help either. What did you suggest to Ralph he take up a shoehorn for? Now the child thinks you can play on one."

"You can — footnotes."

You can understand my surprise at the irritation with which these attempts to lighten the burdens of the morning were met, likewise those I made in the living room from which I called over words of encouragement, advising her to avoid all agitation and to keep calm in the teeth of adversity, which would soon enough be got through. "Oh, go find Ralph and give him his bath," she said.

He was found, easily enough, in the proscribed barn, and was such a mass of filth and bruises that the one could not be told from the other. Nor did I eliminate the one without adding to the other, so brisk was the drubbing I administered in the tub. Tearful howls attested the thoroughness of my efforts, and a faint smile my satisfaction with the results.

I had not been in the children's bathroom for some time, and now found scraps of paper glued to the enamel of the tub, which I paused from time to time to scratch at with my nails.

"What is all this you've got stuck to everything? Are these stamps?" I said.

"You told us to keep our Christmas seals in the bathtub — "

"Oh, for God's sake!"

Fatherhood is an art, and it took as much tact and beguilement as it did muscle to get both the premises and the children spic and span by two o'clock, but we did. I trust the caseworker was well struck by the tableau we presented at the picture window where, in addition to the faces I was making at my family, I believe I also had my thumbs inserted in my ears and was comically waggling my fingers. My wife answered the door, wearing a blue housecoat and leisurely dropping a magazine to the coffee table as she rose to go to it, smiling at the scene we made. "I'm Miss Terkle from Rock-a-Bye," said a resonant voice.

Miss Terkle was a woman of fifty in tweeds the color of summer sausage and with straight brown hair drawn into a yam at the back. She glanced round the living room with what appeared to be approval, and then beamed at the children. They were radiant, and there were glints in the girls' golden hair, undoubtedly the remains of citrus mash.

"Now then," she said, settling into a pull-up chair. Now then indeed.

There are times when parenthood seems nothing but feeding the mouth that bites you. It never seemed to me more so than that afternoon. Phoebe, who knew she had us, led off with a request for eating matter. Which I met by reminding her that, on that head, she had done nothing with her lunch but rearrange it on her plate.

"Sounds familiar," Miss Terkle laughingly remarked. "I guess all parents have different ideas how to cope with the food rebel, but none of them appear efficacious. What do you do when a child won't eat its food?"

"Send him to bed without any supper," I said.

I felt a pressure on an already aggrieved bunion, applied under the coffee table by my wife's foot, as she smiled at Miss Terkle and said, "Would you like a cup of tea?"

"A cup of tea would be fine."

"I hope you take cream," my wife said, rising. "We haven't a lemon in the house."

"Are you going to give her cookies?" Ralph said.

"If you're good," I answered, meeting his ellipsis head on. I glanced quickly at Miss Terkle to see if I'd made another gaffe by thus laying down a pragmatic, or "reward," basis for morality; but her expression told me nothing, that being rather a matter of watching with interest as Ralph's hand advanced toward a bowl of nuts on the coffee table in front of her. The hand closed on a fistful of them, and mine on it. I tried to make him yield his booty, but the hand was as hard to pry open as a clam. I prised a finger at a time away, the nuts dribbling back into the bowl and onto the table. Miss Terkle sat forward, as if witnessing some prolonged and misbegotten act of legerdemain. "Lick the problem not the child," I panted with a smile. She nodded, watching intently. Rather than the principle I had enunciated, I longed to illustrate that more venerable one of "knocking some sense into them" — though if I'd got started on that boy just then I doubt if I'd have been able to stop short of knocking it out of him. I got his hand open at last, but in a final lunge of resistance he stumbled against the coffee table, overturning it at Miss Terkle's feet and emptying the bowl of nuts in her lap.

"Can we go now?" Marco asked, when Miss Terkle had been tidied up.

"You not only can but you may," I said. "Out in the relative sunshine with you! Play nice together, all of you, and when we have tea maybe we'll give you cookies and ginger ale."

I was convinced now that the caller felt herself to be slumming. In the need to recover status, I studded my conversation with as many terms like "substitute situation" and "plastic suggestion" as I could, to show that I was familiar with the latest terrain on child guidance; but I felt her expression to be deteriorating steadily, as though, that is, it were now no longer a question whether *I* should have had children but whether my father should have. A sudden vibration of withdrawal, a lowering of my eyelids, signalized a dangerous glut on my part with this subject, which I now left to the women. Vaguely I heard them talk about the Period of Protest (when the child throws dishes on the floor), then about the Period of Co-operation (when he insists on carrying them in from the dining-room table). I was in my Period of Resignation (the realization that the adults sweep the fragments into a dustpan in either case). Then Miss Terkle was recommending what she considered the definitive volume on dealing with children from five to seven. "I think five to seven is the most crucial period in many ways," she said.

"Right," I said, sliding up in my chair. "That's the cocktail hour."

Miss Terkle glanced at her wrist watch. "I won't keep you any longer than I have to," she said. "This has been very interesting. Now, what about the Pooles?"

"The who?" I said.

"The Pooles. Your friends."

"Oh, yes." We gave our view of the matter, the gist of which was that, yes, we thought it would be fine for the Pooles to have children, whom they could give a good home. What else was there to say? What else was there to think? The Pooles were an intelligent young couple with means, with enough money for a nurse. . . . So we gave our recommendation, and Miss Terkle took her leave, shortly before four o'clock.

"I'm sorry about the nuts," I said.

"Oh, that's all right."

"No, it isn't," I said, and meant it: The nuts that had been swept up and thrown out were roasted almonds costing a dollar and a half a pound, which I had looked forward to nibbling on with my imminent Martini.

I was setting about the concoction of that when the children came tumbling back in, offering to tired spirits a burst of animal health. They talked about Miss Terkle, and I felt there must surely be some substitute situation for this. At last I hit on one. I put on my hat and went out to a bar instead.

The upshot of everything was that the Pooles appeared to have been turned down. Oh, not in so many words of course; they just didn't get any child. By the end of the summer the implications were clear. I took the disappointment resentfully to heart, feeling it one in which I personally shared by having failed to come up to snuff as part of somebody's environmental picture.

"It's hard to tell why agencies turn down couples," my wife said. "It could be some one thing in the Pooles' setup, or a little bit of everything in it. The Hurlbutts haven't been able to find out to this day why they flunked."

"How did it all happen? Where did we go wrong?" I went on, flapping my hands at my sides.

"Don't let it get you down," Isolde said, taking my arm one afternoon as we were leaving their house to go for a drive. "We'll try another agency."

"You're damn right we will," I said. "The hell with Rock-a-Bye."

But Isolde was by no means in perennially level spirits. When October came and they were given neither a child nor a reason for the refusal, she stamped her foot furiously at her home one evening and said, "Why not? What's this all about? Is there some skeleton in our closet or something? That we don't even know about ourselves? How do caseworkers find things out?"

"They snoop," I said. I remember that my wife was watching Augie, who was mixing drinks at the bar.

Snooping is probably the term for what I now undertook myself. For as the Pooles plunged doughtily into a fresh try with another agency, one in New Haven, I thought about them, listened to things about them, asked about them — bent on finding out what I could. My curiosity was thorough and it was systematic. I became a caseworker.

Six

FOR months there was no data — the mystery seemed unsolvable. Then suddenly it poured in from all directions and without my prying for it.

Rather than merely at dinners exchanged in one another's home, we now began to see the Pooles at parties everywhere — the parties I have come to think of as "those Saturday-night strip teases."

How well I remember those Saturday-night strip teases that were such a cardinal part of Avalon social life, yet how they all seem to blur into one: I mean those gatherings at which familiars favored one another with something of the nature and origin of their personality structures, revealing stage by stage the libido or ego or inferiority drives that made them what they were. The next morning they might shudder a little at the intimacy of their disclosures, but not while they were at it; I was often detained by total strangers with accounts of their complexity. "Did I ever tell you about my aberration?" would seem to be the latter-day variant of an old gambit. Women, I think, made freer with themselves than men, stopping short only of some ultimate secret suited to the analyst's ear alone — indeed like dancers one garment short of final revelation, deterred, perhaps, by a warning frown from a husband across the room. At such times it was often all I could do to keep from clapping my hands and yelling, "Take it off!"

There were at these strip teases specialties to suit all tastes. One woman I recall analyzed the whole of her foliation in terms of erogenous zones. This was more interesting to an advertising executive who was present than it was to the rest of us because he listened to the entire story under the impression that erogenous zones were red-light districts. But under whatever skies their peculiarities had burgeoned, in whatever family bosoms they had been separately irked, these people together formed an aristocracy of ills; nor was membership in it to be had merely by being in possession of the glossary, as the ranking neurotics soon gave me to know. There was an implication quite deeply rooted, namely that discomposure is the price of civilized subtlety, and freedom from it the boon of less evolved types. The neurotics were those oysters, so to speak, in whom the abrasive grain of sand had produced the pearl, Sensibility. I myself took this on faith; so that when the neurotics slung an arm around my shoulder, as they often did, and said they envied me my untortured simplicity, I had a feeling of resentment and chagrin. And when they referred to me as "levelheaded," "steady," "a good sort," it was like a goad in my side, for it amounted to being called names. None of this would have carried the sting that it did were it not for a certain professional aspect to this whole matter, which involved a man's pride.

Avalon is full of artists and intellectuals. They set the social tone in the circles in which I found myself afloat. Since artists were so numerous, the connection between neurosis and talent was widely aired, and the view of a genius as someone not accountable to normal standards highly thought of. I found Augie very vocal on this subject.

"Name me one genius who wasn't a son of a bitch," he said one Saturday night at the Blooms'. He was standing at the mantel, waving a highball in one of those gestures that seemed always so patently to typify the Eastern seaboard. "Name one. A son of a bitch in his domestic life, or his sexual conduct, or money matters, or his relations with people at large."

We sat a moment in thought, as if playing a game.

"Plato?" I said at last.

"Very little is known of Plato. Socrates? He wants to know about Socrates," Augie said humorously. Since this mere mention seemed enough for most of the others I didn't ask for particulars, not wanting to appear an ignoramus.

"Shakespeare," I gave him next off the top of my head.

"Shakespeare he says. He wants to know what kind of a bird Shakespeare was. Well we don't really know — luckily for him!" Augie said, smiling at those in primary-colored shirts and wool ties, who smiled back. "Coleridge caused his wife constant embarrassment. Who next? Dickens did I hear somebody say?" He hadn't, certainly not me, but he singled me out as the target of these apparent ripostes because I had sent the goat eating Duncan Hines back to him. "Dickens turned his wife out of the house," he affected to fire back at me. "Gauguin told his family to go to hell. Flaubert had intercourse with a courtesan with his hat on and a cigarette hanging out of his mouth."

"What for?" I asked.

"To show his contempt for bourgeois standards. Wagner had three children by another man's wife, while he was working on his best operas. Byron was a son of a bitch. Smollett wrote all over the walls, or was it Trollope? No, you can't ask a man to be a good artist and a good human being both. The artist is a washout as a husband."

Isolde smiled admiringly up at him during the bulk of this speech.

"And the better he is the worse he is," he finished, and drank. A man in a primary-colored shirt nodded.

"He's right about that," said the man, a painter whose canvases were dubious, but whose inability to get along with other people was monumental.

Now all this began to get to me. Little by little, as the mosaic of implications completed itself, I acquired the sense of lacking caste among subtle and gifted spirits, many of whom were validly that, though with the most articulate it was of course often a case of "howling loudest who had drunk the least." All the artists and intellectuals I knew personally and dealt with editorially had periods when they didn't do a tap of work, which they called, as you know, blocks. Then they would have to go see their psychiatrists, or blockbusters. They frequently interpreted these blocks as sexual, just as they had their drive to produce. It was enough that the real painters talked about their blocks, but when one afternoon at a cocktail party I heard a commercial artist going on about having one, I thought that was a bit thick. This commercial artist had done a series of posters for a chewing gum which were outstanding of their kind. On top of him bragging about his block, his wife chimed in with something about his being "all tied up in knots lately." That did it. I figured if he could have blocks and be tied up in knots, anybody could.

I cast a glance over my life and temper. I could point to days when I just damn well didn't see how I could go in to the office. Why weren't those blocks? I was on salary, true, but there were weeks on end when I was in a "funk" about my work, had no "stomach" for it whatsoever. Those stretches, why couldn't I call them periods of being immobilized about the magazine game if I wanted? As to the shortcomings-as-persons that are the bruited hallmark of talent, why, I could adduce instances in my own case, of which such things as treating tradesmen shabbily and spasms of irritability with my wife and children were only the beginning. There were times when I think I could honestly say there was no living with me. There were other things along these lines. I couldn't reasonably expect much in the way of public testimonials from my wife on that score, but I felt I had a right to at least as much loyalty as the commercial artist got from his. So I brought the subject up as we were driving from the party in question to another party, and we had a spat about it.

"Why don't you ever build me up?" I asked her, out of what she no doubt took to be a clear sky.

"What do you mean, build you up?" she asked.

"You know very well what I mean. The way other wives build their husbands up."

"I don't see how you can say I don't build you up. Why, only tonight, at the card table, I was saying how pleasant you are at breakfast."

"Sure, make me out a cheerful moron," I said. "How about the dumps I get into about my work, and then the states. I'm a dethroned elder child, remember. My temper isn't so damned long as you sometimes like to think!"

"What are you talking about?"

"Sometimes I wonder if you ever know."

She had been slumped abstractedly down in her seat, but now straightened up.

❨ 53 ❩

"*Really!*" she said.

"Yes, really," I said, feeling the wrangle was going well; feeling that if some of our fine-feathered friends could hear me now they wouldn't think I was such a bland mediocrity.

"Have you been drinking?" my wife asked me.

"No, but it's an idea. I need one — all that guff tonight. That commercial artist's wife going on about the stews he gets into. Chewing-gum posters, for Christ's sake! Who the hell does she think he is? I should think *you'd* resent it. Why, there are days when I come home limp as a rag from tension. You know that. I'm just as tied up in knots as he is any day. I'm just as much as any of these bastards around here. And don't you forget it!"

She gave a weak shake of her head and looked out the window. "I never know what you want," she said.

Well, I knew what I wanted. I wanted to be treated with some respect in my home community. I wanted to be regarded as somebody. After all it wasn't as though I was a magazine *hack*; I was creative to a large extent in my work, suggesting changes and even complete switches to artists that they might never have thought of themselves, working with them from the idea stage, and so on. My editorial contributions were thus an integral part of the generative process, in whose extreme ferments I often as not wore my secretary thin. I was in any case fed up with being branded as levelheaded, which I felt certainly to be unwarranted.

I was still brooding on these matters when we reached our destination, a lawn party at some friends named Winchester. The party is important because it was there that Augie gave me my first inkling of the scale on which he practiced what he preached.

There was on hand a nobly hewn blonde who had arrived

with a local painter, the spoils of a recent excursion into the theater, which had consisted of his doing the sets for a musical comedy. She wore a shimmering coral gown which advantageously set off her arms and shoulders and the snowy cleft between. Looking accidentally in Augie's direction I caught his long, carnivorous glance as she crossed the grass to take her seat, but gave it no second thought, there being not a man there on whom her vibrations did not rain. She even made me salivate; I say even me because I am normally plunged into despair rather than excitement by such presences, which are but part of the world's weary wasted stimuli. As intimated, it has become somewhat my pleasure to see women qualify on the more abiding ground of colloquy, and so when I heard the newcomer remark, on her entrance, "Tom has been handing me the usual baloney about how long women take to dress," I knew she was not likely to be among those guests who were regularly seen at Moot Point. Augie was not so given to caviling. Early in the evening he was à deux with her on the lower slopes, helping her to seconds from the buffet spread as well as from his store of learning concerning the living habits of the great. Once I saw her throw back her head and laugh at something he'd said, and it was not much after that that I didn't see either of them at all. I learned afterward that his progress was based in part on her impression that he was a playwright with a work nearly ready for production, a misunderstanding he did nothing to correct and may have done something to create. This all came to a head quickly, to the consternation of more than a few people.

The grounds here were of estate size, almost a small park, an expanse of lawn and manicured privet in the center of which lay an oval pond. Augie in piloting his friend from view had skirted the outer hedgeworks and come up well out of the dusky glow of the Japanese lanterns; but the damn fool had not reckoned with the notorious acoustics of open water. We could hear every word he said, the ten or dozen of us who were sitting just then at the side of the pond near the house. We were presently treated to an aphorism.

"Most women only strike the quarter hour, some the half," came Augie's voice in a murmur transmitted with high fidelity across the calm water. "A few strike the hour. You're one of those."

We writhed as if sitting on nests of ants. Someone called, "Who's for dancing?" To which an eager chorus demanded that the radio be gotten out and going on the terrace without delay. Then there was silence. Into which came Augie's voice again:

"Who was it that said, 'Let us all be terribly Spanish, for there is not enough time to be Greek'?"

It was no doubt the speaker's acting on the injunction to be Spanish that brought the next sound we heard — that of the smart clap of a hand on a cheek. It's one of the most rending adult sounds witnessable, and is almost never heard in real life. Whatever its effect on its object, that on our group was to disperse it like a dropped shell. We scattered in all directions, angrily demanding what was keeping the music.

My wife couldn't wait to get into our car, when the party broke up. She had been among the witnesses to the incident, which thank God hadn't included Isolde.

"Well, what did I tell you?" she said, before I had the car quite in second.

"Hm?" I said, being concerned with a stuck window on my side, and also mentally engaged in weighing the merits of garroting, strangulation and poison for Augie. "How's that?"

"You know what I mean. About your fine friend. I told you so." She sighed and shook her head. "I'm surprised at him."

"You told me so, but you're surprised at him."

"That's just an expression. I'm really not surprised at all. Really! Making a pass at another woman. Well, what do you think of your boy now?"

I steered the car around a large hole in the road. "It goes on all the time," I said.

"You certainly don't sound as if you disapproved of it."

"I'm no censor of other people," I said. "The trouble with you is you don't take people as they are."

"Thank you."

"You're welcome," I said, with as much an air of repartee as the nature of the exchange permitted.

We rode on in silence for a while. I could sense that she was a pod bursting with contention. At last, sighing sharply now rather than meditatively, she said: "That's the male viewpoint all right. Sticking together like — union members!"

"I don't think it was the male sex that started what went on tonight. That dress — designed solely for the purpose of showing off her excellent recreational facilities." My wife made a repressed, grinding noise. I shrugged and said. "It's one-thirty."

"Don't you condemn that sort of thing?" she inquired abruptly.

"Yes, it was a foolish thing to do. At a party and all."

"That's not what I mean and you know it. Don't you condemn it as such?"

All might yet have been well if she only hadn't said "and you know it." That was what stoked me up again. I could not find it in my heart to say, "Yes," and make an end of it. I asked:

"Who was it that said life would be perfectly enjoyable if it were not for its pleasures?"

"What does that mean?"

"Why, that the by-products and botherations that go with pleasures make it hardly worth it. Sex is supposedly life's greatest pleasure and look what it gives you. That," I said, jerking a thumb over my shoulder at what we had left, "and — this."

"Thank you."

"You're welcome. We're the victims of our morality as much as of our sins," I continued acutely, guiding the car around another pock in the road. "Perhaps more. If marriage wasn't made so much a corral in which to confine us we'd all be more content to stay inside it. All you have to do to make Augie forget that bag of sachet is make her available. As it is, he'll probably spend the night tossing and turning."

"I see. Free spirits."

"Oh, for God's sake."

"Maybe you wish you were just dropping me off instead of going home with me."

"Make no mistake about that!" I said, piloting the car into the garage, for we had reached the house.

"Well, go right ahead!" she said, slamming the car door behind her after getting out.

"All right I will!" I said, following her up the walk to the front door.

Mrs. Goodbread took her money, summarized the evening, and left without having to be taken, for she lived only a few houses up the road. I locked the door behind her and turned to find my wife, who had checked on the children, walking into our bedroom. "You're right about one thing," she said from in there. "There are times when you're impossible."

"Thank you."

"You're welcome."

Retirement was a travesty. We occupied our respective beds in one of those marital silences that are so much more corrosive than any words can be. Each lay building up his charge of static electricity, not only out of the friction of the moment but out of the materials of ancient grievances as well: in her case the long maternal grind, thanklessness, fatigue; I as the tethered male who could identify himself with a friend's digression.

"I suppose this isn't just general talk. Maybe you're trying to pave the way for the future. When you might have an affair of your own some day?"

I punched my pillow somewhat and said: "Intellectually speaking, there's no good ground for condemning it categorically. Why is at least one affair almost universal among couples we know? Most anthropologists agree man is not naturally monogamous, remember."

"I'll remember." She settled on her side. "Any time you want to hole up in town with some flea bag, go right ahead. It's O.K. with me."

"Hole up in a flea bag," I corrected her. "With a floozy, in a flea bag. I wish you'd get terms like that straight. It reflects on me."

I spent the night tossing and turning. When I arose the next morning, Sunday, about ten o'clock, I found her alone at the breakfast table. The children were playing outside in the bright sunshine. She was behind the New York Times. I poured myself some coffee and "joined" her. I slipped a slice of bread into the toaster and sat nervously watching for it to pop. She cleared her throat.

"I see Reverend Bonniwell — that minister Mother went to school with, you know — died," she said.

"Death is no respecter of parsons."

It was no good. Her silence on receipt of my reply sharpened the constraint and worsened the mood between us, though she seemed not to notice this. She folded the paper, laid it aside and said, "I've decided to forgive you."

Now this had the misfortune of being precisely what I had planned to do to her.

"Oh, you'll forgive me, will you?" I said. "And suppose I refuse to *be* forgiven. For an argument that's been made a logical female hash of, like every other — "

"Don't give me any more to overlook," she advised, buttering a remnant of toast.

"Overlook, forgive. If there's any forgiving to do around here, I'll do it! What have you got to say to that?"

"Nothing," she replied with spirit, and rose and threw her napkin on the table. "I don't want to talk to you today or even see you."

"That's easily enough arranged," I barked in return, rising and chucking down my own napkin. Since she had taken the dramatic offensive by sailing out of the room, there was no way for me to top it except by sailing out of the house, which I accordingly did — out the open front door and slamming the screen door behind me.

It can be imagined how little placated I was by the sight that greeted my eye — that of Augie and Isolde approaching down the sunlit road, hand in hand. They waved, but awkwardly, for the report of the screen door had echoed like a rifle shot through half of Avalon. I waved tersely back and made for the garage. I climbed into the car and, when the Pooles had passed my driveway, backed out and made off up the road in the opposite direction. I could see them, in the rearview mirror, looking perturbedly after me.

I had breakfast at a village lunch counter. I roosted on an end stool, perusing some fat metropolitan tabloid and sipping infamous coffee. After about forty-five minutes, I went back home. Augie and Isolde were in the living room, talking with Audrey.

"Hi," the visitors greeted me, with some reserve.

"Good morning," I said.

"Warming up."

A few words were exchanged about the threatened resumption of a hot spell we'd just been through. "It's hard on a person. It gets everyone," Isolde said, smoothing out a crease in her skirt.

Augie said, "Audrey here has been telling us you two haven't had a vacation in four years, apart from some visit of hers to her mother's. That's bad. You look a trifle chewed up. Everybody has to have a holiday now and then. Off the old reservation, you know."

"I know," I said, glancing out the window.

"We'd be delighted to take the kids," Isolde said. "No, now, I mean that. You could bring us back something terribly expensive from Bermuda or Lake Banff or whatever."

When they had gone (looking fresh as daisies), I turned to my wife and said, "Well! Isn't that fine and dandy? What did you go and tell them?"

"Tell them? Was there anything left to tell them after that fancy exit of yours? I was in the doorway when they came by, and they waved and stopped, and I told them we had a little spat, to play it down. That at least was better than letting them speculate. By God, I won't have the neighbors thinking we're a couple of brawlers!"

I realized that I had suddenly lost a great deal of ground in the quarrel. And since I had no one to blame but myself, I became twice as hostile toward my wife. Nor did I lose any more time than was necessary in attempting to extract a penalty. I spotted a chance to get even the very next day — by walking the three miles from the station in the broiling heat, under circumstances that I saw a way of pinning on her.

That Monday, the temperature reached ninety-six, and it was well on its way to it when my wife drove me to the station in the morning. My regular train home was the five-thirty. I told her that I was going to try to clean up my work at the office in time to catch the three-thirty, or at least the four-thirty, but that I couldn't be sure. I would phone her from the station when I arrived.

I caught the three-thirty, got to Avalon a little after four-thirty, and entered the telephone booth in the station, sooty and clammy, and hoping that when I rang my number the line would be busy. I needed a grievance of at least that size (the implication that my wife was thoughtlessly chatting on the phone when I might be trying to get through to her) to recover the ground I had lost and get back in the running. Presenting a footsore and bedraggled spectacle at the front door would put her at a distinct disadvantage, one from which she might never really emerge. I dropped my dime in the slot and dialed the number tremulously. I got the busy signal. I clapped the phone on the hook, and, murmuring "Yackety-yack!" gratifiedly, folded my crumpled seersucker coat over my arm and began the three-mile trek that was to punish her.

The sun was still high in the sky and beating down mercilessly. I hadn't gone a tenth of a mile before my shirt felt like a poultice. I crossed from side to side of the road, in quest of shade where it appeared (not to be too vindictive with her), but this was a technique that I presently realized offset any respite from the sun by adding a marked percentage to my mileage. So after that I stuck to one side of the road.

I lifted a wet cuff to consult my wrist watch. Five-twenty. I was not a fifth of the way. At that rate I wouldn't be home before eight o'clock, for much of the journey from there on lay uphill, and it had become increasingly necessary to pause for rest even on the levels. It would be mad to proceed faster than a stroll; a mile an hour was plenty. At that pace, when would my wife begin to wonder? When worry? When grow alarmed? Well before home was in sight, I'd be bound. Two or three motorists slowed to offer me rides, but I shook my head and plodded on.

My clothes were now not only soaked but steaming; at least it seemed so to me. I threw my coat away — or didn't throw it away exactly, but chucked it under a culvert from which I could retrieve it when next I drove by. A wallet I had taken from it made a disagreeable bulge in a hind trouser pocket. I hit a long open stretch where lengthened exposure to the sun had rendered the tar in the road so soft that I had the feeling of slogging through rarebit.

I sat down on a large stone to take a small one out of my shoe. Nursing my foot a moment, I forlornly compared the trite hassle of which this was the fruit with those bright, deftly negotiated spats by which marriage is idealized in drawing-room comedies. I mentally revised parts of our wrangle with some better dialogue (such as might be heard most any night at Moot Point, as a matter of fact). In my breather, there by the wayside, I imagined it as an adroit exchange conducted before dinner guests, which, uncorking a wine or disheveling a salad, I would crown with, "Marriage, my dear, has driven more than one man to sex."

I put my shoe on and rose, and, after pausing to draw fabric away from my person at various points, resumed my march. I sensed the birth of a blister on one foot. Presently, too, I began to have moments of vertigo in which I wondered whether I hadn't perhaps punished my wife enough. I tried to divert my-self by · eating over and over the pun, "You haven't vertigo, you haven't vertigo." I had neglected to water myself at the waiting-room drinking fountain before setting out, and now a great thirst, which a little thought amplified into panic, parched my throat. My general condition, plus heat shimmers in the road and blinding flashes from the chrome of passing cars, re-sulted at last in a fogging of my vision. Fogging may not be precisely the word, for the change took the form of rendering commonplace objects adventurous, and objects visible that may very well not have been there. Thus distant elms and willows appeared for fleeting moments to have the look of date palms, and once I thought I saw a camel on the horizon.

I stepped off the road, crossed a ditch, and sat down on an-other rock. I ran my finger over my forehead in the manner of a squeegee. I noticed several burs on the cuffs of my trousers. I was breathing heavily and feeling a dense throbbing inside my head when a car approaching down the hill ahead of me slowed and came to a stop on the other side of the road. My wife was behind the wheel. I waited for her to speak, prepared to consolidate my gains.

"What's the matter with you?" she asked, through the open window.

"I'll be all right," I said, plucking at my shirt buttons. "It's just my heart."

She put her head out of the window and looked back up the road to make sure nothing was coming. Then she turned the car around and drew up near me. She reached over and opened the door on my side. I got to my feet, made my way across the ditch, and climbed in. I pulled the door shut and she put the car in gear. I made sure my window was all the way down and adjusted the wing glass so the draft would strike me the instant we got under way. "I tried to call you a couple of times but you were busy talking," I said as we did. "So I had to walk. What brings you over this way now?"

"I tried to call the butcher several times — the cold cuts I ordered didn't come — and our party line was busy. That meant you couldn't reach me, and I got to worrying. I figured you might well have been on that three-thirty. I couldn't be sure, but rather than risk keeping you waiting in the hot station, I thought I'd take a chance on a trip for nothing."

We drove in silence for a stretch, and then she said, "Isolde Poole called just as I was leaving. She suggested we all have dinner together."

"Well?"

"An air-conditioned restaurant sounds good."

"I thought you didn't like Augie," I said.

She heaved a long sigh of resignation. "Well, it comes down to what you said," she answered. And, glancing off across the frazzled fields, she added, "You've got to take people as they are."

Seven

FAILING other certifications of his genius, Augie was deep in the long, symbolic process of building himself up as a son of a bitch. I was a willing witness: Curiosity could not resist what conscience must groan over. Our intimacy progressed from uncertain beginnings for Augie's first revelations were not voluntary but the product of incitement. I threw the incident of the lawn party up to him in a sort of peeve for his picking my brains about the spat, as he presently did, not to mention its having been over his sins that I had spent the week-end in the doghouse.

"You're not in any danger of splitting up, are you?" he asked the following Wednesday when he dropped into my office to leave some new cartoons (which I declined to look at in his presence following an editorial rule set up in deference to my nervous system).

"No, we're not in any danger of splitting up," I said with my head bent over my desk.

He set the drawings on a table, where I had motioned for him to put them, and sauntered to the window. "I wouldn't want anything to happen to you and Audrey."

"Just keep your nose clean and nothing will," I answered.

"What the hell are you talking about?"

"How does your garden grow?"

"My garden?"

"The blonde. You were quite smitten with her."

"Oh, that." He shot me a speculative look. "Anything she ever gets, she's asked for. All that come-on."

"Next time remember that water is a great conductor of sound. I speak as a friend," I said. "And, also speaking as a friend, if you mean business put this down as rule number one: Never waste your time with a flirt."

The sagacity of this so got his goat, especially as coming from a tenderfoot as I know he took me to be, that he asked me to lunch and was soon deep in accounts designed to assure me that he not only meant business but was and always had been fairly well established in it. I have listened to my share of males making a clean breast of their conquests, but Augie singled me out as a special confidant in a way that I always felt had something to do with the fact that I kept rejecting his drawings. Some special need must have driven him to play his own Devil's Advocate to a man he knew was down for a character reference for him, even granting that that fact was all a by-product of his wife's having submitted mine. "I suppose I'm a bit of a cad," he said, performing some surgery on a lamb chop. (Why does a man always look so smug when he calls himself a cad?) "But I pay for it."

I fed him the expected straight line, after a leisurely pause. "How?"

"I — no, I've told you enough already."

Tune in next week to this same station and see what happens, I thought. Next week was drinks on me at a Manhattan bar we began to frequent. I wheedled and needled more out of him by taking my wife's line of disapproving; then out came the private psychology. For his explanations were, again, à la mode (it seemed to slip his mind for the moment that the artist didn't need any explaining).

"You see, I have these devilish feelings of guilt," he said. He talked in a quite standard vein for a few minutes and then my ear, practiced from all the Saturday-night strip teases, picked out a complexity it was not accustomed to, a slight offbeat in the popular rhythm. "You see, part of the idea is that I deserve this guilt and when I don't have it I feel uncomfortable. As though I'm being delinquent? There's this masochistic urge to go after the guilt by sleeping with as many women as possible — what other way is there for making myself feel rotten? I feel the guilt, it wears off, and then I get to feeling guilty because I'm not feeling guilty."

"Why sleep around then, if it's that much trouble?" I asked, masking my fascination by breaking a pretzel on the top of the bar.

"It's the only way of getting back to the guilt."

"Why should you want to get back to it?"

"Because I feel I have it coming to me."

"What for?"

"For sleeping around."

I took in a house cat that was arching itself against the leg of a patron in a booth. Augie bent a plastic muddler back and forth. "I've really got myself on my hands," he said. What he wanted me to say was, "Augie, you've got to stop crucifying yourself." Instead I said, "What time is it?"

He looked at me reproachfully. "What do you mean, what time is it?"

I shook my head when the bartender glared at my empty glass. "Isn't it a little rear-end-to? Your complex."

"It's a vicious circle," he agreed, nodding. He plied the

swizzle stick a moment longer. Then he set it aside and revealed, "I'm going to an analyst."

"Does he tell you all this? What you just told me?"

"No — I tell him.'"

There was a pause. I glanced at a wrapped parcel of rejections on the bar, which he had just picked up from the office. Guessing my thought, he said, "This man is very reasonable. And he doesn't dun me for what I owe him either. He's interested in my case."

"I can believe that," I said.

"Not that the sledding isn't tough enough without doctor bills." He shifted his feet and hunched over the bar. He took a drink and for the moment looked the picture of a man with nothing much on his mind. "Divil a penny — "

"I've got to get back to the office," I said. "I'll see you at the P.T.A. thing tomorrow night. Be sure and come now, do you hear, because you're being watched."

Our local Parent-Teacher Association was putting on a fund-raising jamboree for which I had been asked to write a skit preferably satirizing the town Board of Finance which, by cutting the school's appropriation, had put them in the position of needing this benefit. I never went to P.T.A. meetings, they weren't really my speed, but I agreed to turn out a little something for their do. I also let it out that I was not averse to playing the lead. Plans for the project had been some weeks afoot, and now the various committees involved were to get together to discuss the show, the food, the publicity, and the decorations for the school gym in which the shindig was to be held. There was to be an opening rehearsal too — all at the gym, which has a stage at one end.

My piece was a two-character diversion. By the time the evening of the rehearsal rolled around, I had spent many mental hours with my leading lady (Isolde), casting about for the right vein in which to approach my role, assuming she would do hers as Joan Fontaine. I had smoldered in the style of Olivier, had ground my jaws and talked with protracted blinks like Spencer Tracy. With something of Cary Grant's animal charm I had taken advantage of that April heart. I had worked out a system of uttering all my labials with my upper teeth against my lower lip, similar to Humphrey Bogart's, and had even whispered everything like Jimmy Stewart. None of these seemed right for the part. It was while driving to the school gymnasium that I lapsed into an improvisation that struck what seemed to me the indicated mood.

I dissolved to an ocean liner on which we met at table. It was as George Sanders that, taking leave of her in the dining room, I rose and, pushing back my chair said, "If you care to take a turn on deck, you'll find me forward. Possibly even a bit unscrupulous."

That was sailing to the States. When we docked in New York, we made a date for cocktails the next day. "Let's make it fivish," she said.

"Fine," I said. "In front of the Biltmorish."

Five-fifteen found her waiting alone before the hotel door. Five-twenty came and still no me. At five-thirty she found me a block away, browsing at Brooks Brothers' windows. That was how I cured her of that suffix, and, oh, what fun we were going to have if this was any gauge.

I locked the door of my car and walked up the steps to the lighted gymnasium. There must have been forty committee members there, all jabbering away in groups from one end of the floor to the other. Isolde, sitting in the bleachers, raised her head from a script and waved. The P.T.A. secretary, a large woman named Mrs. Blenheim, had said she had connections in the theater and would get us a director. She saw me, and taking a tall, slim man by the hand, towed him across the floor and introduced him as Ernest Mills. He was a TV director who registered omniscience by shrugging one shoulder, and wore a white beret which, on top of a sunburn he had, looked like a poached egg on an order of hash. He was known as Putsi, though not by me.

Suddenly he turned around and, moving his arms above his head as though he were waving off flies, called out, "Kids, we're going to run through the first sketch. So please go out in the hall for your confabs, or if you have to stay inside here, keep it down to a dull roar, so we can hear."

About half of them stayed. Isolde and I mounted the stage. While we were waiting for comparative silence, I spotted Augie in the back of the gym, sizing up the walls for murals and posters with someone in a print smock. Evidently another P.T.A. officer had connections in the art world. But it was all right, I was later assured: two heads were better than one, and the newcomer and Augie were getting theirs together fine. Her name was Cornelia Bly.

The racket subsided and Isolde and I began our reading. Mills and Connections in the Theater sat together on a couple of folding chairs. The sketch was a what-if satire: what if a husband applied the same despotic methods to his family budget as our Board of Finance did to the town's. The M.C. was to set it up with an introduction ending, "Now we meet him as he enters the terrace to join his wife for their annual budget hearing." I explained all this to Mills who hadn't yet read the script.

I strolled out in flannel slacks and a houndstooth jacket and extended an imaginary dry Martini to the lounging Isolde, murmuring as I did so, "One for the Gibson Girl." I then kissed her and sat down with a cocktail of my own, whereupon "my wife" worked the conversation around to how much she had saved on redecorating the house and by skimping on clothes, with me deflating her at every turn in a way that was as foxy as it was deft. In the course of all the persiflage, I fetched her two more Martinis, kissing her each time I handed her one to show that I was flesh and blood beneath this fabulous exterior (and ad libbing repetitions of the Gibson Girl mot, which I assumed my hearers had not caught as they had not laughed). My wife tried to explain to me the difference between cord and seersucker. I reached for my glass and drawled, "I had supposed, my dear, that a seersucker was someone who spent all her money on fortune tellers."

Mills clapped his hands for us to stop and came forward.

"This has been going on for twenty-two minutes," he said. "Where's the action?"

"Why, in the grain, the subtlety of the give and take," I said.

"But this is a skit. It shouldn't take more than five minutes at the most. It isn't a three-act play."

"It isn't?" some card out front whispered.

I said, "There's some conflict coming up in a minute. Where she says she's going to Lord and Taylor's tomorrow. I say, 'What do you have to go to Lord and Taylor's for?' And she says, 'Because I want to go to Hattie Carnegie's next week and I haven't a thing to wear.'"

"And your diction —" Mills continued with his strictures.

"I'm playing him with my tongue in my cheek," I said.

"Maybe that's why I can't hear you."

It got the first real laugh of the evening, and we resumed with some sense of the ice having been broken.

"One more important thing before we go on," Mills said. "Just how do you see this character you're playing?"

"As a sort of George Sanders type," I said.

"George Sanders." He turned with a frown to Connections in the Theater. "Does that strike you as right? For a P.T.A. sketch?"

Connections in the Theater rose and came down, shaking her head. "No," she said, "it doesn't. Not for what we want — local audience identification and all. And I agree with you about too long with too little action, now that I see it on the stage. It bothered me when I read it."

Mills went on to say that he saw the man as a stuffy middle-class suburban husband. Another P.T.A. official joined the discussion and the three of them went into a huddle. I turned back from the footlights and had a cigarette with Isolde, while those with humbler chores looked on.

"Making headway with the Crib?" I chatted.

"Mmm," she responded with an affirmative bob of her head, as she took a light from my match. "I've put your name in, so I expect they'll have someone up your way soon." She laughed. "If this isn't where you came in."

"It isn't that," I said quickly, "but I think you ought to get completely new references. For luck. We sort of jinxed you once. So you feel free to count us out, you hear?"

"You're sweet." She leaned over to kiss the tip of my ear. "And I think you're an absolute genius getting us mixed up in this sort of thing. I hope the Crib has a representative snooping around here. The P.T.A.!"

He glances to the rear and sees that Augie and his collaborator have their heads together indeed, and as duenna it is his task to calibrate the distance between them as they bend consultingly over a sketch.

"I wouldn't think of asking anyone else," Isolde said.

He mops the stage with his withdrawing gaze and wonders, Does no shadow of suspicion ever cross that April heart? Maybe Augie's very openness disarms it. Maybe she doesn't personally condemn the tangents repugnant to Rock-a-Bye? Did these agencies put a tail on a man, like a private eye? He glances toward the bleachers again, and again calibrates the bent heads. The distance between them has dwindled since his last reading. He knows Isolde is looking at him, the tinted-Dresden face in its winsome half-smile, and something shoots along the surface of his heart like ice cracking, and he knows his role at last. It is as Herbert Marshall he must go down the infested years, the faithful friend, somehow loyal to both, suave, meticulous and dear.

"You'll love this. The new caseworker's name is Mrs. Mash!"

He crosses to left center stage and, his back to her, squashes out his cigarette in a soup ramekin.

"I'll do all I can. You know that."

The huddle on the floor breaks up, putting to an end the intolerable scene.

"For this skit to get across," Mills said as spokesman for the trio, "we see him as definitely a conventional middle-class husband. Practical but stodgy."

"In that case, of course, I'm not suited to the part," I said pleasantly, laying my script on a chair, and started to walk off.

"Well, now, not so fast," Mills said. "Your build is O.K. Just boom the lines out — no muttering in your beard — and bang your fists and harrumph around. You can change the lines to suit the character later, but let's just try him for size. You can do it; stuffy — as — the — devil."

Coming on the heels of an afternoon in which Blair had praised me as good at routine details, a relief after all the creative-type editors, brilliant but erratic, who had preceded me in the job, this struck anything but a responsive chord, and I advised Mills quietly not to be optimistic; dryly adding that, as to the diction thing, he may have heard of something in the theater known as throwing your lines away. I didn't catch his answer, but a local electrician who had been asked to handle the lighting, and was already clambering about back there like an eager beaver, audibly remarked that I should have thrown mine away as soon as I wrote them. He was not the worst of the Philistines I was up against. There was additional conferring on how the skit might better depict a recognizable family situation, and Connections had a suggestion. "Putsi, how about putting in a daughter?" she asked him.

"Make him a sort of Edward Arnold type," he said.

"Edward Arnold!" I cried in a spasm of pain and bewilderment.

"The daughter's extravagant, spends money right and left on clothes, phonograph records, runs up telephone bills," Connections went on. "The father huffs and puffs and says, 'Do you think I'm made of money?' "

This excited my tormentors further and they went into how they "saw" this girl as to age, etc. By an odd coincidence it turned out that Connections had a daughter just back from college, where she had studied dramatics. "I could have her here in five minutes," Connections said. "She's home, just up the road."

That was all I needed. To be judged capable of delineating a stuffed shirt was unsettling enough; but the assumption that I could with no trouble suggest deciduous middle age was more than I could take in one night, and, wishing them luck in their plans for a new Ma and Pa Kettle, I turned and strode off the stage. As I did so, I caught my foot in a mess of the electric wire that lay everywhere like spaghetti and pitched into a crate of costumes. Mills sprang forward with the assurance that this sort of thing was the rule in the theater, where tempers were thin and plays not written but rewritten. The battering mine was taking was a measure of its resilience and potential. "This guy a pulp and paper magnate?" I said derisively, disengaging his fingers from my coat lapels. "Or do you see him as a big shot in the trucking game?" Mills and the chapter president, a bull-dozer of a woman who stood solidly athwart my path, detained me long enough for Connections' daughter to be fetched by car, an interval which they improved by assuring me that, as to the age matter, a ponytail haircut to peg the girl as a teen-ager, no more, and some cornstarch in my own thatch to grizzle me up a bit, and the same for Mrs. Poole, should do the trick. Isolde was asked if she'd mind, and she smiled through the wings with a shake of her head. I gave in for the sake of the show when I saw Connections' daughter, who turned out to have been hewn by Rodin, and whose flesh tints were evocative of ripe fruit. I sat down right then and there and dashed off some lines to audition her with, in the frenetic tradition of the theater.

The first speech we gave the girl to try went, "If you don't give me enough money to dress attractively, Pops, you may not find any boys around here to take me off your hands." Mills told her to stand over me as I fumed at a table on which were strewn the monthly bills (wearing on my face that grimace that goes with the legend "Grr!" in comic strips) and also gave her some pointers on how to say the line. "O.K.," he said, returning to his seat. "Go."

The girl read the line approximately as directed. But she prefaced it with a full half minute of aphrodisiac breathing so intense and vehement that I could feel it in my hair and down the back of my neck. It was pointed out to her that the rendition would have been ideal if this were a drama dealing with incest, and she were called upon to sexually inflame her father. It was, however, a cozy domestic comedy aiming at lots of audience identification, so omit the palpitations — and forget about keeping her chest in profile. She caught on and we had little trouble with the remaining lines so far written for her. But she drowned the stage in a perfume so heady that I left the gymnasium with my senses reeling, and dropped into bed exhausted and wretched, and wondering how old the girl really was. Twenty-one or -two probably, if she was just out of college. I was breaking my rule never to get my feathers fussed. And Augie — he was probably in his bed planning a campaign to get into Cornelia Bly's. Some P.T.A.

The show was put on three weeks from that Saturday evening. My wife and kids saw it. My sketch went on between an original ballet and a humorous slide lecture. As finally played it was a satire about a tightwad with a brain like a steel trap, who couldn't solve a simple riddle about a poor mother dividing her apples up. We made him a member of the Board of Finance. The next morning, Sunday, the following scene was enacted at my breakfast table:

MAUDE: (Studiously spooning her cereal about) Daddy, you were wonderful last night.

MOTHER: (Who has obviously been coaching the children and now shepherds them through their exclamations) Yes, wasn't he! The whole program was wonderful, but his skit was the best of all. (Chorus of "Yes, yes!")

MARCO: You could hear a pin drop.

FATHER: That'll be all of that!

MOTHER: (In a tearful collapse of her brave front) The child did not know it was supposed to be a comedy.

FATHER: Who said it was?

For as the hour had approached, and it could be seen how matters might go, I had changed my tune. It was now my story that the skit was a bitter parable of misguided thrift rather than a comedy aiming at easy laughs. The switch was made just in time, for the result had been precisely as the boy had said — you could hear a pin drop. Our hopes had been briefly nourished when one of the flats wobbled and threatened to collapse on the stage, to resolve in that way the conflict with which the drama grappled; but someone back there (no doubt the electrician who'd had it in for me all along) righted it in time, and we'd had to play through to the end. In front of an audience, Connections' daughter couldn't resist the chance to show what she could really do with her teeth in a part, and returned to Cheyne-Stokes breathing, fluttering my hair and offering me advantageous views of her hocks, which I had already repeatedly and exhaustively ratified. She wore the subversive perfume again, and wherever I walked on the stage or sat, she had just been and left her spoor. In the demoralizing boredom, I had an impulse to seize her in an incestuous embrace and then maybe extemporize to some sort of O'Neill finish. But we finished as rehearsed, and the audience gave us a pretty good hand at that, no doubt in a flood of gratitude for their deliverance.

MOTHER: Why do you object to the child's saying you could hear a pin drop? You've been claiming it's a savage indictment.

FATHER: (Rising and leaving the dining room) Oh, what's the use trying to talk to this family? (He slams the door behind him, starting the refrigerator.)

I was sitting in the living room when the dining-room door opened and Marco was gingerly piloted over to apologize. Which he did.

"That's all right, Marco," I said. "Forget it."

He drew his mouth taut and said: "My name's not Marco any longer. I've found the name I want to change to."

"Oh?" I said, glancing at my wife. "What do you want us to call you from now on?"

"Alphonse."

As the choice of one who had soured on his own name because people laughed at it this was a substitute for which we were hardly prepared.

"Alphonse!" I said. "Where did you ever get such an idea?"

"Your play."

It was true; I had used it for the husband. The thing was, as the hour drew near and it was plain how things were going, every expedient for injecting comedy relief into the skit had been advised, including that of funny names for the characters.

"But Alphonse is a *humorous* name — " I began to explain to the boy, but that avenue was forever closed to me; the tribe of Digger Indians to whom we had apparently been playing had greeted the principals' open-armed exchange of "Ermingarde!" "Alphonse!" with such gloom that the watchful Marco had decided that here, certainly, was a name void of comic implications, and it had winged its way straight to his heart. I held my breath all morning, fearing a similar announcement from the dissatisfied Phoebe — we had called the daughter in the skit Melba. But that at least was spared me.

"So from now on, you might as well call me Alphonse," Marco said levelly. "Because I won't answer to any other."

That alone would have been a disastrous enough result of the Avalon First Annual P.T.A. Supper and Jamboree. But there were grimmer dividends to be reaped.

Eight

ON a day otherwise unmarked except for Phoebe's circulating a report among the neighbors that I was dead, I saw Augie lunching in a New York chophouse with someone who looked familiar: it was the conjunction of the heads. He had spotted me too, and the next time we met he spoke of her.

"She's got something I can't put my finger on — at least not yet," he said.

"Everything takes time," I said dryly.

It wasn't long before he had progress to narrate. Two weeks later I ran across them in a midtown restaurant called the Somerset, and this time I got caught in a traffic jam beside where they were sitting and had to stop.

The Somerset was a packed grotto among whose tables, which were the size of throat lozenges, the waiters flowed by some kind of osmosis, and the celebrities, wearing dark glasses in an already crepuscular gloom, picked their way by a power presumably like that of the bats they must be blind as. Some illumination was afforded by the incendiary dishes that were eaten there, but that was fitful. The customers were about equally divided between celebrities and people wearing dark glasses in the hope of being mistaken for one; but they must all have by now developed that eerie dexterity by which bats are said to "feel" things just short of touching them, because they never bumped into anything, except occasionally one another. It was a new, contemporary habitat in which I was less adept with the naked eye. Add to the perils of darkness those of wires getting underfoot from telephones being plugged in at tables, as well as the flaming skewers borne aloft in the general press, and it was worth your life to go in there. Only the wonderful food drew me. I never saw menus squinted at from so many angles — because while the celebrities removed their glasses to consult them, the third-string columnists and unemployed bit players kept them on so as not to be unmasked in the interval as nobodies. There was an incessant waving from table to table, though I don't know what anybody thought he saw, or whether it made any difference. Unless it was owls they resembled after all.

I didn't immediately recognize Augie, because he was behind a pair of smoked goggles himself — he had just sold us a two-inch spot page decoration of a cornucopia full of frozen foods, which we might find a place for next Thanksgiving. He affected instability, throwing his charcoal down and grinding it underfoot when the cornucopia wouldn't come right, in repairs to it at the office.

"Hello, hello," a familiar voice said. "*Setzen sie sich.*" And there he was, looking like a hunted gambler. "Sore eyes," he said, a little self-consciously, and lifted the cheaters to rub them. "You remember Cornelia Bly." I congratulated her on the party murals, as I already had Augie.

"Thank you," she said. "How did your skit go? I couldn't make it that night."

"You could hear a pin drop," I said. It got a laugh. She invited me to sit down, though God knew where I would have, unless in one of their laps. I said I had to get back to the office.

"Your artists have it easier than you do," she smilingly suggested.

Augie said: "We must all have lunch together sometime. And I want you to see Cornelia's paintings. She might do a cover for us."

"Love to," I said, taking my leave, and inside of ten minutes had gained the street.

Cornelia Bly was on the short side, shorter than I had remembered her, with her hair done — or I should say left undone — in one of those tossed salad sort of close crops. Her smile was a pink and white semicircle of short teeth and bright gums, which rather put me in mind of a slice of watermelon. She had a habit of ducking her head when she laughed. She wore no make-up and her finger-ends were square. She was dressed in snuff-colored tweeds, and a brick-red porkpie, which I took to be hers, hung on a peg over Augie's head.

"She doesn't have your obvious kind of attractiveness," Augie said to me later. "A woman like that totally escapes your callow romanticist. They wouldn't look at her twice."

"I don't know about that," I said, picking up my beer, for we were at a bar.

"You realize what a fraud the whole sexual paraphernalia is, your Hollywood sexless cakes and pies. How much more mature the French are — throwing a disheveled heroine at you on the screen. A man is like a moth driven insane by indirect lighting, by the interfering fixtures of glamour. Then he finds that bright light that's shed best by the naked bulb."

There was a little more to it than that. Cornelia had a glamour that wasn't alone anti-glamour. She had at the moment a kind of prominence. She had leapt into vogue on the crest of publicity springing from legal action she was bringing against a firm for one of whose advertisements she had done a semiab-stract portrait which, she claimed, they had changed without her consent. She charged that the face had been mutilated by the addition of a second eye. The case had gained wide newspaper attention, and one news magazine had run a picture she had drawn over, showing the face as she had orginally done it with its single eye, side by side with the mutilated version containing the two. "The Eye for an Eye Girl" she was called, and was pointed out in restaurants and theater lobbies. So Augie liked to be seen lunching with her and strolling through art galleries.

When it reached the point of my trying to phone the boule-vardier at home and being told by his wife that he was staying in town that night, where he had business, and would I like the number of the hotel where he was staying, I laid the cards on the table.

"Look here," I said, after a few pre-lunch drinks had loosened me up, "I've got something on my mind. Let me begin by saying that my personal opinion has nothing to do with this. I don't care who you play house with, but circumstances have made it my business and I can't beg off or back out. To beg off would in itself be an answer to the people I'm accountable to, and one not in your favor. You must know by now what I'm talking about. Have you forgotten that you gave me for a reference?"

He frowned into his cocktail. "I've been meaning to talk to you about that," he said. "Putting you on the spot is the last thing in the world I want to do. It was of course Isolde who gave you two for a reference."

"I assumed as much. Also that it's mostly Isolde who wants a child?"

"Not at all," he said with an injured air. "I want one just as much as she does."

I'd like to have seen the expression on my face as I answered, "You act like it. Do you know why you flunked out at Rock-a-Bye?"

"They knew I was an artist with no regular income. They think it's too risky to put a child into a home with a financial picture like mine."

"Does Isolde know how much trouble you go to to keep contrite?"

"Did you ask me to lunch or was I subpoenaed? Isolde is broad-minded."

"Isolde is not a caseworker," I answered. "I'm broad-minded too. But the Crib isn't. The Crib is just folks, the same as Rock-a-Bye. If they hear about the husband sleeping with other women, they don't understand that he's doing that to keep his guilt feelings tuned up. And I don't want to be the one to explain it to them, though I'd like to be around when somebody else does. Neither do I want to have to explain to them the tradition that the artist is part son of a bitch. Agencies size a couple up by asking, for one thing, if the husband is a good provider — yes, granted. But they also ask themselves if a child they give them might one day be the victim of a broken home. Lots of children are, you know."

"Yes, I know. And when I can no longer bear to think of the victims of broken homes, I begin to think of the victims of intact ones." He had me there, and I was grateful he didn't pause for an answer but went right on, with some heat, "I don't see what the hell my sex life has to do with whether I'll make a good father. If Isolde and I have an understanding about these things why isn't that enough for the rest of the world? Why must people go around looking for fleas in one another's hide, like monkeys? Our marriage works as good as anybody's we know with natural children. Look at the Arkwrights with their three, and the Johnsons with their six. I wouldn't give ten cents for either of those homes. Let welfare workers go to homes like that and make them deserve their own children or give them up. Why don't they give all couples tests before they let them have children, or stop trying to find flaws in marriages that don't exist? Western culture! The way it mauls and mangles the individual to save him for society. It's time we turned it around and organized society to let the individual live — yes, let him indulge impulses that don't hurt anybody. Soon enough we'll all be dead, or what's worse, old. When are we going to get civilized and let the whole man live? The French — "

"I know. But this isn't France. And if it was I'm not sure Cornelia wouldn't be chaperoned till she was safely married. Is she married?"

"Certain African tribes — "

"There's no time for certain African tribes. A woman named Mrs. Mash, who lives in Haversham, is coming to see me any day and ask for a clean bill of health about you. So answer yes or no — are you keeping your nose clean?"

"Of course I am. I'm walking the chalk line these days. It shows how much I'm willing to give up to have a child."

"What about Cornelia Spry?"

"Cornelia Bly. I'm not sleeping with her, if that's what you mean."

I looked at him and then looked away. What good was the question? How could I tell whether he was lying or not? He even owed it to me to lie, to clear my conscience and get me off the hook. But it didn't get me off the hook. Our talk only lashed me into a state of curiosity bordering on prurience itself. I was now that censor whom if you scratch you will find a satyr. In the half-wretched relish with which I now threw myself into the role of snoop, it was all I could do to keep from picking Augie's brains every time I saw him. Then a totally unforeseen incident occurred which uncorked my friend without any prompting, as well as shed some light on him from a fresh quarter.

It happened at a party, a typical Avalon evening studded with intellectuals who listened only to jazz and read principally the avant-garde funnies. In addition, there was the beautiful and jumpy Monica Stern, the dress designer; old Thaddeus Hall, the connoisseur of doorknobs; and Sid Walters, the clear poet. Mills, my director, was on hand. Whether or not he came with the beret I don't know because I came late and left early. He was there with his wife, a large, pleasant chandelier of a woman, covered with costume jewelry. It kept falling off her like decorations from a Christmas tree, and once I saw her angling for something in her Tom Collins, though that may have been a cherry. At one point Monica Stern sat next to me, rapidly draining me of interest in the servant problem. I had slipped away to Moot Point and was deep in didoes with her there, altering her to suit the tenant, when I became aware of a peculiar thunderhead building up out of the conversation around us. It went like this.

There was a bachelor named Morley who ate ice. He had brought up something he called mannerism tests, in a discussion about the sexes. When pressed for details by interested guests, he rang Mills into the discussion.

"Oh, you have a subject do three or four things." Mills explained. "There's a typically masculine and typically feminine way of doing each. You give the person a score accordingly."

"Let's try it," a woman proposed. "Who'll be It? Morley?"

"I know the tests, or at least one of them — how you drink

from a glass," Morley answered, grinding up the cubes out of his fourth or fifth highball. "The rest'll come back to me the minute I hear them. What we want is a fresh subject."

"How can there be two ways of drinking?"

"There's two ways of doing everything. And you can't cheat. Come on, who'll volunteer?"

Everybody was cagey. But at that moment who should turn from a *tête-à-tête* he'd been deep in with a woman a little apart from the group but Augie. He extended an empty glass to the hostess. "Could I have another?" he said. Everybody laughed.

Morley rose and spread his arms like a traffic cop. "Make way for the gent," he said, and taking Augie's glass went to the cellaret himself. "What are you drinking?"

"Scotch and soda. What's the matter with all you people?" Augie asked, grinning. Here a small knot gave off twitting Sid Walters about the clarity of his verse, and we became one. Morley shouldered his way back with a hastily conjured highball. The company watched in silence as Augie took it, glanced into it, and drank.

"Female," Morley said with a consulting look at Mills. "Women look into a glass before they drink, men not. Right, Putsi?"

"Not female — feminine," Mills corrected him. "It's not sexual as such — just strains in the make-up, characteristics. Like — well, masculine and feminine endings in poetry."

"Augie does move the needle to the thread, not the thread to the needle," Isolde said with a laugh. "Remember that business in *Huckleberry Finn* where the woman sees through Huck's disguise?"

But Morley was not to be put off. "I just remembered another one — *the way you look at your nails*. That right, Puts?"

"Well, yes," Mills said, sauntering toward the cellaret with his own glass.

"What the hell is this?" Augie asked, his smile a little frayed.

"Just look at your nails," Morley said. "Don't be bashful. Go on — they're yours."

"Let somebody else. I don't want to hog the show."

"What good is the test if you let everybody do a part of it? Go on, look at your nails. Don't be a spoilsport."

"All right if it'll make you happy." Augie obligingly spread the fingers of one hand in a fan and examined the tips.

"I think I'd like a drink too," my wife said, rising and making her way over to the bar. "And, Julia, do you still have the shuffle-board downstairs?" she asked the hostess. "I'd like to play."

Morley screwed round in his seat to find Mills, who was trying to bail out of the lark. "Puts, he looked at his nails like this. Isn't the idea that that's the way a woman would examine a polishing job? As distinguished from closing your hand up in a sort of fist?"

The latter was what Augie was now doing with both hands, having set his drink down. "For God's sake," he said, giving his belt a hitch. As we sat wondering how we were going to dismount this tiger we'd gotten aboard, Augie shook a cigarette from a pack and twisted a match from a book, remarking that Morley had probably had too much to drink — a fact which had also penetrated the rest of us.

"What's the next test?" my wife called over. "Let me be the guinea pig for the next one."

"He just took it," Mills put in, nodding at Augie. "It's the way you strike a match. Most women strike the match away from them, men toward them — the way Augie just did."

"So what score does that give me?" Augie inquired.

"Sixty-six and two thirds," Morley said. "It's all in fun of course," he added with a nervous laugh.

"Don't laugh in that tone of voice," Augie said. "It ain't ladylike."

"Now look here, pal."

"If you're so interested in masculine behavior, I've got a suggestion. Step outside and repeat that score."

"We are outside," someone said in a hopeless whisper. It was the case; we were out on the terrace, where we hung suspended largely on canvas in attitudes of stylish prostration, behind screens which moths had begun to batter in the late-summer-evening half-light. "There's boxing gloves in the basement," the hostess said facetiously.

"You people run this stuff into the ground," Augie said. That's what the rest of us thought too, suffering there in the gloom, and he should have let it drop. "All this bushwa."

"It's not bushwa, exactly," Mills said, strolling around behind a stout chaise longue from where he now proceeded to try to make peace by pouring oil on the flames. "The point is this: everyone is, and *should* be, a mixture of the two. Now wait a minute! A perfectly masculine man would be a monstrosity, just as a perfectly feminine woman would. Van Appledorn has worked all this out in exhaustive studies. The ideal is a balance of ingredients, is what Van Appledorn says."

"I don't give a damn what Van Appledorn says. Just watch your own lip. I fished a miller out of my last drink, so why shouldn't I look in the glass first?"

"You were quite right. Oh. Women usually hold a cigarette between their fingertips is another. I notice you've got yours well down against your hand, like a truck driver," Mills added graciously. "Of course these tests aren't Van Appledorn's. Schmidlapp's working on that."

"You can have Schmidlapp too."

Someone whispered in the ruined twilight: "Abraham Lincoln wore a shawl."

"I still think — " Augie went on, ignoring the emollient and kindling his expired fag from a table lighter someone had the presence of mind to extend — "I still think a man is a person who likes women and a woman is a person who likes men." He thanked the guest who had given him the light and glanced down at the unattached Morley, who now sat in a dejected slump, as though a jag had worn off. "That's perfectly true to a point," Mills said. "It doesn't hold for your Don Juan. He's trying to prove something. . . . "

The discussion, to still call it that, was going on when several of us went downstairs by way of falling in with Audrey's shuffleboard suggestion. We had been playing for some time when there was a muffled hubbub overhead, and a woman's face appeared at the top of the stairway. "They're at it!" she called, and was gone again.

We clomped upstairs and out to the yard where we found a circle of spectators standing on the grass, watching something in the center that wasn't instantly discernible. By an accident of confusion I thought first that Augie was fighting Mrs. Mills. Then I saw that in the cleared space were Augie and Morley, supporting one another in a comradely embrace.

"They're pooped," our stairway narrator explained. "Should we break them up? Most people think not."

"It started all over again when Morley accused Augie of symbolic virilization," someone else said.

"And then Augie called Morley a battle-ax."

"My daphne," the hostess moaned, glancing worriedly at a flower bed.

"Look, could you come over more this way, fellows?" her husband said, drawing the pair toward the house. The two staggered over together, interlocked.

"Isolde, put a stop to it."

"Why? It's what they want," she had sense enough to answer.

"*I'll* put a stop to it — the second he's sober," Augie said with great honor.

"I'm sober," Morley retorted. "What are you going to do about it?"

"Let go of that and I'll show you," Augie said, trying to wrench free his necktie to which Morley clung like a swaying subway rider. "More toward the house, away from those flowers," the host insisted testily. The combatants swerved obligingly down a slope in the lawn, with elaborate menace but around opposite sides of an intervening sour gum, as though they were stalking a common foe rather than spoiling for one another. Suddenly Morley took a cut at Augie that caught him straight on the nose. Augie cocked back a lean arm and planted one in Morley's middle, dumping him over backward into a clump of bushes. Augie stood over him and inquired after his health. Morley rose and grasped him around the waist with such determination that what they were doing changed to wrestling. Dancing erratically, they carried on an insulting banter full of epithets like "bigot bastard," and during which they stumbled about more or less buttressing one another. The host and I tried to pull them apart, but they were inseparable. By now a subtle bond had developed between them which seemed to consist of *their* being linked against their discouragers. At length, however, they stumbled against the sour gum with such impact that they were not only shaken free of one another but knocked, breathless, to the ground.

"It's a draw!" Isolde declared. We rushed forward and hustled the antagonists inside into separate bathrooms, from which they emerged cleaned up, and ready to shake hands, which they did with foolish grins. Everybody felt better all around. Everybody, that is, except Mills. He sat with a preoccupied look, which I later learned arose from his not being sure there hadn't been an error made in the drinking-glass test. It turned out that it's men who do tend to glance into a glass first — women by and large not.

But the incident did not lose its importance as a cause. At our weekly luncheon, the following Wednesday, Augie was not long in getting around to the triviality of the entire occurrence. "Mean, of course, there are these differences between the sexes. It's just that I don't like the idea of guys that lay their palm on their chest when they laugh being umpires," he said. "Or look at the toe of their shoe and waggle it, like women."

"Have you ever noticed that women pick a flake of tobacco off their tongue while a man sort of spits it out?" I said, sprinkling salt into my soup.

"Women have a different walk from a man," Augie said, looking away. "A woman throws her leg forward from the hip. A man from the knee."

"Yes, I remember that from physiology class."

I bit off a crust of roll and chewed it thoughtfully.

"Women and men get into bed differently," I said. "You've probably noticed the way a woman does that."

"Mmm," he said with a nod. He twisted round in his chair. "Where's that damned waiter with my beer?"

"A woman sits down on the bed first, then sort of swivels her legs around under the covers. Unlike a man who thrusts himself in foot first."

I have said that Augie was not prompted to the revelation he now made, but I guess I did irk him again with my insight into women and knowledge of their ways and all. However, I knew he had come stoked up and ready to tell me how many women he had slept with even without my cueing him by remarking: "I was thinking about your point regarding just plain taste for women being the real male gauge. What would be your guess is the number of women the average man sleeps with? The average American let's make it. In his lifetime?"

"That's hard to say," Augie answered. He took a pull on his beer, which had been served him, and looked away. "I've slept with forty-three."

"Forty-*three!*" I exclaimed, lowering a laden soup spoon.

"Isn't that many?" he asked with a negligence that I thought was really too much.

"Do you keep *count*, for God's sake?"

"I won't swear to the figure. Mean I happened to be thinking about it the other night, wondering where the women I'd known were that very minute, the way you do, and I started to count them."

"How many of these are since you've been married?" I asked. "If I'm not being too personal."

"Not at all. Ten."

Ten. So he had gobbled more sex on the side than I had partaken of in my entire thirty-five years, wild oats included. "What's the largest number of affairs you've had going at once?" I asked, biting down on an aching tooth.

"Three."

"Three. And do you think," I demanded indignantly, setting my soup spoon down altogether, "do you think I should be asked to give you a reference in the light of this information? Do you sit there with your bare face hanging out and ask me to recommend you to Rock-a-Bye and the Crib and Itsy Bitsy and God knows what else yet, as they flunk you out one after the other, do you ask me to say of a man who has laid over forty women, 'This is my idea of family timber.'? Do you think this is the sort of thing we want in our community? Do you now? What will people think when they find out I turned a goddam ram loose in the P.T.A.! Forty-two women!"

"Forty-three. Shh! People are looking. Now then. *Don't you think these very facts speak in my favor?* Because they show what I'm willing to give up to be a family man."

"You're not giving up Cornelia Bly. Because I phoned your hotel that night you stayed in, and they said you had left a message not to be disturbed," I put up to him. I hadn't phoned that night — it was just a trick. In my wretchedness and my wrath I wanted all the facts, however they might discommode my conscience. "I never asked to be a reference," I said. "But the only way out of this is straight through it."

"That's the way I look at it too," Augie answered. "So O.K. I'll tell you about Cornelia Bly." He studied his shrimp cocktail with that kind of frown that precedes the birth of an intricacy. "I can only put it this way. It's Cornelia Bly who's put me back on the straight and narrow."

Sensing a fresher nuance than those with which I was normally visited by articulate friends, even Augie, I spread my elbows on the table and listened keenly.

"You see, even if my wife might stand for a certain amount of nonsense I have a mistress who won't. Cornelia Bly is — how shall I put it? — a Puritan of the intellect. She doesn't care that much for conventions, but imposes her own rules on human relations outside of them, like your true radical. No promiscuity for her! So while my wife wouldn't mind my sleeping with Cornelia, Cornelia wouldn't stand for a minute for my sleeping with someone else."

"You mean you feel morally accountable to the woman who's led you astray?" I asked.

"Exactly," he said, gratified by my grasp. He shifted forward in his chair and went on eagerly, "You see, I wouldn't dare two-time her."

"Is she a battle-ax?"

Augie laughed, but gently, as if the walls had ears. "There's this, that most men do want a certain amount of domination. It's what I've always missed in my home life. I never got it from Isolde. Can you understand all this?"

"I may in time. I could understand it better now if it was the other way around — that you were married to your mistress and sleeping with your wife."

"That's exactly the way it feels! That Cornelia *is* my wife and Isolde's the Other Woman." Augie smiled. "We have a little domestic joke, Cornelia and I. I call her C.B. Like a vice-president?"

"What about your guilt feeling?" I asked. "What ever became of that?"

"That's been transferred to my marriage."

"You mean it's when you're with your wife you feel pangs of conscience?"

"That I'm cheating on Cornelia," he said, nodding.

"But won't this undermine your marriage?"

"Undermine it?" he said, with a tolerant smile for my opacity. "Just the contrary. Don't you see, it gives my home life the quality of an affair, and what takes longer to wither than that? Isolde's even suited to the role physically — sitting around the house in those velvet slacks and subversive necklines, greeting me with cocktails and roses in her hair. It's for her I buy the jewels and the expensive perfumes, believe you me!"

"I believe you," I said.

"So now I think I've answered all your questions. I've settled down into a reasonable groove, and my marriage is in no danger as every hour I spend with my wife has this tincture of cheating on another woman. Must you leave?"

"I have an office appointment. I can't finish this sandwich, but you take your time. Here's my share of the check," I said, tumbling some money on the table and rising. "I'd like to hear more about this later."

What did I think of what I'd heard, after settling down in my office (and combing the snarls out of my hair)? This. That if Augie were put out for adoption, preferably to C.B., who would brook no nonsense, and Isolde married someone else, we might hope for a reasonable solution to all this. But failing that, I figured I might as well go along with Augie's elucidation and see what we'd see. For if Cornelia Bly had succeeded in pruning his trespasses to within that degree of rectitude, that degree of the stern standards by which the agencies were bent on measuring man, who was I to quarrel with the alchemy by which these ends were gained? Furthermore, once he and Isolde got a child there was every reason to believe the progress would be completed by the responsibility that alone perfects growth. For who of us is mature enough for offspring before the offspring themselves arrive? The principle of society is forced growth. The value of marriage is not that adults produce children but that childen produce adults.

It was on the basis of this thinking, and a few of the points Augie himself had validly made in his anger, plus a dash of mercy and a pinch of hope, that I at last made a settlement with my conscience. I would give him the testimonial.

"When," I therefore impatiently asked my wife, "is that woman Mrs. Mash going to get here?"

Nine

SEPTEMBER slipped into October, summer into fall, and still no Mrs. Mash — except at the Pooles' where she called for repeated interviews. She preferred to go slowly, letting her impressions steep and simmer. "It takes nine months this way too," said Augie, who chafed under what he called the woman's X-ray eyes. The exhilaration of the turning year was felt in the city's quickened tempo. Autumn is the spring of the spirit, when the sap flows once again in wilted urban man. Also in wilted urban man who lives in the country. Audrey and I went for Sunday drives with the Pooles, improvising rides along the blazing back roads and through little towns whose names we didn't catch and to which we fled without the aid of maps. There was an epidemic of some respiratory nuisance which all the children caught. Phoebe got it first, and she was pumped so full of penicillin that the fumes from her cured a cold I had. The others followed, and in addition to the miracle drugs, electrically driven croup kettles were set going in various corners of the house. There were so many hissing plumes of steam on all sides that the place looked like a roundhouse. We had no fears about leaving the children with Mrs. Goodbread, a skillful mechanic, who watched the croup kettles with all the care with which in the old country, she said, she had tended smudge pots to guard the orchard fruit from frost. You have an instinctive faith in anyone who has sat up all night with trees. Dr. Vancouver was all right in there too. He carried a supply of surgical masks which he put on the *patients*, when examining them with stethoscopes, explaining that this was indeed an epidemic and his first duty was to the community, for whom he must keep himself in fettle. Setting out on one of our foursome jaunts, we saw him parked beside the road in his car, taking his temperature. He waved as we went by, the thermometer sticking up out of his smile.

It was on that trip that I first began to notice Augie wasn't himself. He sat slumped in the back seat beside Audrey, managing to look glum even in the yellow tartan cap and houndstooth jacket which comprised his plangent motoring gear. Cornelia Bly was in Florida for a month. Did he then miss her that much? Isolde said the picking, poking painstakingness of the agency was wearing his nerves down, as it was hers. It was an awful mental hazard. Augie, who had claimed such attunement to the autumn season that he could smell the leaves turning in their faint combustion, "exactly like something burning," and held reveling in her melancholy to be the highest joy open to man, didn't feel like reveling in the melancholy now. He was too miserable. "*Wenn du fehlen willst, fehle gut,*" he said.

"Don't talk like that," Isolde said. "What does that mean — something about not feeling good?"

"No, it's from one of the great Germans. 'If you're going to be a failure, be a good one,' " Augie said. In the rearview mirror in which I could see him as I drove, he seemed to be disappearing into his getup, like a turtle into its shell.

We were to lunch that Wednesday and discuss his latest try — a drunk lying in the gutter of a bowling alley — but there wasn't much to say about it. "Make him look dreamy and happy there, and you might put in a spectator — someone looking over and doing a 'take' on it," I suggested. He nodded vaguely. Our food came — a sandwich and a bottle of ale apiece. Pouring myself a glass, I asked: "Heard from Cornelia Bly lately?"

"I got a letter Friday," he said.

"You get letters from her at home?" I asked.

"No, I pick them up at general delivery, Norwalk."

"How's she doing? Still down in Florida?" I was sure from his expression that she'd given him the air, but I sensed that he wanted to talk about it and was doing my best to prime him past his reluctance.

He brought the letter abruptly out of his pocket.

"You might as well know the whole story," he said. "It's all in this. First she tells some gossip about where she's staying, local history and one thing and another. How we're still technically at war with the Seminole Indians." He poured himself some ale. "The tribe was originally formed by splitting with the Creek Indians. The name means 'seceders.' They fought the United States bitterly in 1817–1818, and later under Osceola. Toward the middle of the century that was. There aren't but three hundred Seminoles left in Florida. It seems a treaty was never signed with them."

"But that's not what's eating you."

"No." He bent his head again over the letter. "I told you Cornelia went down there to paint, but that's not the whole story. She went down there to think things through. Come to some conclusion about 'us.' That's all right, ours is a special relation, outside the pale. She felt she had to go over the whole thing objectively and without any emotional kibitzing from me. And now she's come to a conclusion about 'us.' Only down here she explains what she never told me before she left. It seems 'us' will soon be three."

It was a moment after his words reached me that his meaning did. There was an interval of dreamy disbelief during which the meaning floated dreamily toward me, like a shuttlecock over a badminton net well after the drive that sent it there is finished.

"I see," I said. "And?"

"And she wants to have the child and keep it."

"I see," I could only unresourcefully repeat. Then I asked: "How do you feel about that? Don't you stand on the right to live your own life, outside the pale as you say?"

"What is the matter with you?" he reproved. "A child . . ." He raked his hair and wet his lips. He shook his head distractedly. "I blame myself. . . . What's so funny?"

"Blaming yourself. I'm sorry."

"Who else is there to blame? I don't know what's the matter with you sometimes. Put yourself in my shoes."

I kept a straight face by pretending to probe a molar with my tongue. I said:

"It seems to me this is her own affair. She's sort of tricked you, hasn't she?"

He seemed not to have heard me. "My old will to fail," he said.

"How many months is she pregnant?" I asked, smiling helplessly now.

He held up three fingers, as though he could not utter the word. "Too late to do anything now but see it through."

"She knows you're married of course?"

"Of course. But that has nothing to do with it in her view. She feels she has a perfect right to be a miss mother if she wants."

I asked: "Can she afford a child?"

"She's banking on the ten thousand dollars she's suing that

flour company for. Her lawyer says it's a sure thing. He's got a critic who'll testify that there's been damage to her reputation. Thousands of people who never heard of her before have read about the case. So she figures the ten thousand she's asking will see her through the first few years, and by that time she expects she'll be making enough on her paintings to support the child. And of course she's hoping to get more advertising commissions as a result of the publicity."

The case was by this time already on the circuit court docket in New York. It came up very soon — in fact Cornelia's lawyer called her back from Florida by wire.

We all followed it with great interest. It was a libel suit, that being the category under which damage to professional reputation comes. The trial consumed two full days of expert testimony, disputed opinion, and legal and aesthetic wrangling. The pictures were of course placed in exhibit, and a long argument raged as to which looked more mutilated, with distinctions drawn between literal and artistic mutilation. The audience was all ears. The critic who testified in Cornelia's behalf was the editor of a surrealist quarterly called *Bloodshot*. I was in court with Augie the afternoon of the second day, and also two afternoons later when the judge rendered his verdict. He awarded damages to the plaintiff in the amount of twenty-five cents — in other words, Cornelia had lost the case. Augie gripped my arm and hauled me to my feet. "Let's go have a drink," he said.

"How the hell is she going to support that child now?" he said, in the bar to which we hurriedly repaired. "In France she'd have gotten a judgment. The artist has some rights there — what they call *moral droit*. Not here. I tell you, this country is a nest of Philistines."

"Won't she get more work, as you said?" I asked.

Augie shook his head. "Not a chance. The advertising agencies are laughing up their sleeves." He took a long pull on his beer and lowered the stein to the table. "She's got to give the child up now."

"Would she lay it at your door?"

Augie gave me a slow burn; and when my face began to get out of control I hid it with my hands and said, "Oh, God," holding them there till I had steadied myself enough to remove them and ask: "She has no other moneys?"

"Not enough. She lives with her brothers in a sort of homestead they inherited from their parents, who are dead. In Norwalk. She comes from a fine family," he added a trifle smugly. "I've never been there — we only met in New York. And where would I get any extra dough?" We glanced simultaneously at an envelope full of rejections in the pocket of his topcoat, which hung on the wall, the week's rejections which he had picked up from the office that morning. I remembered what I'd told him that night in his studio, about all the potential cash there was in his files, if he ever needed any. The same thought must have crossed his own mind because he brought his fist down and said, "She's got to give it up."

"Don't tell me," I said, "tell her."

He did, the next night. His report was that she tended to agree, but he didn't trust her. Women were too emotional. "Look at the cold, calculating way she sat down and figured this thing out from beginning to end — about having a child," he said. She needed further persuasion, he was sure, pressure perhaps from another source. "I mustn't run the risk of being seen with her from now on," he told me across the table at which we were again lunching. "I'm being watched closely — very closely — by the agency at this stage. So I've got to keep my nose clean, as you say. I don't suppose you'd talk to her?"

He had another guess coming if he thought I was averse. "I'll be glad to," I said, emptying a bottle of ale into my glass. He turned on me a look of canine gratitude, which I must say ill became a stormy petrel. "You're a brick," he said.

That was only part of it. What appealed to me was the opportunity of acting as proxy for a rogue. It was not only a role to which I was temperamentally drawn and by nature inclined, but one in which I was thoroughly grounded and even finely trained by the practice in which this picaresque side of me had been developed: I mean the hours spent at Moot Point honing my wits on just such romantic imbroglios as this. They had been literally without number, as I have perhaps adequately suggested. I had been embroiled there with women of all ages and from clinging vines to flinty intellectuals like Cornelia Bly, with no demonstrable damage. With this one a summer's dalliance, through a squall of passion with that, and out of it all had come a fund of dexterities and attitudes, aphorisms and ripostes all ready and waiting in a reservoir of dialogue at which I was letter perfect. Put myself in his shoes indeed! When was the week in which I had not? Lucky for the collapsed rebel that there was someone available to step into his role who had been thoroughly rehearsed.

Sympathetic as I was and ready with my good offices, however, I could not forego one final, somewhat reproachful remark as I rose from the table at which my deflated radical yet tarried.

"I guess you realize now," I said, laying a hand on his shoulder, "that you've been living in a dream world."

Ten

TAKING over for Augie was a grave responsibility. I felt that. I spent the next days getting myself in the mood for the part. What did that call for as I saw it? Strict conformity to the character in which it had begun — that of a moral independent. Of that I was convinced. It was all right for Augie to reform in his private life, but any show of faintness on the other front, any faltering, gelatinousness of heart would be instantly taken advantage of to the possible detriment of the innocent. Perhaps beneath the girl's bravado I would find another soft center? Then I must the more show no soft center myself, in taking it from here at the point where the rapids remained to be shot. There is only one way to shoot the rapids if you want to keep afloat until you're past them — you must paddle faster than the current.

I set to grooming myself for the part on these lines. I imagined that I was an international cad about whom there must be no mistake. In brushing up, I practiced on my wife, with some old capers of mine that were familiar to both of us. I often pretended that we weren't married but were only living together, or had just met, or some such. I often tried to look not married when we checked in together at hotels, signing the register furtively and what not, to see if I could arouse suspicion. Well, driving her to town to shop for an aunt's birthday present, that Thursday evening when the stores were open, I imagined that the family station wagon we were in was a low-slung open Jaguar in which I had just picked her up. I was wearing a tweed cap anyhow, and now slouching raffishly behind the wheel I said, "Let's go up to my place and do a little hard breathing."

"Take this road here, it's shorter," she said. "Then cut over to Main Street."

I began to jab with my thumb at a jammed press latch on the glove compartment, to make my wife ask me when I was going to fix it. I jabbed at it several times, reaching across her to do it, and at last she said, "When in God's name are you ever going to fix that thing — or take it down and get it fixed?"

"Women nag their husbands about what they don't do. Men nag their wives about what they do," I said, settling back. " 'When are you going to fix this or mow that?' women say. And men, 'Why must you put chives in everything, what are you forever rearranging the furniture for?' None of that for me."

I prowled down Main Street, steering with my hands on the bottom of the wheel. My wife was poking around in crannies looking for the mate of a glove she had in one hand. "Why can't women lose gloves by the pair?" I debonairly chaffed.

I was feeling my way around in the part, circling for the right vein, and now I felt I pretty much had it: that of a light and informed rascality, a profligate charm that was irresistible even to its victims.

"We ought to pick up a little something for the children, if Maude says they've behaved," my wife said.

"Children! How can you conceive of such a thing? No children for me, you may as well know. The human species is the only one that is devoured by its young." For all this she would soon be at Moot Point, protesting weakly that my kisses drew the marrow from her bones. I dug up a paper-back novel that had got wedged under me. "What the hell is this?" I asked irritably. "Good God, you're not reading that woman?"

"Dip into it waiting for your train. I thought it was up your alley, that sophisticated sort of idiom."

"Every idiom has its idiot." I drew to a stop before the gift shop and reached over to open her door and let her out. "Don't take too long in there. And then let's go up to my place and do a little hard breathing."

Augie arranged for me to see Cornelia the following Wednesday evening. The encounter was to be lubricated by the assumption that I wanted to look at her paintings; having seen which I would proceed to the main purpose of my call. At half past seven on Tuesday evening Augie phoned and asked me to come right over to his studio.

When I climbed through the hatch leading to it, I found him in shirt sleeves, sorting through piles of drawings and sketches which lay everywhere on tables and on the floor. Two new electric heaters had the place hot as a kiln.

"What are you doing?" I asked.

He pointed down at a stack larger than the rest. "Can you let me have a thousand bucks advance on these? There's at least thirty more that you've expressed interest in over the years. I mean the ideas of course."

"What's up?"

He drew a long, harried sigh and hitched up his trousers with his wrists, his hands being black with dust.

"Mean there'll be expenses in any case. Whatever's done in the end, there's things I ought to foot. And if I give her the money — all in a lump sum, and enough — there's less chance of anybody coming around here and *asking* me for it. You know — some relative or friend, maybe stirring up trouble or suspicion. I've got to keep out of this."

Now Augie had remained an artist, not by selling his pictures, but by refusing to sell his jokes. Once he took a nickel for them his status would be confused and polluted, not to mention the unlikelihood of a gagman's ever eluding those bourgeois moral laws from which the artist enjoyed exemption. But he was in a spot, and there was no alternative. Was a mistress to force him to take that first long step toward the estate of wage earner? . . .

I stared at the stack. From my point of view, this was the bonanza for which I had been waiting — ours just when the magazine needed ideas, a good new jokesmith. How Blair would rejoice! I didn't feel much like rejoicing now. "I hardly know what to — " I began.

"Oh, the hell with that. You once made me an offer. The letter must be around here somewhere. Fifty dollars apiece for ideas if I went into production, with a quantity bonus if I sold over fifty a year. This is the same as production," he said, waving at the masses of work. "Twenty usable ideas would cover the thousand and I'm sure there's more than twenty there. Go on, take a look."

I could read the caption on the top one from where I stood. One missionary to another in a cook pot as they are about to be eaten by cannibals: "Our work hasn't been entirely in vain. They're going to say grace."

"Look here, I don't see that it's this much your responsibility," I said. "If she wants to be a miss mother, let her be one."

"Don't," he warned me nervously. "I want to do this. The thousand should see her through — well, the first stage. Beyond that let's not look. I owe her this much. So don't go making any bones about this part of it." I realized that he was scared of C.B. — scared, at least, of what she might do — and was determined to put himself in a position of owing nothing, and clear of provoking an erratic action. As he argued about it, he kept glancing instinctively toward the house, and it was vouch-safed me that the philanderer was scared of his wife too! Like any good American husband. "Cornelia can have hostilities. Masculine protest and one thing and another. Showing the world she could get along without a husband was undoubtedly part of that whole plan of hers, at bottom. I understand she's overshadowed by her brothers," he chattered, pacing the sweltering loft.

"Will they be around too?" I asked him.

"Well, they're O.K., from everything I hear. A very cultured sort of family. One's a musician, the other's a literary scholar."

"What's the other one? You said there were three."

"He's a minister," Augie said, looking for his cigarettes. "But they tell me he's not orthodox."

So I had my work cut out for me. I knew what I was to be pitted against. But Augie gave me no time to think about my own problems. "So the poor kid's probably been reacting to her environment. So handle her with kid gloves. Mean butter her up about her paintings," he said. He was pale. Don Wan. The tilted blue eyes had a fugitive look, and the normally neat reddish-blond waves had been thoroughly plowed. Augie was really a very good-looking egg despite a somewhat spoonbill nose, and no doubt there were women who thought that gave him the look of an intellectual Bob Hope. He drew a deep breath and turned again to the drawings. "Now do you want to take these with you and go over them on the train in the morning? Because time is of the essence."

"I don't have to look at anything first. I'll have the agreement drawn up and the check for the advance ready by noon tomorrow. Then you can cash it and — do you want me to take the money along tomorrow night?" I asked.

"I'd appreciate it. She's got a cold and can't meet me outside the house, and I don't want to be seen there. I have other people to think of in this."

"Certainly. Bring the drawings with you when you come to the office tomorrow," I said. I had started to say good night when I thought of something. "By the way, what are you going to tell Isolde is happening to all the money you'll be getting? Because you'll have to tell her you're selling your jokes. It'll be no time before she sees them coming out in the magazine, because I'll be turning them over to the artists right away."

"God, I never thought of that. Yes, she knows all my stuff. What'll we do?" he asked hollowly.

I thought a moment.

"Well, suppose I do this," I said. "Suppose I make the advance a little more than a thousand — the best Blair'll do, say — and you'll have something to show Isolde. Or put in the bank. Keep dividing what you make between the two women, for as long as you have to." I backed gingerly through the hatch and started down the precipitous stair. I paused with my head at floor level. "You'll have to work like a son of a bitch now," I said, and disappeared from view.

The Blys lived in a large white rambling house on the outskirts of Norwalk, the address of which I found in the phone book, and to which I was directed by three cops. Norwalk is built on more hills than Rome, and nothing in it, uncannily, is descended to but only attained by climbing. I had the thousand dollars on me, but to keep in the mood I pretended I had cadged it from a rich uncle who had written me off as a rotter and was only doing it for my family. "This is the last wench I'll buy off for you — from now on you can tidy up your own messes," he'd said, and stridden from the drawing room. I parked the car a block from the house and walked up to the door, unregenerate still.

Cornelia was, of course, expecting me, and it was she who answered the door. "Come in," she said. She was wearing a loose-fitting artist's smock like the one she'd had on at the P.T.A. business — maybe the same one. She led me into a living room lined with books from floor to ceiling, in which two men in their middle thirties were sitting, one sideways in a deep chair, with his legs slung over the arm, reading a book, of which he turned a page as I entered; the other on a sofa before a fire, reading a musical score. "This is my brother Carveth," Cornelia said of him. "Are we interrupting a concert?" she asked, for it turned out that Carveth derived the same pleasure from reading a score as other people do from hearing the composition played — more. "And he'd rather read a recipe than eat the dish," said a voice behind me. "This is my brother Hubert," Cornelia said, indicating the reader who had risen with the book in his hand.

Carveth had studied at Juilliard and Rochester, and abroad at the Paris Conservatory and in Germany and Italy. He was now at home working on a history of music which he said Knopf was going to publish in twelve volumes. He was married, but his wife, an anthropologist, was at present on the Zambesi on a Guggenheim, studying Rhodesian taboos. Hubert was another in a family who had jet-propelled themselves from one scholarship to another. "The best things in life are free," he said, having, at thirty-six, never paid for his tuition. Carveth frequently taught between courses, but Hubert had never sat anywhere but on the student's side of a lectern. No one in the family could enumerate his degrees on the spur of the moment, nor extemporaneously recall the colleges and universities he had attended, which included Oxford, the Sorbonne and the Free University of Amsterdam. He had grazed wide among the humanities, but would seem to have settled on literature, in which he would continue to conduct research until a suitable teaching post turned up. Faculties in the main tended to be chary of him because he appeared to have no specialty. The other two brothers gave him what aid was not supplied by scholarships and grants. He was currently in the East to catch some lectures at Yale, which was his alma mater and to which he had offered to bequeath his brain. He had made this offer several years before, but had not received formal acceptance, only a series of interim replies advising him of the status the matter had reached in the departments among which it was being bandied for consideration.

"Won't you sit down," Cornelia said to me.

We were given brandies in large inhalers, and cigars were passed round. Cornelia declined those Hubert proffered in a humidor, and lit a Between the Acts of her own. I took a cigar, but did not immediately light it. Setting aside his score, Carveth remarked that he'd have been farther along in his work if his old room hadn't been stolen from him by his brother. "You know — the one overlooking Norwalk Bay," he said with a meaning glance at Hubert. "I had thought there was no advantage in the view," replied the other, "since the Bay is something to be overlooked in any case." The fire was prodded and Carveth was coaxed to the piano. He composed impressionistic pieces in the tradition of that pleasant homogenized dissonance come down from Debussy through Delius. He played a suite of three numbers called "Night," being a series of sweet qualms on that subject, then struck out into a group of take-offs. Using the air of "Three Blind Mice," he parodied first a Bach fugue. Then he did the tune as Berlioz would have done it, and lastly, Hindemith. We set down our brandies and applauded when he'd finished.

"The Hindemith needs work," he said, reaching for his own drink which he had set on the piano.

"No, I like it best," Cornelia said, taking another cigarello from its flat tin.

"Oh, really?" Carveth said, rising from the bench. "I thought it needed touching up."

"Oh, come now, that's pure affectation. You know it's perfect," Hubert said from the armchair, over one side of which he again had a leg slung. I saw that there was a tradition of family persiflage here, at which Hubert was most active. He had a way of bringing his head down when he laughed that resembled Cornelia's, except that in his case it often took the form of appearing to dodge an expected blow for his jokes.

"Hubert thinks everything is affectation," Carveth said. "He takes nothing at face value."

"But nothing can be taken at face value. Least of all pure naturalness. That's the ultimate affectation. It's the attempt to cover our masks with a bare face."

"Nonsense. I appeal to the rest. What do you say?"

Cornelia chose to follow the dispute with her musing slice-of-watermelon smile; so they all looked at me. I swirled the brandy around in my glass a moment. "There's a lot in what he says," I said.

I set my glass down and suggested to Cornelia that I ought perhaps to see her paintings, for which I had prefabricated some remarks. She rose from her window seat and, letting Carveth give me another spot of brandy, I took my glass and followed her through a door to the rear of the house.

Her studio was a large, high-ceilinged, sky-lighted room, the walls of which were as covered with paintings, etchings and drawings as the rest of the house was with books (there were bookcases along both walls of the corridor down which we had come).

"Just go right ahead and look around," Cornelia said.

The canvases, which everywhere met my eye, gave me the sensation I often get from extreme modernity in painting — that of smothering under a crazy quilt. The succession of bisected squares and triangles and other mathematical forms were utilized in rendering man, machinery and nature alike. There was a Cubist study of three dancers; a mélange of gears and pistons suggesting visually the roar of many means of transportation; and everywhere color represented as refracted light. Having completed the tour, I took a drink of brandy and turned around.

"These are excellent, but don't you painters ever feel you'd like to break out of your prism?" I said, to find that there was nobody in the room but myself.

I took a stiff slug of what remained in my snifter and returned to the living room, where I found Cornelia curled up on the window seat, listening interestedly to a discussion about poetry between Carveth and Hubert. Sitting down beside her, I leaned toward her and whispered, "They're excellent but don't you think — "

"Oh, thank you," she said. "Did you really like them?"

"But they're not for us. We can't use that type of thing for a cover."

"No, I supposed not." Our attention was drawn to the discussion. At the moment, Hubert was analyzing the transition from Victorian to modern poetry.

"Poets used to be obvious with obscure words," he said. "Now they are obscure with plain ones."

There was a silence in which he acknowledged my return by looking in my direction; it had the effect of an inquiry as to what I might think of this. I set my brandy to rocking in the snifter again, and said, "They go too far."

Carveth saw that there was precious little to rock, and came over with the bottle and gave me another splash. So the civilized evening wore on. Hubert walked the room, drawing on his cigar.

"Of course the whole discussion, our whole view of poetry, is so restricted to what we know of the English that we don't understand there are other traditions. The French, what an entirely new vista they open!" he said. "How much more pure poetry there is there. And how didactic and moralistic so much British poetry seems by comparison."

"The French for the simile of beauty, the English for the simile of health, as it were," Carveth said, carrying the bottle back to the table.

There was a sound of feet coming down a stairway.

"Here comes Emory," Cornelia said.

I stiffened. This was it — the minister. These two chaps I could handle — broad-minded, educated, reasonable liberals both. But Emory was a horse of another color. I gulped down my brandy and steeled myself as he entered.

The cleric was a roan. He had a billow of chestnut hair flecked with gray, and bright blue eyes like glazed berries. He wore a black velvet smoking jacket and carried a pipe in his hand. He was at forty a crystallized bachelor (unlike Hubert who was "interested" in a woman in nearby Stamford). He rapped out the pipe on the underside of the mantel, after we had been introduced, and said yes to Carveth's offer of a brandy.

"I've been on the phone the whole evening with the trustees about that new steeple. Ours blew off, you know," he told me, "in that hurricane last fall. Act of God," he added dryly, and there was a gust of laughter that could not have been less hearty than the gale which had toppled the spire. "I suppose," he continued, spreading his hands to the fire, "I suppose the termites in the beams come under the same category, as well as that plaster that fell out of the ceiling in the committee room."

Hubert winked at us and said, "Maybe each is a punishment for not taking the last more seriously."

"Now, now, let's not have any more of your stuffy theology, Hubert," Emory said, taking the drink from Carveth. "I get enough of that from my parishioners."

So now I saw that the whole family represented the sophisticated progressive tradition, Emory as much as the rest, if not more so. I learned later how advanced he was; how he had no creed, refrained from public prayer, and was known to heckle street-corner evangelists for giving the church a black eye. "Don't you know the Gospels don't harmonize? Don't you see you're stressing nonessentials?" he would fling at them on Saturday nights.

Hubert drew him into an argument about the existence of a personal Deity, which Hubert said there might be more evidence of than Emory admitted. "Tommyrot," Emory said. "In any case, I have never thought of Him especially as a saint. He is a symbol of the whole world's upward struggle — the hard knowledge, not the easy salvation." He went on to say that his quarrel was more with the churchmen he was left of than the scientists he was to the right of. All science had given us is the the specter of a meaningless universe, but its very meaninglessness ennobles our own values, which are the bootstraps we raise ourselves with, and which must be love, not fear. Sacred must not be an anagram for scared, etc.

He sat down and crossed his legs. "Well, getting back to our church problems, let us hope," he said somewhat sardonically, "that a kind Providence will put a speedy end to the Acts of God under which we have been laboring. But enough of my botherations." He looked over at me. "So this is the chap who has our wench in an interesting condition?"

Cornelia opened her mouth to set him right, but an impulse took hold of me. Squeezing my cigar from its cellophane sheath, I said: "Suppose I have."

"Why nothing at all, dear fellow," he said. The others assured me they were not medieval about these matters either; that they did not regard the idea of seduction as psychologically valid. They vied with one another in not regarding the idea of seduction as psychologically valid. Hubert rose and went over to a shelf of books, at a row of which he peered. "Is it Faulkner who has one of his characters point out that women are not seduced, men are elected?" he said, running his finger along a number of titles. "Confound it, where is all my Faulkner?"

"That's beautifully put," Emory said, producing pencil and paper. "I must use it for a text some day."

I sat up in my seat. "It's not a view I share," I said, reaching for my inhaler, which was empty. Carveth replenished it for me, observing that I was a brandy partisan. "I drink to make other people interesting," I said, showing them at a stroke what their aphorisms were beside those of a man like George Jean Nathan.

"Can't find it. Oh, well," Hubert said, coming away from the shelves. "That's what comes of loaning books."

I bit off the end of my cigar and checked the draft. I was aware of Cornelia watching me with an anxious frown as I paused to take another drink from my glass. "You boys haven't seen my latest picture. I've finished it. Why don't you go have a look at it?" she said. "It's still on the easel."

"I prefer the double standard," I said, striking a match. "It enables one to retain the luxury of guilt."

A couple of the men rose. "I'd like to see the new picture," Carveth said.

Having lighted the cigar, I rocked my brandy, cradling my inhaler in one palm. "Affairs are like watermelons. They leave more mess than they're worth."

"Yes, perhaps you two have things to talk about," Carveth said. "Please remember we'll do what we can, which of course isn't a great deal. It's a pity Cornelia lost the suit. She was banking on that rather, and now things have been knocked galley west. I guess she feels now she can't keep the child. We realize you're married — bit of a poser that. Agree with Shaw that mating shouldn't have anything to do with marriage, necessarily. However, if she decides it's best to relinquish the child, that's probably the most intelligent and enlightened thing to do, from the child's point of view as well as everyone else's."

"Just as it's been proved that two dissimilar stocks produce the best offspring, so being reared by a third is very likely an added advantage," Hubert put in. Cornelia sat smoothing out a pleat in her skirt with her palm. "Well, let's go see the picture then. You'll excuse us."

When they were gone, Cornelia said:

"What did you do that for?"

"Augie's name must under no circumstances come into this," I emphasized, pointing the coal of my cigar at her. "As you know, he's trying to negotiate an adoption."

She gave a nervous laugh, ducking her head.

"They mistook me for him. That's all right. That's fine. I have nothing to lose, and I'm glad to do this for Augie. Just as Augie's glad to do this for you." I drew the money out of my pocket and went over and set it on the table beside her. She looked at it without taking it.

"But I don't want anything from him. I'll take care of this myself," she said.

"It's a thousand dollars. It should see you through. If it doesn't, get in touch with me — not him. He must be given a wide berth, now and forever. Is that clear?" I said in firm tones.

"You're very sweet."

I smoked the cigar till I was nauseated, which point was reached when the band which I had left on it caught fire, then I dropped it into an ashtray.

"It's your money. I'll bet it is — isn't it?" she said. "Augie hasn't got it to spare."

"It's his — every mortal penny, and I won't go into what it's cost him here, in terms of his career."

I watched her a moment as she sat with her head bent, smoothing out her skirt, which was flat as a table-top. Overshadowed by her brothers indeed. Was she one of those who must always distinguish themselves heretically — sue clients for defacing her work with the normal number of eyes, get pregnant as a spinster, smoke cigars?

I rose and stood over her again. I spoke quietly and deliberately.

"Some day, mark my word, you're going to meet a nice fellow and fall in love. You'll want to marry and settle down. Have a home life and children," I went steadily on. "But that'll be out forever if you already have one. Don't be a miss mother." I let this sink in. "So do the right thing, by this one as well as by yourself. I mean make it possible for it to have two parents instead of one. Well, now, if you want this — I mean if you want this child to have two parents instead of just one, and yourself to be a wife as well as a mother — now get this because it's important — there's a wonderful place in New Haven called Rock-a-Bye. That's where you should go. I recommend it highly. It's a first-rate place, which you can rest assured is very particular about who they give babies to. They turned Augie down, and so that's why it's absolutely essential that *this is the one place you go and nowhere else* so that — are you listening?" The head bobbed. "So that Augie won't end up adopting his own child."

I followed her responses sharply, ready in case she said anything unreasonable or was in any way emotional or illogical, in which event I would say, "Women! How much easier it is to chase them than to follow them." But I was given no grievance on that head, which irked me to some extent, as I had gone to a great deal of trouble preparing for this interview. Cornelia was the soul of compliance, repeating "Rock-a-Bye" after me as I asked, to make sure it was firmly printed on her mind. And when the brothers came clomping back it was with the same enlightened bonhommie and badinage and broad-minded tolerance as when they had left. I stood ready and waiting for them with my back to the fireplace, now gone cold, holding the snifter in one hand and the retrieved and rekindled cigar in the other, with a forbidding expression. It was the look of a man accustomed to buying his way out of every scrape. Instead of bristling, they "quite saw my situation," that it was "just one of those things," and regarded the thousand dollars, left visible on the table and explained by Cornelia, as damned handsome of me — better than lots of chaps would have done considering the trouble was mostly Cornelia's carelessness and unfortunately ill-timed impulse.

As I went out the door, taking my leave about eleven o'clock, gluttonous for the night air after all those brandies, the cleric called, "Come drop in at my church sometime." The invitation did not pass off without a rejoinder.

"Oh, don't let him do that," Carveth chaffered as I picked my way down the stairs to the sidewalk. "The poor chap might lose his faith."

Eleven

"WHAT happened? How did you make out? What did she say?"

Augie's questions tumbled out.

"Women are like lobsters," I said. "The tenderest meat is in the claws."

"What's the matter, are you stewed?" he asked, raising his voice into the transmitter, for I was reporting to him by phone from a tavern booth later that night. "How was she?"

"Having a mind of one's own doesn't necessarily imply having any mind as such," I felt constrained delicately to lay before him. What a hoodwinker Sex was! C.B. indeed!

"But what *happened?* The coast is clear for a minute so I can talk — but hurry."

I told him. I explained that it had gone quite well on the whole and that everything looked to be under control. There was nothing to worry about that I could see, barring the unexpected. Accounting from a phone booth wasn't very satisfactory, but I had wanted to reassure him. I told him I'd give him a full report the next day.

The excitement of the evening in general conspired to murder sleep, or at least inflict serious injuries on it, in my case, and hours later I was still wide awake. I thought of the days when I had nothing to worry about but a rat in the wall. Would that time come again? Don't lie here revolving on a spit, I told myself — sleep.

I remembered something I've heard from time to time all my life, namely that the last thought we think before we go to sleep is important because it is amalgamated into the subconscious. I'd read it recently in a magazine and a short time later heard an inspirational counselor on television, expounding it, say, "Dwell on some worth-while or uplifting thought as you drop off. Maybe just a line of poetry. I once lulled myself to sleep with the phrase, 'the darling buds of May.' The sheer beauty of a line like that, taken over the brink with us, can't help permeating us with its moral or aesthetic merit."

While lying in bed, waiting to fall into the arms of Morpheus (or into his hands, rather, as I prefer to think of it, and as you would, too, if you had some of my dreams) I remembered the counselor's suggestion and acted on it. Composing myself between the sheets, I set my mind to the task of selecting something to dwell on. I fetched up with several possibilities, famous sayings and fragments of poetry and one thing and another, but discarded them all for various reasons — not suited to meditation, too flippant, etc. Among them was "Say not the struggle nought availeth," which I felt to be rousing rather than mesmeric in its effect. A capital thought to get up with, say, and face the new day. For some reason, I recalled Samuel Johnson's "Patriotism is the last refuge of a scoundrel," and also that it was he who first said Hell was paved with good intentions. Neither of these seemed quite right for the purpose at hand; one did not want anything "trenchant." I could see that this method was not as easy as it sounded. Then suddenly there swam into my mind a line of poetry that I found as felicitous as the TV counselor apparently had the fragment from Shakespeare. It was from a poem by Dylan Thomas that I'd heard someone read aloud at a party the week before: "Altarwise by owl-light in the halfway house."

I dwelt on that awhile. The cadence of the words and the gentle profundity of the mood they evoked utterly charmed and, gradually, soothed me. An excellent idea, this. I would make a regular practice of it, taking a thought or a line a night and immersing myself in it, giving myself over to its overtones. How much better than indulging in some flabby reverie full of wool-gathering and wish-fulfillment. I reiterated the line hypnotically to myself: "Altarwise by owl-light in the halfway house . . ." Just as I was getting pleasantly drowsy, I sensed something nagging the back of my mind; something about the line. I didn't know what it meant.

I lay with my hands laced under my head, looking up at the ceiling. Did the poet mean to convey the idea of religious experience in middle age under nocturnal conditions? Or was the owl designed to suggest a pagan element (as the bird traditionally linked with Minerva) rather than mere physical nightfall? Or was a note more funereal than either of these intended to be struck? Was the symbolism all private and obscure? After maybe half an hour of this, I glanced at the dresser clock, which was not obscure, being phosphorescent. It said a quarter after two. (I hadn't gone to bed till one-thirty.) This was a hell of an hour to get into textual criticism.

I lit a cigarette from a pack on my nightstand and, propped on one elbow, lay on my side smoking. Was the trouble that the line was torn from its context? Maybe if I had the entire poem, or a stanza from it, it would help, provided it did not open exegetical vistas that would keep me till dawn. I mentally ran over the poetry collections in my library, without being able to think of one that was likely to contain any Thomas. Nor could I remember a word more of the poem as the man had read it at the party, or even what it was about.

My arm felt strained and I straightened to a sitting position. Perched tailorwise on the bed, I myself stared like an owl into the gloom. I was stark awake now. Tailorwise by owl-light in the half-awake house. "The hideous clarity of insomnia." Who said that? Wasn't it Chesterton? Know any more Chesterton? No. How about Chesterfield? "The pleasure is momentary, the position ridiculous, and the expense damnable." Not a very edifying thought, nor one the TV counselor would have been likely to sanction. Turning my back on the deep waters into which I had permitted myself to be lured, and fixing my mind firmly on the names of Longfellow, Whittier and Holmes, as on the lights along the shore, I made for the havens of corn. "Build thee more stately mansions, O my soul." I should have picked that. Or better yet, "Tell me not in mournful numbers life is but an empty dream." Yes, that was the ticket. I would switch to that.

As I mentally intoned my substitute selection, however, curious and persistent alterations kept creeping into it — "Tell me not in mournful owl-light life is but a half-baked dream," and so on. There was no getting ashore; like a firm undertow my original selection drew me back. A question of sportsmanship, the pluck to see a thing through, came into it too. "Altarwise by owl-light in the halfway house." How could a line so analgesic to the ear be so exacerbating to the intellect? "Not by eastern windows only, when daylight enters, comes the light," would soon cover the situation.

I threw back the quilts and groped my way into the hall. Snapping on a light, I squatted before a bookcase there and ran my eye along the volumes on a lower shelf. Through the open bedroom doorway I could hear my wife stir.

"Whah you doing?" she mumbled.

"Looking for a book."

"Can't sleep?"

"No. Do you know where that anthology of criticism is I bought last week? You know, the one with the section on modern poetry."

"Oh, I dah noh. . . . " Her words trailed indistinguishably off.

"Look, are you awake? You heard Fred Hume read that poem of Dylan Thomas's. What does this line mean to you? 'Altarwise by owl-light in the halfway house.' "

"O my God you raven bow this sour a night?" she said, and turned over with a violent groan of the bedspring. "Stew o'clock."

I found the book and took it to bed with me. Tilting the shade of the lamp on my nightstand so the light wouldn't bother my wife, I burrowed down in the chapter I wanted. It had, as I'd recalled from having flipped through the volume when I bought it, several pages on Dylan Thomas.

"The Welsh bard's rich kaleidoscope of images projects a highly personalized, memory-charged idiom," I read, "through which is restored the virginity of the lyric impulse. . . . " There were a number of passages quoted from his poetry — none, however, containing the line in question.

But the reference work turned out to serve its purpose nevertheless. A page or two of "the cistern of Self" and "perpendicularity as distinguished from horizontality of feeling fund," and I felt my eyes grow heavy. I laid the volume aside and put out the light, the raveled sleeve of sleep already half knit up. Drowsily wadding my pillow under my head, I remembered something

Disraeli had once said, to the effect that he didn't know to which he was the more grateful — the books that kept him awake or those that put him to sleep.

And with that thought I drifted off into the Land of Nod.

I awoke from a dream in which I was to get a medal provided I could endure having it pinned on my skin. Didn't make it. Looked over to my wife's bed. Sprawled out on her side with one leg arched up, her thigh exposed under a rumpled blue silk nightgown. A beautiful sleeper, quiet as a Cadillac. I reached a leg across the aisle between us and prodded her with a toe. She twitched awake and smiled.

"I suppose you expect me to marry you now," I said. She yawned and stretched voluptuously, curling her fists over her shoulders. "Well, don't get any ideas, Liebchen. I prefer things strictly à la carte."

"So do I. I don't plan to spend my life washing a man's shirts and bearing his children," said my wife, who occasionally fell in with my rigmaroles when she had the time.

"Can you bear children?" I said, sizing her up.

"I can bear children all right. It's men I can't bear."

I went into the bathroom to wash. She meant well, but she didn't know how to hold her end up in a rigmarole — always said things that were out of character.

I made breakfast, as I frequently do. I brewed coffee and squeezed oranges. As Audrey and I were sitting at the breakfast table, each sipping his coffee and with his separate ruminations, the children began to troop in. First little Phoebe, naked except for a tweed vest; an old salt-and-pepper affair of mine. The implication that she had slept in it was one that I did not care to explore.

Maude said when she came in: "Tell us that joke about Mrs. Obenhaus."

"We mustn't make fun of people's names," I said. "After all, we know the Obenhauses."

The thing was that last night's mood curiously persisted, and I found it difficult to throw myself into the family japes. I could not shake myself free of the role. These poor children, did they dream their father was a viper? How would they take it when one of his numerous scandals broke at last, making his double life front-page knowledge? Would they forgive him in later years?

"Go on," Maude persisted. "We never tell any of these jokes outside the house."

"Oh, all right. Why, we're going to visit the Obenhauses tonight. They've been married ten years and are having Obenhaus," I said, unwillingly. "Is that what you mean?"

Ralph said: "What's a father vexation?"

I looked accusingly at my wife. "I thought we were going to restrict them to kids' programs — no television after dinner. It's bad enough having to explain what a jeopardy sheriff is, but at least Westerns are boys' speed."

"We heard this on a Western," Ralph said. "The bad guy in it had a father vexation."

"Somebody on a dude ranch? For heaven's sake?"

"No, regular out West. He kept holding up the Wells Fargo over and over because he had a father vexation. What is that? There's father vexations and mother vexations I know."

"Just what it sounds like," I explained. "His father vexed him when he was a child, that means got under his skin. Can you understand that?"

"I think I can," Ralph said, giving me a thoughtful look, and returned to his cereal.

I felt more and more isolated from all this; not part of a family picture at all, but separate from it, a stranger to it even, whose sins might be visited upon his children unto the third and fourth generation. I saw it all: the lawyers filing at last into the house, the youngsters being spirited from the vicinity of disgrace, my wife exclaiming, "How could you?" as she paced behind drawn blinds. The scene was so vivid to me that I shuddered and shook my head, as if to shed it from my mind's eye.

"What's the matter with you?" my wife asked, watching me across the breakfast table.

"Nothing. I'll be all right."

The illusion was not lifted — nor the sense of apprehension dispelled — by a couple of the children coming over, as they presently did, and tousling their Pa. That these scenarios were premonitory was revealed in the course of the next week, several days which preceded the descent of Mrs. Mash, but followed certain events out of which was being brewed, unsuspected, a little hellbroth of my own.

Twelve

AMONG the Saturday and Sunday spring and summer suburban nights, germinal to these follies, in which I have tried to show Augie as going from strength to strength, was an occurrence more directly relating to myself, whose role was not always a spectatorial one. It arose out of that old pain in the ischial protuberance that the self-designated peers of the Age of Foible gave me, in particular with that fancy categorical singular, "the artist," which they were forever using on themselves. I decided not to let that one pass the next time it came round.

It came round next in the course of a barbecue, on the beach at Avalon, on a night now so lost among the moral dog days of that summer that I would be put to it to fix it chronologically amid the lawn parties and fist fights that also helped form its social tapestry, except that my wife was at her mother's in Pennsylvania at the time, with the children, on what was supposed to be a last holiday before school started. So it was probably the end of August. I was giving a light to a matchless blonde, not to put too fine a point on it, when someone remarked, "Of course the artist is at odds with the culture of his time."

"So is the editor," I piped up.

Everybody turned and looked at me as if they thought I was nuts.

"So is the what?" someone asked.

"The editor," I repeated, snapping the match away into the sand. "You know. He's at odds with the culture of his time too, very often. So are the auditor and the architect, for all I know, but I can speak for the editor. I can name you several, all top men in their field, who wouldn't take a plugged nickel for ours."

I pestered them systematically with this heresy for the good part of ten minutes, a long lecture for me. I went on to say that I didn't know of an editor worth his salt who was really integrated with the prevailing mores, that at least two editors of my acquaintance had imperfect domestic backgrounds and even histories of sexual digression, as well as other of the stigmata of creativity — not too extreme a word, I submitted, for a profession that often as not involved whipping somebody else's work into shape. Being compelled by modesty to leave out of the discussion what I might have in my private craw, I spoke of the compensatory part the work of editing might play, for the individual. I submitted that the drive to get out a magazine every week could be basically sexual in nature, a kind of sublimation for the person in question. I said I liked to think of the editor as a kind of pimp who brought the artist and his public together.

They nibbled on this with long teeth at first, but gradually came to take a less dim view of it, and to treat me with more respect. I detected thoughtful glances from several, thoughtful pauses in the chewing of chicken meat, that seemed to foretell one's being able to hold one's head up a little higher in one's community.

There was an immediate tangible upshot of the disquisition.

A girl on the edge of the group whom I'd noticed, in the light of the fire round which we were ringed, to have been listening with particular attention, crept across the intervening sand and wedged her way in beside me. The majority (not including me) were dressed for swimming, and she had on a dark blue suit which was still wet from a recent dip.

"I was interested in what you said about editing," she said. "I've written some articles that need cutting and maybe a little other working over — whipping into shape, as you say. A fresh eye is important, don't you think?"

"No doubt about it," I said, running one over her hair, which was like corn silk; her long, luxuriant and, I was sure, native, lashes; her full if somewhat pulpy mouth. She had one of those faces that remind us that prettiness is not a degree of beauty but something else again. While far from pretty she just missed beauty, with the kind of plainness in which you feel that a stroke or two more of the chisel would have meant divinity. I swirled a can of beer I had in my hand — one whose half-dozen predecessors had lubricated my tongue for the harangue, as a matter of fact — and looking into it asked, "What kind of articles are they?"

"Sort of memoirs. About my family?" She had that habit of ending declarative sentences with an interrogatory inflection, as if to add "You know?" "Mainly my father, who was a sort of character? In the town where I grew up in Massachusetts. The sort of thing you use a lot of in *The Townsman*." She cleared a strand of hair out of her eye, and settling down beside me on the sand said, "I need someone who can sort of look at them objectively. Someone who's not too close to the subject?"

I drank the lees of my beer and pitched the can on a nearby pile of empties. "I'd be glad to look at them," I said.

"Would you?" She clasped her hands, on her knees again. "God, if I dreamt there was a chance of getting in *The Townsman*. Sort of all jelly at the thought?"

A beer later I heard her remark that she loved the country so much every time she got out to it that she didn't see how she lived all alone in the city in a stuffy apartment. Two beers later, and in the dying firelight, I heard myself say, "Perhaps we can discuss them over lunch one day."

She sort of mislaid a hand on my arm and said with a laugh, "There's a whole book of them."

"I eat every day," I assured her with an arch smile. I threw another can on the pile. "This is what is known as a publisher's advance."

"Ish kabibble about that if I can just get some good sound professional advice." She looked into a beer of her own, holding the can in both hands in a way that gave it the quality of a temple vessel, and asked, "Are you here alone?"

"Yes. You alone too?"

"Yes. That is, I came with the McBains. Week-end guest. They're cousins. Do you know them?"

I didn't, except by sight; I hadn't met them till tonight.

The chiaroscuro broke up, with some of the Nereids and old youths charging in for a last dip. The water was so shallow here and the beach sloped so gradually you had to run a quarter of a mile to get your feet covered let alone attain a depth sufficient to fling yourself into with any éclat, so that these dramatic dashes petered out into bathos. A man had tried to commit suicide here once — a local artist who'd had a painting rejected by the Avalon Hardware Company, which hung canvases as a way of displaying wares in its picture-frame section — and had gotten so tired and discouraged walking out in search of deep enough water that he'd turned around and gone back. Gotten a little self-conscious too, as there'd been parties on the beach watching. A few hundred more feet and he'd have been under Long Island jurisdiction.

The girl and I hesitantly rose. "Look, are your people — ?" I began.

"I'll tell the McBains to go on, if you can drop me."

She went to the McBains' station wagon where she also changed back into her street clothes. Carrying a last beer apiece, we went for a walk down the beach.

Strolling along, I recalled my last summer holiday from domestic life, two years before; how I'd begun it in a ferment vaguely related to the hearsay about the "trouble" husbands "got into" when their wives were away. My debaucheries had ultimately consisted of an hour spent in the shooting galleries along Sixth Avenue with a friend named Al Standard; the consumption at Lindy's of great bleeding wedges of strawberry cheese pie and a party at the home of a neighbor, to celebrate his revision of a hymnal for a denomination whose name escapes me. The interlude of lotus eating had been interspersed with plays and movies frenetically gobbled in the drive to "get as much in" as I could, and had ended, one final evening, in the company of an air pilot acquaintance, who confessed a secret desire to write obscenities on the sky.

It was my memory of the general tepidity of that fortnight (and of the sheepish kind of shame that constituted its aftermath) that added, I suppose, a slight undercurrent of resolve to my mood of tingling expectation as we scuffed along through the sand. We fetched up near a breakwater a half mile from where we'd started. We sat down on the sand, turning our faces to the water and hearing nearby the tidal river pouring itself forever into the gluttonous sea; the same sea that wallowed softly or flung its pitiless spume against the rocks at Moot Point.

"A nickel for your thoughts," she said. "Inflation."

"I was just thinking how in all this Everything, there's Nothing," I said. "The more Everything, the more Nothing." It was the old *Weltschmerz* act, which no longer worked with my wife. One arm flung out above my head, I lay back on the sand and went on, "Never to pluck the fruit of meaning or longer be permitted to eat the lotus of illusion — that is the curse of modern man. Never, never and again never to decipher what is written in the stars, or whispered in the ever-murmuring sea shells."

She pushed back the lock of hair the better to scrutinize me worriedly. I dropped my arm down over my eyes, gorging myself on her concern.

"To think that death comes to species as well as to individuals; to worlds as well as species," I continued. "That as we lie here the earth under us is cooling toward the clinker it's bound to become — like the moon."

"Are there then no what-do-you-ma-call-its — values?"

"None whatever," I replied inclemently. I gave a small, bitter laugh. "Except those we scratch out our farcical little day with. Philosophy is the attempt to pick at a wet knot with boxing gloves."

"Are you sure?"

"Positive. Think of the dreams and fancies set humming in this walnut hull." I tapped my skull. It was considerably south of that point that my own fermentations were going on, but anyhow. I stretched a hand upward. "There's nothing or nobody to whom all those boiling stars mean so much as a four-minute egg."

"My father is an atheist too." She rolled away and smiled reminiscently. "You and he are a lot alike."

I was wearing denim slacks, a soiled T-shirt, and a switchman's cap, clothes not exactly suited to the elucidation of *Weltschmerz*, but I did my best to recover the offensive.

"Life is a jigsaw puzzle with half the pieces missing. Millikan tried to add up the number of molecules there are in the Universe, and ended up with a cigarboxful of zeros. There it is — take it or leave it — the Universe."

"The Universe isn't everything," she consoled me.

"What are your articles like?" I sat up.

"Never mind them now."

"Tell me about your family."

I had drawn the bung from a rather capacious subject. She went into detail about her ancestors, who had been fishing people on both sides. An uncle was now curator of a marine museum of natural history in Massachusetts — he had reconstructed an entire whale skeleton from two corset stays, or something; a grandfather on her mother's side was a captain who had gone down with his ship (rocked in the Credo of the deep?). I heard this while Arcturus slipped an inch toward the abyss, and the moon rose like a bloody cliché. She brought it up to date, the story, with an eccentric and wonderfully picturesque father, in the tradition of salty characters, who was the main subject of the memoirs she was working on. "He sues everybody," she told me hilariously. "And always grumbling about the way things are. A lot like you."

Our hands met up like crabs cruising in the sand between us. I lay over toward her as, now, she settled back.

"Are the eyelashes home-grown?" I asked, propped on one elbow.

"Mm," she said, nodding.

I studied her with a morose intoxication. I tried to put a

check on myself by flunking her out of Moot Point, that touch-stone. I had been supposing to myself that Le Corbusier had designed the house, and now I imagined asking her whether she liked Le Corbusier, and her replying, "Love some — with a little Benedictine if you've got it." Thus my imp and guardian floated above me, to sabotage and save. But it was no good. In her eyes was the splintered light of stars, and her voice seemed to echo the murmur of delinquent waters. Her eyes were blue, her skin fair, her lips strategically placed. After I had kissed her, she sat up and fanned her face in tribute to myself. "Whew," she said. "Sort of absolutely flabbergasted."

I could have kicked myself as I drove her out to where she was staying, clear in Southport fifteen miles away, and I knew that I was going to feel more like kicking myself when I got home to my place. So, figuring I might as well be hanged for a sheep as a lamb, I kissed her again and again, when I dropped her.

She sat musing on me from her corner of the front seat. "I had a feeling right from the start that you were going to play on my black keys." She got out a comb and tidied up the mess of pottage for which I had sold my birthright. "Such a Schopen-hauer." She smiled, raking the long soft fleece. "The last boy I went with was a sort of moral fatso?"

I came round and opened her door. "It's been very nice — what is your name?" I said. "I didn't quite catch it at the beach."

"Terry McBain," she said. We walked up to the house. "About the articles. Supposing I phone you at your office. Sort of next week?"

Thirteen

I SPENT the days till then with a nagging conscience. My pricks of remorse were especially keen in the empty house, where my wife's blank pillow and empty bed, the framed photographs on the mantel, the clock ticking into the silence drenched with absence filled me with a sentimental regret. Oh, if I had only kept my rovings to Moot Point! How many pleasant hours, ruminantly alone in my fortnight's bachelorhood, might I not be spending there even now. In the coral gardens of my thought life the figure of Terry McBain did supplant that of Isolde Poole — just as Isolde Poole's had that of her predecessor — like those hermit crabs which inhabit vacated univalves, but only brokenly and unsuccessfully: reality always routed me to account. More than that, my conscience dunned me with claims even for peccancies committed at Moot Point, now, a thing previously unheard of, for Moot Point had always been a sanctuary where I could tell the illusory hours unvexed. "There is nothing wrong," I evoked myself as chatting on the terrace there with Terry McBain, "there is nothing wrong with the birds and bees as a metaphor for sex. For what man has not felt himself pecked and stung to death?" Oh, how I wished I could recall those words now; even that phantom wrong to my wife was gathered into the general circuit of guilt.

This state of mind continued until I found myself in an endless round of wishing I had the truant evening to live over again.

So obsessed did I become with this idea of having another chance that I finally began to ask myself, Why not? Why couldn't I relive that evening? It should be perfectly simple. I would reproduce as closely as possible the circumstances under which I had erred, lead up to the point where I had succumbed, and then not succumb. This, I felt, would not be a mere ritualistic repair of my spirit but an actual moral victory, since the same physical indulgence would be open to me.

The urge to make this token demonstration of fidelity put me in a fume of impatience when half a week passed without Terry McBain calling me at the office, as she had promised. The need to get this whole thing over with before my wife and family got back made me decide that, if Terry McBain didn't phone by the following Friday, I would call her. By Friday noon she hadn't phoned, and, having found her in the book, I rang her up. She was home.

"Oh, hello, hello," she greeted me, instantly recognizing my voice. "I was going to call you. How's tricks?"

"Fine? How are the articles coming?"

"Why, I was polishing and cutting three of them — I wanted to get them in shape before I showed them to you. Sort of trimming away the fat?"

"Well, swell. How do you feel about dinner tonight? Are you free?" Naturally my plan wouldn't work if she just brought the stuff into the office. I had to have an actual temptation.

"I'm free, yes, and I'd love to. I don't know that I'll have the articles done by that time, if that makes any never mind."

"That doesn't matter. How's seven o'clock?"

"Okie doke."

We ate at a place of her choosing called Mrs. Ainslee's, this being a bower of chintz garnished with potted palms and cooled by mechanical zephyrs, where the liquor had to be fetched from a bar next door. Terry was dressed in a navy blue faille suit of provocative sibilance and a blue and yellow ascot that, under the eaves of a floppy yellow hat, set off her amber skin and blue eyes. I watched her mood closely for any signs that her country relatives had supplied a dossier of me at variance with the idea of an unattached man I had permitted myself to be mistaken for, but there were none. Maybe the cousin McBains didn't know me any better than I knew them, if indeed Terry had reported on the sequel to the barbecue at all. She chattered sociably over a dinner of roast beef and Yorkshire pudding, largely about her father, who sued everybody. I asked the waiter whether his neighbors could scare up a bottle of red wine, and one was obtained. We had a dessert whose identity was never clearly established, but it was a kind of cobbler in which apples figured principally. Picking at mine, I said, "Let's go up to your place."

Terry sipped hot coffee through pursed lips.

"I've been thinking, after the other night," she answered gravely, lowering her cup to its saucer.

So she had a moral reclamation of her own to make. Good God, I'd never thought of that! But, of course. In addition to the normal female wish not to seem to be too easily had was the hazard of her appearing to be offering amorous favors in return for editorial ones. Casting couches. On top of all this loomed my owing it to her to tell her that I worked in the art department and had nothing to do with text, hence could be of no use to her. But I couldn't do that quite yet. What a muddle this was getting to be — and with only tonight to play it out. Resistance was the last thing I'd bargained for. If she was going to play hard to get, I reflected as I set fire to a cigarette, we were faced with a hopeless stalemate: she withholding what I would wait forever for the opportunity to decline. Yet without my reclamation the evening would be a total waste.

I began to get nervous and fidgety. When the waiter hove into view again I signaled him over and said, "Have they got any Corbusier? I mean Courvoisier?" He trotted out the front door, and presently trotted back with two glasses of cognac. Dreamily breathing in the fumes of hers, Terry closed her eyes. "Trying to ply me with liquor?"

There was something to that: I would have to seduce her into a state of compliance advanced enough for me to extract some moral credit from it. I turned over the check which the waiter had left. Seventeen dollars and twenty-eight cents.

"Come on, let's go up to your place."

She closed her eyes again and shook her head with a playful smile.

"What if I said it meant a lot to me?" I asked.

She set her glass down. "What if I said it meant a lot to me not to miss a picture that's running uptown? A revival of *Mutiny on the Bounty*."

"I've seen that."

"Well, so have I. Wouldn't you like to see it again?"

"Of course."

The film absorbed us both. Halfway through it, Terry peeled off a glove and slipped her arm through mine. She scratched my wrist lightly with her red talons. We held hands till the end of the picture. Then we walked to her place, which was only a few blocks away.

"Father's a dear underneath. He's paying my rent for a year

while I try my hand at these crazy articles, as he calls them,"
she said. "Of course Mother's a scream in her own right. I think
you'll love her. Mother always says Father's the most even-
tempered man she ever met — always surly."

I was unco-operative. "Is he discombobulated? Does his epi-
zootic sagatiate?"

"What's the matter?" She appraised me. "Such a gloomy.
Living out there in the country all alone probably. . . . My place
is right in this next block."

Slowing my pace, I cast an eye up at the stars.

"Nickel."

"Oh, I was just thinking of the Fourth Law of Thermody-
namics, or whichever one it is that says matter is running down.
Matter is running down and the universe itself will one day become extinct. An everlasting and immitigable nothingness, in
the void of black and absolute — "

"Don't." She gave my arm a maternal squeeze. "You're better
off not thinking about those things. We can go so far and no
further. Don't torture yourself by delving too deep."

"I can't help it."

I was feeling lousier every minute, because this was among the
old routines with which I had wooed my wife, on whose black
keys I had also played. It was a vicious circle, this having to use
sentimental coin to square myself. Like hocking your wedding
silver. But what was I to do?

"This is my door," she said as I sailed on by, upward gazing.
"Well, it's been a wonderful evening."

I had once seen a play by J. B. Priestley in which the audience
is given alternative endings. One is an unhappy one, the fruit
of a chain of revelations about the characters brought on by a
trivial question about a cigarette box, early in the first act. The

other is a happy, "what if," ending, such as might result had the question not been asked, but some other, equally trivial, deflection intervened, and set the course otherwise. I had to get that optional ending, and get it tonight.

"Just wonderful. Thanks so much."

"Some people wonder how people can do themselves in," I said, looking down at the ground. "I don't wonder about it. That's the only thing I do understand."

"Come on up," Terry said.

I mounted the dark stairs behind her, swinging my hat in my hand.

Terry's quarters consisted of a small living room, a Pullman kitchen, a bedroom and a bath. There was a tiny entrance hall with a chair in it on which I put my hat. She switched on a table lamp in the living room and disappeared into the bedroom, taking off her hat. "Fix us a drink," she said. "You'll find everything in that chest next to the typewriter. And ice in the refrigerator. Make yourself at home. I'll have a bourbon and water."

I mixed two, and carried them to a coffee table in front of a sofa. I sat down on the sofa. I could hear Terry stirring about in the bedroom — a drawer, the jingle of wire hangers, something zipped. Somewhere in the building there was the muffled sound of a door shutting. I glanced nervously at my wrist watch. It was five minutes to eleven. Too late to catch the eleven-twenty home. There remained only the twelve-thirty — the last train to Avalon till the milk runs.

There was a rustle of, I think, Swiss batiste, and Terry appeared in a blue and white dotted dressing gown. She joined me on the sofa. "Sort of making you the host." She picked up her drink and sipped from it. "Strong." She lounged, partly away from me, with one shoulder against the back of the sofa. I was aware of the whisper of negligee and of my senses drowning in perfume.

"Too much nose candy?" she said and laughed. "It's a little stronger than I usually use. Somebody gave it to me."

I wondered had it been the "moral fatso" of whom she had spoken. Something puzzled me.

"You said your last boy friend was a moral fatso," I said. "Just what does that mean?"

"Oh, he thinks, like, Mother's Day has become too commercialized, and the government is getting into things that are none of its beeswax?" She sat closer and slipped an arm through mine again. "I can imagine what marriage to *him* would have been like. The type who'd be out every other night because he'd be sort of secretary-treasurer of everything? And the rest of the time he'd be downstairs with his woodwork hobby, making the sort of trays you'd have to have standing around on end."

"And when you went on vacation with him, he'd mail everybody live turtles," I said, feeling I was getting the hang of this thing. "Kind of a Mortimer."

"His name *is* Gerard."

We laughed together, having Gerard's number so.

I stole another look at my watch. Still too early to go, without appearing abrupt. I said, "What was the one before that like?"

"Him. He was a genius, but he had two pages missing."

"He had two pages missing?" I said softly.

"He invented things. He'd invent something you'd attach to an open window so that if you weren't home it would close automatically when it rained, by the wet shorting out the electrical circuit. Only it turned out that the dew shorted the circuit the same way, so the bedroom windows would keep sliding shut all night?" She smiled up at me. "Jealous?"

"Tell me, Terry, did your father ever see either of these guys?"

"Father!" She sat up, sloshing her drink in the hilarity of remembering something. "I'll never forget what he said about Albert — that's the inventor. Well, Albert worked his way through college selling magazine subscriptions, you see, and when I told Father that, to build him up, Father said, 'And after he graduates from college he'll *still* be selling them.'"

I laughed, a soft laugh of private security. The whole thing had resolved itself into a kind of double or nothing, so to speak, and Terry's apparent willingness to have me stay the night would leave me with the debt paid off and a substantial moral balance in my favor. Cautiously I tested my position. Running the ball of a forefinger along the rim of my glass, I asked, with a tongue grown surprisingly dry, "What time is breakfast around here?"

"Breakfast is any time anybody wants to get up, but it won't be around here quoth she. Not with a Schrafft's nice and handy in the next block." She watched me, sipping. "Have you ever eaten their grilled Johnnycake?"

"Very often indeed," I said. "I love it."

I finished my drink and then waited a few minutes more. Then I stood up.

"Look, I think I'd better be getting along."

But the retrieval of my self-respect was not to be effected without a grave hitch: the loss to Terry McBain of her own.

"Well, will you make up your *mind*?" she said, her eyes brighter than I had yet seen them. She set her drink down on the table. "Is this a habit of yours — flipping through samples to find something that strikes your — "

"No, it's not that at all."

She rose. "I'd like to know exactly who it is you're trying to make a fool of," quoth she, tucking together the lapels of her dressing gown in a gesture not without truculence. I seemed to see ranging, generation on generation behind her, the granite New England spirits out of which she had professedly been hewn.

"Myself, I guess. I'll probably hate myself for this in the morning," I went on, attempting a humorous subtlety that I was far from feeling, and, to tell the truth, far from comprehending myself.

"Just what the devil does *that* mean?"

I smiled and looked at the rug, pinching my nose. "It's just that I think you were right earlier in the evening, back at Mrs. Ainslee's — where, by the way, I was amused at their having to run out for liquor all the time. Incidentally, I wonder what the legal arrangement is in a case like that — who pays the tax, or what."

"Where were we?"

"But the thing is, people shouldn't lose their heads."

"They shouldn't blow hot and cold either," she tersely answered.

"You're right there. You've a perfect right to call it that," I said fairly. I shook my head. "Sex," I said, as though the grievance and the weariness were equally mine.

It was, I sensed, my apologetic air rather than my philosophical one that somewhat mollified the girl. Undone of my aplomb, even of my *Weltschmerz*, of which nothing remained but a hangdog look, she felt a little sorry for me. At least she relented. But the revival of our footing was only temporary. "Well, let's forget it this time," she said. "Run along if you want. What I was going to ask was if you're interested in going to a cocktail party at some friends' of mine in town here. It's a week from Sunday."

Panic clawed me, in the need now to get everything cleared up.

"Look, I don't know whether you know I'm married or not —"

"Married."

"Yes, I thought the McBains told you."

"The McBains don't know you from Adam — but they may," she said flintily.

"Oh, Terry."

"They couldn't place you when I asked them about you —"

"But I took for granted — I mean all of us at the same party. Of course it was a large party, one of those enormous affairs, sponsored by local groups, that are so typical of Avalon community life, especially, I might add, in the summer, with our miles of beaches. But what I meant to say is, I sort of took it for granted you knew the dope about me. That I only meant I'd come to the barbecue alone — not that I was single. Had I only dreamt — I mean if that angle was important to you." I gave this up and now did hang my head. "I suppose I'm a rotter."

"Oh, don't go giving yourself airs!" Terry turned smartly to the window. "*Well* — married." She turned back again, and, her arms folded, regarded me with displeasure, "Can you give me a little better idea what this is all about, including the double talk?"

"Why, yes, I'll do my best." I drew a long breath and looked up, like a public speaker preparing an answer to something put to him in the question period. "I've seen you twice," I began.

"The first time was accidental, as you know, a case of where one thing led to another, as they often do. I was sorry for it."

"I'll bet you were, the time it took you to call me back."

"I'm coming to that. So we have a sheep-through-the-gap, a husband momentarily fallen from grace. Oh, a thing common enough in itself, but still, leaving an aftermath of regret, for basically we are moral creatures, however emancipated we pride ourselves on being intellectually." She breathed sharply and rolled her eyes up at the ceiling. "Now we come to why I called you back. You see, I wanted to prove to myself that I wasn't a cad. That I was made of better stuff. And besides, I owed it to my wife."

"What about what you owed me?" she said, tucking shut the negligee with the same bellicose gesture. "When are we coming to that?"

I was like a man who, thinking to pluck up a negligible strand of briar, finds he has hold of a mile of twisting root. I pursued the subject with a kind of tense interest, wondering how I would handle it. Moving a step, I caught sight of myself in a wall mirror. My complexion blended harmoniously with the color scheme of the interior, which was an off-white, very attractive against drapes of oyster and a bottle-green rug.

As I was collecting my thoughts, Terry started toward me with deliberate steps. "Do you know what I think I owe you?"

I shot a glance at a vase on a nearby table. Among my Moot Point délicatesses was a scene in which a spitfire I have up for the week end aims a piece of earthenware at me and I duck. "Darling!" I nimbly return. "I didn't know you were domestic." It wouldn't have worked in here, that much was clear.

"Did you ever see a play by J. B. Priestley with two endings?"

I jabbered in a dry voice, backing into the vestibule and toward the door.

"I can think of a lot of things to do to you —" Terry said, still advancing.

"A grim ending and a happy one. I just wanted to run through this incident again up to a certain point, and then sort of switch to the happy ending, like in the play. A very skillfully woven thing it was, the sort of thing the British do so much better than we. Think of my intentions!" I protested. "Get this thing in its proper perspective. I might as well have come up here to put you on a pedestal."

" — but they're all too good for you. Like hanging!" she continued, ignoring my rebuttal as she had my parallel.

"*Dangerous Corner*," I said, feeling for the doorknob behind my back. "That was the name of the play. It ran for quite a while," I added, feeling as if I had done so myself — or as if I might.

"I could call a cop to say you're annoying me. Or the janitor to throw you out." Terry was talking like that.

I opened the door, snatched my hat off the chair, and scurried for the hallway stairs. I picked my way down them gingerly but rapidly, in a tailwind of invective for "my sort" that grew in volume and intensity as I negotiated the two twisting flights to the street, and drew tenants to their doors as well as sped my departure. A rather muscular and formidable-looking woman in a dark bathrobe glared at me as I shot on down. The words abated as their author apparently sensed spectators to be accumulating on the lower landings, but they echoed in my ears as I scuttled through the one remaining door into the safety of the street, and continued to echo long afterward: the sound, justly respected, of an injured woman.

Fourteen

SO now I felt rotten about Terry McBain. Now it was she I had on my conscience. I felt I owed her something. I could still see the hurt in the fronded eyes, in the anger of that skirmish I couldn't shed the recollection of. It was with a view to now paying *that* account, and if possible closing the books on this entire matter before my wife got back (in five days), that I phoned her to offer my good offices with the articles.

It took no thinking out to decide that that was the one clear kindness I could do her. No strings attached, no ulterior motives, nothing in it for me. Just a favor.

I went out to phone her, not wanting to put a call through the office switchboard girl, who had a sharp ear for the rhythms of folk speech. I slipped out for a late lunch, winding up in a Howard Johnson's that had just been opened in the neighborhood. I wasn't terribly hungry and my stomach was upset, but I'd have liked something like a broiled chop of some sort. "Could I have a lamb chop?" I asked the waitress, waving off the menu she extended. "I don't want much to eat and so as little vegetables and so on as I can get."

"I can give you the children's portions if you'd like," she suggested. "In fact, the lamb chop happens to be our Simple Simon Special."

"I'll have that and a bottle of ale. Bring me the ale first, please."

"Well, now, I couldn't give you the ale on the Simple Simon — I mean if you're thinking of a substitution for the milk. You have to take the milk, and a little ice cream for dessert, if you want it on the lunch."

"That's all right. Just bring me the Simple Simon Special and a bottle of ale," I said, feeling we had reached the nadir of human relations. I was mistaken. She was back in a trice with no ale and to announce, "We're all out of lamb chops. Would you like to see the children's menu?" She held out a small bill of fare which I declined. I leaned back against the wall of the booth I was in and viewed her.

"I understand there are twenty-eight of these places," I said.

"That is the number of flavors. There are over four hundred restaurants."

"All as good as this, I trust?"

"I was only trying to help. You don't have to bite my head off."

"How else would you suggest getting anything to eat around here?" I took the menu wearily and donned my spectacles to consult it. I was persecuted by a flow of designations such as the Peter Piper Plate, Little Boy Blue and the Humpty Dumpty Lunch. My stomach gave a low growl, like a displeased dog. However the Humpty Dumpty looked O.K., the entree being described as "small chicken salad," which seemed to be on the snacklike scale I was in the market for.

"I'll have the Humpty Dumpty," I said, handing the card back to her, "and a bottle of ale. Black Horse if you've got it."

"We have," she said, making off.

I spied a trio of hens watching me from the next table with

that "the types you meet in public" expression. As I pocketed my glasses I cowed them with a slow burn, which scattered their regard. The ale came, and then swiftly the Humpty Dumpty, with roll and butter.

Having restored myself on these viands, I went to the telephone booth and called Terry McBain.

"This is me," I plunged in the instant I heard her voice. "Look, I'm sorry about last night and the whole thing and all, but let's forget it. Now what about the articles? I'd still like to see them."

There was a long pause. Then, "You would?"

"Very much. Of course it isn't my department, I'm in the art end — " I rattled off at high speed, to get that debt of clarification out of the way — "but I can see that they get into the right hands, and maybe give you a little steer on them myself."

"Of course last night was one of those ridiculous businesses — better forgotten."

"When can you drop the pieces at my office?"

"Sort of after while? I've been touching up the first few chapters, enough to give you an idea what the series will be like. Fifteen in all. I could be there at fivish, if that's O.K."

She spent the first five minutes in my office browsing among the mulch piles of sketches and drawings on every desk and table and on some of the chairs.

"Sort of a pool of blood last night."

"Well . . ." I shrugged.

"So this is the funny-pitcher factory. Fascinating, to see all this stuff in embryo stage."

I could see she was interested, so I said, "Would you

mind if I took one second to get this memo off? Then I'll be free."

"Go right ahead. Love to rubber."

I drew the mouthpiece of a dictaphone toward me and said into it: "Memo to Mr. Blair. On the attached idea-to-be-worked-on, suggest the bus conductor be changed to two barefoot street fanatics in sackcloth and carrying the usual 'Repent' placards, watching a colleague down the street whose sign reads, oh, something like, *Patronize the Gotham Ecclesiastical Supply House — Hymnals, Collection Plates, Other Religious Accessories*. One of the two fanatics saying to the other, 'I never thought I'd live to see Ebenezer go commercial.' "

I paused and saw that her back was listening. I released the catch on the dictaphone and showed off some more:

"Memo to Mr. Blair. Catch no fetal heartbeat in attached fencing-school idea, however offer this notion which I'm afraid is a rather complete switch. Two fencers in dueling school having a fist fight. Their rapiers lying on the floor. One observer to another: 'It all started when one of them made a crack about the other's form.' "

I rose, handed the dictaphone record through the doorway to my secretary and came back in, closing the door behind me.

"Well, then."

We walked on a light crust of formality and tact, like a snow crust you try not to step through. She wore a brown suit and had a silk ribbon in her yellow fleece; she struck at my vanished youth and my disreputable sorrows. She was holding a brown Manila envelope, disquietingly fat. Seeing me appraise it she suddenly took a tighter grip on it and moved to the door. "This is ridiculous."

I reached over to prise the envelope from her grasp. She

jerked it behind her back, and in my struggle to snatch it she banged against the closed door with a thud that rattled the latch. We scuffled against the door. I heard my secretary's typewriter stop in the outer office, and the sound of a chair scraped back as by someone rising in alarm.

"No," Terry said. "Don't."

I pinned her against the door. Holding one of her arms, I reached behind her with my free hand for the envelope. My embrace crushed a cloud of scent from her clothes. At last I wrested the envelope out of her clutch and dropped it on my desk.

"I'll look forward to reading it," I panted, smoothing back my hair.

She tugged her coat and skirt to rights. "Well . . . You'll call me?"

"Yes."

"Well, good-by then. And thanks a lot. You're very sweet."

She had not reached the elevators when I had the envelope open and the manuscript in my lap. It began:

"Father was always suing everybody. At the drop of a . . ." I shuffled through the pages reading sentences at random. "Father would say, 'The mean temperature for July has been ninety-one point five, and that's pretty mean. . . .' For years Father put no stock in 'this allergy business,' but later came to believe in it to the extent of being convinced that he was allergic to his own hair. . . . Dressed in his fur coat and coonskin cap, Father was a sight to behold. . . ."

I put the manuscript down and walked to the window. I looked down into the gulch of Forty-seventh Street, twiddling the Venetian-blind cord. Father was that star codger and ubiquitous nuisance who had still not been written out of the national system. Father McBain was a trifle overpicturesque for *The Townsman,* that much was sure — and his daughter not yet out of the building.

I phoned Father's daughter shortly after noon three days later, by which time I'd read the manuscript through and so had the fiction editor Hackett, who'd sent it back to me with the note "Too reminiscent."

"Look, this is good stuff, but not just up our alley. And they're stocked up on reminiscence at the moment." I made a slip of the tongue and said "reminuisance" first, or almost did.

Long silence. "I see."

"I enjoyed reading it myself. A lot."

"I'll bet."

"Come, come now. There are lots of places you can sell this."

"I know. I've tried them all."

"Well . . . " I hesitated. It wouldn't do to just mail the stuff back to her, or leave it at the receptionist's for her to pick up. I couldn't seem to get my foot out of this thing. "Can you have a drink?"

"Can I *have* one! I need one."

We met in the Biltmore lounge, and this time she had on a salt-and-pepper tweed suit and a "courageous" little hat of butterscotch color with a pompon on it.

"It's junk," she said instead of hello, as I set the envelope on the table where she'd been awaiting me. "Junk, junk, *junk!*" she repeated accusingly, with such ferocity I thought she was going to reach across the table and scratch me.

"Stop this nonsense," I said. I signaled a waiter and ordered a Manhattan. She was already drinking a Martini. "You act as if your whole life was at stake."

"Well, it is. I'm twenty-five, time to find out if you've got anything or should go back to Squeedunk. What's the matter, don't you like my hat?"

"Yes. I was just admiring the way you wear it — so nice and casually." I made another *lapsus linguae* and said "casualty." She called me on it and also brought up the one I'd made on the phone, which had not escaped her.

"What have you been doing, chewing slippery elm?" she said. "Well anyhow, if the stuff was only good for some magazine. I was always afraid to try *The Townsman* because that was where I wanted to be. Now I know." She sighed and broke her hands apart. "I suppose I might as well quit."

I wished she would quit — quit talking like this. And I wished that damned woman at the next table would stop too — she was delivering one of those "ices" monologues to a female friend. "So ices if you think you deserve a better job, go in and tell him ices. Ices you've been in the bathroom-fixture game long enough to have that right, and if you don't blow your own horn nobody will. Right ices? Ices nobody ever got anywhere hemming and hawing — take the bull by the horns ices to him."

"Let's get out of here," Ices to my own companion, after ten solid minutes of this. "What — what are you doing for dinner tonight?"

She gathered up her bag and gloves and the Manila envelope. "I'll fix dinner for us. We'll stop by and get some veal for scallopine. Don't try to talk me out of it. I have to do something with my hands when I'm in a stew."

Outside in the street, she threw the manuscript into a city trash basket, taking for granted of course that I would fish it out, which I did; but I felt very put-upon having to dive in head first, as I did, because the basket had been recently emptied and the manuscript lay at the bottom. I almost fell in. I carried the manuscript the rest of the way to her apartment, where I gave it to her. She threw it into a wastebasket. I ignored these proceedings.

She clattered to work in the tiny kitchen, conjuring utensils out of an area no larger than a phone booth. I tied an apron on myself, but then sat reading a newspaper because every time I offered to help I was jostled out of the way. At last, after much beating of flour into the veal with the rim of a saucer, she had it simmering in sherry in the skillet.

She turned and took me in. "Nickel," she said.

"I'm reading the newspaper."

"Nickel," she demanded.

"I was thinking that we all learn by experience, but some of us have to go to summer school," I said, with an air of aphorism that was undone by a wet paper napkin sticking to the bottom of my cocktail glass as I raised it to my lips.

"What would you tell your wife if she came in here now?"

"That we were cutting capers in the kitchen," I said with a rather engaging smile, and slipped another inch behind my newspaper.

"We ought to have some wine with this. Besides this sherry." She turned and stooped, and from a lower drawer dug a bottle of claret which she said someone had given her the previous Christmas. (I wondered was it the moral fatso, or the chap with two pages missing.)

"Have you ever had mulled claret?"

"Well, hell." I crossed my legs under my apron.

"I'd like some now. That's just what I feel like." She got out spices and began to mix them briskly into the claret. "You know what mulled claret is, don't you?"

"I know what mulled claret is. It's a cure for alcoholism." I wanted to read my paper. "You need a poker to heat it with anyway. We don't have one."

"The janitor has. Downstairs in the basement, a poker left over from the coal furnace."

"But that's ten feet long!" I protested.

"What of it? If you want mulled claret, do it right. Go on down and get it. If the janitor isn't there it won't make any difference. He won't mind. Just go through that door you've seen in the front hall and down the stairs. Go on."

"Oh, all right," I said, with that reluctance familiar to husbands when they are routed out of their easy chairs on some domestic chore. "I'll get it."

The janitor wasn't around, but I found the poker. Carrying it up, I met a woman on her way down. I stood back in a corner of the landing to let her by, holding the poker up like a spear. "Mull some claret," I explained with a giggle, so she wouldn't think I was up to some kind of violence.

The poker wasn't ten feet long, exactly. But I stood clear in the living room in order to heat the tip over a kitchen burner; and to plunge the hot end into the claret, which was on a table in the living room, I stood in the bedroom doorway. But it made a fine hiss, and I suppose the cups of claret tasted better for the observed ritual.

"There's an autumn tang in the air," Terry said, in defense of our doing this.

There was no autumn tang in that apartment. I went around in shirt-sleeves opening windows. Superimposed on the spirits in the scallopine, the mulled claret made me begin to feel a little mulled myself. Bustling about setting the table, we'd accidentally touched hands and felt a spark fly between us from the electricity scuffed up by our feet in the carpet. Terry found this amusing and wanted to do it with our lips. I did not feel these kisses "counted"; indeed, since they represented bodily contacts which I made no effort to develop, I saw them as actually piling up additional credit in the moral balance I had on deposit.

Suddenly she said, "All junk," and sat down and dropped her head on the table, after clearing a space in which to do so.

"Now, now," I said. "It isn't that bad."

"Isn't it? I told you my father agreed to pay my rent for one year. The year's up, without me coming through. And now I've got to 'give up that nonsense.' But I don't want to do anything else. You're right — we're better off dead."

"Don't talk that way," I said, putting my hand on her shoulder.

She rose and was around, and I felt the clutch of a hand that advertised her warmth and demon. "Put me to bed."

This affair, then, had no status and cohesion of its own but was purely a framework for its emotional concomitants, in which alone it had any shape and perseverance, like those old barns which, themselves in a state of collapse, are supported by the vines to which they have given rise.

I staggered into the bedroom with her and laid her on the bed. "Thanks for the dinner," I said. "It was swell." Starting for the door, I was arrested by the thud of a thrown shoe, which clattered to the floor after making a lesion in the wallpaper.

She removed and threw the mate, with a vigor which gave new force to the professed need to be doing something with her hands when upset. I hesitated in the doorway. "Close it," she said.

I stood there as she peeled off her stockings and then the

rest of her clothes. I still hesitated — I couldn't offend the girl. She stood on a rug in the middle of the room, and through no fault of my own I saw the teacup-sized breasts and the lyre-shaped loins, the whole symmetrical edifice of youth in the light which dimmed when she came over and swung the door closed almost.

"Why are you an atheist?" she said.

Her hair hung down like the velvet in old collection bags.

"God only knows."

I couldn't get the knot out of my tie — my hands were shaking so. I slipped the noose over my head. My teeth chattered like castanets. Somehow I got my clothing off. I felt a cold breath from Betelgeuse, and somewhere a chunk crumbled from the Polar Cap whose thawing would one day flood the continents and blot us all from view.

"Hurry," she said from the bed.

My knees knocking together, I picked my way across the cold floor, stepping carefully over Myerstown, Pennsylvania, where my mother-in-law lived, to the bed. I lay in it shivering from head to foot.

"Sorry," I said later. I wished to Christ I was at Moot Point, where all this was so much easier.

"It happens to everybody." She lay back smoking a cigarette, the sheet drawn to her chin. I watched the coal of her cigarette, like a pulsing jewel when she drew on it. She put it out and said, "Guilty wilty?"

She threw back the covers and went into the living room from which she returned with a bottle of whisky and a couple of glasses. She poured and handed me a drink. I took it like a man receiving medicine, and drank it off. A spark shot between our hands again, reviving her interest in that lark.

"You're a regular dynamo on this rug," she said. "Come on, get up and try it. Relax, for God's sake."

I climbed out of bed and stood on a shag rug with her, compliantly wiping my feet on its nap, to work up electricity.

"Say, I've got an idea," I said, as I did. Some association, some accidental connection in my mind, had given it to me.

"What?"

"About where to send your articles," I said, steadily generating current. "Or the first one anyway. *The Reader's Digest.* Your Most Unforgettable Character. Lots of people have done their fathers or some other relative."

She stood openmouthed with pleasure. "I never thought of that. But, of course — it's a natural. Why, what a wonderful idea. Why didn't I think of that myself?"

"Because you kept thinking of him as a book. Forget that. He's a one-shot."

As she digested the proposal, I slipped over to where my clothes were and started to pick my way into a cold shirt.

"No, no," she said, seeing me. "Let's drink to the idea."

Three or four drinks in rapid succession produced a bonfire in the pit of my stomach; which warmth soon spread up my limbs and into my head, suffusing me with a delicious drowsiness; on the crest of which I floated off with the last reflection that, when I awoke in the morning, it would be to the assurance of having slept with another woman only in the literal sense of the word.

I awoke to find myself on the living-room sofa. How had I gotten there? No matter. Some filament of conscience, some tropism in the dark, had led me to it — to finish the night in a tableau of rectitude. Twisting about under a slipping quilt, I felt a crick in my neck, cramps in my legs, all morally usable miseries. Was that a dream of having been at Moot Point that I vaguely remembered? A clock on a desk said two-thirty. How could it be this light so early? And with all the shades drawn. I got to my feet and stole a look into the bedroom. It was empty; so was the apartment except for myself. My head ached and my tongue was parched.

I went into the bathroom and there met a poltergeist in the mirror. I took a closer look at him. My hair was mashed every which way, like grass after a storm. My eyes looked like swatted moths. I drank cold water and doused my face with it. I felt a relief that was a kind of crystal exhilaration: I had come off all right. In fact I was glad it had all happened — it put me in the light of having better instincts than I'd supposed. I was like the doors on that Italian church which had all along been assumed to have been bronze, but were discovered on cleaning to be gold.

When I went back into the living room, I took a look into the wastebasket in which Terry had thrown the manuscript. It was empty.

Fifteen

I HAD just been to the latest 3-D movie and was resting my eyes on some bas-relief at my favorite museum, and chatting with its curator, a man in a white coat who was polishing the establishment's collection of crystal. His name was Frank.

"Experience is the shortest distance between anticipation and regret," I said.

He nodded noncommittally, and looked out at the moist, suddenly autumn-like street. "It's been an all-day drivel," he said. He set a furbished glass on the back bar. I dug a handful of change out of my pocket and set it on the bar.

"The coins of desire are counterfeit; those of love have numismatic value. Neither can be spent." I shoved a fraction of my wealth across the wood and said, "Give me another Rhine wine and spritzer."

"I like these all-day drivels," he said, contentedly scratching his briskets. "Pleasant." He came over for my glass and refilled it. "I'm glad to see you switching to white wine and soda. I don't make as much out of it, but it's a damn sight better for you." Pouring in the soda, he asked: "What made you so philosophical? What started it?"

"Oh, many things, Frank," I answered, "but mainly, I think, flunking philosophy. It was my first intellectual disappointment, and gave me that sense of proportion about myself that one so sorely needs. Had I lightly mastered those great German noodle floggers, I might have gone on indefinitely without acquiring that philosophical viewpoint that is so indispensable.'"

"It comes in handy around here all right." He set the drink in front of me. "You sure get all kinds in this place." He rang up the money, glancing at me in the mirror. I was wearing a reversible raglan which was new but showing the strains of repeated adaptations to the fickle weather prevailing previous to today's (which had been largely as Frank had said). For the better part of a week, we had been through such abruptly alternating fits of sun and shower that, weary of reversing the raglan, I had put it on tweed-side-out and left it that way. "How come you got a topcoat that's part raincoat and then when it rains you wear the topcoat part on top?"

"How much wood would a woodchuck chuck if a woodchuck would chuck wood?"

"And then no hat to boot."

"I like the gentle rains myself." I drank. "They speak to me of peace. Of the peace at last when these upholstered bones — " I broke off and said, "All right. I know. Let there be no moaning at the bar."

But my heart was not in this. Because now I found that I had my wife back on my conscience again — to some extent. And now that she was home I wanted to make some final, resolving gesture of affection, something in the way of a coming-home present.

The present idea, I thought, turning it all over in my mind, would blend very nicely with the anniversary of our first date, which, searching for some occasion that she probably wouldn't remember and that would hence put me ahead of her, I recalled was to be Saturday, tomorrow. The day would most likely go unnoticed by her, as she did increasingly forget the incidental occasions she had once set such store by. But this was the eleventh hour, and I was still racking my brains in vain for something to give her.

I had left the bar and was hurrying through Frank's drivel to catch the five-thirty home when my eye was caught by something in the window of a liquor store. It was some bottles of a variety of Moselle known as Piesporter, which were on sale as a closeout for three dollars and eighty cents a bottle. The year was '37, a great one, which meant that at this price, and thirty-five dollars a case, the stuff was a steal. I went in and snapped up a case.

"Can you get it out to Avalon, Connecticut, tomorrow?" I asked the salesman, an oppressively natty man in blue pin stripe, and with a blond mustache waxed and twisted into two tines. "I need it tomorrow and I'm not driving."

"I'm sorry, we can't deliver across the state line," he said. "Regulations."

"I see." I pondered my problem. There was only one solution, short of making a special trip by car for the goods, if I wanted it for the week end. "I'll take it with me," I said.

"The whole case?" the salesman said, boggling at the thought. "Can't you take a few bottles home at a time — I mean if you come into the city regularly?"

I explained that the purchase was for a present, and that I did not want to dissipate the gesture by executing it piecemeal. I had made more forbidding portages on Christmas Eve, I had him know, and wasn't going to be daunted by twelve bottles of Piesporter. Besides, I had a plan all doped out in my mind. "Make two parcels of five bottles each," I instructed him. "I'll carry one of those in each hand, and a bottle in each of my raincoat pockets. Make the parcels good and strong with lots of stout twine to hold them by. And I'll phone my wife while you're doing that, if I may, and tell her I'll be on the next train."

It was a figure laden on the above lines that the rush-hour throngs saw toiling down the ramp at Grand Central Terminal, bent over double and plashing audibly, his eyes popping and the veins in his neck standing out like whipcord, his hair pelted into absurdity by the sudden downpour into which the all-day drivel had changed. Moselle is a reasonably light wine, but not by avoirdupois, and I was now proceeding on the remnants of strength left by sprints for cabs which had punctuated the quarter-mile walk in the rain (fruitless sprints, with all that ballast), dashes across traffic intersections, and that broken-field running that makes up so much of a commuter's life. My pace, as a consequence, had slowed to the next thing to a dead stop. My arms felt as if they were coming out of their sockets, and the parcels grazed the floor as I moved. The effect was a little like that prowling gait that is the trade-mark of Groucho Marx, except that it didn't go very well with a wet sheep dog look. Bangs to my chin, I continued down the incline. I paused and set the packages down to brush my hair back, and also to button my raincoat; the two bottles in it made that feel like a millstone around my neck, and I thought that by fastening my coat they might be less of a "dead" weight. But fastening the coat only made it bind unendurably, and I stopped to loosen it again.

I had exactly two minutes to catch my train. What remains in my memory is a small nightmare of exertion. Somehow I got through the main waiting room and, strolling exhaustedly through the gate, heard the conductors yelling "All aboard!" A train let out of its air brakes a series of snorts not unakin to my own stertorous pants. How we pay for sex! I thought. Still I experienced a certain pleasure in my pains, feeling them to be giving me "what I had coming" and thus to that extent closing the score against me. Yet had I dreamt that this was not the end of what I was to pay but only the beginning I believe I would have sunk to the floor and died. In a final spasm of effort I swung aboard the forward platform of the last coach of my train, which was the first platform open to me. I dropped my cargo in a corner of it and stood with my back to the door.

Breathing heavily, I thought of the affectionate dedication behind the production of such wine as this, how the workmen in the German valleys climb the steep terraces on which the vineyards grow, nursing the fruit into maturity by constantly rearranging individual pieces of slate in the soil so that each grape will get the benefit of reflected sunlight, effort more painstaking and back-breaking than what I was going through on this end to acquire the product, but not much. But now I had the bottles, to take home and lay at my wife's feet, which, God knew, would be about as high as I could lift them.

Lurching through the tunnel, I felt a hand on my shoulder. "Are you all right?" a man asked. I saw out of the tail of my eye, as I turned my head a little, that it was a conductor.

"I'm O.K.," I said. When he hovered, solicitous, I repeated testily, "I'm O.K."

"All right. I was only trying to be helpful. It's my duty when somebody looks — " He hesitated, then went on, "Last week we had a case of acute indigestion."

"This is a case of Piesporter," I said, without turning around.

My arms still hung in a simian fashion for I hadn't yet straightened my back — I couldn't. Add to this the fact that he was seeing me from behind, and I suppose there was sufficient ground for his anxiety.

"A case of what?"

"Piesporter."

"That's a new one on me," the conductor said, removing his cap and rummaging in his hair. "Piesporter. What's it like, if I may ask?"

"It's a growth in the Middle Moselle."

So apart from the stiff back I was quite myself again, such as that may be, and by the time we rumbled out of the tunnel and up the grade toward the 125th Street stop I was seated in the car, near the front door where I could keep an eye on the vestibule, for I had left the packages out there. My coat with the two bottles in it was folded carefully on the luggage rack overhead.

The walk from the Avalon platform to the station wagon in which my wife was waiting for me was no problem, being only ten feet. Though I could feel the parcel cord biting into the crop of water blisters I had sprouted in the course of my New York heats. The rain had stopped.

"What are those?" my wife asked me as I stowed the packages in the back of the car.

"Don't you know what for?" I asked mysteriously. I set my raincoat out of sight on the back seat. "Don't tell me you've forgotten what day it is tomorrow," I said, springing into the front seat beside her.

"Tomorrow?" she puzzled, starting up. "What day is it?"

"Why, the anniversary of our first date." I looked wounded. "You've forgotten."

She looked at me suspiciously. "It is at that, isn't it?"

"Yes. Oh, don't feel too bad about it," I said, reaching to take her hand. "Anybody could forget." Everything was going well; going according to plan.

"What did you get me?" she said, withdrawing her hand.

"Now, now, just be patient. Tomorrow's the day, not today."

However, that evening as we sat in the living room reading, I began to wonder what the Piesporter was like, and a marked thirst came about. I put my book down and rose.

"Look, I know you're dying with curiosity," I said. "It's only an hour and forty-five minutes till midnight and, well, I wouldn't mind. It's also a kind of coming-home present for you. So want to open it?"

"Could I?"

Well, nothing would do but that I get the packages out of the closet where I had them hidden and bring them into the living room. I kept the two separate bottles out of sight as they would have tipped the present off. "I can't wait to see the expression on your face," I said as, with an eager smile, she knelt on the floor to open the first of the parcels. She drew out one of the bottles.

"Well, wine," she said. She read the label. "Piesporter?"

"It's that Moselle you're so crazy about."

"I am?"

"Yes. We had it at Hans Hoffman's that night — remember?"

"I see. Well, gee, thanks." She looked over at the other package. "Now I'll open this one."

"That's Piesporter too," I said. "I got you a whole case.

You'll notice it's a '37. A great year for German wines, and for a lady too," I added prettily. She got to her feet and dusted off her skirt. "Also, it's a *Spätlese*," I pointed out, tapping the label of a bottle which I had picked up. "That means it's from selected grapes which have been allowed to become dead ripe, which is another — where are you going?"

"Just back here and sit down."

"Which is when those grapes are at their best," I continued. "It's a condition the Germans call *edelfaul*, when the grapes are *edelreif*."

"Yes. Well, thanks a lot. That's wonderful."

She picked up the magazine she'd been reading, from the floor where she'd dropped it; but it lay unread in her lap. At last she said:

"Did you mean that women are at their best too, when they're — what did you call that when the grapes are dead ripe? *Gestalt*?"

"No, no — *edelfaul*. I believe that's the way Hans pronounced it. Hans went into the whole thing with me after dinner while you and Elsa were playing duets. It's a fascinating subject. I'd like to know more about it. Why, certainly women are at their most attractive when they're mature. That goes without saying."

"Then why say it?"

"I didn't say it."

"No, but you implied it. With that remark about the vintage year and age and all." She dropped the magazine on the floor again; I put the bottle back and sat down. "This is the fifteenth anniversary of that first date already. Do I look thirty-seven?"

"You do not," I answered with sincerity and alacrity.

"When are you supposed to be middle-aged? Thirty-five?"

"Oh, I don't think till forty. And even then . . ."

"Even then what?"

"Even then a woman is only just beginning to get into her, to get into this — " I wriggled restively up in my chair. "Well, into this *Gestalt* — I mean *gefülte* — Oh, damn it, you've got me doing it now. The French have a term for it too. What do they call it again? Oh, yes — *pourriture noble*, I believe. It means a noble ripeness. When the grapes get so they're ready to fall off the vine."

There was a silence.

I said: "Age is a guarantee of body and perfume."

The silence deepened. She looked over at the cellaret on top of which stood a bottle of Canadian Club. "I think I'd like a drink," she said. She rose and started for it.

"Why not open one of these?" I said, indicating the Piesporter. "Come on, let's start celebrating! I'll have one chilled in a jiffy," I added, picking a bottle up and bustling into the kitchen with it. "I can't wait to see the expression on your face when you taste it."

We sat regarding one another moodily across an ice-filled saucepan from which the neck of a bottle of Piesporter protruded like the muzzle of a gun. However, I had a fresh white napkin if not a wine cooler, and I poured and served the Moselle with style. I toasted the occasion, and we drank.

"God," I said, working my lips. "Beautiful?"

"Mm," she agreed, nodding. "Quite nice."

"Get that delightful fruitiness characteristic of all your fine Moselles." I was relieved to find the wine good, because I'd suddenly remembered something about Moselles having to be drunk young, which meant that mine was pushing senility, and also shed a little light on it as a shopping coup.

"What did you do while I was gone?" my wife asked, looking at the largess strewn about the floor.

"Oh, nothing much. Like I told you — movie or two, dinner here and there, and once I ran into Al Standard and had drinks with him. Like I said. Why do you ask?"

"Oh, nothing," she said, stroking the stem of her glass between her fingers.

Holding my wine aloft and appraising its hue, I said, "A very funny thing happened at one of the restaurants I tried, down in the Village — a misprint on the menu. It was one of those hectograph menus? It said, 'Dreaded veal cutlet.' "

She shook a cigarette out of a package and took another tack. "You're really getting to like wine, aren't you? Especially white wines."

"What do you mean by that?"

"I mean you like white wine," she answered, a flintiness in her voice which recalled the great Chablis. "You'd love to lay in cases of it, have a cellar, but it's too expensive. Unless you're buying a present for somebody that you'd be expected to spend that much money on anyhow — "

"I think that was uncalled for," I said, going over and giving her a light. But it was what I wanted. I moved cautiously in quest of a grievance, luring her inch by inch toward saying something she would be sorry for. "I remember distinctly you were crazy about the wine we drank at Hans's. You exclaimed about the Piesporter we had first, and you exclaimed about the bottle he opened later. It was a 1937 Rüdesheimer Hinterhaus Riesling Auslese — "

"You have to exclaim at Hans's. Or he sulks."

"I'm not through yet. I remember that bottle because I memorized the label, as a sort of a gag." I started over from the beginning. "It was a 1937 Rüdesheimer Hinterhaus Riesling Auslese Wachstum und Original Abfüllung Grafen von Francken-Sierstorpff."

"Don't make so much noise," she shushed with a warning jerk of her head toward the sleeping children. "Why, do you bone up on the subject during those tough three-hour lunches you have to go through in New York every day?"

Now she was close. In a moment she would wound me, if I worked it right. Then I'd be in the catbird seat. Carefully, I cued her; carefully because this called for egging, and a hair's-breadth too much could in a twinkling reverse the advantage by making the other one the injured party.

"You mean while you're curled up here reading a book? Like that one there?" I said, pointing to a volume spread-eagled on the ottoman.

"Not curled up with it, exactly, but trying my best to wade through it — it and the rest of that set of Trollope you bought me on my last birthday because you were dying to reread him."

That did it. That was the shaft that went home.

I turned a hurt face to the window and said, "I don't think that was a very nice thing to say. What puts you in such a defensive mood? I don't understand it, darling." I faced about with a hand spread. "Is it because you thought I'd mind your forgetting our little anniversary? How could you know me so little as to think I would?"

"And speaking of anniversaries, there hangs my last wedding-anniversary present." She nodded to a Reginald Marsh over the mantel. "That painting you just had to have. I can't wait to see what I get on the next one. A nice silver ice bucket probably."

That stung me to the quick; so much so that I could not be content with wounds but must take up spears.

"This is the thanks I get for carting this whole damn case home," I said. My arms still ached for me to wave them to any great extent. "Are we going to start appreciating some of the finer things of life, or are we going along on the level of taste here in Subourbon Heights?" Since the gag was a visual one it made no sense to her whatever, and I was too proud to spell it out. I expanded on the subject of the portage. "All the way across town during the rush hour and in a downpour, and then halfway across two states. At least the conductor on the train showed some concern — he was really worried. Why, the distance I lugged this stuff to get it home on time is big enough to put in all the vineyards between Braunsberg and Schweinfurt!"

She may have thought I was swearing at her, because she ground out her cigarette, rose and started to leave the room. I stepped athwart her path.

"Take a look at these," I said, spreading both hands to display the rows of blisters I had acquired. "Talk about edelfaul!"

My wife passed around me, after an accommodating glance at the lesions, and marched on into the bedroom with great dignity.

"Good night," she called back satirically. "Sleep tight."

"Don't worry, I will," I said, drawing the Piesporter from its ice even as I reached with my other hand for my glass.

Well, I patched it up though. I smoothed it over. I smoothed it over with another present. It was a series of recordings, by Casadesus, of all, but all of Ravel's piano music. Three records — six sides, that is, and long-playing — which I was lucky

❨ 175 ❩

enough to pick up in Avalon the next morning. It made a nice remembrance, I think, because it's the sort of thing I can't abide.

And a couple of weeks later Terry McBain phoned me in an absolute tizzy to say that the *Digest* had bought her Most Unforgettable Character.

"Episode," I said to myself, "closed."

Sixteen

SO things were back to normal again. And back to normal up at Moot Point too.

With what nostalgia had I not in the interval hankered for its enveloping graces, and how tonic now the resumed hours there among my growing ranks of guests! It was on one of the evenings soon after my return that we invented, a group of us, in a spate of extemporaneous mirth, something we called Loony Latin, the idea of which was, of course, later pirated and transposed into Gallic as Fractured French. It was basically the same thing. For example, a *hic jacet* was, we said, a sport coat worn by a person of provincial, or corny, taste; *ad nauseam* meant a sickening industrial advertisement, and the like. We didn't mind the theft; indeed, we followed with amusement the solemn commercialization of what had sufficed us purely as an evening's toy. "Limitation is the sincerest form of flattery," I laughingly observed to my circle as we passed the plagiarism around one night. But we never publicly belittled the volume, or the foolish napkins and highball glasses that succeeded it either, as that would have been rather a breach of suavity in the brightest constellation, as our set had by now come to be called, in the Eastern social skies.

How did things stand in Avalon, and what of Augie Poole? He was far from being without interior resources of his own, as

I very soon came to see. One evening I went over to his house to borrow an ice crusher and found Isolde in tears. Now what? Everything had seemed under control. Augie had kicked in with another five hundred dollars, which I'd taken to Cornelia the day before. Augie was laying low, as was proper since he was under very strict surveillance now in the Crib's final checkup before approval. Cornelia had told me she'd gone to the Rock-a-Bye people, as I'd urged, and they were fine; all confidences were honored and nothing demanded, but anything putative fathers felt they could give was appreciated. Hence the extra five hundred, the original thousand being regarded as covering medical expenses as such. Augie walked the chalkline, holding hands with his wife in public and being knightly in many other ways and at all times. Then, happening to glance in the window after ringing the bell to get the ice crusher, I saw Isolde drying her eyes as she rose from the couch and came to the door. My heart sank: all the beans had been spilled.

"Oh. The ice crusher. Audrey did call about it, I forgot. Come in."

"I hate to . . . " I stepped inside, closing the door.

"No trouble. I'll get it."

She went into the kitchen. No Augie in sight. I thought I heard a creak in another room. Was the ex-satyr in hiding?

Isolde was in the kitchen long enough to touch up her face as well as get the grinder, without very good results.

"What's the matter, Isolde?" I said, taking the ice crusher.

"You know." She dove into the couch and buried her face in the cushions.

"Augie?"

The head bobbed. "I suppose you've known about it all along."

I set the ice crusher on a table. I reached down and touched her hair awkwardly. "Augie's basically a good egg. . . . "

"Good!" She tossed around into a sitting position, her hair flung up at me as if in reproach. "Is that all you can say? Is that all you can say for the most wonderful guy a woman ever had? To do a thing like that."

"To do a thing like what, Isolde?" I said, confused.

"Sell his ideas of course. What are we talking about? Give up his career and settle down to being a hack idea man. A gagman! So he'll have the kind of family-man, steady-income quality the agency wants in a husband. He's doing it all for me." She broke into fresh wails, giving me time in which to collect my thoughts.

It didn't take me long to get the pitch. The old bastard, I thought, angrily navigating the room. Making moral capital out of what his sins had made inevitable. Getting on deposit a lump sum so big he could draw on it indefinitely — pretty sly. Why, it would keep him liquid till the day he died! For when would the time come when his wife must now not be grateful to him?

"Where is he now?" I asked, wondering if he was around here but too ashamed to come out.

"He's in his studio." Isolde gave her nose a tweak with a hand-kerchief. "He's pretending he doesn't care, the lamb. Did he seem to you to be cut to pieces?"

"Not exactly. Well, in a way." I veered bewilderedly in my loyalties. I had a sudden flash. Was he even more saintly-like-a-fox than seemed? There was the likelihood, my intuition told me, that Augie had come to realize at last that he didn't have what it takes, and would have sold his ideas anyway. So it was next to nothing that he had managed to parlay into martyrdom. Maybe this was speculation, but it was valid speculation, and

I felt Isolde had a right to any consolation it might afford. Therefore I said:

"Baby doll, don't cut yourself to pieces. Because there's this about it. Eventually — well, let me put it this way. There comes a time in every man's life when he realizes he isn't wielding a rapier, but only laying about with the kitchen poker — "

"Oh!" she brought out in a reproving gasp, and turned away. Then she said: "But of course that's the way you've felt about him all along. This is what you've always wanted."

"I was only — "

"I know. Trying to make it easier for me. I'm sorry." She stood at the window and worried a handkerchief through her hands. "I wish I didn't nave to take this from him. I told him I wouldn't have it, but he insisted. He almost got angry about it. But I sure wish I didn't have to take it from him."

"You may have chance enough to pay him back," I said and, picking up the ice grinder, beat a hasty retreat.

I couldn't get home fast enough.

"Well, Audrey," I said, carrying the crusher into the kitchen where she was preparing for a couple of after-dinner callers we expected — people who liked stingers and frappé drinks, which is what the ice crusher was for, "Guess what your wicked Augie has done now."

"Been arrested with a chorus girl?"

"He's given up his career for his family," I said, a trifle smugly. I hadn't mentioned any of this yet, having hesitated to break the news before Augie did. "It seems the agency would feel better if he had a steady income, soo he's selling his ideas and becoming a gagman. A gagman! You know what that means. Burying his dreams of becoming an artist. Forever," I added when there was no response.

"Well, that's fine," my wife said, reaching into the refrigerator for something.

"Is that all you can say? It's fine? Why don't you admit 'my boy,' as you've ironically been calling him, has come through with flying colors? I hate to say I told you so, but I think you ought to give credit where credit is due."

"I do." She closed the refrigerator door and turned. "I give him plenty of credit, if this is what he's really doing. But is he giving up for Isolde any more than Isolde has given up for him?"

"What do you mean?"

"Her acting. Or have you forgotten? That was a career too. I won't say she has a terrific amount of talent, but it's as much as Augie's any day. Maybe more — because Isolde at least has had a few bit parts."

"Augie's sold things."

"What?"

"To us. That cornucopia full of frozen foods — probably other things in the future."

"That cornucopia." She smiled. "Really now. That dinky little Thanksgiving spot. You called it a one-shot yourself. No faces to draw, which is the real test of a cartoonist — you keep saying that yourself. Don't go away yet. Oh, you've started the oil furnace again. One second, I want to make this point. It makes me so furious I can hardly talk. When a woman gives up something to be a housewife and mother, it's taken for granted — that's just Nature. But let a man make the least concession and there's all this hoopla. It's always the man marriage is a trap for."

"I'll keep my own shut and save ours," I said, and walked with a broad smile to answer the door, for our guests had arrived.

On returning to the office from lunch the next day, I found a telephone message on my desk:

Miss McBain called at 12:35. Would like you to call her back. Urgent.

What could be urgent? Probably some revisions on Father that she wanted help with. Well, that was hardly urgent from my point of view; I had a few pressing matters of my own to attend to. I was deep in a raft of correspondence I'd let pile up when the phone rang and it was Terry again. Her voice said "trouble."

"I hate to bother you," she said, "but something's happened and I just had to tell you. Something terrible."

"What?"

"Can't you guess? Think hard."

There was a pregnant silence.

"Does it concern me?" I asked.

"Indirectly. Have you guessed?"

"Terry?"

"What?"

"Have you been drinking?"

"No. I'm so embarrassed and — ashamed. Such a *fool*. I might have known."

"Known, Terry?"

"That I was asking for it."

"Yes."

"You've guessed — the inevitable. . . . Hello, are you there?"

"Yes. You mean that when I was drunk and didn't know what I was . . ."

"What do you mean when you were drunk? The thing is, I've told Father — "

"What?"

" — and he's already talking about lawyers."

"Bu-but." I rose on rubber legs, gored on a vision of armed nuptials; except that no blunderbuss in Father's hands could bring about our union. Blunderbuss: a mistaken kiss. "I'm already ma-ma — " My voice bleated away into a thin squeal, like Laurel's of Laurel and Hardy when he is about to cry. I picked weakly at a kink in the phone cord. "Your father won't shuh-shuh-shoo — "

"What on earth is the matter with you?"

"Will he shoot me?" I laughed feebly.

"Don't worry," she said, laughing herself. "I won't even mention your name." I felt a partial relief — but only partial; like a genuflecting pack beast relieved by ten pounds of a load a hundred in excess of his capacity. "You're a brick, Terry. Look, can I call you back? Are you home?" I wanted to get off the office line.

"Yes, but I won't be here long. I'm waiting for a plane reservation to come through, and if I can't get that I'm going to catch a late afternoon train home. That's why I wanted to get in touch with you right away. I wondered if you had any ideas."

"It's too late for what would have been my main thought — not to tell your father."

"I know." She sighed. "But he would have found out anyway."

"Not necessarily. Those things can be . . ."

"He'd have found out. Somebody would have told him and then it would have been twice as bad. Of course it isn't a sort of desperate rush. It'll be months before — "

"I'll call you back, Terry. You know how terrible I feel about it, of course — "

"Don't. It's not your fault." She heaved another long sigh. "But it is the ruination of everything. It's just the end."

"Courage," I babbled. "I'll call you back."

My legs growing steadily number as under a prodigious dose of Novocain that was freezing me from the feet up, I sat staring at the blotter-pad on my desk. Papers materialized upon it and were removed by my secretary's hand. It had a lace cuff at the wrist. My secretary found me, sometime later, affixing my signature to letters of which I was the recipient, and reading without comprehension correspondence I had just dictated.

"What's the matter?" she asked at last. "You look pale."

"I'm all right. I don't feel so hot. Open a window, I'm roasting in here." I lay down on a couch I had in my office and said, "I won't take any calls for a bit."

I heard the phone ring in the outer office and my secretary's crisp voice, "He's out just now. Is there any message?"

After a while I went downstairs and into a drugstore, where I hauled myself into a phone booth and dialed Terry's number. There was no answer. I let the phone ring several times and then hung up. Back in my office, a telegram awaited me:

COULDN'T GET YOU AGAIN TO SAY GOING HOME TRAIN THIS AFTERNOON SORRY NOW BOTHERED YOU BECAUSE YOU SO UTTERLY DUMPS BUT FELT HAD TO TELL YOU AND PROMISE NOT BOTHER YOU AGAIN SOMETHING MUST SEE THROUGH MYSELF.

So she was leaving the burden of gallantry up to me. She was giving me an out, but only after I had learned the facts. I couldn't honorably take it. I would call her back, of course, next week, and the week after that if she hadn't returned. Meanwhile what? Meanwhile how much money could I dig up and where? I couldn't pay out anything like this called for without it showing on my bank balance. Too much to smuggle under Miscellaneous in a family budget. I'd have to touch the office for it. Pay it back a few dollars a week; go without lunch maybe; or such fancy ones; or pick up a little fruit at a Sixth Avenue delicatessen. We all overeat. *There are lots of good reasons for being good.* Get hold of yourself is the main thing at the moment. There mustn't be any sign of this *Angst* to anybody. *Angst*, there's a word for you. Say it over and over to yourself till everything becomes a joke. *Angst, Angst, Angst. Weltschmerz.*

At home, we got the notification from the agency that Mrs. Mash was coming to interview us about the Pooles. Now the whole picture was changed. Now it wasn't the danger of Augie adopting his own child, but of his adopting mine. Mathematical "odds" are no comfort to a man in *Angst*. Not this type of *Angst* anyway. A possibility is a possibility, and the submicroscopic mote of this one bloomed into monstrous likelihood: Terry, sent into the snow by a Biblical Father (like the girls in the cartoons we were always running), coming out to stay with the only people she knew who could take her in, the McBains, friends near Avalon who would see her through, help her get in touch with some nice local agency — *Angst*. Did I have the whole thing to do over again? Why didn't I die in Grand Central, lugging the Piesporter? Why didn't I die on the walk home in the heat, back in that other time?

No wonder I lost my voice (in more or less the same fading squeal as on the telephone) when the Mrs. Mash woman marched into the bedroom.

I got it back the next day. But I didn't let on to anybody. I didn't want to be quizzed on why it had conked out. Not till

I had the answers all worked out. I wanted time to think. I continued, on the whole, in bed, jotting bulletins and words of encouragement to my wife and such of my children as could read — Maude and Marco — and the story was given out that their father had been stricken with quinsy and might be laid up indeterminately, this being also the explanation phoned in to the office when Monday came and my absence from it had to be accounted for. Of my Moot Point considerations nothing remained; "escapes" never avail us when they are really sorely needed — they appease only the gray hours, not the black. I sat in a cockpit of the bedclothes and drank highballs. Tuesday afternoon I heard my wife on the phone when Blair called. "Why, he's under the weather, Mr. Blair. Quinsy . . . How's that, Mr. Blair? . . . Because he's allergic to it." (To penicillin, which he'd asked why I hadn't taken.) When my wife suggested she call Dr. Vancouver for another look at me, I rolled my eyes as if to say, "That hypochondriac." However, she called him.

He peered gingerly down my throat again, asking me not to breathe on him as the epidemic was still going strong and many there were who depended on his good health. I held my breath, but gagged on the stick he put down my throat, causing him to avert abruptly. He sat facing away from me till my gasping had subsided. His examination over, he rose and said, "Again I can't find a thing. A thing, that is, but a little tightness of the anterior muscles that you might get with *globus hystericus*. But *globus hystericus* couldn't possibly last this long, so maybe you've got an aphasia. I've never seen a true aphasia." I glanced at my wife and then modestly at the counterpane — for a true aphasia would give us great status in the psychosomatic belt. Vancouver stowed his flashlight in his bag and snapped the tongue depressor in two and gave it to my wife to dispose of. Then he went into the bathroom to gargle.

"If there's anything troubling you, tell me," he called later above the sound of washing his hands. "Or if you don't feel it's any of my business I'll have Dr. Printemps look at you."

"Who is Dr. Printemps?" my wife asked.

"He's a psychiatrist."

The very word was like magic. I cleared my throat. They turned and looked at me speculatively. I put a hand to my throat and smiled: not able to talk yet, but it seemed to be loosening up in there. Before Vancouver left, I was able to whisper a word or two. Well, good, but it still might be wise for him to give Printemps a ring and — I shook my head and waved him off. I would be all right.

The ringing phone was a further tonic: every time it did I jumped, wondering whether Terry, if she'd returned, would be indiscreet enough to call me here; I must be getting back to New York, and calling her to forestall any such thing. The possibility of Mrs. Mash's reappearing gave further spur to my recovery, though I devoutly hoped I had been washed out as a witness.

That evening, my wife and I sat in our wonted living-room chairs. I drew on a cigar of the size, smaller than a panatela, known as a doll. I had a flannel rag around my throat which gave me a vaguely tragic air. She occasionally paused in her knitting to watch me.

"Now that you can talk," she said at last, "what's it all about?"

"I was hoping you wouldn't ask me that. I'd really rather not go into it," I whispered, my voice threatening to depart again.

"You've got to."

"No."

"Yes."

"Our union has been blest with issues," I said with great good humor, fingering the rag around my throat. "No, I feel it's fairer to all concerned to drop it." I drew on the doll and, frowning at the coal, let a trickle of smoke out of the side of my mouth.

"I'm your wife," my wife said, hooking up a strand of yarn with her little finger. "It would never get any farther as far as I'm concerned."

It was of course no use resisting; her curiosity would never let me rest. I twisted the cigar out morosely in an ashtray; then suddenly buried my face in my hands and said, "Oh, my God." I peered at her through a latticework of fingers, and saw that she was knitting steadily, her face overcomposed; a little pale.

"How do you feel about — well, extramarital affairs, as they're called?" I said. My plan was to pay out as little rope at a time as I could, till she was satisfied. "Kinsey has shown us that the majority — "

"You mean Augie's been sleeping with another woman?" I nodded. "Yes."

"That's all?" Her manner was suspicious. "That sent you into such a tailspin?" I would have to pay out more rope.

I rose and, flapping my hands at my sides, said: "I suppose it's no use trying to hide anything. The woman is with child. That was it."

Standing at the window made no sense: the drapes were drawn. But I couldn't bring myself to turn around. My shoulders may have hunched a little as I steeled myself. I heard the click of the needles stop, and a rustle as she put her knitting in a basket on the floor beside her chair. Then I turned around.

We can seldom adequately foretell how people will react in an emergency or to extraordinary tidings, even people whom we know intimately; I had supposed my wife's disapproval of Augie's deeds would ring out proportionately to this their fruits. Nothing could have been more mistaken. She sat quietly a moment, after my announcement, greeting it with only a stare into her lap. "I'm sorry to hear that," she said.

She reached over for a package of cigarettes and dug one out. "Yes," I said, "so am I."

She sighed with her whole body.

"Well," she observed philosophically, yet at the same time a shade more censoriously, "people sleep together with their eyes open."

Seventeen

BACK in town once more, the next day, I drank three whiskies in rapid succession and dialed Terry's number. I shut my eyes and gritted my teeth as the ringing phone drilled into my brain: once, twice, six times, eight. No answer. This failure was blessedly repeated the next day, and three days later — five times in two weeks. And then the operator said, "That number has been disconnected."

It would be idle to disguise my relief. It was as though a stone had been lifted from my chest. She had been as good as her word then, "seeing it through" herself; and I as good as my vow to meet the demands of honor. Terry had undoubtedly gone back to her family, and I had not the remotest idea where in Massachusetts that was. There was nothing more for me to do — but try to forget.

My agony sloped off to a vicarious concern, once again, with Augie's. My wife did not press me for details; in fact, she wanted to know as little of them as possible now that she knew the gist, out of a feeling of loyalty to Isolde. I gave her to know that the situation was "contained," and proceeding toward a satisfactory resolution. Of the good this ill wind blew she needed no reminder: that was obvious in Augie's conduct. The account he gave of his reconstruction, on standard breadwinner lines, was enough also for Mrs. Mash, who troubled me no more. I suppose the woman had concluded that the opinions of a zany such as I were worthless in any case. The Crib O.K.'d the Pooles. It was now simply a question of settling down and waiting till the agency had "something that seemed right for them." For such an institution goes to as many pains to choose the child for the parents as it does to choose the parents for the role.

Typical of the new Augie were certain burning moral wants, a tendency to take inventory of himself in preparation for the role; in particular, to contemplate the awful symmetry of the circumstances under which he was about to assume it. We had long ethical discussions, of which the fruit was the conclusion that this was all a moral charade which had elicited his best and must now be forgotten, in favor of preparing himself for his new duties, the faithful discharge of which would give him quittance in full. This was a premise to which he clung, but one he insisted tirelessly on rehashing, like a man punching out a pillow on which he is trying to rest his head. We recapitulated it on long hikes we took with the aim, also, of fatiguing him so he could sleep, and on which he insisted on dragging me along (the word is an apt one for I am no lover of walks) both to keep him company and help hammer out a coherent position. So while we chose varying terrains to traverse on foot, we covered the same philosophical ground so often we were letter-perfect.

"You see, it's a sort of moral charade, no more," I puffed as we mounted a stile and struck out across an open field, one Saturday afternoon. "Your right hand will cancel out the debt contracted by your left."

"How can I be sure?"

"Because every man fathers a child and then rears one. You will do no less."

"But the two are not the same. Someone else will rear mine."

"And you will rear another's. All life is random. We conceive in blind happenstance even what is our fleshly own," I replied in a fairly turgid passage we had worked out in numerous marches across the stony meadows of Connecticut. I built dutifully to my climax, though breathing hard from exertion. "What are we but ciphers in the manswarm, grains in the anonymous dust. Nameless we come out of darkness, nameless return to it." Some of this was Augie's, some of it was mine, and some of it was Thomas Wolfe's. "But there is no point in flailing ourselves with fruitless reproach."

"You certainly seem to have done a lot of thinking about this," Augie said.

"Yes."

"Tell me the fable of the Roman mother and her child."

"Oh, not that again," I groaned, making for a stone wall. "Let's sit down here and take a breather."

We did. I took off my hat, a gray homburg. I have a great difficulty with hats which stems from the shape of my head, which is long and narrow like that of a football, so that a hat which fits from front to back will be too wide. I had recently gotten a haircut and so this homburg kept slipping down with each impact of my heels on the hard ground — the way you bring an ax down on its helve by pounding the other end on something. There were times on these marches when it dropped down over my eyes. This naturally obscured my visibility and once nearly cost me my life when I stepped out on the road in the dusk and into the path of a car whose driver had not yet turned on his lights.

I squeezed off a shoe and nursed a foot which had a large blister (*edelreif*) on it. "Life is a fortuitous conglomeration of Adams," I said. I looked up at the sky. Augie followed my glance. Appraising the dark wooliness of the clouds he said, "I wouldn't be surprised if we got one hell of a snowstorm. There's one due, you know."

"Yes," I said. "Does look like it. Let's go home."

Hobbling along down a road along which cars whizzed steadily, I said at last, "I don't know about you, but I'm going to flag a ride." So we hitchhiked, and at last a man we knew named Hal Mansfield came by and, recognizing us in the dusk, stopped. He took us both home. I remarked that it looked like snow, and Hal said heartily, "Yes. That reminds me of that sleigh ride party we've always talked about getting up. This time let's do it."

"I'm game," I said, glad for the lift in the warm car.

I had once defined Reality as "a shuffled deck of cards." That sleigh ride party turned out to be the Joker in the pack.

There were close to twenty of us half-yokels in it. Sleigh rides were constantly being gotten up or talked about, there in Avalon; the impulse at work was, I suppose, that nostalgia for simplicity that motivated a population a third of whom lived by taking in one another's antiques. Forgetting that true simplicity that lies in the flip of a thermostat switch on a cold winter's night — and reminded by Hal Mansfield of my promise — I agreed to turn up at his house the following Saturday night, "if there is still snow." There was, a frozen coat of it, in a temperature plunging toward zero and below.

A few feelers were put out about postponing the lark, but bravado carried the day, and half past seven found me upstairs sheathing myself in successive layers of cotton shorts and shirts. At this point my wife, whom I had thought busy scratching together a getup of her own, came into the bedroom where I was dressing and lay down, with the statement that she believed she had a cold coming on. Murmuring persiflage about the Spartan spirit, I drew on vest after vest. I donned a coat and then wormed into a mackinaw I remembered I had in the closet. When I crowned this improvisation with the homburg — the only "old" hat I had — my wife turned her face to the wall and pleaded a sick headache. "You're the doctor," I said humorously, and feeling more upholstered than clothed, descended the stairs, pocketed a pint of brandy, climbed into the station wagon and drove off. The Pooles were visiting Isolde's grandmother in another part of the state.

I found a sleigh in the Mansfields' yard, and standing beside it a man in a decayed blazer, flapping his arms. A cap that he wore with the earlaps down, a muffler one end of which was flung over his shoulder, his guarantee that he had newspapers under the blazer, and a mustache on which icicles had begun to form indicated that no detail would be lacking in our search for an Arcadian pattern.

"Where's everybody?" I asked.

"Inside," he said, pausing to adjust the harness on a steaming roan. I turned to the house with visions of warmth, eggnog and cancellation dancing in my head, but at that moment the door opened and people came tumbling and laughing out of it, their arms laden with blankets and heated bricks and stones. Hal Mansfield led the way to the sleigh, on the floor of which muffed and mittened people disposed themselves under quilts. "Hop in," somebody said, and handed me a tepid rock.

The possible alternations of sexes having run out, I scrounged down between a former tax assessor of perhaps forty-eight to fifty and the tail of the sleigh. He and I were supposed to share a warm stone, as well as a blanket, but the stone became speedily indistinguishable from our shoes, with the result that the former tax assessor and I kept feeling for each other's feet under the robe. Tiring of this rigmarole, he finally kicked the rock into the middle of the sleigh with an oath. He talked briefly about how the speedometer of his car had squeaked on the way up, owing to the cold's having rendered the grease in the mechanism ineffectual; then conversation died between us.

There was some friendly ridicule of those who had begged off. To the insinuation that their courage had failed them, someone replied that it had served them — we'd not the guts to back out, nor the sponsors the intelligence to call it off.

"We couldn't," Hal Mansfield said. "We've made arrangements to meet the other bunch, you know."

"What other bunch?"

"There's a party heading this way from Southport. We're to meet up somewhere between the Yacht Club and Grove Corners, on Grackle Hill Road. That gives us about eight miles apiece."

The connection between group misery and mirth is a boon on such occasions, but I never reached the stage evidenced by the hoots and buffoonery of my companions. Mile after mile I lay quivering under the robe, my teeth chattering, the homburg crushed indifferently under my head. I began to feel what is, for me anyhow, the first symptoms of really bitter cold — a pain in the eardrums. High time for a nip, I thought, and bit off a glove. But my fingers were too frozen to fish the bottle out, and after a few moments of fumbling among the stratifications of my clothing, I laughed weakly and said to the former tax assessor, "There's a bottle in my right inside pocket. Maybe you can get it out."

No maybe about it. In three seconds he had rummaged it out

of my ribs and was unscrewing the cap. "Ah, brandy!" he said, taking a pull.

"Brandy!" someone else shouted. Word went round and then the bottle, with many a lusty slug and many a good word for me. More impotent than either hurt or angry, I saw it passed from one mittened hand to another. There was some left when it got back to me, but my hands were so stiff half of it trickled down my chin, where it speedily froze. Then, settling down as far under the blanket as I could, and as nearly in the shape of a hoop as is humanly possible, and in a state of hopeless discouragement, I tried to concentrate on the localized glow in my stomach.

A sister-in-law of Hal Mansfield's, a woman named Mrs. Kipling, revived the spark of life in me with something she said. It was a reference to "the real sou'wester" she had on, which someone was admiring. I remembered her having once related being aboard ship "in a terrific nor'easter."

I hauled myself around and into a sitting position against the side of the sleigh. The woman was opposite me and one to the right. Pushing the homburg out of my eyes I asked, "Are you originally from New England?"

"Yes. Well, that is, Papa and Mama moved up to Vermont when I was eight." She smiled. "Are you?"

"No. I'm from the Mi'est," I said. "I went to Nor'estern."

This wasn't definitive parody being largely due to my jaw's being so stiff I couldn't manipulate it well enough to talk any better than that; but I stood a hundred per cent behind the way it came out.

"Have you lived in New England all your life since then?" I pursued.

"All my life except for three years when I was abroad."

"Oh, you were a broad at one time. How long ago were you a broad?"

"In my twenties."

"That's the best time to be a broad," I said. "What's it like, being a broad?"

"Oh, wonderful."

"I imagine it must be."

I gave this up, being engaged in another foot joust with the former tax assessor who had hijacked a hot jug from his neighbor. We were rewarded with a warm trickle on our trousers cuffs, having kicked the stopper loose. I reorganized my limbs on the floor again. As I did so, I heard someone up front ask Hal Mansfield, "You're sure they're on their way? This is Grackle Hill Road," and Hal Mansfield answer, "Positive. I talked to Ned McBain on the phone just now before we left."

That rang a bell somewhat louder than those tinkling on old Dobbin's harness. Rigid as a figure on a catafalque and steadily more garnished with ice, I lay in a fixed stare, contemplating the brass tacks in Cassiopeia's Chair. A young woman next to Mrs. Kipling, imagining herself to be guessing my thoughts, glanced up at the sky and said softly: "Isn't it majestic? Think of it — in just the Milky Way alone, all those billions and trillions of stars."

"I don't have my glasses with me," I said.

"Each one a world. And all billions and trillions of light years away. All swinging through inconceivable reaches of space."

"It's all right if you like that sort of thing," I said.

"Doesn't it fill you with reverence?"

"No. It just makes me sick to my stomach."

"Then what have we been put here for?"

"To freeze."

"You think everything is futile?"

"Yes."

"Then why not commit suicide?"

"That's futile too."

My jaw having worked itself loose a little in this colloquy, I turned to see what other groups in the party I could throw cold water on; but almost all the rest were clustered now at the front, watching the road ahead for the other sleigh. I turned to Mrs. Kipling.

"Have you ever been to We'inster A'ey?"

"No," she said, giving me an icy stare; and heaving herself to her feet, picked her way to the front.

A cry went up. "Here they come!"

Bells on bobtail rang as we sailed to the summit of Grackle Hill and slid to a stop. A second horse snorted and stamped nearby, and the merrymakers boiled down off the sleighs and mingled on the road, shouting and laughing and thumping one another on the back. Those in our sleigh stumbled out past and over me, till only the former tax assessor and I were left; then he climbed down. "Coming out for a stretch?" he said. I murmured something negative. I had caught the name McBain again.

When our sleigh was empty, I raised myself cautiously on one knee and peered over the side. They jigged and chatted in the snow. Everyone had that tearstained and kind of fiendish look that people have in extreme cold. Which of them were Terry's cousins? Suddenly my eye caught a glimpse of a face above a woolen scarf, which made me duck down out of sight again. A moment later, I heard a voice that went with it.

" — Mother always walked into the house backwards in

winter, because she claimed that kept her glasses from steaming up? Never did though."

I lay in a paralytic trance, hearing the bright cries shuttled in the air around me, like swirling flakes of sound. We were there five minutes, ten, maybe more. I didn't concern myself with time. Because now I began to feel an ominous comfort, and I thought of that slow-creeping, delicious warmth with which doomed travelers are said to lie down in the Alpine snow. Remotely, I heard something about going to Shively's for hot chocolate. Then figures came pouring back into the sleigh, tumbling over me and taking their places again. Then we were off, again in a tinkle of harness bells. We took another hill, and I kept my eyes on the stars, for it was toward these that we seemed to be mounting.

"Excelsior!" the former tax assessor said. "Why couldn't somebody think of putting excelsior in this damned thing? Pad the floor as well as warm it up."

I turned and gave him a dull look, fancying that my neck squeaked as I did so, like his speedometer. I knew what the "Excelsior" meant. I felt a pleasant sleepiness, now. Things receded; all words fused in a general babel, and had that remote and elfin sound of voices that trickle through to you on the telephone from another connection. Indifferently, I remarked the fluency with which two women gossips clacked their tongues; because at this point I felt that my own would retain any position into which it was bent, like lead. I put it out weakly to wet my upper lip; it slid across it, there having occurred under my nose a marked thickening of the filigree that goes with death by freezing. I laughed softly at a rotting star. Already I could feel my spirit, like gas let out of an uncorked bottle, drifting toward the blue pavilions of eternity. I turned my head toward the open tail of the sleigh. A moon was rising, like a bad orange.

Shively's was a large ice-cream place on the Post Road. I heard them piling off the sleigh, and, still more dimly, off the other one, and into the store.

I thought, after a moment, I mustn't lie here. I must get up and take a bus home. Maybe I could even find a cab. But I remembered — I had no money. I laughed helplessly as my hands fumbled at a pocket, then crept to a standstill, like some numb arachnids.

Two figures hove into view at the tailgate. "There he is. What's the matter?"

"I have no money."

"We can let you have money. You can't stay here — you'll freeze to death."

I smiled. It took quite a while, being like something making its way through silly putty. Yet I had at the same time, as they helped me over the tail of the sleigh, the most extraordinary sense of lightness, like a window mannequin any one of whose limbs could be disjointed and laid aside. They helped me across the sidewalk and through Shively's door.

I sidled into the first booth I saw empty, hoping Terry wouldn't recognize me even if she saw me. I couldn't pull the brim of the hat down over one eye as it was a homburg. There was little danger of her spotting me immediately in the confusion; a mauve nose and generally *glacéed* features kept me incognito for a good ten minutes. But then, as I was raising a cup of hot chocolate to my lips, I happened to glance into a booth in which Terry was looking over, her elbows cocked up on the table and a cup in both her hands, studying me. Her mouth opened in an inaudible cry of recognition. She excused herself to some companions I couldn't see, rose, and carried her chocolate over. Dressed in a buttoned coonskin coat, she slid in across from me.

"I didn't know you were here," she said. "How've you been?"

"I tried to get you, I tried every which way," I said, looking her steadily in the eye. "How are you?"

"I'm fine."

"Let's go over where we can talk," I said, pointing to where a group of teen-agers were making enough noise around a jukebox so no one could have overheard us. But just then the jukebox started up, and it seemed all right to stay where we were. A loud vocal streamed across the huge premises:

> The way you bugged my heart
> You snowed me from the start,
> I was a cornball and a cow;
> But now I'm in a puff
> Over one who's got the stuff
> And everything is Roger now.
> So don't try to bug me back
> Or wig me when it's slack
> 'Cause everything is Roger now.

"I tried to phone you, oh, many times. Your phone is disconnected. You — came out here?"

"Yes. I have a room at the McBains' now. That's them right over — there." She pointed at a middle-aged couple gotten up largely in leather. "I earn my sort of keep around the house a little, sit for them et cetera — and scribble a few hours each day."

She bent her head to sip from her chocolate. Raising her head, she parted the hair away from her right eye and made a study of me. "You're blue."

"Just what did you expect of me?" I asked.

She watched me, drinking.

I slid down as far as I could in the booth, till my chin was almost on a level with the table-top. "How many months are you gone?" I asked in a hollow voice.

"What are you talking about?"

"The child."

"Child? What child? What in God's name are you talking about?"

I slid up again in the booth. "Isn't there a child?"

"Where did you get such an idea?"

"What was all the — what was it you called me in such a state about?"

She opened her mouth on an unuttered laugh, then put her hand to her forehead. Then she said, "I thought you understood what I was talking about. That was about the article. My Most Unforgettable Character?" I nodded impatiently. "Father threatened to sue."

"Sue you?"

"Well, *The Reader's Digest*, actually. He wasn't going to be anybody's Most Unforgettable Character. Soo, they sent the article back." She spooned up the frothy chocolate. "I was sorry I bothered you about it, but I felt so low I just had to tell you."

My mind flew back over the telephone conversation. "Have you guessed? The inevitable. The thing is, I've told Father. I'm so embarrassed — so ashamed. I might have known. . . ."

I asked her, "What are you writing about now?"

"Mother." Her face lit up and she leaned across the table. "Mother was always trying to outwit pests in the house. Like the other night, when the McBains found one of Ned's suits all chewed up by moths, I remembered how Mother would always throw an old piece of flannel on the floor of the closet, so the moths would eat that instead?"

I laughed heartily. "That's rich," I said.

"Mother won't think being somebody's Most Unforgettable Character is a disgrace to the family. I've already cleared it with her. So when I'm finished, if you could find a minute. . . ."

The jukebox boomed out across the room's expanding hubbub:

> You played me for a schnook,
> You're blotsky in my book,
> You never built a bonfire in my hall.
> You're soggy and you snowed me
> And he's the one who showed me,
> I know that he will fizz me with his call.
> Now that I really dig you
> Don't wait for me to wig you,
> 'Cause everything is Roger after all.

Members of both sleigh parties rose and began to draw on mittens and mufflers. "Right home for me," somebody said.

"What's the matter?" I called, hysterical. "We soft?"

I got home about a quarter to twelve, to find my wife reading in bed.

"What kind of a time did you have?" she asked, looking up from her book.

"Terrific." I took a hot bath, drew on flannel pajamas I'd set to warm on the bathroom radiator, and returned to the bedroom.

My wife set her book aside. "Did you really?" she asked me,

interested. "Because, you know, I didn't actually have a sick headache or anything. I got cold feet at the last minute."

And none too soon, old girl, I thought as I pulled the covers back and popped blissfully in between the sheets.

Eighteen

THE peak of Augie's conventionalization took, in terms of outward symbols, the form of his joining us all for a church supper one evening. Seated on folding chairs in the church basement, we put our minds to cutting roast beef without dissecting the paper plates on which it was served; and this with meat only moderately amenable to surgery. A jab of particular force not only cut through my plate but made a slight incision in the trousers fabric of the knee I was holding my food on, and I felt a trickling warmth which gave new meaning to the term "lap supper." This was in the early spring. I had on a white linen suit for the first time that season, and lifting my plate I saw a stain the color of hemoglobin spreading on the pants. My companions fared better, having asked for and gotten well-done meat instead of rare. My emotions remained pent up, as we were seated within earshot of the minister, a pale, seraphic man with eyes the color of lentils. Still, what words I would have cared to utter would have been unfit for a brothel, let alone a house of worship. To some profanity that did escape under my breath my wife said under hers, "Please. We're in church." To which I answered, "Only in the basement." I looked around me, and wondered what their religion really meant to the commuters I saw on every hand. I have never heard of anything being converted in Connecticut but old barns.

Looking a little like an intern calling it a day, I rose and, with Augie, took all the empty plates back to the serving counter. There we got four dishes of ice cream and four cups of coffee, and joined our ladies with them. They were deep in a conversation during which Isolde, as we approached, cast an admiring glance at her husband in the course of something she said. Sitting down, we learned what they were talking about: the slowness of the agency in not having, even yet, come through. She was clearly chafing under the delay. Which the Crib explained by saying that at the moment the demand exceeded the supply, and anyhow they hadn't had anything that seemed right for the Pooles — for, as they emphasized more than once, they made a point of matching the parents with the child as closely as possible. This concerned the latter's extraction (what was known of it), color of hair and eyes, and other details of general appearance on which comparison might reasonably be made. Audrey was quick to corroborate this to Isolde, from her own experience with friends who had adopted, and so was Augie, out of what appeared to be widespread private researches of his own.

"Augie's certainly gone out of his way to find all this out," Isolde said. "So interested." She blew him a kiss across me.

A moment later, as we were watching a diversion at the serving tables where somebody had dropped a loaded tray, Isolde suddenly set her dessert spoon down in her dish and said: "I know what we'll do."

"What?"

"Try again with Rock-a-Bye."

Augie's face turned the color of the ice cream he was raising to his own lips, which happened to be pistachio. "Why do that?" he asked.

"Why not? Lots of couples try more than one agency. Or even more than two, before they succeed. That right, Audrey?"

"Well, yes, that's true. The Haleys tried I don't know how many agencies before they got something."

"Well then." Isolde spread a hand as at something elementary. "Why should we stick with the Crib?"

"But would shopping around be fair to them?" Augie protested. He laid his ice cream aside.

"Yes, why hurt their feelings?" I chimed in.

"Feelings!" Isolde laughed. "What's that got to do with it? I've got feelings too. Look how long they're taking. They might keep us on the string indefinitely. What can we lose by getting our name on two lists? If the Crib has something for us first, fine. If Rock-a-Bye, fine too. There's every reason to believe Rock-a-Bye should change its mind now. Augie's changed. And so has his whole financial picture. We never did get a clear answer on why they turned us down the first time, but I think a lot of it was this stable breadwinner idea. Besides, I think we owe it to Augie himself to make them reverse their verdict. I'll call them tomorrow." She emphasized this with a "so there" nod of her head.

I started to protest again, but Augie warned me off with a shake of his head, for fear of arousing suspicion.

Some suspicion had been already aroused several weeks before, when Augie's 1099 form arrived from *The Townsman* office — the statement for Federal income tax return, which specified how much he had earned from the magazine as a free-lance contributor the year before. Isolde had fished it out of the mailbox and opened it, to find that he had earned considerably more than he had declared to her. He explained the discrepancy by saying he had been putting money a little at a time into a separate savings account with which he had wanted to surprise her.

"It's like flaws turning up in a perfect crime," Augie'd said to me. "I sure as hell never thought of that. I wonder what next." To cover his story, I arranged for another advance from the office, and he hurriedly put the money into a new savings account which he did thereupon start.

The next link in what Augie called the infamy of events was revealed at a folk dance in Bridgeport to which we and the Pooles went, separately, early that summer.

For a long time people in our crowd had been trying to get me to folk dances. One of the most persistent was Sid Walters, the clear poet. Sid's obsession with things of that nature formed, as is often the case, part of a generally political concern with society, and, conversely, my indifference to them has been vaguely deplored as somehow indicative of scrawny thinking and bourgeois leanings. Just how my refusal to watch large numbers of strangers exert themselves rhythmically in upstairs rooms is evidence of how I vote has never been clear to me. My blind spot on the colloquial arises in part, I suppose, from folk singers I have heard in New York night clubs, where though the entertainment may be produced on a zither the charges are not necessarily computed on an abacus. But it also dates back to a milking certain Avalonians, myself included, received at the hands of a minstrel with a guitar, who wandered into town off of a freight car and thence into our hearts with the story that he was an ex-convict, a detail which gained for him an extra status among a small but discerning minority. A purse was gotten up for him to which I contributed twenty-five dollars. Intimations that Solitary, as he called himself, was better than any predecessors, including Lead Belly, were liberally nourished by himself and others, and he had acquired a substantial vogue among the intellectuals before he was exposed as an impostor who not only had no criminal record but possessed a background spotted with nothing more than a fear of work and a few jumped hotel bills. I always thought the bastard should have been arrested. However, he disappeared from local view and was never seen again. Uppermost in his repertoire was a number entitled "I was a stranger and you took me in," a ditty that I always think would have a fine relevance if I ever met him long enough to sing it back to him.

Sid Walters and my wife, in the end, whisked me off to a dance by conspiracy. He broke into the house one night flourishing a mimeographed handbill for a Hungarian revel when I was asleep in an armchair. "It's tonight! In Bridgeport! Let's pile into my car and go," he said. Audrey clapped her hands with what I was too dopey to see was a faked extemporaneity, my shoes were fetched, and before I knew what was happening, Mrs. Goodbread materialized and I was being led off between the two plotters to the waiting automobile. It was raining. "Some night to drag a man out to a recital," I grumbled, climbing into the back seat behind my wife.

Studiously buttoning a glove, she said, "It's not a recital, actually, but a real dance."

I reached for the door handle but it was too late.

"This will be the real thing," Sid said, shooting away in second. "Ah, those czardas rhythms. What they do to a man."

"Czardas — didn't Hoagy Carmichael write that?" I said, determined to be as much of a Philistine as possible.

Sid sketched in something of the history and background of Transylvanian forms, and as we headed up the Post Road toward Bridgeport, talked at length about ancient folkways. I have had enough about folkways, especially when dished up with psychiatric-anthropological analysis. I slumped down in the back seat and spent the remainder of the trip trying to think up some new folkways.

One folkway I thought of was an annual so-called Week of Good Report, during which people would go from door to door repeating nice things about their friends, to "atone" for the gossip spread the balance of the year. During this week the populace would eat nothing but tongue in penitential admission of the length of their own; thus they would "take everything back" for the twelvemonth by symbolically eating their words. Then I imagined an annual ceremony involving the hanging of an anthropologist. Another possible folk custom that occurred to me was something that would fall on a day known as Maybe Tuesday, a day nationally observed by building on the already emerging folklore of the quiz show. The quiz show would be reversed. Television crews in every city and town in the country would enter homes and instead of giving away money and gifts for questions answered correctly would take away some article of furniture or other possession for everyone that was not. This would be a long ceremony, lasting all day or till the family were completely stripped of their belongings. Neighbors would gather to watch. This is of course a modernization of the scapegoat ritual, and is called Maybe Tuesday because, as the expression would go, maybe next time it would happen to you.

The dance was held over a restaurant called the Romany Café. I knew from this that it was probably genuine, all right. All authentic folk affairs are held on the second floor. Anybody taking you to one that is on the first floor and representing it as the real thing is either lying or himself the victim of a misunderstanding.

The hall was large, and filling up as we arrived. We met a man in a pea-green jacket who was doing a thesis on some aspect of the dance for his master's, a friend of Sid's who showed my wife how to skip. "That's damn well what I'd like to do," I mumbled in an aside. My wife shot me a glance which enjoined me to either keep my mouth shut or stop acting like a peasant. "Get around and mix," she said, and disappeared on one foot. I did, and presently found myself running into friends from Avalon. We stood out, not favorably, by contrast to the many Old World costumes of the neighborhood folk; in our herringbone and banker's flannel we were dreary to a degree. One by one, or rather two by two, the suburbanites stepped out onto the floor, and were lost in the avenging swirl.

I drifted over to a table where a heady wine punch was being served, and had two or three. There I made the acquaintance of a girl of Slavic extraction named Anna, who spoke a patois derived from coast-to-coast hookups, Broadwayese, and official bebop. "That orchestra is cool," she said, rocking her head. The band was playing a popular favorite at the moment, but she expressed appreciation of a polka that followed in the same terms, and belittled czardas with, "Why don't they get it off the ground?" She taught me a few of the folk steps. The Tokay in the punch reached my head and my feet simultaneously, fostering an illusion of acquired skill; my fourth drink was soon my seventh; single sensations dissolved, over the flying hours, in a general haze of wine and rhythm. About eleven o'clock I happened to glance toward the main doorway and saw the Pooles arrive with another couple. Isolde said something in my wife's ear and they embraced happily. I guessed what the good news was from Augie's long face.

"We've been accepted by Rock-a-Bye," he said, taking me to the sidelines.

"I see."

"We got the report today."

We sank together onto folding chairs which bore the name of a local mortician.

"Let me think," I said.

I was in a mixed frame of mind. Only half of me seemed to sober up while the other half continued to revel, like a street shaded on one side and in sunlight on the other, or possibly moonlight.

"You couldn't steer Isolde away from it?" I said.

"You know I couldn't. It was for me she did it."

"Then we've got to steer Cornelia away from it — if there's still time."

"Would you?"

I got to my feet. "I'll call her right away," I said, oblivious of the hour. I looked around for a phone booth.

"Are you sure you're in shape to?" Augie assessed me worriedly. "You look three sheets to the wind again."

"I'm all right. There's no time to lose."

I found the booth and put in my call. Hubert answered.

"Cornelia's not here, old man," he told me. "I just got back myself from a lecture tour. I can't tell you where she is, but I expect to hear from her. I'm leaving again the first of the week."

"Is Carveth there? Maybe he can tell me."

"He's up at a planning committee meeting for Tanglewood, old man."

"How about Emory?"

"Popped off to Rome on a Fulbright. Got it all of a sudden and arranged for a year there, while his assistant takes over. He's studying Papal history."

"Well, when you say she's not there do you mean she's in New Haven?"

"Oh, yes. She's packed up and gone."

I sat a moment in the booth after hanging up, wondering what to tell Augie. I decided not to tell him anything that night, since he couldn't do anything about it anyway. I would take counsel with myself tomorrow, when I could think more clearly. He was waiting for me near the booth when I came out.

"Everything's O.K. Don't worry about it," I said.

"You talked to her?"

"Yes. There's time to work something else out. Come on, have a drink."

I had three or four myself in an effort to recapture my earlier vinous mood. I danced a couple of polkas with my wife. Everybody was having a good time. I remembered nothing much from midnight until the next morning when eight o'clock struck, like a hammer on my head. I was reassembling the night's impressions in the shower, later on, when I placed what was weighing on my mind — Augie. I spent the next two days mulling over whether to tell him the truth. After all, there was nothing he could do about it. But maybe there was and I couldn't think of it. Or maybe he would want to know, or should. What a responsibility. I stepped over to a mirror to see what an effect this was all having on me. I looked very discouraged, and not a little bitter. No, it was too much to shoulder alone: I would tell him.

"I've been trying to decide whether to break this to you," I said to him, "and I figure you probably should know. I didn't talk to Cornelia. She's already settled in."

"God," he said, clutching his head, as though he were a newel post about to come apart.

"Not necessarily," I said. "Now let's take a good, hard and calm look at this thing. What are the chances of — well, the Sophoclean windup to it? I take it you understand what I mean — you've read Sophocles?"

"Easy does it."

"To begin with, there's only a fifty-fifty chance that Rock-a-Bye will be the one to call you first. Right?"

"They said something about thinking they'll have something for us soon," he said in a dry falsetto.

"Secondly, even if you do draw Rock-a-Bye, the chances of Fate doing what we're afraid of are mathematically so — "

"And the time'd be just about now . . ." he went on to himself. "And the way they make a special point of doing everything in their power to match . . . Christola."

Here I began to rummage for the moral in Augie's life. Did it lie in this burgeoning irony, that the very virtue he had come to present might at the last make him vulnerable to calamity? Was the point that he had not been a complete rogue, only half a one? That if he had really told everybody to go to hell he wouldn't be behind the eight ball now? I had hoped it was the reverse: that it was in the fires of illicit fatherhood that he was to be shriven for the respectable. I had to believe that.

"Well, anyway, there's nothing you can do about it," I said. "There's a kind of relief in that — in pure helplessness. Nothing to do now but wait and see."

"Yes," he sighed. "I guess you're right. It's in the lap of the gods."

Nineteen

IT was a viewpoint from which I would have distilled more comfort had I not the sense of its being partially in my own lap. From being merely privy to Augie's affairs I had progressed to a condition of intimate involvement in them, so intimate that the same quivers of apprehension charged us both. We were emotional Siamese twins, to the extent, at least, of being in a three-legged race for whose duration we were fraternally lashed. And one of the length of whose course we had no foreknowledge. It was, therefore, with a simultaneous plummet of fear and wave of relief that I heard Augie say, having called me at my office from the suburbs, "I've got news for you."

"Make it brief and end on a note of hope."

"One of the agencies just called. They've got something for us. It's a boy."

Tracing with my eye the spirals of the phone cord, I asked: "Which one?"

"Rock-a-Bye."

And so out of whatever reserve of fortitude, caution, poise, or maybe just capacity for outrage, with whatever we had between us to give that this might yet take, we prepared to face the final step. The agency expected Mr. and Mrs. Poole the next afternoon at one o'clock sharp. By noon both of them were in such a swivet that they asked us to drive over with them.

It was Saturday and I was home, so we all piled into our station wagon, which would better accommodate the five we expected for the return journey, or even the four of us going out, than the Pooles' coupé. I drove, and sitting beside me Augie chain-smoked. "The nervous father," Isolde laughed from the back, where she and Audrey sat with bunting and other gear. Augie essayed some sign of amusement too. "Probably have to carry me in," he said.

It was not true — we had to carry him out.

Rock-a-Bye headquarters was a long, narrow, one-story building of white clapboard, set in a square of clipped privet. We were greeted in the reception room by a smiling gray-haired woman named Mrs. Larch. Audrey and I stayed behind in the reception room while the Pooles went back together, ushered by Mrs. Larch.

I lit a cigarette and walked the floor. Audrey smiled at me from a chair. Both were pleased by the stew their husbands were in.

"You look funny," she said.

"I feel funny."

"This happens every day."

I let it pass. I was twisting out the butt of my cigarette in an ashtray when Mrs. Larch thrust her head in and cried, "Come quick!"

I shot through the door ahead of Audrey and pursued the trotting Mrs. Larch up a broad corridor and through another door beyond which a nurse in white was throwing water on Augie from a paper cup. Augie was spread out in an overstuffed chair with his head back. The nurse was dipping her fingers into the paper cup and baptizing him as a housewife does her ironing. Mrs. Larch took the cup from her and dashed the contents into Augie's face. His eyelids began to flutter, and I looked elsewhere.

Disposed nearby above a silk coverlet reposed a blue and gold parody of the features being sprinkled and slapped, unless strain had laid both Augie and me open to hallucination. Yes, that must be it, I told myself sternly, taking in the tilted blue eyes and the blond hair with reddish glints. I blinked, as though to clear my head of a mirage. With a sudden cavernous yawn on the infant's part, the mirage did vanish. Or had *that* been an illusion?

Behind me they were feeding Augie brandy from a regular glass.

"Are you O.K., sweets?" Isolde said, chafing his wrists as Mrs. Larch tipped his head toward the brandy.

He nodded and tried to get up. Mrs. Larch persuaded him back with a firm push of her hand on his chest and said, "Let's move him to the front, there's a sofa there he can lie on." Augie made a gesture of protest, but she signed for me with a shake of her head to ignore him, and I took him by the ankles while Mrs. Larch grasped him under the arms, and we bore him to the front.

"These make the best kind of father," Mrs. Larch stated. "You can keep your casual husbands."

"*In other words there's nothing unusual about this,*" I said, walking with my back to my burden. "You keep brandy on hand."

"You'd be surprised what we use brandy for," the nurse said.

"What are some of its other uses?" I chatted.

"Are you all right, lamb?" Isolde asked. She walked flanking Augie, like a handler talking to his prize fighter in cartoons you have seen of boxers being borne from the ring.

"Certainly I'm all right. Let me down."

"All the strain, and now the excitement."

The collapse of an iconoclast is not among the more impressive sights in the world. Pain has been called a natural anaesthetic, once it gets unbearable, and I suppose some such process made me begin to giggle now that this thing was getting really awful. Presently I shook with laughter. I laughed so hard I damn near dropped my end of Augie. I had to pause to secure my grip on his ankles. He kicked and squirmed. "Let me down," he ordered.

We let him down only on the sofa, where he promptly sat up. The nurse gave him the rest of the brandy. We watched him as he finished it. I felt I could have done with a spot myself but didn't dare ask for it.

"What are some of its other uses?" I persisted, when I'd got my voice under control.

"We rub it on the gums during teething," Mrs. Larch told us. "Matter of fact, we sometimes put a drop in baby's formula when it won't sleep at night." She laughed. "You might remember that when you're walking the floor some night, because I can see this is one daddy who's going to take his job seriously."

"I think I'll report you to the state authorities, serving liquor to minors," Augie said. We were all glad to see him kidding again.

The nurse brought in the baby.

"What, *what* a dumpling," Isolde said.

"He's asleep," Audrey said, over the nurse's other shoulder. "Sweetest thing I ever saw. So aloof and kind of amused."

The nurse beamed at it. "I don't suppose you want him."

"Why, have you others?" Augie said.

"Oh, sure, take your pick," the nurse said, really going along with this joke. "Who'd want him? Angel."

"Yes. I think we've done you proud," Mrs. Larch said. "He even looks a little like you."

"Water." Augie held out the empty glass which I took and filled from a cooler that was pointed out to me in a small adjacent office. "Little chaser," Augie said, taking it. I walked over to the group of women clustered round the child. I thrust a hand in and chucked it under the chin. "Kitchy kitchy coo," I said, a delicate chill going up my spine.

We had to wait while Mrs. Larch took the parents into the small office for a few final formalities. She closed the door, but I couldn't help overhearing snatches of conversation that were none of my business.

"As I've said to your wife, Mr. Poole," Mrs. Larch said, "we can tell you that the mother is a fine intelligent woman with artistic background, like yourself. We try to match all those things, you know — intelligence and all, as well as physical similarity. But of course any woman can make a slip. The wrong company — you know."

When we got away at last, I drove home as though I was trying to claw my way out of an opera. "When the duke discovers that the child he has adopted is none other than . . ."

"Not so fast," my wife called from the back seat where she and Isolde sat with the new addition. "Do you want to kill us?"

I had work to do and lost no time.

"I see what they mean about a vague resemblance," I said. "He does have Isolde's coloring, sort of; her complexion. And of course those blue eyes."

"Augie's too," Isolde said.

"Mm, yes. Yes, I see what you mean."

"I thought that was what Mrs. Larch meant — that it was Augie he looked like."

"Oh, really? Perhaps so."

"Those slant eyes and that hair that isn't quite blond or quite red," Isolde said.

"Don't be deceived by reddish hair in a baby," I said. "Remember, dear, how we thought every one of our kids was going to be redheaded, till we realized it's because it's so thin and the scalp shines through it?"

Augie snapped a cigarette nervously out of the window. "I never saw a baby they couldn't see resembled everybody on both sides of the family. Babies look like everybody because they look like nobody. You can't tell anything about a baby that age. Let me hold the nipper awhile."

I thought we were handling it rather nicely. Now if the women could continue in their sentimental and rather touching belief that Augie had gone to pieces out of excitement, and meanwhile just go on dithering so over the infant they couldn't see what they were looking at, why, everything might yet be all right.

But Augie himself was far from confident. He started to take me out on those long hikes again, to hash things over. I did my best to reassure him. "Stop and consider the odds against such a thing," I said, and when I said stop I meant just that. I led the way to a large rock, where I sat down to nurse another boiled foot. The sun was sweltering, and I had spots in front of my eyes as thick as shad roe.

"You know damn well the odds are just the other way — we've been through that," he said.

"Shall I try to call Cornelia again? She may be back now."

"No. I'd rather be in doubt."

"Well then be in doubt. Don't be so stubbornly sure."

"It struck you that way, the first look. You admitted it."

"Why didn't it strike the women that way?"

"Because they weren't looking for it."

"And we were. So we ended up seeing things. You always end up seeing what you're afraid you will."

But Augie was not convinced. "So now I set out across the high wire," he said presently as we rose to resume the walk. "Because if there's any resemblance, time will bring it out. Not blur it."

"Don't even think of it," I said, grasping his arm — more in the need of something to hold on to than to steady my friend.

Because now we needed everything we had. This would take all our nerve and caution, all the faith and courage we had between us and that high reasoning we had pledged in our earlier walks and talks, everything we had thought and said and stolen from Thomas Wolfe. For while our position had been cooked to a cinder by the turn of events and we had suddenly to reverse the direction from which we drew our strength — having to exchange the philosophical peace implicit in the idea of a patternless anonymity for the solace of apparent Design — a great deal of what we'd settled on was still true. The lines fit anyway, and that was a God's mercy, because if we'd had to work out an entire new routine I don't think I'd have been able to face it.

"Think that you turn out in the end to get what was always yours," I said, galloping along a step behind him. "That out of all the manswarm — "

"Cut it out about the manswarm," Augie said. "The important thing is to watch the women. Watch them like hawks, to see if they suspect."

"Well let's start back," I said. "It'll be getting dark soon."

Dark brought the added risk of his being moved by the stars to some cliché about Infinity, whose infested reaches and galactic turmoils I so deeply deplored. Even allowing for the likelihood of "pattern," and subtracting such histrionics as there were in my *Weltschmerz*, there remained a legitimate irritation with the Cosmos which, if I had to put it in a word, I would describe as the basic indignity of being constantly required to look up into bottomlessness. It's not the kind of thing to which I am by temperament suited, though everyone, of course, to his own taste.

We got home before dark, all right, and when I did I found a letter from the new president of the P.T.A., outlining some projects she had been turning over in her mind for the coming season, soliciting my earnest and active co-operation, and expressing the hope that we would all put our shoulder to the wheel to make this a banner year.

Twenty

AUGIE seemed now, rather than the contrary, to have acquired a certain dignity. An added stature, if you will. We might once, for his truancies, have called him "small." There was nothing small about the scale on which he was now cast. The thing is, he had become invested with a sort of classic Greek irony. He had adopted his own son, and if this does not cloak a man in the Grecian absolutes then nothing in this world will.

Watching Augie go down the street in his too-short top-coat (and the soft hat, pulled down over one eye, to which he was partial that season) you would not have suspected that here was a man who walked in the cool Sophoclean symmetries. Pushing the pram in which reclined the cargo that made it so, he would have struck you that much less as a character headed for rhetorical doom. But he knew he was and I knew it. The child grew daily more the spit of his trundler, with the jolliest impersonation of his father's grin. Strangers pausing by his pram, and neighbors also ignorant of the adoption, invariably remarked on the resemblance. "Chip off the old block," they would say, slapping Augie on the back. Now there was no need for us to watch our wives like hawks — that was how they watched us. Audrey was the first to suspect, or the first to come out with her suspicion. One evening I was aware of her looking at me over the rim of a magazine. I picked one up and got behind it myself.

"It's Augie's, isn't it?" she said.

"Augie's?" A thin smile clung to my lips, like a postage stamp insecurely pasted to a letter.

"I didn't see that was why he behaved the way he did at the agency because I didn't want to see it, I guess — one of those things your mind shuts off. But it's getting clearer every day. It's true, isn't it?"

I refilled my highball glass and then went into the kitchen for some ice. "I won't say it is or isn't," I said, returning. "I'll say, suppose it is? Result: the Pooles have now got what they've tried — how long is it now? — to get. Leave Augie out of it for a minute. Just think of Isolde. What used to stand in the way of their getting their heart's desire was the fact that he was irresponsible. Now it's because he was that they have."

"How do you figure that out?"

"It's the fruit of his lechery — "

"If we can't discuss this without using words like the fruit of his lechery then let's drop the whole subject. How do you reason all this out — that they're getting their heart's desire thanks to his wrongdoing?"

"Because if it hadn't been for his having a child out of wedlock they wouldn't have any in it," I said.

"They'd have gotten another."

"Not necessarily. In fact very likely not. If you'll recall, what finally cleared them with the agencies was his reform, fiscal and otherwise. But he reformed and settled down and became a breadwinning husband, because he was scared into it. And he's becoming more of one every day, as I can tell from the books. Well, if he hadn't sinned on the scale he did the chances are he wouldn't have reformed on the scale he did. Think of Augie — this will help — as a kind of Everyman, combining the good and bad in us. Remember that if it weren't for babies born illegitimately there wouldn't be any for the salt of the earth to adopt. Augie was just his own source of supply."

We talked like this long past midnight, and when we gave off were a long time getting to sleep. I was feeling ragged the next day when Augie phoned and asked me to go for a walk with him. It was a Sunday afternoon, and he was going to take the little mimic out for a turn. That meant an easy stroll, rather than one of our grueling marches, and I agreed. I was waiting for him at the road in front of our house when he appeared, pushing the buggy at a brisk clip at that.

"Isolde suspects," he said as I fell in beside him. "What does Audrey make of this? She looks at me oddly. You've told her, haven't you?"

"I couldn't get out of it," I said.

A man carrying a fat Sunday paper was walking toward us up the road, smiling broadly. It was Mr. Goodbread, husband of our sitter (now also the Pooles'). Goodbread had been a gardener for an estate on the Sound which had been recently closed and put up for sale, and he was now working a day apiece for several of us more modest home owners. He stopped to say good afternoon and to dote into the pram. He had on his working dungarees. A brown cardigan full of blowouts and a knit cap bound at the tip like a wurst expressed his indifference to nonessentials.

"Is nize boy," he said, with an accent that was the product of his having lived in both Germany and Russia. He grinned and bent to pinch a cheek. "Look just like Daddy. Everybody say."

"Oh, God," Augie said when Goodbread was gone. He

clenched his fists and looked where God lived. "I can't stand any more of this. I can't stand Isolde's not coming out with it. I'm sitting on a powder keg, waiting every day, every minute, for it to blow up. There's only one way to end the suspense."

"How?"

"Set it off."

I clutched his arm. "Now cut it out," I said, "and get hold of yourself. You'll set no powder kegs off and maybe have something get back to the agency."

"Why?"

"Because if they find out it's your child they'll take it away from you. What ails you? Have you forgotten this is a probation period? It's a year before you sign the final papers. You can do what you want then; until then, *shut up*."

But Augie knew what there was for Isolde to put two and two together with: the discrepancy about the income declaration; a mysterious and hastily terminated telephone call or two to think back on; nights spent in town. Singly they meant little; together and in the light of the growing resemblance, they formed a basis on which to reassess the fainting fit. And Augie didn't have enough of a moral balance in the bank of domestic relations to cover what they added up to. He felt it to be only a matter of days before Isolde blurted out a query of some sort; and he sensed, too, the at least slight advantage to be gained by confession, as against being called to account; and so he warned me not to be surprised if I heard him blurt something out first. "Yes, I might very well do it when somebody's around — cushion the shock. I don't think I could stand it just the two of us together. But I want to get the explosion over and done with, and let the dust settle and see what we'll see. Get the damned thing on the agenda."

Isolde accosted me in the hardware store and told me that Augie had been acting "queer." He went about with an abstracted, at times distracted, look. "He tells me things he's said before," she related. "He'll get at things around the house he's already fixed. He talks about moving back to New York." She paused, frowning at the floor. "And now he has this idea he should be playing the piano all hours."

I gave her what reassurance I could: that suburbanites thought continually about moving back to the city, that it was no rarity for people to become suddenly obsessed with hobbies (which were in any case a preservative rather than a threat to stability) and that as for repeating things, everyone did that — I did it myself, now and again, when tired.

"Have you ever taken the car down to have it greased twice in the same day?" she asked. "Or been so tired you got up to play the piano in the middle of the night?"

No, I admitted, I hadn't. Nor had I seen Augie for some weeks. "Has this come on all of a sudden?" I asked.

"Yes, more or less. Drop over tonight if you're free, and see for yourself," she suggested. "Isn't tonight when Audrey's having the Brownie mothers?"

It was, and so I promised Isolde I'd look in.

I arrived about eight o'clock. Augie was sitting at the piano, playing Christmas carols.

"Rushing the season, Augie?" I said, shaking off my topcoat.

"I guess I am," he said. "The middle of October."

Isolde and I exchanged glances. It was the last of November.

"But I like the old carols," I said, rubbing my knuckles on my palm as I entered the living room. "I don't see why we shouldn't play them oftener."

Augie swung round on the stool. "It's funny nobody writes

any new Christmas carols — except old Mrs. Likely. Remember her, Isolde? I ran into her the other day. That's a handsome jacket you've got on," he complimented me.

"Thanks," I said.

We sat down with brandies; Isolde and I did, that is — Augie walked about the room.

"How's little Augie?" I asked.

Augie turned vague eyes to me. "Who?"

"The little nipper."

"Oh, he's fine."

We talked about him some, and I learned his latest achievements. Which reminded Isolde to slip in and see that he was covered. When she returned, Augie said:

"Did I tell you that I ran into old Mrs. Likely on the street?"

"Yes, you did."

There was something wrong here. And it wasn't long before I thought I had my finger on it.

Augie had recently phoned the magazine office about a cost-of-living adjustment check he had coming, and I remembered the punctuality of his inquiry as well as the notable accuracy of his estimate of the figure due him. No want of mental clarity there. Nor in other details relative to business matters, other dates and sums pertaining thereto. So it was borne in on me that I was witnessing a performance, like that conducted at Elsinore. His object was, of course, to portray himself as not responsible for his actions. He was using a broad brush because there was no time: events were closing in on him.

Presently I perceived something else.

"Augie hasn't been sleeping well lately," Isolde said.

"Not just lately," Augie put in. "It's been over a year, actually, though I've tried to keep from worrying you with it. It goes back to when — " He hesitated, then went on: "Maybe you remember the fantods I had once last July? I never told you about it, but at that time I sank a thousand dollars into some stock that turned out to be worthless. It was the first of July. I don't know what could have come over me. I suppose even then I wasn't myself. . . ."

So that was part of the plan. He was trying to establish his incompetence as pre-existing far enough back to cover the time of the act responsible for the pickle he was in; was trying, in other words, to make it retroactive. But good God, I thought to myself, don't lay it on so thick. For now he bent down to peer at and finger the goods in my coat. "That's a mighty handsome jacket you've got on," he said. "Did you have it tailored?"

"No," I said miserably and a little resentfully, looking into my brandy glass and crossing my legs. "I bought it at Rogers Peet. They had a sale."

Isolde set her glass down. "Who'd like a game of Scrabble?"

"I would!" I said, glad for any escape from the form of scrabble we were in as it was. Augie excused himself, pleading fatigue. "I'll kibitz," he said.

He sat down and rambled at the piano, however, soon after Isolde and I had started a game. Giving that up, he went over and turned the radio on. He got some recorded classical music and, shading the volume to our joint liking, went over and stretched out on the sofa, which he affected not being able immediately to locate. From there he kept up a sporadic chatting.

"Guess who I ran into in town the other day, looking exactly the same as ten years ago. Old Mrs. Likely. I asked her if she was writing Christmas carols and she said yes — the church choir was going to sing one this season."

This attempt to offer a disintegrating façade was one I was

able to be tolerant of as well as see through, because of my own *Weltschmerz* act which was a degree of the same bid for consideration. But it was a difficult transaction at best, and I was dying to tell him that better men than he had failed to bring it off, and for God's sake in any case to put on the soft pedal. At this rate it wouldn't be long before Isolde saw through it herself. Even already, I felt some response on her part to my own ill-concealed skepticism. Finishing a turn at the Scrabble board, she leaned back and said: "Augie, what was the stock you bought?"

"I don't want to bother you about it, baby," he said. "It's water over the dam. I don't even remember the name of it."

"But you remember the date you bought it."

"It was around the Fourth of July." He laughed through his nose. "I guess some connection about burning money up, like fireworks. Oh, well." He went to the radio, on which a recording of a quartet by Bartók had begun. "Do you mind if I get something else?" he asked. "Bartók always makes me want to walk sideways."

I felt Isolde looking at me.

"That's exactly the effect he has on me, Augie," I said and, laying out my letters, sat back. "Your turn, Isolde."

She pushed back her chair and rose.

"I'll be right back," she said. "I want to take another look at that baby."

So Augie saw that Isolde saw that he could tell a hawk from a handsaw, all right, and that he wasn't bringing this thing off. Yet he abandoned the act with the keenest reluctance. Isolde's refusal to credit his lunacy was a bitter blow to him — in fact it almost drove him out of his mind. I suppose his pride was involved. The two lived under a steadily mounting voltage of constraint, exposed to one another's nerves as to live wires. Somebody had to give, and soon. That was why I avoided going to the Pooles' as often as I could, remembering Augie's stated hope for a buffer when the situation broke. But I couldn't decline invitations indefinitely, and so at last I let my wife accept one for dinner on an evening in the middle of the week.

There was a *Turf Guide* in evidence when we got there, suggesting that Augie had lapsed into an interest, long suspended, in the horses. That was when I made the famous crack about posting with such dexterity to racing sheets, putting us all in stitches at the table. Augie, however, resumed a look at once remote and edgy, and when, as we settled down to coffee in the living room, he cleared his throat to say something, I threw in hastily: "Have you ever noticed what a ringer Mr. Goodbread is for Tito? One of those amazing resemblances."

"Oh, you must hear Augie's imitation of Mr. Goodbread," Isolde said. "Do it, Augie."

"Oh, no."

"Please do," we all said.

"Oh, all right. De sep feeds de gress like de blod de vessels. Dis wary good ting, big horse lawn mower ronning over de gress make de blade lay down flat if no sep — but if sep, springs ride beg op again."

"Priceless?"

"Wonderful."

Augie drew a deep breath and continued nervously:

"So de otter day I was over to see Hinkle de dog catcher aboud how much topsoil he'll need in his beg yard, wants to seed it, and I was explaining how de gress needs deep ort what can nourish de sep, when who should ring but de phone. Hinkle rons in de house a while, and pretty soon comes beg out mad. 'Woman calling me op because dead dog in de road in front of her house,' he says. She says, 'Can you come right over and pick it op?' I says, 'No.' She says, 'Why not?' Says 'Big horse.' She says, 'Big horse why?' Says, 'Big horse I only dill wit live dogs. Dad's my jurisdiction — I'm de dog catcher.' She says, 'Who shall I call?' Says, 'I don't care, lady. Call de ondertaker. I only pick up what I have to catch.' She gets med flies off de handle. Dad's the poblic for you every time. Dey're worse dan anybody' — Look, I'm the father of that child."

I don't know why Augie chose that particular moment. His take-off had gone well, we were having a good time. Maybe that was why — an impulse to spring it in a state of grace. Or maybe the very unreality of the moment was useful to him. Maybe it was for both of these reasons, or neither, or one altogether different. But he sprang it and there we sat. The damn thing was on the agenda. Not only on the agenda, but before the house.

Augie went over and raised a window. He wiped his brow with a handkerchief and came back to his seat. Isolde was running her forefinger round the rim of her cup. My wife and I were looking into our laps.

"There was a child, you know. This is it. There's no doubt about it. Why try to hide it, why pretend? I suggest we hang me from a sour apple tree. I suggest we cut me up into little pieces for fish bait. I hate to do this to Dick and Audrey, but they wouldn't be spared it anyway — I'd have to face them finally, so why not now? I figured we might as well get it all over with in one crack." He rose and walked toward a crib in a far corner of the room where Junior was parked tonight. "I'll do anything you think fair. This little cherub — "

Isolde came over and thrust herself between them, her back to the crib. "Don't you dare touch that child!" she said.

"Now, Isolde," I said rising, not knowing quite what line I was taking.

"Get out," Isolde said to Augie.

"Forgive me."

"I'll forgive you if you get out. Get out and don't ever let me see you again."

Augie stood looking at her with his mouth open. I stood with my hands spread. Audrey got up. "I think we'd better go."

"No, stay. I'm glad myself about that part of it — now I won't have to tell you myself. And I'd rather not be alone tonight," Isolde said.

"Well, then I'll leave with Augie," I said. "Audrey and you can stay together."

"You want to do that then?" Audrey said. It was all getting idiotic — as though we were discussing who would ride with whom to a party or something.

Augie turned to us. "I have a few more things to say." I supposed he meant in castigation of himself, but couldn't be sure; because Isolde strode to the door, flung it open, pointed through it, and said: "Get out! You — coyote!"

There was once a movie — perhaps it was *All About Eve* — in which some actress had done that to George Sanders and he'd said, "You're too short for that gesture. Besides it went out with Mrs. Fiske." Isolde was short, but she wasn't too short for the gesture. And Augie got out. But he hesitated first and said, "I ought to pack a few things."

"I'll send your things. Just get out now."

"Forgive me."

"Later."

"Then we'll let it that way. I'll let you know through Dick where to send my things. I'll probably stop at the Algonquin."

"You wouldn't stop at anything," was another rejoinder I recalled, this one from a musical comedy, in a brisk exchange also involving hotels. The mind has its own shock absorbers when emotions are under stress.

When Augie started for the closet to get his coat and hat (having shut the door a moment because of the draft) I went for mine too.

"Wait," Audrey called to me. "I'd like you to stay a minute and tell Isolde all the things you told me the other night. You know — how if it hadn't been for Augie's bad side there wouldn't be this good, and so on. How it's thanks to that and all."

"Well, all right," I agreed, though I'd have liked an hour or two alone to prepare a few notes. I was certainly more than happy to do all I could to help my two friends get this straightened around. I stood with my overcoat in my hands. "But shouldn't I at least drive Augie to the station, if he's going to New York?"

"I'd rather walk," Augie said. "It's only two and a half miles."

So we watched as he got into his coat and put on his hat. He opened the door and then paused, as if waiting for something. I felt we were waiting too — for what? For something more substantial than a mere exit, perhaps, something more clarion and conclusive, as befits a man who through Spanish living had come to a Greek end. But there was nothing, and the moment passed as a hesitating doubt whether he should wave or not. And at last he didn't wave, but gave us a rather charming smile and then, glancing into the corner where the crib was, went out, closing the door quietly behind him. We heard his footsteps a moment on the gravel outside and then no more, a faint sharp dwindling sound which seemed to give us something of the recessional touch we missed, like the last color fading from a sunset clothing some particular doom, leaving to us a silence in which we could only suppose that we had seen the last of Augie Poole, a figure already vanishing up the road, a memory and a means, a phantom digested by the evening shadows.

Twenty-One

CONFESSION is good for the soul only in the sense that a tweed coat is good for dandruff — it is a palliative rather than a remedy. Augie's admission solved nothing and helped nobody. It eased one tension only to create another as bad, or worse. What was to become of the Poole family, now three? Isolde, who must be judge and jury, realized soon that this state of affairs could not continue without reaching the ears of Rock-a-Bye. Agencies by no means relax their vigil of a house after they have given it a child. Rock-a-Bye would still be many months on the watch. A representative dropped in less than two weeks after Augie's expulsion, as a matter of fact, but it was during the day when there was no need to explain his absence from the premises. But Isolde knew agencies have ways of finding things out and was constantly afraid theirs might get wind of the rupture. Still she could not find it in her heart to take Augie back. So she delayed: hesitating, doubting, weighing. And waiting. As though something would turn up to help her make up her mind, or make it up for her.

"But those things don't happen," Audrey and I remonstrated with her, time and time again. "You've got to make your mind up to take him back or that's the end of it."

Augie, meanwhile, lived unhappily at the Algonquin in New York City. His work went poorly. He got no new ideas. We gave him a steady part-time job at *The Townsman*, developing germinal ideas we had in the office, or ideas that were nebulous or imperfect; situations of the kind to which Blair always attached the memo, "Something here. Work on." Augie was very creative on these. His "switches" were often completely new contributions, and he saved many a joke we had been ready to scrap. He worked on the captions of bought cartoons, too. He came in three days a week to the office. He languished. He loved Isolde — that was plain now. And he loved the child. There was no doubt he missed them more acutely every day.

"He's dying to see you both," I reported to Isolde. "Isn't that worth something?"

She smoothed out a pleat in her skirt with a stiff hand and frowned. Pride held out. Augie had now been gone five weeks.

"What'll I tell him?" I said. "I'm going to have dinner with him in town Thursday. Any message?"

No message. She needed time.

Thursday I quit work early and had several drinks at as many bars in restless preparation for meeting Augie at a bar we had designated. The higher I got the lower I got, as it were. When I turned up at the appointed place, which was my personal favorite, the curator looked at me narrowly.

"I see I got competition," he said, wiping a glass. We were again momentarily alone.

"Give me a straight rye," I said.

"I don't know."

"Come on now. I'm a steady customer here."

"You're not very steady tonight."

"Then give me a white wine and seltzer."

Frank complied, but advised I make the drink last as it was all I was likely to get from him in the very immediate future.

He went silently back to his work. I nursed the drink moodily, turning over something extra I had on my mind. Moot Point had fallen off.

All the grace and charm seemed to have vanished from that pleasure dome, now apparently past its modish peak and sloping into its long decline. The sequels to those delicate humoresques, each an étude illustrative of some aspect of the sexual harmonics, with which I had so often detained myself in times past, had become unremittingly banal and gross — mere carnal intervals, encounters with shopgirls whisked up there for the most elementary of purposes. Why? Was my fancy not what it used to be? Or were its latest products secretly willed, out of that hankering for the vulgar, that nostalgia for the loam of things, that haunts overspun man? In any case I was spared nothing. I visualized to the last detail the breakfasts which, once the last fine fillip of communions given and taken there, were now the penalties of its debauches. Indeed their horrors were often the whole of my scenarios. Thus I imagined myself, in trying to render somewhat more literate the conversation going on over bacon and eggs with one of these grisettes, as wondering aloud whether Proust would live, and her replying, "Is he sick?"

I slumped across the bar with my hands to my face.

"What's the matter?" Frank asked.

"Unholy mess."

He shook his head.

"What defeats me about you educated fellows is you have everything a fellow could ask for, well-spoken, good jobs, fine families, and you sit around here like the last rose of summer. I don't know. It's too many for me. Believe me if I had your job."

"I know," I said. "I've got everything."

"Then get that mailbag off your lower lip."

Frank turned and watched something on the sidewalk outside. I followed his gaze and saw a blonde six feet tall and wearing a mink stole, looking in.

"She meets a guy here once in a while," Frank explained.

"I tell you what you do, Frank, if she comes in here. I'll be sitting here like this, my tie straightened, new homburg on, a drink in front of me, my briefcase on the next stool — a fellow outwardly prosperous, you understand, and yet with a definite touch of something lost and lonely. Then you go over to where she's sitting and say to her, like a bartender in a cartoon, you see — now, get this. You look over at me and say to her: 'It's a sort of Marquand story — a basically independent nature sacrificed to the externals of achievement.' Have you got that?"

"Oh, go to hell," Frank said. "Here she comes now."

The woman went to the farthest stool and set a gold mesh evening bag on the bar and drew off a pair of pink gloves, which she folded and laid as carefully on the evening bag as she had the bag on the bar. She was smooth-featured and clear-skinned, with durable Panelyte laminated plastic top designed to resist stains, scratches, heat and moisture. Finely crafted, meticulously detailed, legs tipped with satin brass ferrules. Complete with synchro-mesh, spatter shield and automatic three-heat timing switch. All this plus the wonderful economy of Frank's budget-pleasing prices. Hurry! Hurry!

"*C'est l'époque*," I said, lightly tapping the ashes from my cigarette.

"What did you say?" asked Frank, who was mixing her a whisky sour she had ordered.

"It's the age we live in. A general, almost stylized, ennui has taken hold of us. Security, intellectual attainments, these mean

nothing; subtlety is a hindrance to peace as often as its source."
I saw from the woman's reflection in the bar mirror that the
ripe mouth had fallen ajar. It closed, however, on a cigarette
presently thrust into it. Every hair was in place. She had obviously never been hissed at by a lamb chop, or by anything else
in a frying pan. I got her in trouble. *O my God!*

"The human mechanism," I continued, "has become too
finely tuned. We are shattered by vibrations from which denser
natures were exempt. The path to death and decay is not an
easy one, and to presume to untangle the skein of things is
worse than in vain. It is vain."

"I thought you di'n't feel good," Frank said, serving the newcomer her libation. Watching him strike a match for her cigarette, I thought to whet her interest with something in a lighter
vein, something from my store of incidental quips and sallies.

"You change that bar rag about once a year, Frank?" I twitted.
"He changes that bar rag once a year — on New Year's Eve.
Every New Year's Eve he wrings out the old, wrings in the new."

The woman took a sip from her sour and scratched an instep.
I tried a fresh tittup.

"Man in a small Southern town killed his mother-in-law, his
sister-in-law, two cousins and an uncle. He took the bodies down
into the basement, boiled them in washtubs, and puréed the
remains through a sieve. What was the upshot?" I twisted my
cigarette out in an ashtray. "Strained relations."

The woman presented a face wreathed in smiles. I was about
to smile back when a pair of masculine shoulders three feet wide
brushed past mine from behind and the woman was joined by
a new arrival. A better example of the "denser natures" to which
I had just alluded could scarcely be imagined. I'm not saying
his eyebrows and hairline merged, but the image will be met-

aphorically helpful. He was dark, and weighed at least two hundred and fifty pounds. He patted the woman's head with a little endearment, from which she drew back. "Can't a fellow touch the girl he's in love with's hair?" he said.

"Get me all mussed up."

"I like those eyes even when you're sore," was his rejoinder. "You hypmatize me."

I beamed benevolently on the scene and winked at Frank. "Let us all be terribly Spanish, for there is not enough time to be Greek," I said.

The primate who had just come in stepped over to me.

"What was that crack, Bud?" he said.

"That was no crack," I said. "I was just — "

"I can hear. I got ears. I don't like remarks passed about nobody's nationality. See?" the primate replied, helping himself to a handful of my lapels. "In this country we don't care where people came from. This is a democracy."

"It was in the spirit of that assumption that I — "

"And talk English."

"Yes, sir. Yes, siree."

"O.K."

He released me and went back to his hypmatist. The bartender scowled at me and I scowled back. I would take my custom elsewhere were it not for the appointment I had in this dump — that was what my glare said. Finally the door opened again and Augie hurried in.

"Sorry I'm late," he said. "But I just had a phone call from Isolde at the hotel."

I was instantly tense. "What about?" I asked.

He gave a nervous shrug. "You got me. She just said for me to come out, she wants to see me. Something's up."

"Wants to see you when? Tonight?" I said apprehensively.

"Tonight. Give me some Bourbon and water, will you?" Augie turned to me. " 'Had to see me' was the way she put it — not wanted to see me. What could that mean?"

"God, I don't know. I hope the agency isn't on the warpath."

"Don't even say it." Augie glanced over his shoulder at a wall clock. "It's seven-thirty now. The next train isn't till eight ten. Time enough for a couple. I sure need 'em."

"I told you not to stir this up."

"Cut it out. Mean only a storm could clear so foul a sky."

Augie had a couple, in the course of which I phoned Audrey and told her I'd be on the eight ten with Augie instead of on a later train for which we had made arrangements that morning. "Isolde wants to see him. Something seems to be up. What's going on?" I asked.

"You'll find out when you get here," she said. "I can't talk about it over the telephone."

"Well, what is it?"

"You hurry home."

Augie and I walked the three blocks to the station. On the train we buried ourselves behind magazines — not that we read them. We were both on tenterhooks. The train was a local and the trip an eternity. But at last we arrived at Avalon, and there were Isolde and Audrey both waiting for us on the platform. Their eyes were red. They had clearly both been crying.

We got into our separate cars and started for home. I could see the Pooles' car tailing us in the rearview mirror. We had gone a short distance from the station when Audrey burst out with:

"You'll never guess what's happened."

"What?" I said. "What the devil's going on out here? Is it something about the agency?"

"No."

"What then?"

"Isolde's going to have a baby."

As everyone knows, childless women often become pregnant after adopting an infant. The experience of maternity itself supposedly thaws out the fears and self-doubts that had previously thwarted its accomplishment. That had happened to Isolde, in only the few months' time in which she had been a practicing mother. She had always wanted a child at the same time that she'd feared it, and naturally the swell of emotion released by the realization of her long-hungered-for condition swept her back into a tide of feeling for her husband. She had suspected her condition for a couple of weeks, but only today had medical reports proved it beyond a doubt.

I don't know what reconciliation scene was enacted in the Poole home that night. I can only imagine it — the tears, laughter, protestations, embraces.

On that night, which now seemed so long ago, when Isolde had called Audrey and told her of their wish to adopt, Audrey and I had been lying in bed unretired, in the way we have — she reading a book, I smoking and musing and listening to sounds in the plaster. Neither of us was reading this night. We nursed a drink apiece and talked long past midnight about the Pooles. I thought I heard a faint rustle in the wall and remembered the rat that had visited me the other time. We had no more rats now — they were gone. No thanks to either Nebuchadnezzar (who had died a few months before) or the cat the Pooles had loaned us; thanks only to a terrier we had acquired. Jake was his name. Perhaps it was only Jake, scooting and scrabbling about in the basement, who had made the noise. Our four children were of course long asleep, dreaming their peculiar dreams. Phoebe (now firmly representing herself as Alice) often dreamed of letters of the alphabet, or so she told us at breakfast.

The phone rang. Audrey bolted out of bed and got it on the third ring — par for that distance. It was Isolde. They talked for half an hour or more, and when Audrey returned she said: "They want to celebrate. All of us together."

Celebrate we did. We made a night of it in New York. Our old foursome. Happy once again, with a difference perhaps — but happy. The Pooles carted Augie, Junior over to our place in a carrying basket and Mrs. Goodbread sat with all the children there. We dressed. The girls were visions in new frocks; the men, in tuxedos now slightly tight for them, looked like exploded baked potatoes. We had dinner and then went to a night club. We drank champagne. We raised our glasses.

"Here's how," Augie said.

The child was born in the early fall and was a girl. Anita is her name.

That was only a few years ago and yet the children seem to be already growing up — the Pooles' and, certainly, ours. Mrs. Goodbread sits regularly with the Pooles' two, but our Maude is now old enough to leave with the rest. Old enough also, though, to be going out on her own now and then. Mr. Goodbread still mows lawns for several of us and detains us widely as a raconteur. Dr. Vancouver has left general medicine and settled in pediatrics; there is still a lack of baby doctors in growing Avalon and he has made a good thing of it. Isolde takes her kids to him and reports he is O.K., but still a good deal of a hypochondriac — though less apprehensive about catching things from babies than he'd been from adults. Terry I never saw again. The McBains moved West, and they and she have dropped from sight. Now and then I pick up a copy of *The Reader's Digest* and look for the article about her mother, but I never see it.

So Augie was gathered into the orbit that claims us all at last. So the damnation is that there is no damnation; the peal of doom is a penny whistle, the Good Humor bell calling the children at evening. So the years glide along. I never go to Moot Point any more. There is nothing doing there. A new six-lane highway goes by the door, and Moot Point is a silent ruin. It would have been much better had the state survey hit it directly — then it would have been condemned by eminent domain and torn down, with reasonable remuneration at market value. But the government does not recognize near misses or what they call consequential damage to property deflated by scenic blights. So my old haunt stands, throttled by the encroaching forests, choked with bushes filled with guzzling bees or tufts of winter snow. Cars and fume-dispensing trailers bowl past the front all day; the Maine waters murmur everlastingly behind. I hardly think about it any more — I can't stand to. But sometimes I'm reminded of it, and then my heart breaks. As a valley dweller drinks from streams which bear rumors of the cold purity of mountaintops, so I can in chance moments of daily life catch echoes and glimpses, intimations of that ideal typified by Moot Point at its best. A woman's wit and animal ease, splinters of hotel gaiety, these quicken memories of that lost Babylonian grace, that quicksilver common to all those who were seen there in the old days.

I've been looking for another site; or I should say we are — because my wife has taken the initiative in our search for a summer cottage. We've had our eye for a long time on a lakeside plot up in New Hampshire, and it looks as though we're going to buy and build on it. Nothing pretentious, you understand, nothing fancy, just a little place we can call our own. It won't be named Moot Point, by a long chalk, but probably something like Pines and Needles, or even Drowsy Dell. Because instead of the suave adulteries and worldly company for which Moot Point was famous in its heyday, this will be strictly a family affair, with youngsters romping on the lawn and splashing in the water. We'll have the Pooles up a good deal, I expect, for long week ends and summer holidays with all the children, of whom ours are approaching the age when they'll have friends and school-mates of their own to ask up. Maude already has a boy with a popping car, which leaves half its organs in my drive. Incidentally, I often come upon Maude making entries in a book which she refuses to let me see, and keeps locked in a drawer. She says it's a diary, but I don't know — it looks more like a notebook to me. Could that, then, be the end? "Father always started the oil furnace when he stamped his foot. . . . Father would make Mother presents of his favorite wines and of the books he wanted to read. . . ."

"Everybody has to get away," Mother remarked over her needlepoint one evening, as plans for the summer cottage were being completed. "And don't you think it'll be a real retreat for both of us?"

"I don't know about you," Father said, pouring himself a glass of ale as he settled back with a sigh in his easy chair, "but it's certainly a retreat for me."